NICHOLAS J. RIPLEY

A WINTER FOR DOVES

PART II

First paperback edition January 2024.

Cover design by Nicholas J Ripley
Editing & Proofreading: Rachel Oestreich, from The Wallflower Editing, LLC
Typesetting: Ines Book Formatter
Author photograph © Kirstin Dietza, from Dietza photography

ISBN 979-8-9887588-1-5 (paperback)
ISBN 979-8-9887588-3-9 (eBook)

Published by Project Suncloud LLC
www.patreon.com/ripleyjnick

This book is dedicated to:

Steven Gordon and my mother, Diana Tennyson. Thank you for believing in me. Couldn't have written this without either of you.

Content Warning:

It is only fair that I, the author of this book, forewarn you of the content you are about to read. The Project Suncloud series is not for the light of heart. Readers, please be advised, these books contain: alcoholism, animal death, castration, child death, despair, domestic abuse, drowning, drug usage, extreme violence/ death, gore, gun violence, homophobia, infidelity, mentions of miscarriage, mentions of rape/attempted rape, profanity, sexual content, sex work & human trafficking, suicide, suicidal ideation, racism, religious imagery, and torture.

The purpose of these being included in the Project Suncloud series is not for shock value but rather to explore darker, real-world themes. Views of characters do NOT reflect the views of the author. Project Suncloud is a work of fiction. While some of these aspects may be upsetting to some, I felt that they were all important to the stories I sought to tell. You have been advised.

Table of Contents

EPISODE 10

A White-Haired Reprisal

AYLEN

The girl known as Aylen Monro sat in the back of an ambulance roughly an hour after she found her roommate and roommate's boyfriend murdered in her college apartment. A blanket had been wrapped around her as she stared at the ground. How did this happen? Legion was supposed to come after *Aylen*. Only Aylen. She felt ashamed and stupid. Of course, if she was always protected by Jared, the next logical step would be to attack her best friend. Her *best* friend. A shiver of guilt rolled through her, making her wish she hadn't already cried her eyes out. She killed her own best friend. She had told Jared about Legion, which was specifically what it had told her *not* to do. Aylen was at fault for Beth's death.

She remembered her best friend's final look, the helplessness as blood gushed from her mouth and her throat. Then she had a sickening thought: Did Legion disguise itself as her? If that was the case, then Beth would have witnessed her own best friend killing her boyfriend and slitting her throat. At best, it had only happened five minutes prior to Aylen getting there, depending on how deep the cut went. The killer was still close by when she found Beth. Unless Legion was like Jared, there was no way that it'd been far away by the time she got there. If only Jared and Aylen had gotten there sooner. If only they hadn't talked to Eric. If only—

"Hey, A, you okay?" Jared asked, sitting next to her, trying to console her. Soon after she found the corpses, Jared was the one who found her bathed in her best friend's blood. He'd told her he knew to hurry to the apartment because he found some kind of mechanical bug in his own. It had a mini camera and audio recording abilities. Jared said he thought Legion only revealed it to send him a message. Assumedly through that bug, it heard every conversation they had. It knew everything about Jared already, yet still wanted Aylen to give it a notebook full of bullcrap. She felt sick. Why was Legion trying to use her? *Why?* Jared was the one who pulled Aylen away from Beth's body. He was also the one who called the police and reported the incident. He was the one talking to police this whole time, being questioned about how the bodies were found and whatnot. Aylen looked at the crowd gathered around the emergency vehicles. "Aylen?" Jared asked.

She searched around. "Yeah," she replied quietly, watching the crowd talk among themselves.

"You're lucky. The doctors told the police you weren't in the right state to be questioned."

"Lucky?" she asked quietly.

"Well, maybe lucky isn't the right word," he agreed. Jared looked to his side, toward the crowd. "What do you think you'll do now?" he asked. "Go live with your mom, or—"

"I'm going to join the Saint Organization," Aylen replied stiffly.

"Aylen . . ." Jared started sympathetically.

"I fit all the requirements, don't I? I'm a victim of the Devil's Deviants. A victim that's sick of this bullcrap." She turned her glare on Jared. "I'm joining the Saint Organization. And you're going to help me." He saw how sincere Aylen was. She could see it in his eyes that he wasn't expecting that kind of intensity from her. He knew there was no talking her out of it this time.

Two black body bags were pushed out of the college dorms via stretchers. This was the last time Aylen would see Beth. She kept that in mind as they watched the bodies be carried off into the emergency vehicles. She would never see Beth again.

"All right," he stated solemnly. And now Aylen had a mission: She would stop the Devil's Deviants. They had gone too far. Taking her best friend from her was the final straw. No matter what, she would find the mutated bastard that had wronged her. And one day, she would get her revenge.

Legion would pay.

CERBERUS

Cerberus drove through town on his motorcycle. It had been a long day making sure the outer deviant colonies had enough rations to survive. Sneaking in and out of Salutem had, in truth, been the bitch of the day. The outer limits were always tough to sneak through. The UWF kept a tight hold of whoever went in and out of Salutem, so you could only sneak by the outer wall's forces easily if you knew the sewer lines well, not to mention you couldn't be afraid of getting dirty.

The night air blew through Cerberus's long hair, sending it back as his motorcycle roared lion-like out of the exhaust pipe. The streetlights painted the way for him as he drove to the darker part of town, but eventually the lights stopped and he found himself having to rely strictly on the light generated from his motorcycle. He knew exactly where he was going, though. One lone streetlight shone above the parking lot of the abandoned buildings. This part of town was *mostly* abandoned buildings: Old signs of old businesses stood around like a graveyard of tombstones, old chain-link fences stood as grisly reminders of days past. A porno shop remained on one corner, a greasy hamburger joint on another, and finally the place he was going to lingered on another corner.

Cerberus stopped in front of it. It was packed tonight, or so the number of cars in the parking lot told him. He looked up at the red neon sign. *The Ninth Circle*, in bright red letters. Also on the sign was a naked red lady with devil horns and a trident. Cerberus dismounted his motorcycle and lit a cigar. Home sweet home.

He walked up the steps of the building, his heavy boots stomping on the wooden stairs as he walked to the first set of doors and opened them. The room inside was dark and there was a large man, larger than even Cerberus, standing before him, blocking the next set of doors. His beard was braided, he had long hair tied back in a ponytail, and the sides of his head were shaved. The bouncer's stomach was portly. Hmm. Cerberus had never seen him before; must've been a new guy. The Devil's Deviant attempted to walk past the bouncer, and the man stopped him.

"Whoa there, tiny," the bouncer said, a cocksure grin on his face. "What're the words? Or are you on the list?" He sized up the tall Cerberus, who felt only mild annoyance at that point. Dumbass should know who he was.

"'Be sober, be vigilant; because your adversary, the devil, as a roaring lion, walketh about seeking whom he may devour,'" he grumbled. Cerberus rolled his eyes and attempted to walk past the bouncer again, but now the man's hand found a home on his chest. Now this was getting really annoying.

"Whoa there. Wrong Bible quote, tiny. Are you on the list or are you gonna go home?" the bouncer said, getting in his face. Cerberus looked around the room.

"Quote has remained the same for over seven years. It hasn't changed," he said calmly.

The bouncer grinned. "Yes it has, tiny. Now get lost before I get angry."

Cerberus sighed. A loud crack popped suddenly in the bouncer's leg. He screamed in pain before he was slammed into the ceiling and then the floor by an unseen force. Cerberus puffed away at his cigar. The unseen force lifted the bouncer into the air and made him hover before him. Cerberus grabbed him by the shirt.

"Listen, *tiny*," he growled calmly. "I'm really not in the mood for dick measuring. Also, I'm not sure what they've told you, but I'm one of your bosses." He put the lit cigar to the bouncer's face. The man's flesh sizzled, causing him to fidget in agony. "Consider this your letter of resignation." The bouncer grunted in pain and response. The invisible force Cerberus controlled flung him into the ceiling again and let the man crash to the floor. Cerberus looked at his handiwork as a beautiful waitress rushed out wearing a very revealing outfit and holding tray.

"Sorry about that, Mr. C. New guy," the waitress said, rushing to check the man for a pulse.

"New *fired* guy. Give him the serum, Gwen." Cerberus scoffed, taking another puff of his cigar.

"Sure thing, Mr. C. They're waiting for you inside."

Cerberus walked through the door in front of him. Loud rock music from a wildly distorted guitar played in the background. Naked and half-naked women danced on poles in front of a crowd of perverts, the strippers all wearing little devil horns atop their heads as they gyrated in seductive ways. Some of them were giving lap dances to loyal customers. Familiar faces tonight. Few new ones too. The room was dark, the shadows broken only with multicolored flashing lights. Cerberus looked to the stage and saw the band playing the noisy music. Some sort of underground metal or rock band, gathering a small crowd around the stage. He looked to his right, at the bar. It looked like Blasphemer was busy bartending, as usual. His naturally blue skin seemed to fit the lighting in a complementary way. It worked out for the better too; people thought it was part of the gimmick of the nightclub. In the corner of his eye, he eyed an Asian woman making out with a man atop a barstool. Oni was working her tongue down the man's throat while dressed in some kind of leather outfit. Her elongated tongue licked the side of the man's face as she looked back at Cerberus. Poor bastard had no idea what he was in for.

The large Devil's Deviant made his way to the back of the nightclub, where there was a section labeled *VIP Lounge*. In front of the entrance was War. He stood roughly eight feet tall, his bald head and muscular physique gleaming in the dim light. War's crimson skin appeared even redder in the club's lighting. "You're late," he said, crinkling his nose. "And you smell like shit."

"And you smell like hookers and blow," Cerberus responded to the larger man. "I miss anything?" War opened the door and motioned for Cerberus to step through. He complied.

"A couple things," War said, shutting the door behind them and locking it. As soon as he locked the door, the floor sank down into the underground bunker that the club was built on top of; the true base of DD operations. Before Cerberus were the cold metallic walls of the gigantic bunker, well-lit by lights on the floor and the ceiling. He looked at War. The ginormous hulk-like freak walked alongside Cerberus as they made their way farther into the depths of the Devil's Deviants' base of operations. His compatriot's footsteps made large thuds as they walked. "Pestilence's assignment has been going swimmingly, got word from our contact that the processor that Pluto needed was retrieved, Legion returned from its . . . extracurricular activities. Oh, and Lucifer requests your presence immediately," War said calmly.

"Right now? Do I at least get to shower before I go?" Cerberus muttered in annoyance.

"Afraid not. It's a Ritual," War said calmly. Shit. Cerberus sighed. He had gotten tired of these goddamn things. War led him to the lobby of the bunker. The inside was built almost like an old-time prison, with the rooms being the deviants' private quarters rather than prison cells. There were at least five levels in the living section of the bunker. That meant five walkways filled with blood-thirsty deviants on every level, looking down to the ground floor, watching the scene occurring there. And in the center of the pit-like lobby on the ground floor, there he stood: the leader of the Devil's Deviants.

Cerberus watched Lucifer, who was standing in front of a chained man kneeling on his knees. Lucifer looked up at the cheering deviants with a sort of smug look upon his face. He had slicked-back dark brown hair, small horn-like mutations protruding like half of a crown from his forehead, and a worn look upon his face. Tonight, he was wearing a long coat over his usual buttoned-up shirt.

"Brothers and sisters," Lucifer said to the cheering deviants. Cerberus stood in the corner of the room with War, staying out of the limelight. "These days we have reasons to rejoice." Lucifer looked around, scanning his audience. "General Rob Harper of the Saints is dead. Our funds from the nightclub have been profitable. Pluto says that his progress on the machine has been slowly but steadily coming along. But, brothers and sisters, these are temporary times. Our enemies, the Saint Organization and the UWF, still remain at large. For now, the Saints have been beaten back. This will not last long, though. Soon enough, they *will* be back on their feet again, attempting to thwart our attempts at revenge." Lucifer shook his head while looking down. "However, right now we have a time of peace." For a second Lucifer looked devilishly at the crowd. Then he pointed to the man chained up on the ground; the man looked only lightly beaten up, but very frightened. "Tonight, we got ourselves a UWF soldier: Corporal Abraham Judge. He was said to be the top of his class in the military academy. . . . *Shall we test him against the top of our class?*"

Cerberus recognized his cue. He tossed off his leather jacket and threw it to the ground, then proceeded to walk up next to Lucifer. "Abraham Judge, meet Cerberus, our own personal hound of hell. Unchain the prisoner!" Lucifer commanded. Cerberus knew the score: fight to the death, no abilities. These Rituals had become a sort of circle jerk for his kind over the years. Definitely not his first rodeo either.

Two deviants unchained the UWF soldier, and the soldier cracked his neck. In his eyes was a mixture of fear and anticipation, evidenced by his heavy breathing and wide eyes. The man was ready to fight for blood. All right . . . Cerberus removed his tank top and threw it to the floor. "Go kill each other!" Lucifer barked out with a smile. All of the deviants on the ground floor backed away and cheered. Cerberus looked at the ceiling and rolled his shoulders. Here he went again.

Whack.

He felt a fist sink right into his face. Then a knee struck him in the gut and he ended up on the floor. The corporal's boot kicked across his face. Blood trickled into Cerberus's mouth and he spat it onto the ground. Deviants around him booed and cursed the corporal as he grabbed Cerberus's hair and raised him up. Despite being apparently beaten to a pulp, Cerberus made no sound or yelp of pain. The corporal was cocky now, whacking away at him, even going so far as breaking Cerberus's nose. The UWF soldier smacked him in the face again, taking him down to the ground, and Cerberus heard a clang as someone tossed a knife into the pit. The soldier picked it up as the deviant lifted himself from the ground and staggered to his feet. The corporal swiped at Cerberus.

In a moment, Cerberus held the corporal's wrist firmly. He looked into the UWF soldier's eyes squarely. "Now we're even," he uttered darkly. A sickening thud echoed throughout the room as the two men's skulls connected. Cerberus twisted the corporal's arm and a sickening crack rang through the room. The large, Viking-like deviant then brought an elbow down onto the same arm, and the corporal screamed in pain before Cerberus elbowed the man in the ear. The man screamed in agony from the vicious assault, crashing to the floor. Cerberus grabbed the man's sweaty head and slammed his fist across the man's face, sending blood flying from his mouth. The hellhound flipped the soldier over and knelt on top of him, planting sticky, red-soaked punches into the man's face, knocking out his teeth. The corporal managed to shake the deviant off him and punched Cerberus across the face. Acting as if the punch barely affected him, he hardly reacted and proceeded to continue pounding on Corporal Judge. Then Cerberus got up and wiped his bloody beard and mouth while looking up at the crowd. The deviants were cheering for him in a way that showcased that he clearly had the home team advantage. He looked at the corporal on the ground, crawling and bloody, and thought to himself for a second. The large deviant then undid his belt and held it in his hand.

He watched the once proud warrior, Corporal Judge, crawl like a sniveling coward. Then he stomped on the man's back, relishing the cry of agony. He wrapped his belt around the man's neck. "This ain't personal," Cerberus muttered as he pulled on leather, entrapping the corporal's windpipe like an anaconda strangling its prey. The corporal struggled the best he could as he fought for air. Cerberus watched the man turn pink as he put his foot behind the man's neck. Saliva slipped from the man's mouth and a vein protruded in his forehead as he helplessly gasped for air. The hellhound looked up at the ceiling as he felt anger rise up in him. Then he roared and pulled the man's arms while pushing his foot forward.

Crack.

The corporal lay lifeless as Cerberus untangled his belt from the man's neck. The deviants roared and cheered at his victory. "It's just business," he said to the broken-necked man lying on the floor. Lucifer approached Cerberus and raised his arm, looking at the crowd with a smug look on his face. Then he whispered in his champion's ear.

"After you get cleaned up, meet me in Pluto's lab. We have much to discuss."

"Gotcha. I'll take out the trash first," Cerberus said to his boss as the crowds cheered. He lifted the corporal over his shoulder and began his way toward the exit. Deviants cleared the way for him to enter the metallic hallway beyond, the dead man hanging limp on him. After turning some corners, Cerberus found the room he was looking for: the bunker's cargo bay. The room was dimly lit and had rusted pipes on the ceiling and a gigantic hatch in the center of the room with yellow-and-black striped tape surrounding it. To the left was a control pad with a variety of buttons. He pressed the green one. There was a hiss of compressed air being released and the clank of mechanical pulleys from the sides of the room. The hatch opened, shaking the ground slightly under his feet. A loud metal screeching sound echoed in his ears and he looked into the hatch. There they were.

Eating each other, screwing each other, seeing Cerberus at the top, snarling at him. He looked down at the Brainless in the pit. They had obviously bred more, since there were more in the pit than the last time. He watched the misshapen figures act out humans' most basic animalistic instincts, then he tossed the dead corporal into the pit. The creatures at the bottom worked their way over each others' bodies to reach the corpse. They pulled at it every which way, tearing off bits of the body and disemboweling it, ripping off skin with their teeth and claws, gnawing through bone and flesh alike. The Viking-like man walked back to the control panel and closed the pit.

"Well, that was . . . inviiiiigorrrrating," a sexless voice behind him said. Instantly, he knew who else was in the room with him. He didn't turn around.

"Don't you have anybody else to bug, Legion?" the large man grunted.

"Unfortunately, no. We did, but then ourrrrr fun ran out. We had to make a few, um . . . necessary cuts," it said as its naked, sexless body crept into view. Cerberus turned around to see both the brown eye and the blue eye of Legion's bodies staring at him.

"Piss off, I'm busy," Cerberus grunted.

"I would, but seeing you *manhandle* that UWF soldier, it just . . . turned me on so much!" Legion smiled, wrapping its arms around Cerberus's neck seductively. It morphed into a beautiful naked woman "What, do you prefer this?" Legion asked. Then it switched into a naked man. "Or this?" it uttered with a seductive smile. Cerberus pushed it away.

"Hank, tell Stephanie to knock it off," Cerberus said, unimpressed. Legion morphed back to normal.

"Actually, believe it or not, that's Hank, not me," it said in a woman's voice, closing its blue eye.

"I can't help it, he's so fuckable," Legion uttered in a man's giddy voice, closing its brown eye. Cerberus walked away, rolling his eyes with a sigh, used to this treatment from Legion.

"Ya should've let me handle it, you scared him away!" Legion's female voice scolded.

"Please, as if *you* could seduce *him,* dumb bitch," Legion's male voice replied. Cerberus sighed; their arguments would be so funny if they weren't so pathetic.

"Bitch? *Bitch?* That's rich! Can't believe I used to sleep with a fuckin' loser like you!"

"'Cause you were *such* a winner yourself, weren't you? Miss used-to-stalk-ex-husband?"

"That was just *once!* Hank, if we weren't attached, I swear to god I would—" Legion's voices continued back and forth, fading as Cerberus increased the distance between them.

Cerberus exited the cargo bay and went back to his private quarters. He made his way into the shower and turned it on. He hissed when the cold water poured onto his body, as he began to feel the pain from the earlier fight. His ribs and nose were definitely broken, he had a black eye, welts and bruises on his torso and face, and his lip was busted. The cold water felt like ice on his skin as it dripped down. He was getting too old for this shit. Soon enough, he would be hitting the big five-oh. Not this year, but in a few more years. What would he do once he could no longer fight for his side? What would he do when the pains in his bones became unbearable? It had been about ten years since Project Suncloud. For ten years, he had sought revenge for his dead family. How much longer could he work toward getting revenge? It was a scary thought that they may never win in the end, that all that the deviants had done had been in vain, that all the people they had lost would have died for nothing.

Cerberus heard Morningstar knock on his bathroom door. "Hey! You almost done in there? I gotta patch you up and then you gotta meet with Lucifer," she called.

"I'll be out in a minute, goddamnit," he said gruffly. He turned off the shower and wrapped a towel around his waist before walking out into his living room.

"Ahhh! Old man naked! Old man naked!" Morningstar said, covering her eyes.

"I'm wearing a towel, for Christ's sake. Hurry up and patch me up," Cerberus said, annoyed.

He sat down on a chair and Morningstar knelt in front of him. She took ahold of Cerberus's face. "Man . . ." she said, wincing.

"What?"

"Did you have to let him beat on you in the beginning like that?" she asked while shaking her head.

"Can you fix it?"

"Yeah," Morningstar replied, putting her hand over Cerberus's lip. A bluish-white light emanated from her hand. Before he realized it, his lip ceased hurting and felt normal again. She put her hand over his nose without touching it. "This is going to hurt," she warned him. He nodded. After the light emanated from her hand, his nose suddenly cracked with a sharp pain.

"Goddamn!" he exclaimed.

"Told you. Now, what else is broken?"

"I think at least one of my ribs . . ." Cerberus grunted while sitting up, showing his bare torso to Morningstar. She winced as she looked at his ribs, the skin over them a dark purple.

"Slap my ass and call me Susan . . ." Morningstar said quietly.

"Jesus, you and that expression—"

"Well, I mean damn, Cerby, you really let him kick the crap out of you! If you ruptured any organs, I'm not sure I could fix that!" she stated firmly.

"It was no more than usual," he grunted.

"Why does Lucifer keep using *you* for the Rituals, though? I mean, you could've gotten killed tonight!"

"Enough!" Cerberus firmly stated, which shut Morningstar up. "I'm fine. Just patch me up so I can make my meeting." The room went quiet and she put her hands in front of Cerberus's ribs. He watched as the bluish-white glow of her ability exited her hand, then cringed when he felt a crack, but otherwise remained silent. Morningstar looked seriously at Cerberus.

"That's all that's broken from what I can tell. Now, the black eye and bruising might take a while to fix; skin and muscle are always harder for me to heal than bones. Want me to fix 'em?"

"Nah, keep 'em, Lucifer will be pissed if I make 'im wait. Thanks, as usual," he said while getting up.

"No problem. . . . Hey, Cerby?" Morningstar asked solemnly.

"Yeah?" he turned to her. She thought for a second, then shook her head.

"Never mind," she remarked quietly.

"All right. You should get out of my room now, I gotta get dressed." She nodded and exited the room. Cerberus put on some clothes and headed for his meeting with Lucifer.

Cerberus walked through the hall until he stopped in front of Pluto's lab. Misshapen teeth immediately lunged at him as he turned the corner. It would've made him jump if he weren't so damned used to it by now. He stared darkly as Pluto's pet Brainless, Sheila, tried to move toward him in vain. Sheila had been a woman before she turned Brainless. She was an ugly thing now: dark brown skin, bird-like feet, no arms, two gigantic nostrils where her eyes should've been, malnourished body, and a long human-like arm sticking out of her head. A chain in front of the door held her back from Cerberus. He took some beef jerky from his pocket and threw it to the ground. The Brainless followed the beef jerky and attacked it, allowing Cerberus to enter Pluto's lab. Dog-eat-dog world.

"Ah, Cerberus! If it isn't our reigning champion!" Lucifer said, smiling. The lab was a large room with tanks, screens, computers everywhere, machinery, and the massive contraption that Pluto had been working on. It was menacing and looked like a gigantic metallic ball or cracked egg, with lots of gadgets and gizmos that Cerberus didn't recognize. The egghead had been busy. "Come in, I was just discussing things with Pluto." Lucifer motioned to the figure next to him.

Pluto was a slightly overweight man wearing a tie with the Disney character of the same name. The front of his forehead looked as if his brain had been pressed hard against his skull and left an imprint. Pluto looked up at him from his office chair through extremely thick glasses.

"Cerby! Good, you're here! I was just discussing with the boss man about what we'll be doing next," he said in a friendly voice, chuckling in the back of his throat.

"What's up, then?" Cerberus replied gruffly.

"Well, essentially, as you know, in order to get the machine to operate, I basically gotta reconfigure a quantum plasma reflector all by head, since we don't have any real knowledge about the original itself. Not to mention to get the desired effect, I'd require rectometer cylinders that're bigger in diameter to make sure the gravitational intake and altitude don't intervene with the anti-matter, so therefore—"

"Get to the point already. In English, preferably," Cerberus said firmly.

Lucifer chuckled at his response and placed a hand on the hellhound's shoulder. "Cerberus doesn't have time to look through a thesaurus, Pluto, he is a *warrior*. He just needs to be told what to do and the best method of attack," he said with a grin. Pluto looked up at both Cerberus and Lucifer from his office chair with a degree of uncertainty. The heavyset man then turned to his keyboard and typed something. Suddenly, a hologram appeared in the middle of the room, roughly ten feet tall. Cerberus's eyes widened.

"*That* is where I think we'll be able to find the remainder of the resources for this thing." Pluto smiled.

"How the *hell* would we manage *that*?" Cerberus said in shock. Lucifer smiled.

"That is what we brought you here for." Lucifer looked at the hologram with a grin. "To discuss our plan of attack."

ESMERALDA

It was early in the day when Esmeralda stepped out of the Saints' main building and headed for the mess hall. Outside, birds chirped and the air had a certain amount of nip about it. It was fairly dead today, cloudy too. No new recruits in training yet, though there was talk that a new batch would be arriving soon. Because of this, Ezzy thought she should enjoy the peace of this morning. The sound of new recruits training in the morning was never pleasant.

The Columbian woman rubbed her eyes and yawned, still feeling tired. Upon entering the mess hall, she saw Saints sitting everywhere as normal, eating breakfast. She grabbed her own breakfast from the line, sat by herself in the cafeteria, and began quietly munching on her food in silence. It wasn't too long before her silence was interrupted by the arrival of Gail sitting at her table. She gave the woman a puzzled look.

"Mind if I sit here?" Gail asked. Esmeralda's mouth was full but she shook her head before she swallowed her food.

"Not at all," she replied quietly. There was a minor silence as Esmeralda continued munching on her food.

"Goddamn, Ezzy, feel like I haven't seen you in forever. How've you been?" Gail asked, breaking the silence.

"Been all right," she responded almost immediately. "You?"

Gail seemed to notice Ezzy was rushing the conversation, and she stopped and thought for a moment. "I'm, uh . . . actually gonna have an assignment soon . . ."

Esmeralda stopped. "You? On an assignment?"

"Yeah, in a few nights. Kinda a special errand sorta thing. I, um, was actually wondering if you wanted to come along. There's gonna be a few of us going on this thing . . ." Gail trailed off again.

Esmeralda was puzzled at the suggestion. "What *is* this errand?"

Gail twisted her face. "Afraid mum's the word unless you accept. Abel wishes to keep it on the down-low," she admitted. Esmeralda didn't like the sound of that. Secret errand? Who knew what levels of bullshit that would entail. "It'd be awesome if you did. I remember how well we worked together back in our days of training together. It'd be cool to go on a mission with you. Haven't been on one in a long time," Gail said pleasantly.

Esmeralda sighed and shook her head. "Thanks, but . . . I have things to tend to here. Plus I'm not really a *secret mission* type of gal. There's better people suited for that kind of thing."

Gail twisted her mouth and nodded. "Fair enough." There was a momentary silence again as Gail seemed to gather her thoughts. "So, uh, has Morgan told you the news yet?"

At this, Ezzy flinched. She squinted her eyes. "News? What news?" she asked, feeling herself tense up slightly.

Gail looked around to see if anyone was listening. "About his promotion?" she asked, keeping her voice lowered. Esmeralda breathed out slightly.

"Wh-what promotion?" she asked. She was surprised. Normally she'd be the first to hear of such a thing. It *was* Morgan, after all. Gail seemed excited though, grinning slightly and getting more erratic in her movement. She looked around again.

"Gabriel is gonna get *pardoned* from his training duties . . ." Like a bolt of lightning, the words struck Esmeralda. *What the fuck?* Esmeralda stopped eating and pushed her food aside, now invested in what Gail had to say.

"*What?*" she asked.

"Yeah. Apparently Morgan convinced Abel that because of the Ronald Brown incident, he isn't fit to train new recruits anymore. I guess Morgan will be in charge of new recruits now. That's a pretty big step up for you guys, right?"

No. Ezzy was mad. Furious even. That fucking . . . she breathed out.

"Apparently Gabriel doesn't know yet though. He's gonna get told at the end of the week."

"Thank you for telling me . . ." Ezzy said, rising to her feet. "Good luck on your mission," she added before rushing off. After putting away her food tray, she rushed back to her and Morgan's shared quarters. On her way to the building, she passed a drunk-looking Brenden, who noticed her and looked like he was about to say something. "Not in the fucking mood, Brenden," she growled, hurrying past him and catching him off guard.

"Love it when you talk dirty to me!" he called out before she entered the building.

In a matter of seconds, she arrived at her door and burst through it. Morgan was still asleep on the bed. She slammed the door as hard as she could, jolting him awake. "*What the fuck did you do?*" she yelled.

"E-Ezzy what . . ."

She grabbed some of the fruit sitting on their dining table. "You *snake!*" she yelled, throwing some at him. He guarded himself against the incoming fruit, squinting his eyes.

"Hey!" he growled.

"You used the Ronald Brown incident to get Gabriel fired from training recruits? How *low* can you get, Morgan?"

Immediately, the larger man jumped up from the bed, scaring her. "I do something for *us*, to give *us* more importance in the Saints, and you're gonna fucking yell at me?" Esmeralda's breath came harder as he pushed himself into her face. "*You're gonna talk that way to me?*"

Thwack.

Esmeralda lost her breath as Morgan's fist struck her gut. He threw her to the ground, where she crashed into the lower cabinets. Immediately, tears welled in her eyes and she began shaking. He knelt down and yanked arm, grabbing it hard, making it hurt. "What do you say to me? Huh? What do you say to me?" he barked.

Just like that, fear made Esmeralda's resolve diminish. "I-I'm sorry. *I'm sorry!*" she cried desperately.

"Louder!"

"*I'm sorry!*"

He let go of her arm. "That's better . . ." he said, calming down. Esmeralda broke down, crying in front of him. Goddamn it. Why was she doing this? "Now look what you made me do . . ." he said softly, coming in closer to her. He pulled her into an embrace and she shook in his arms. "Shhh, it's okay," he assured her. The woman clutched him, but her eyes were drawn to a certain dresser drawer in the room. It wouldn't take too many shots of the revolver that was stashed in there to kill him . . . and herself. She didn't have the strength to do it right now . . . but maybe one day.

She sobbed as he hugged her and kissed her cheek. One day.

AYLEN

It had been three days since Beth's untimely murder. Aylen looked around Jared's apartment as he brought in the last of her stuff. After the UWF police spent the last few days searching her apartment, they found nothing. Jared told her that was no surprise. Not just because the government covered things up, but apparently Legion was that untraceable. Even though they had reopened her apartment to her, Aylen was unable to go in. *Physically* unable to go in. It was rather embarrassing for her, actually. She didn't want to see Beth's blood on the wall. Didn't want to see the apartment that she and Beth had fashioned together defiled in the way it had been. Jared had been nice enough to get her stuff for her, but she felt terrible to be such a burden. She felt like she was a burden to everyone. She had just gotten off the phone with her mom, who offered to drive her home. Politely but firmly, Aylen refused. If she went home, Jared wouldn't be able to take her where she wanted to be. Aylen thought about this as she looked out at the university. What was once a vibrant, hip, and exciting place to her had turned awful and dreary since Beth had died. She hated this place now, a fact that made her sad. She used to love this school. Used to love it with all of her heart.

She heard footsteps come closer to her but didn't look their way. "Think I got everything of yours . . . you'll need to sort it out, though, what you want mailed to your ma," Jared said gruffly.

Aylen didn't look at him, but rather continued staring out the window. "Thank you," she said solemnly, looking down into the courtyard of the university. How many times had she and Beth walked across that courtyard, chattering like schoolgirls about nothing? "D-did you make the call?" she asked, still watching outside.

"Yeah. We're just in time for you to join the latest batch of new recruits, apparently. We go there at the end of the week," Jared stated firmly. Aylen nodded, still not looking Jared's way. "Aylen . . ." he started.

"Yeah?"

"Won't you even look my way?" he asked. Slowly and with uncertainty, Aylen turned toward Jared. She didn't want to look at him. It hurt to look at him. "Tell me honestly. Do you blame *me* for what happened? We haven't made eye contact in days," he said. Aylen thought for a moment. Was she mad at him? In truth, she didn't know. She couldn't feel anything. She felt numb.

Aylen stared at him blankly. "No," she replied simply.

Jared sighed. "Three days . . . you haven't really said anything in three days. Not so much as a whimper or a full sentence. Just want you to know if you need to talk . . ."

Aylen shook her head. "I don't," she stated firmly.

Jared thought for a moment and nodded. "Well, if you do . . . you don't gotta deal with this alone," he said quietly. He headed into his bedroom. "You know where I am if you need anything."

With that, Jared closed his bedroom door, leaving Aylen alone in the living room of his dorm. Slowly, she got up off the leather couch and made her way to the cardboard boxes her new roommate left on the floor. Quietly, she knelt next to the nearest box and opened it. In it were things that seemed trivial now: her figurine collection of Sonic the Hedgehog characters, the scarf she'd been knitting, the funny hat with cat ears and googly eyes she found at the mall that one time. Then she found something she wasn't expecting: a familiar framed picture. She lifted it and saw two teenage girls looking back at her. Two fifteen-year-olds, both wearing stupid hats and making the ugliest faces they could. Aylen studied the picture. One of the girls was slightly taller than the other, with blonde hair. Her purple tank top and green pajama shorts matched the googly-eyed dragon hat she wore. Her leg was on the bathroom counter, and in her hand was her pink cellphone, which was pointed toward the bathroom mirror. Her tiny tongue protruded from her mouth as she made the most unflattering face she could while looking at the mirror. The blonde girl's free arm was wrapped around the shoulders of a slightly smaller brunette who was wearing an oversized purple T-shirt and the cat hat Aylen had just found. The brunette girl had her eyes crossed and her cheeks were sunken in to make a fishlike facial expression.

Aylen clutched the photo for a moment and rubbed her thumb over the glass frame. She remembered when this was taken . . . her and Beth's second sleepover. She studied the picture and how happy they were.

"Beth!" Aylen screamed, rushing to her friend and lifting her as she gurgled and shook. Dark, warm liquid seeped over Aylen's hands as it poured freely from a gash in Beth's neck and spewed from her mouth, rushing over her chin. Her bruised and welted face looked like that of a drowning person gasping for air, but unable draw breath. Her eyes stared at the ceiling, widely but vacantly, while she squirmed weakly.

Aylen's breath shuddered as she stared at the picture. Her hand shook slightly as she continued to study it. She killed. . . . Aylen dropped the framed picture back into the cardboard box. She sniffed in, but no tears came out. Her heart pounded, yet her face remained stone. She killed her best friend. Aylen killed her best friend. She had to get into the Saint Organization. She had to make this right. She had to make it up to Beth.

Aylen breathed in and looked at the boxes. All of these boxes were her life with her best friend, a life she could no longer be a part of. She'd have to separate herself from Lindsey and the remainder of her friends . . . had to separate herself from anyone that was close to her in this life. She was going to be a Saint, a hero, and she was going to stop the Devil's Deviants. She was going to fight and kill the monsters. It was the least she could do, after what had happened. She was going to avenge Beth, no matter the cost.

ABEL

Night fell yet again on Salutem. A slight mist from the drizzle earlier filled the chilly air as two black vans drove through the glimmering streets. Abel watched through the front window from his seat in quiet anticipation. Tonight was the night. He hadn't seen action since Widow's Mountain, but his skills were still sharp. Would he need them tonight? A feeling of unease lurked among the Saints that rode alongside him, preparing their weapons as the van twisted down the winding road. Everyone was dressed in black tonight, not knowing where this late-night adventure would take them. Abel looked briefly at Gail, who seemed to be watching him intently. It had been a while since she had seen action as well. If anything went wrong, could she still hold her own?

"Cheery mood tonight," a familiar voice in the van said. Abel looked over at Corporal Greenfield, who was looking at him with that cocksure grin he liked to wear. Abel swallowed. "So, I gotta ask, General," the young man began. Gail shot Eric a look, which he noticed and didn't seem to mind. "I don't see Captain Webster around anywhere. I gotta say, I'm curious where he is," the blond man said before grinning wider.

Abel breathed out, glaring at the young man. "Captain Webster couldn't make it. Not that it's any concern of yours."

Eric shrugged. "Just wondering. After all, he *is* the man that got me suspended. Speaking of which, is this little mission your way of saying the suspension is lifted?" the young man asked, squinting his eyes.

"It's my way of saying I'll think about it," the Saint leader stated firmly.

Eric lifted his eyebrows and nodded. Then he took a moment and looked around. He sniffed and looked at the soldier to his right. "Get ready in a hurry, did we?"

Abel sighed and turned his attention back to the road. Eric Greenfield was many things, a pain in the ass being one of them.

"Fancy seeing you, Gail, thought you were Faith for a second," Eric said as the car rocked back and forth. Gail glared at him from her seat. "Then again, you have a distinct quality about your face she doesn't have . . ."

Gail sighed and rolled her eyes. "Bitchiness. I think bitchiness is the term you're looking for, Eric," she said with annoyance.

"Nah, was about to say it's a slightly prettier face," he said with a smirk.

Gail grinned at this, too widely. "You think you're so sly, little boy."

"Only if it's working," Eric replied. The woman's smile turned full-on flirtatious.

"Down, boy."

Abel cleared his throat, getting their attention. "Mission," he said gruffly. Eric quickly winked at Gail and Abel could swear that woman slightly blushed. Those two haven't . . . ? Abel shook his head and turned his thoughts away from the idea. Eric was still Eric, apparently, for better or worse.

After Eric quieted down, Abel's stress began to overcome him. He could see the construction site they were to meet Dupont at in the distance. An ache of anticipation came over him as the van slowed to a crawl. It was a skeleton of a building, surrounded by dirt. The driver of the van stopped and got out, opening the gate that closed it off from the rest of Salutem. They passed through, and Abel watched as the driver of the other van in their small convoy got out and closed the gate behind them. There were barrels filled with fire on the half-building, their glow coming into focus as they got closer to it. Between them were tractors and such, and between those were figures that began appearing among the half-built building, holding assault rifles. Dupont's men. They wore tan enhancer armor and looked vaguely menacing in the dark. Abel gulped as the men stepped out in front of the van and held up their hands, telling the vans to park. Here went nothing.

In moments, they opened the back of the vans and Saints poured out onto the dirt. Abel left the van last, accompanied by Eric and Gail. The air was cold and a slight breeze blew right through the black turtleneck and jacket that he was wearing. Carefully, he and the group began heading toward the building. On the highest level above, the men in tan enhancer armor looked down at the Saints as they approached. There was a ledge in the building that was roughly ten feet off the ground, which had stairs leading up to it. It was there that Abel could see a casually dressed weasel of a man with a thin face and an equally thin mustache. He stood in front of a barrel crackling with fire, warming his hands. The man took notice of Abel and the other Saints approaching the foot of the stairs.

"Ah! Monsieur Quinn! At long last! Come, stand by the fire with me, it is a cold night," Dupont said cheerfully.

Abel briefly exchanged a glance with Gail, who was equally unimpressed. "Thanks, I think I'm comfortable where I am for the moment," the Principal Overseer stated. *Just him? By himself? On the same floor as Dupont* and *his soldiers? No, thank you.*

Dupont grinned and wagged his finger. "Cautious man, I like it!" he said before beginning to head down the stairs. "Very well, I come down to you, my friend," Dupont said cheerfully enough. As it stood right now, Dupont had a few more men than Abel, but the Saints had Eric, so he wasn't quite as alarmed he normally would've been. The men in tan enhancer armor kept a close eye on the Saints as their leader headed toward them. "Caution is a sign of a good businessman. I like good businessmen, they make business . . . well, more of an art than business," Dupont mused.

"You have something of mine," Abel now said firmly.

"Technically a little more than one something, though. Am I right?" the Frenchman said, tilting his head. "Yes, that's why we're here. To renegotiate. Come, walk with me." The man beckoned the Saint leader to follow him. Abel gave him a look of dissatisfaction, then looked toward the men in enhancer armor that stood above them. Dupont curled his lips. "All this distrust . . ."

"It's warranted. You have three of my soldiers," he said bitingly. Dupont sighed, then looked at his men and spoke in French. The men in enhancer armor on the higher levels jumped to the dirt below, right next to Abel and his Saints.

Dupont turned to Abel, slightly annoyed. "There, now my men can get to know your men better. Will you follow me now?" Abel exchanged a glance with Gail, who gave him a look with a furrowed brow and a frown.

"How do I know you don't have more up there?" Abel said before turning back to Dupont.

The Frenchman twisted his face. "Tell you what. We just go up here, in full view of your troops. And we talk like that, then?" the man suggested, frustration edging further into his voice. Abel looked at Gail again; she shook her head no. Abel breathed out and nodded, tapping her shoulder before walking up the stairs. Her gaze seemed to follow him, even as he kept his eyes off her.

Dupont smiled at this. "I see your lady friend worries about you," he said with a sneer.

"She's a loyal comrade," Abel grumbled.

With that, Dupont and Abel climbed the stairs together. "So . . . you're Monsieur Martell's cousin."

"On my mother's side, yes," Dupont responded as they got to the top of the ledge. The building was large, with a deep vacant shadow, preventing Abel from seeing too deeply into the almost tunnel-like structure.

"The Saints had nothing but a healthy working relationship with Monsieur Martell. What is all of this about?"

Dupont smiled. "Innovation. Monsieur Martell's empire crumbled to pieces. As the successor to my cousin, I must make sure that every facet in this rebuilt empire is sturdy."

"Is that why you killed Tautou?"

"Tautou was stuck in the past. Afraid of change." Abel thought for a moment at this statement. Just what the hell did that mean? "I am sure you can sympathize, being a new leader of an empire yourself."

Abel sniffed in. He didn't like that Dupont was comparing the two. "I don't kill my people if they don't agree with me," he said flatly.

"Ah, but how does the saying go? 'Can't make an omelet without breaking a few eggs'?" Dupont responded pleasantly. The Saint leader scrunched his face and looked down at his Saints, surrounded by Dupont's men. They were sizing each other up.

"I see you have your men wearing enhancer armor. Wouldn't happen to be *our* enhancer armor, would it?" Abel said before turning back toward Dupont.

"Observant. Yes, it was desert armor, hence the *horrible* color. Not quite as stylish as the green you Saints like to wear." He chuckled.

"You're trying to make a deal with me and you're wearing *my* enhancer armor?" the Saint leader said sharply.

Dupont seemed to note the hostility. "Well, to be fair, when dealing with a group that wears enhancer armor, no doubt it's a good idea to have armor yourself?" he asked. "That, Monsieur Quinn, and I'm not here to make a deal with you. *You* are here to make a deal with *me.*"

Abel lifted an eyebrow. "Oh?"

Dupont shrugged. "There aren't many buyers in the market these days, but I want *you* to convince *me* why the Duponts, no longer the Martells, should do business with you," the Frenchman said, shrugging.

"You're joking."

"Non, Monsieur, I no joke," Dupont said firmly. "You Saints were short your last two payments."

Abel scoffed. "We paid the exact amount for those shipments."

"Yes. But you did not pay *my* interest."

The Saint leader was already sick of this punk. "Interest?" Abel asked, a wry smile now on his face.

"Something we can overlook once you pay an initial fee, then we will continue doing business as usual if I deem it worthy, with added rates, of course," Dupont said pleasantly.

Abel blinked. "And how much are you bumping up prices?" he asked.

"Mmm . . . twenty-five percent."

The Saint leader cocked his head. "Twenty-five percent."

"Oui. Twenty-five percent. What? I thought you Saints had *money.* Shouldn't be a problem, no?"

Abel glared at the pompous Frenchman. "You expect me to pay twenty-five percent more—hell, even do business with you still—after kidnapping my men?"

"Is there a problem with that arrangement, Monsieur Quinn?"

Abel scoffed. "I'll tell you something about me, boy," the Saint leader began. "You may think that because I am the new leader, I'm weak, like some petty thug you normally deal with." Abel shook his head. "But you can't bully me. I have *no* fear of you." He stepped closer to the gangster. "I have killed Anthrodi in blade-to-blade combat. I have faced hordes of Brainless. I have slain my fair share of Devil's Deviants. Me. *Personally.*" A pleasant feeling rushed through him at Dupont's sharper breaths, at the fear that widened his eyes and made him swallow. "What have you got on an Anthrodi foot soldier, boy?"

Dupont scoffed with an unconvincing smile and shake of his head. "Is that supposed to scare me, Monsieu—"

"*General,*" Abel interjected. "I am a general and you will address me as such. Your cousin was a man of honor. I respected the business we did with him because of it. You have no honor. You're just a dumb punk trying to strongarm me into a faulty deal," Abel said, staring into the eyes of the younger man. He didn't seem as sure of himself as he did before.

"My cousin . . . was a little circus *freak*. A pathetic, petite little *midget* who got killed by his own men—"

"Oh, but I bet you never dared say that to his face did you? I know what used to happen to anyone who would comment on his dwarfism." Abel was within kissing distance of the Frenchman, and could smell a foul odor about him. "Your cousin, despite his size, was more of a man than you will ever be, boy. Now, I'm done playing games and I'm not gonna do business with you, so tell me: *Where are my soldiers?*"

"Such a temper . . ." a female voice spoke suddenly at their side, catching Abel off guard. Footsteps echoed from the deep, dark shadows. Abel squinted and made out a female figure walking forward. Immediately, Abel began backing away, down the stairs, recognizing who she was by her shock-white hair. "I think we've played this out long enough, don't you, Dupont?" the woman asked.

Abel was on the steps when the female figure emerged fully into the light. Pestilence. She wore a leather crop top, exposing her tattoo-covered arms and a little of her tattooed belly, as well as leather pants and boots that matched. Her white hair was tied in a braid of some sort, and in her hands were three familiar severed heads. The two girls' heads were in one hand, held by their hair, and the bearded man's head was in her other hand, propped against her leg. One of the girls' heads looked worse than the others. A revolting gash had opened up Corporal Day's face, along with multiple cuts, and her eye was completely mangled. "Here are your troops, Quinn. Take 'em."

With that, Pestilence rolled the heads down the stairs. Abel stared in horror at Pestilence's presence and continued to back down the concrete steps. He looked at Dupont. "You made a deal with the Devil's Deviants? *You betrayed humanity*, Dupont?" he yelled.

Dupont shrugged. "There's only two real customers on the market anymore. And *they* pay better," he said with a slight sneer. Abel backed up to his Saints now, and Gail grabbed his collar and pulled him backward. Within the upper levels of the half-built building, he could see glowing eyes. Brainless.

"You will burn in hell for this, Dupont!"

But as the words left his mouth, a crowd of inhuman men and women with assault rifles appeared on the ground from the shadows behind them. Deviants. They were boxed in.

"I think you need to worry a little about yourself, Monsieur Quinn," Dupont said, cocksure.

BANG.

Abel was blinded by a bright flash and felt a hand press his belt. Enhancer armor enveloped his body as he felt himself being rushed away by someone else. The same hand that released his armor pulled him down to his knees. When his vision returned, all he could see was a man in green enhancer armor next to him. His hearing came back, and now he heard blaring gunfire from his side. He felt a hand on his other side.

"General! *Are you okay?*" Gail yelled. Abel blinked. What just happened? Abel briefly looked over the top of the block of bricks they were hiding behind. Pandemonium had erupted in a matter of seconds. DDs, Dupont's men, and Saints were on the ground dead. A chaotic firefight had erupted. He barely had a chance to see where the enemy soldiers were before a hand pulled him back down and he heard bullets zip by his head.

"*Sit down!*" a familiar voice from the soldier next to him beckoned. Eric? Was it Eric that had pulled him this way? He and Gail exchanged looks.

"Eric threw a flashbang to get you out of there!" she yelled to Abel as sparks flew next to them. Abel looked up again. Pestilence was calmly walking down the stairs, her skin fading into a shade of chrome. Bullets bounced off her as she marched forward. Eric returned behind cover to reload.

"We need to find a way to get you back to those vans. Those vans are bullet-proof and our only shot out of here," he said, breathing hard.

Gail pressed a button on her armor. "Saints, priority one is to get General Quinn to the vans. I repeat, priority one is—"

Just then a man with blue skin turned the corner, holding an assault rifle, looking directly at Gail. Before Abel could even react, a knife appeared in the deviant's head and he fell down.

"I'll make a distraction," Eric said, rushing past the two, sword fully extended. "Get Abel to the van, Gail." Abel watched as Eric rushed toward three of Dupont's men with assault rifles, each pointed at the Saint. He was fast, though. Before the men in tan enhancer armor could react, the young man swiped off the arms of one of them and cut off his head before stabbing the one behind him in the stomach, then shooting him in the face with a handgun.

"*Come on!*" Gail said over the gunfire. She helped pull Abel up and began rushing through the chaos. Saints were all over, either killing Dupont's men and the DDs or getting killed by them. Abel spared a look at the building above; the Brainless were still up there, waiting. He turned to look at Pestilence, whose chrome skin glowed in the firelight. She was holding a Saint woman in the air by her throat with one hand; her other arm was shaped like a blade. Without any hesitation, she put her hand through the Saint's body before looking Abel's way. They weren't that far from the vans. Saints began circling them as the Saint leader continued toward their escape. They were almost there when Gail took notice of Pestilence. Oh no . . .

Gail broke off from the Saints, stepped toward the woman, and raised her assault rifle. Pestilence began toward the group, walking calmly even as Gail screamed a primal howl, pointing her rifle at Pestilence.

RATATATATATATATATATATATATATATAT—

Pingpingpingpingpingping—

Pestilence didn't seem to react at all to Gail unloading her ammo into her. Abel tried calling for his comrade, but his voice fell upon deaf ears. That idiot! She was gonna get herself killed. In moments, the Saint ran out of ammo and threw her rifle to the ground, reaching for her sword. Just then, another Saint with a sword appeared in front of Gail and pushed her back, causing her to fall backward to the ground. Abel quickly rushed to her side and pulled her up, helping her toward the vans. In moments, the man swung his sword at Pestilence's neck but was blocked by her hand. She swung her arm toward him and he jumped backward, avoiding her blade. The two exchanged blows for a moment before the man eventually kicked her back and began backing away slowly. Angered, Pestilence pointed her finger toward her enemies. The Brainless above began jumping to the ground, running past her to get to the Saints. The man with the sword retracted it and ran to the vans.

"Time to go!" Eric yelled as the remaining Saints rushed into the vehicles, shooting at the incoming Brainless. Abel pulled Gail into a van and other Saints filled it behind them, with Eric being the last to enter before they shut the doors and sped off. Abel looked into the side mirror. The Brainless were all left behind as both vans raced forward, eventually crashing through the chain-link fence that closed them off.

Abel looked at the woman in his grip as she held her head in her hands. Her helmet was off and she was sobbing. Then he took off his own helmet and looked at her.

"*The hell were you thinking?*" he barked at her. "*You could've been killed!*"

Gail shook her head. "I-I'm sorry Abe, I'm so sorry . . ." she said, still sobbing hysterically, tears rolling down her cheeks. He knew why she was crying. He put his arm around her shoulders, then looked around at the other remaining Saints.

They were all staring at him with their helmets off, defeated looks on their faces. Abel was almost killed tonight. He and the others here were almost slaughtered like Rob at that ambush. This was a close call. Too close. Those damned DDs . . . they tried to kill him like they did Rob, and he had been stupid enough to fall for such a trap . . . he felt embarrassed. He should've seen it *was* a trap. Should've known something was wrong. He had to keep this quiet. The Saints couldn't afford to know of this horrible mistake that almost claimed his life. "None of you can tell anyone what happened here tonight," he said firmly. Then he shook his head. "No one can ever know just how close that was." The group remained silent to this order, looking at him grimly.

"Uh-uh," a familiar voice said. "'Fraid you're gonna have to buy my silence this time, General Quinn," Eric said, with a catlike grin on his face.

Abel glared at the younger soldier. "What do you want?" he asked darkly.

Eric smiled wider at this. "Back in."

JARED

Jared awoke in the middle of the night to hear wailing in his apartment. On instinct, he used his super speed to get out of bed and rush into the living room, immediately turning on his lights. There, on his leather couch, Aylen was curled up into a ball, wailing her heart out. Jared stood in slight shock for a moment. It had been five days since Beth's death, and not a single tear had dropped from her since it happened. She had been quiet, very quiet, and she had barely eaten a thing. Now, she clutched her blankets and scrunched up her face, cheeks wet with tears, as she let out a nearly screaming wail. Jared rushed to her side.

"Aylen?" he asked. Aylen she saw him, but she continued sobbing, shaking her head.

"I-I killed my best friend . . . I-I killed . . ." She shuddered before sobbing some more. Jared felt his heart drop.

"Hey . . ." he said, putting his hand on her shoulder. She continued sobbing as he rubbed it. He softly hugged her as she remained lying down.

"Sh-she's gone. M-my best friend is . . . she's . . ." Aylen mumbled before letting out a another huge wail. Jared knew her pain. He knew it too well. After that last sob, Aylen sat up and he backed off. Her eyes searched around. "I just—I just see her face, Jared. It—it never leaves," she said while sobbing. "It's my fault she's—It's my faul—" Her words turned incoherent.

Jared hugged her again and she clutched him back tight, sobbing into his chest. "Shhhhh, it's okay . . . it's okay . . ." he said to comfort her.

After a moment, he heard only sniffles again, and he backed away when Aylen did. Her eyes were red. "I-I'm sorry . . . th-this is embarrassing . . ." she said with her face flat, wiping away tears. "I—I don't know what came over me. I—"

"It's okay. Better you cry, A," Jared said solemnly. "Better out than in."

Aylen shook her head and swallowed. "I-I'm not ready to talk about it. I—I don't want to talk about it . . ." she said, her lip quivering slightly.

Jared nodded. "Okay . . ." he stated. "You haven't eaten much in the last couple of days . . . want me to cook you something?" he asked.

"S-sure . . ." she said, nodding.

He studied her face. "What do you wanna eat?" he asked. She looked deep in thought for a moment and looked up at him.

"Mac and cheese, please . . . if you have it . . ." she said meekly. He did. Jared quickly started cooking up the food she requested. She sat on the couch silently, blankly staring at nothing. He studied her and twisted his face slightly. He didn't like seeing her like this. He understood it—if anybody understood it, he did. He sighed. She was too nice of a person to suffer this way.

After he finished preparing the food, Jared got out a plate and fork for Aylen and brought her the meal.

"Thanks . . ." she said quietly. He sat next to her on the couch.

"No problem," he said in response. He watched her eat. She was hungrier than she must have realized. At first, she delicately nibbled on the food, then she was shoveling it. He smiled slightly. She was getting her appetite back.

"So . . ." Aylen began in between bites. "What's that hairstyle you like to wear called?" she asked quietly.

Jared blinked, lifting an eyebrow. "What?" he asked, chuckling.

"Your hairstyle . . ."

Jared leaned back into the couch, not sure what to make of her subject change. "Well . . . I've styled my hair like Sid Vicious . . . or at least, I've tried to," he said, putting his hand through his messy hair.

"It's cool," she commented.

"Thanks."

She finished the meal and put the plate on his coffee table. "Wanna watch anything?" Jared softly asked.

"Uh . . . yeah. *Adventures of Dumbcat*, if that's okay . . ." she said meekly. Obeying her wish, Jared turned on his TV and turned on the show she wanted to see. At some point, she leaned in to him and put her head on his shoulder. Jared breathed out and looked down at her as she watched the show. Before long, she was lying on her side, facing away from the deviant. After Jared finished the episode, he looked over and found her fast asleep. Quietly, he placed her blankets over her and stared at her for a second. He wasn't sure the Saint Organization was the best thing for her, but after what happened, how could he tell her no? Still, he wondered if Aylen could survive the Saints. It wasn't an easy life, and it certainly didn't seem like the sort of life Aylen, of all people, should get involved in. Hopefully, she had enough strength in her to keep herself alive. The war had claimed much fiercer characters than her in the past. What was this nerdy bookworm gonna do?

As Jared went back to bed, he dreaded their drive to the Saint Organization in the morning. Hopefully, Aylen could survive. Hopefully, he wouldn't come to regret letting her join. Hopefully. Either way, tomorrow was a big day.

EPISODE 11

MONSTERS

PESTILENCE

Pestilence came back to The Ninth Circle, followed by her men. It was early morning and the music was a slow and rhythmic beat, and the remaining strippers in their last few hours of work danced almost lazily for the few remaining perverts in the room. Of course, of the remaining patrons was the overweight drunk named Bugsy. He had been a loyal customer of theirs since the beginning so his presence throughout the night was to be expected. Lately, he had been drooling over a girl who called herself Eevee Sapphire. The stripper briefly looked up at Pestilence with a furrowed brow and sunken cheeks. To this, the white-haired woman merely nodded her head. From what she knew of the girl, her time to pay certain debts was quickly running out. The girl had nothing to worry about from Pestilence, but sooner or later, somebody would make her disappear. Pestilence expected her to no longer be around within the week. Such was normal around this place.

Pestilence and her men trekked forward toward the VIP Lounge, where Dejon, otherwise known as War, waited in front, a smirk on his large face.

"Sexy as ever, Pestilence," he said with lust in his yellow eyes. Pestilence remained stone-faced. The red-skinned man moved in a bit. "You know . . . if

Death isn't man enough for you, I'm always happy to oblige," he said, looming over her, blocking her path. She coldly stared at him, then gave a slight, wry grin.

"The day I see your cock is the day I cut off your balls, Dejon. Get out of my way."

The larger man chuckled. "So vicious! Whatever happened to that sweet li'l thing I knew back in Neolympus?" he said, leaning down, almost within kissing distance of her. She smiled seductively, putting her hand on his cheek, then turned her hand into metal, her fingers into blades, and slowly began cutting his flesh.

"She grew up, Dejon."

Softly, War grabbed her hand and moved it away, looking slightly disappointed. "Mmm, damn shame." He backed off, wiping his cheek of the blood leaking from the scratches. "Lucifer wants to see you. Talk to you 'bout what you've been up to lately," War said, changing his tone. Pestilence breathed out. *That can't be good.* She and her men passed War, and he added, "Don't keep him waiting." They exchanged glares before the doors to the VIP Lounge were shut and the elevator began descending. Pestilence scowled. She would never forgive him for what he tried to do all those years ago.

Once arriving in the bunker underneath the strip club, the other deviants got to return to their quarters, to their families no doubt, yet tonight Pestilence had to make a stop before that luxury. It was dimly lit in the bunker, signifying nighttime. She furrowed her brow as her boots clanked upon the metal walkways. Lucifer hardly slept; when he did, his sleep patterns seemed somewhat random and inconsistent, a bit of an enigma to everyone in the bunker. Unfortunately, Pestilence had no such sleep schedule. Her body felt heavy as she continued forward, body aching from the bullets she'd deflected earlier. No doubt Lucifer wanted every detail of what happened tonight and how plans had gone awry.

Once she arrived at Lucifer's quarters, she knocked on the steel door. It took a few moments before the door made a sound and a familiar face peeked out. His brown hair was slicked back, the horns on his forehead pointed toward the ceiling, and the whites of his eyes seemed slightly reddened. It looked like he was wearing some sort of satin robe over pajamas. As his eyes met hers, a smile rose from the corner of his mouth.

"Pestilence."

"Hello, Lucifer."

"Come in."

Lucifer widened the door. As Pestilence entered the front office of the DD leader's headquarters, she looked around at the familiar walls. The only fireplace in all of The Ninth Circle crackled to the right side of the room. Oak bookcases filled with literary classics took up the majority of the space on the walls of the room. Where there weren't bookcases, landscape paintings of forests covered the walls. A red, persian rug was in the middle of the black marble-looking floor with red leather couches leading up to it. Next to the couches were end tables with lamps that lit the room. Toward the end of the room was a desk. It was large and oak and had a big, comfortable chair behind it, as well as less comfortable chairs in front, just to remind everyone who was in charge in this room. To this side of it was a door that led into the rest of his living quarters. The office in its entirety looked out of place from the rest of the bunker, but she supposed that was exactly the way Lucifer liked it. He was the king down here, after all.

"So . . . the Dupont deal was successful," Lucifer remarked, indicating for her to sit in front of his desk. Without hesitation, she sat in the chair and breathed out uncomfortably.

"It was indeed. Officially speaking, the Saints are now without their gun contact."

Lucifer circled around and pulled out some brandy from a nearby cabinet.

"Hmm, good. But . . . I hear our other bit of business failed," he said, disappointed. Pestilence breathed out through her nose. "Quinn escaped," Lucifer added coldly. "You don't usually fail me, Pestilence. I'm shocked." Pestilence swallowed hard, fearing what may happen to her. There was a brief silence in the room before Lucifer chuckled slightly, lowering himself into his chair. "Don't look so glum, Pestilence. I know there were other factors at play than any incompetence on your behalf. The Bastard Saint, so I've heard, is the only reason Quinn escaped with his life." Lucifer leaned back in. Pestilence breathed out slightly, relieved.

"His presence was unanticipated, sir. He's been an inactive member for the last few months according to our intelligence."

"So you're saying intelligence is to blame for the folly?" Lucifer asked calmly. Shit. Pestilence didn't want to be responsible for anyone's death.

"No. *I* should've killed the Bastard Saint in combat. He caught us by surprise with the flashbang he used . . . but I went toe to toe with him and couldn't kill him. The blame falls on me."

Lucifer smiled at this. "You say that like it's not impressive you're still alive after that encounter. The Bastard Saint is one of their two best soldiers, only rivaled by Azrael. The fact you can walk away from a direct fight with him unscathed is a miracle. It is said he is the best swordsman in the world . . ." Lucifer trailed off and took a sip of his brandy. "Well, I suppose, at the very least, we've weakened their resolve somewhat. No doubt they'll be scrambling to find a new source for supplies now that we've officially cut off their main supply line. It should buy us some time. We'll need it for what we're going to do in the near future."

There was slight silence between the two. Pestilence merely nodded, shocked that Lucifer was so forgiving of her failure to kill Quinn. She didn't wish to look a gift horse in the mouth, however. She would be thankful that he decided to not punish her. "You've done a lot for the cause lately. Rest up. Enjoy your family. I'll be contacting you when I'm ready for us to start preparations for the next step toward Project Reckoning," Lucifer said pleasantly. "You're dismissed."

With that, Pestilence nodded and got out of her chair. "Oh, and Pestilence?" Lucifer said, getting her attention. "Next time you find yourself in one-on-one combat with the Bastard Saint, you'd better kill him." His tone was serious, yet he maintained his smile.

A shiver went down her spine as she looked at him. Then she nodded her head again. "Yes, sir."

With that, the white-haired woman made her way out of the DD leader's quarters, feeling his lingering, hawk-like gaze still upon her. That man always made her nervous. Despite her abilities, she always felt mildly powerless in his presence. Yet he gave her permission to relax for a bit, and that was a relief. She needed some time off.

Excited to get home, Pestilence walked hurriedly through the halls of the bunker toward her quarters. She hated the leather outfit she was wearing; it was tight and uncomfortable and she wanted to change as soon as possible. While walking home, though, she passed a familiar sight: A skinny, blue-haired Latin girl with extremely short hair and an oversized blue sweater stood where she normally stood almost every night. The irises of her eyes were blood-red and the girl's ears were long and pointed from Project Suncloud. Pestilence furrowed her brow to see the girl where she was. It had been years and she had done this way too often.

"You ever get tired of staring at that door, Famine?"

The younger, blue-haired girl sighed and turned toward Pestilence. "Ever get tired of commenting on it?"

Pestilence walked up to her and the girl willfully ignored her as she approached. "It's unhealthy, J," she said sympathetically. Famine barely reacted. The three small stars tattooed under her red eyes twitched slightly in the dark. "He's been gone now for years."

Famine curled her lip at this. "When I was going through the worst of my addiction, where were *you* when I needed you, Em?" she snapped. Pestilence closed her eyes and breathed out.

"That's not fair and you know it."

"I know, but . . ." Famine indicated toward the door. "*He* was there when I needed someone most. *He* helped me get clean. Haven't touched anything bad in a long time . . ." Famine paused, seeming to relive memories while staring at the door. "I don't come here because I miss him, I know that bridge is more than burned. I come here . . . to remember." Famine turned toward Pestilence. "Remind myself why I'll never have anything to do with the stuff again."

Pestilence analyzed Famine with her eyes and nodded. What the hell was she going to say to that? Famine had been clean for years now. "Fair enough. Don't let anyone else see you out here, though, if you can help it. Might give people the wrong impression."

"Thanks, Auntie Em," Famine replied sarcastically as Pestilence continued walking. That girl . . . Pestilence sighed. She was doing a lot better now, but what a shitty life that girl had led. There was a time when Pestilence had tried to look after her, but there's only so much one can do for someone who is out to destroy themselves. It really was *him* who got her on a good path, oddly enough. Life was funny that way. Nothing was ever simple, and it definitely was never black and white.

When Pestilence arrived at her quarters finally, she felt a wave of relief come over her. A genuine smile grew across her face as she began to dig out her keys. She didn't have to be Pestilence behind these doors. Behind these doors, she could be plain old Emily Gilmore. No intimidating façade, no having to be tough. As she unlocked the door softly, she found her quarters dimly lit by a yellowish light. She had done her best to make this bunker seem like a regular home. Rugs were laid over the hard floor, paintings and potted plants sat next to the walls, and comfortable chairs were placed in front of the TV set. On one of the side tables was a photo of three familiar figures, smiling back at the camera. As Pestilence softly closed the door behind her, she could see a familiar dark-skinned man, fast asleep on the recliner. His hair was curly and he wore a robe over his pajamas. Paul tried—and failed—to stay up late for her again.

She smiled at this and walked over to him, leaning over and kissing him on the forehead.

"Mmmm . . . was wondering when you'd come home," her husband said sleepily, eyes still closed. He opened his eyes slightly and the two looked at each other with smiles before meeting lips. The kiss was a loving and tender one, and soft. The two then pulled away. "How'd it go?"

Emily twisted her mouth. "I'll tell you about it in the morning. Is Stacy asleep?"

Paul smiled. "Out like a light, no tossing and turning." Emily lit up at the news. That was good.

"I'mma check on her, you go to bed, mister. I'll join you soon."

The two kissed again and Emily made her way to her daughter's room. Quietly, she opened the girl's door.

When she saw her equally white-haired daughter fast asleep, the full-grown woman smiled wearily and crept toward her sleeping daughter, eventually lying down and curling up beside the girl on the bed. She watched her and breathed out, lightly untangling the sleeping little girl's hair. Everything Emily did, every horrible thing she would ever do . . . at the end of the day it was all for *her*. Emily watched her daughter sleep. Despite the hellish night, Mrs. Emily Gilmore was finally home.

AYLEN

Aylen sat in the front passenger seat of her car and stared out her window. Under the circumstances, both her mother and the university understood her taking time away from school. In order to keep up with all of her coursework she would have to take online versions of the classes, but physically, she did not have to return to the campus until she was ready. Aylen thought that this was beneficial; she would need that time away from school if she was to do what her heart and mind had set on doing.

She looked over at Jared, who was driving the car. They had barely spoken since the night Aylen declared she would become a Saint. Since the night that Beth was murdered. Last night was probably the most they had said to one another in a while. It was still strange to talk to him, though. They both remained quiet as a grave as Jared drove through Salutem with some of Aylen's personal belongings in the back. The other half of Aylen's belongings were still at Jared's, since she was now to stay at his place whenever she wasn't on base. Aylen wasn't sure where her emotions stood at the moment, but it didn't feel right to talk to him these days. She didn't hate him, but she didn't necessarily like him anymore either. It wasn't anything he did. Lord knew he had been nice enough. He'd taken very good care of her depressed and quiet state over the last week or so. But perhaps it was because she blamed him, or blamed herself? More likely the latter. It was because she told Jared—about everything—that Beth was dead. It was her fault. Legion's knife may have slit her friend's throat, but her blood was on Aylen's hands.

Aylen looked through the front window. A ginormous black wall taller than a skyscraper had begun to come into view. They had been driving for roughly an hour through Salutem to get here. This was the border of the city, a place Aylen only vaguely remembered passing through back in her childhood. She and her parents had crossed into Salutem through it during the Great Assimilation in 2046. She remembered being fascinated by it as a kid, and it still fascinated her now. As Aylen and Jared drove up to the wall, she continued to study the massive blockade. It was an impressive structure that had to be at least five hundred feet tall. On various balconies on the wall stood armed guards and mechanized gun turrets. At the ground level, there was a gate on the wall that blocked the road. Armored men with German shepherds were on standby at the entrance. Jared slowed the car as a guard with black armor waved for them to halt. Jared applied the brakes, stopping the car entirely. The man with the black armor walked to the car window and Jared rolled it down.

"Hi there, how can I help you today?" the man in the black armor said in a mechanical voice through his helmet. Aylen observed the armor; it was thick and tank-like, obviously meant to withstand heavy firepower. Over his heart was an insignia that looked like a rook chess piece attached to a fist. On his shoulders were the signature snowy mountains of the United World Federation with the words "Peace on Earth" encircling them. The sun made the armor glimmer the way it would on a black car. He carried some sort of automatic rifle, something slightly more advanced than she'd seen in video games, though Aylen had no idea what the exact model was.

"We wanna pass the border," Jared said calmly.

"Do you have a license to?" the man in black armor asked. Jared nodded and pulled a card from his jacket's chest pocket. The armored guard took it in his covered fingers and looked down at the license. Lasers emerged from the helmet and scanned the barcode on the card, then the armored man looked at his comrades who were closer to the wall. "He's good!" the armored man yelled. The gate began to open, revealing the road behind the wall. The armored man handed Jared back his license. "All right, sir, you're good to go. You and your lady friend have a wonderful day." The armored man nodded and made way for the car to pass through.

"Thank you," Jared said. Then he lifted the brakes and they passed through the gate.

Aylen looked at the area beyond the gate, mesmerized. Miles of untapped wilderness stretched out in front of the car, the likes of which Aylen wasn't sure she had ever seen. The car sped down the road as she stared out the window at the lush green fields and trees that surrounded Salutem. Majestic green mountains filled the background of the beautiful scenery. She looked in the side mirror of the car and watched as the gigantic wall of Salutem drifted farther and farther away. The child in her wanted Jared to stop the car so she could run out into the wilderness. Perhaps she would've if what happened to Beth hadn't happened. Then again, she wouldn't be traveling to the Saint Organization's base if that were the case. The car twisted and turned down the road, and soon they vanished into a dark forest. Jared noticed Aylen's admiration for the greenery of the forest and smiled lightly.

"This forest is called the Forest of Sorrows. Apparently, some decisive battles of the Anthrodi War were fought here. Some of this war's battles have been fought here as well. It's beautiful, but it's also a deadly place. Brainless, Deviant colonies, and other unknown dangers roam these woods."

"How long till we get there?" Aylen asked quietly. Jared squinted his eyes and searched ahead of him.

"Maybe another thirty to forty minutes," he replied. Aylen continued to watch the seemingly ever-expansive forest. The Saint Organization was only thirty to forty minutes away.

GABRIEL

Gabriel made his way to Abel's office and opened the door. What could Abel possibly want with him now? He did not like the spontaneity of the summons for him, especially considering that Abel already had stern words for him after Ronald Brown's execution. He entered the office, clenching his teeth and tightening his muscles. His friend looked rather haggard behind his desk, as if he hadn't had any sleep the night before.

"General, you summoned me?" he asked sheepishly. Abel watched Gabriel from across the room, an unreadable look on his face.

"Yes, sit down."

Gabriel obliged and shifted uncomfortably within his seat.

"Why the, uh, why the summons?" the captain asked his superior. Gabriel watched as Abel studied him up and down.

"How long have you been training Saint Organization members?"

"Roughly around five to six years, sir."

"I see," the general said calmly. "Well, there's no easy way to say this, so I'll just say this outright, but . . . understand we all are grateful for your training services. You've even trained my son, for which I am thankful."

"Wait . . . what are you saying?" Gabriel snapped, feeling a well of anger spur within him. There was a moment of awkward silence as the two men stared each other down. Of course. *That* is what this was about. Gabriel breathed out through his nose. "Are . . . are you *terminating me* from instructing the new recruits?" Abel paused for a moment, then nodded.

"Yes," he said firmly. Gabe scoffed. Figured. "You will still keep your title as my right-hand adviser, and you still are a captain, but that particular responsibility has been removed from your repertoire. Now, if you want to take someone in as your personal pupil, you can do that, but you are no longer in charge of training new recruits."

"So who's in charge now?"

"Captain Gatton."

"Morgan?" Gabriel complained. He chuckled wryly. "That's rich."

"He's the only other one of us with as much military background as you. I'd even dare say he has more."

"If I may, sir, why am I being taken off from instructing duties?"

"Well . . . I don't think you are capable of continuing the training. Due to recent events, I think you are no longer fit for the task."

Gabriel took a moment to process this, then nodded. "I *understand* your decision . . . due to how the execution of Private Brown went recently . . . but *Morgan?* If I may, sir, he is *not* qualified to take control of training. Man is a troglodyte, sir, I don't think he's well suited to—"

"Captain Gatton is taking over the position and that is final," the Principal Overseer said sternly. "You're too soft in your treatment of new recruits and you let your feelings apparently get in the way of your judgment. I can no longer trust you in the training of our new recruits, not after what happened. You and I both know Ronald should've been trained better." Gabriel was about to say a response when the general cut him off. "This is not up for debate, Captain." Gabriel shut his mouth and shook his head. Unbelievable. "Now, I will not deny that you were a good teacher at a point in time, so I will allow you to take one new recruit and train them yourself. According to our units spread across Salutem, there are at least four new recruits coming in today. Think of the recruit you choose as a way to redeem yourself in my eyes. You are dismissed."

The captain saluted his superior. "Sir," Gabriel stated before he left the office. There wasn't a question of whether or not he would take someone under his wing. The captain *was* going to find his recruit. Whoever the recruit would be, Gabriel would choose them carefully. He would show Abel and that rotten bastard Morgan who the better teacher was.

MORNINGSTAR

Morningstar took the trash behind the nightclub and put it into the dumpster. In order to avoid obvious detection to any normal people who may have been around, she had wrapped her head in a medical wrap, thereby covering her deformed eye. It was a nice-looking day outside. Despite being within a desolate and rundown part of Salutem, the sky looked absolutely beautiful. Luckily enough for Morningstar, she was able to enjoy the sky with only one eye. Her other eye had lost its ability to see a long time ago. She supposed she should feel horrible about that, but it didn't bother her in the slightest. She had long forgotten what it was like to have the use of both eyes, so there wasn't much for her to miss.

Meow.

The deviant teenager turned around and saw a black-and-white kitten looking at her, meowing as if to get her attention. Morningstar smiled.

"Hey there, what's your name?" she asked the kitten while kneeling down. The kitten quickly ran away, looked behind it, and meowed again with a tiny, squeaky voice. Morningstar held out her hand and the kitten went up to her arm and rubbed against it. "See? You can trust me," she said in a cute little voice. She picked the kitten up and it squirmed within her hands. "Look at the little baby, look at the little baby . . ." she cooed as she cradled the kitten in her arms and kissed it on the head. "You wanna stay with me, baby girl? Hmm?" She hugged the kitten. "I think I'll call you . . . Jelly. You like that name?" The tiny kitten meowed at her, making the girl smile. The young deviant made her way back into the nightclub, kitty in tow.

"Uggh, what're you doing with *that* in here?" Oni asked Morningstar, looking disapprovingly as she entered the door. Oni was a Japanese girl in her twenties, covered in tattoos. She always wore revealing clothing that revealed the beginnings of a gut, and her black hair usually looked fairly unwashed. She was leaning at the bar with a beer bottle in hand as Blasphemer cleaned the counter. Looked like she'd had another rough night, judging from the pronounced bags under her eyes. This didn't bother the teenage deviant, though.

"I found her outside near the dumpster. She looks hungry, so I thought I'd take her in."

"Morningstar . . . you can't just take in strays. Put the damn thing back where you found it. Thing could have a disease," Oni said, curling her nose and twisting her mouth.

"Easy there, Oni," Blasphemer spoke before turning his attention to Morningstar. She studied his skin: it was a suffocation-blue in normal lighting and his completely black, alien-like eyes made it hard to tell where exactly he was looking except for where his head pointed. "Don't mind her, she's got a bit of a hangover, not to mention she's had a rough morning."

"Shut the fuck up, Blasty!"

"Had to clean up another of her *victims* this morning. Not pretty."

"I said shut the fuck up! It's not my fault my mouth gets big when I'm turned off, all right?"

"It *becomes* a problem when you rip out a man's throat with nine-inch teeth during intercourse. But what do I know, right? I'm just a bartender."

"Gimme a break, Blasty. He tried to stick it in the wrong place. Fucker got what he deserved." Oni pouted before taking a swig.

"'Kay, did *not* need to know all that . . ." Morningstar said quietly, sighing and chuckling softly while looking at Jelly. Oni scoffed, setting her attention on Morningstar. The glare was piercing, and immediately the teenager knew she had said something she shouldn't have. "Um, it's just . . . it seems kinda personal—"

"Please, fuckin' *virgin* over here. What, *you* gonna judge me? The fuck gives you the right to be judgy? Not like anyone's been fuckin' *you*, One Eye. Too scared that thing in your head will pop out," Oni said bitterly. Morningstar felt a sting there. Ow, that was a low blow. Blasphemer quickly said something about Oni being cut off and the two bickered for a moment while Morningstar still processed the comment. The woman was right, she was a virgin. She had never had sex with anyone and there wasn't anyone that *wanted* to have sex with her. Not that she thought she was ready or anything, but. . . . Her eye was certainly something that kept anyone from being even remotely interested. It was too grotesque. Too ugly. No one would ever want to. . . . Morningstar blinked repeatedly, shaking off the comment.

Oni began walking away. "Fuckin'— I-I'm goin'. Don't adopt that kitty, Star. I'm serious. Little furball just gonna make this place even more *disgusting* than it already is," she said with a mean chuckle, dragging a beer bottle behind her. Morningstar frowned, watching Oni walk off. She hadn't meant anything by what she said . . .

"Hey, don't let her get to ya. She's . . ." Blasphemer said quietly, looking in the direction Oni left. ". . . been through things, and drinks heavy 'cause of 'em. Her words have less to do with you, more to do with her being unhappy, 'kay?"

"I know. . . . Thanks, though, Blasty." Morningstar smiled. She could always count on Blasty to be kind to her.

"So, what's the kitty's name? Come up with one yet?"

"Jelly."

Blasphemer raised his eyebrow. "Were you hungry when you made that name up?"

"No . . . why?"

"No reason. Jelly is just kinda a silly name for a cat, eh?"

"I guess. . . . I don't know, I like it," Morningstar said, trying to manage the squirming kitten in her hands.

"Guess that's the kitty's name then, as long as you like it," Blasphemer said, continuing to clean the bar counter. After a moment of thought, a question came to Morningstar's mind.

"Hey, do you know if Death and Pestilence are home?"

"Well, I know for sure Death is, being the stay-at-home husband and all. Pestilence might be still working on an assignment, however. Hard to say, though. You should go show them the kitty, I'm sure their kid will love it."

"Oooh, good idea! Stacy will probably love her!" She smiled. Then she went on her way with a huge grin on her face, excited to show Stacy the kitten.

AYLEN

Sleep had almost overcome Aylen when Jared stopped the car. She shook the cobwebs out of her head.

"We're here," Jared stated blandly. Aylen looked out the window at their destination. In a clearing in the forest there stood a large group of buildings guarded by chain-link fences and a gigantic wall that encircled the structures. Behind the fence were two guard towers connected by a bridge as well as to the wall.

"The Saint Organization base is a prison?"

"Nope. It's an old Anthrodi War base. 'Scuse me for a sec." Jared stepped out of the car, leaving the open-door signal to beep in a steady, metronome-like tempo. He put his hands up to whoever was watching from the tower, something in hand. Jared put his slightly clenched hand to his mouth and an eagle-like sound pierced the air. The gate began to open and Jared went back to the car silently. "Ready to meet the cavalry?" he asked almost sarcastically. Aylen didn't answer as he started the car. Her stomach clenched as she was reminded just what she was here for. Immediately, she was thankful that she took the cast off her ankle the other day.

It was once they were past the gates that Aylen truly grasped what she was getting herself into. The ground was mostly dirt, but the base was vast with concrete and wooden buildings scattered throughout. Trees also filled the grounds, making the base look almost more like a summer camp than an actual military base. People in dark blue T-shirts and olive-green pants roamed this way and that as her SUV followed a dirt road. It was . . . amazing, for lack of a better term. Its own small community. It was bigger than Aylen had expected it to be too. People in blue jumpsuits jogged together, kids as young as fifteen years old hung out in small groups, men and women in thin, dark green armor stood guard with machine guns. All these people were here, and virtually no one in Salutem really had a clue. She was shocked.

Jared guided the car to a nearby large rectangular building that looked roughly four stories high. At the top of the building were menacing gun turrets that looked significantly older than the ones the UWF had back at the barricade. Without a doubt, this was definitely the main building of the base. Jared parked and the two exited the car, stretching their limbs wordlessly.

"Let's get going," he instructed Aylen, who people-watched as they walked.

The two went up the concrete steps of the main building. When they entered it, Aylen was surprised at how clean the interior was, especially considering the dirt outside. Jared grabbed her hand and went to the front desk, where a young man sat dressed in the same outfit the men and women outside seemed to wear. Up close, Aylen could see a crest over the shirt's heart. A skull over a silver cross with wings, two spears, and the words "Honor, Vigilance, Duty" written underneath. Aylen couldn't help but think the crest was somewhat peculiar. The man at the front desk took notice of them.

"Jared, I see. How may I assist you today?" the young man asked, seemingly annoyed.

"I brought one of the four recruits. Her name is Aylen Monro."

"Aylen Monro . . . how do you spell that?" the young man asked sharply, grabbing a pen and paper.

"Aylen is spelled A—"

"Can the girl speak for herself?" the man behind the desk interrupted, obviously not tolerant of the boy who brought her.

"Aylen Monro," Aylen replied quietly. "Aylen is A-Y-L-E-N. Monro is M-O-N-R-O." The young man wrote the name down and then handed a form out to her.

"Fill this out and wait in the waiting room. *Jared* knows where it is, he'll take you to it," the young man said with a glare. Aylen looked around to see various people of different ages giving them dirty looks while walking by. Well, this was a friendly environment. She looked at Jared, who had donned a more demonic look than usual on his face: his brow furrowed, nostrils flared, and eyes blatantly orange. It was as apparent as a sore thumb that a lot of people didn't care for him here, and vice versa.

Jared took Aylen by the hand and led her to a cold waiting room with uncomfortable metal chairs. The only people there were the two of them. "You're doing fine," Jared assured Aylen, who was now feeling very uneasy. Suddenly, the entrance opened.

"Oooh, is this one of the new recruits?" Aylen heard a male voice say. She looked behind her to see a long-haired man standing at the doorway. A scruffy beard lay like a canvas across his face and dark circles were present under his eyes. He wore jeans and a dark blue T-shirt with the Saint crest. A kind, somewhat vacant expression graced his face as he lazily slinked forward. His eyes were glazed over, but the smile on his face was welcoming.

"Yeah, Brenden, she is," Jared said, seeming annoyed. Brenden's eyes widened as he scanned Aylen. He moved surprisingly delicately for a soldier of the Saint Organization.

"Ah, a cute one too. What's your name, darling?" Brenden asked, now heading for the seat next to her. He plopped down with a smooth movement.

"Aylen," she spoke quietly.

"Well, that's an unusual and pretty name. What's its origin?"

"N-Native American."

"Native American!" the man said, seeming to find some amusement. "Are you Native American, my dear?"

Jared sighed. "Don't you have somewhere to be, Brenden?" he asked, stiffening his face and rolling his eyes. Aylen smelled the alcohol on Brenden's breath. He stopped and laughed, apparently finding Jared's annoyance amusing.

"Unfortunately, none of the good bars are open in town and quite frankly, ninety-five percent of the men here are too straight to flirt with."

"Ain't that lucky," Jared remarked.

"I would say! So, since I have nothing better to do than sit around on my *ass* till there's another battle, I figure I'd meet the newbies," he said with a low chuckle. Brenden studied Aylen. He seemed to be looking at her as if he knew the punchline of some joke she wasn't in on. She honestly didn't feel enough energy or life within her to care, though.

Jared sighed. "Yeah, great first impression for her you are: a drunken loudmouth." Then he chuckled.

Brenden laughed. "I *do* make a good poster boy for the Saints, don't I?" he said coyly. With that, he turned his attention to Aylen. "Welcome to the Saints, where we eat, drink, and fuck until we go out and *die*!" He laughed. Jared breathed out with slight frustration. Brenden continued, "Hey, might make a good campaign. Who knows, maybe we'd get more recruits." He pulled a flask out of his pocket and began sipping from it. Aylen looked on in concern. He . . . he was allowed to do that? Brenden continued observing the girl. "You're a quiet one, aren't you? Why you here, girl? Tell me your *life story*. Why is a tiny thing like you here with the rest of us suicidal maniacs?"

"To join the Saints."

"No, no, no. I mean, *why* do you wanna join us?"

"Brenden . . ." Jared warned, trying to come to her defense. The man kept talking, flat-out ignoring him.

"Usually it's either to be some sort of hero by killing deviants, utter racism against deviants, or to get revenge on a Devil's Deviant. Deviants, deviants, deviants! Which one are you? You don't strike me as the glory-seeking type."

"None of your business, Brenden," Jared growled slightly.

"Oh come on, she can indulge me. What *brings* you to our band of merry men?" Brenden asked before taking yet another sip of his flask.

"Revenge," Aylen replied firmly. As soon as the man heard this, he stopped drinking from his flask and looked at her. A sobering, much more flat look dropped on his face almost immediately.

"My condolences for whatever the DDs have done to you. . . . May I ask what they did?" he asked with his tone more sincere as he looked Aylen up and down. Jared shot him a look but kept silent this time. Aylen thought for a moment before deciding to speak.

"They took my best friend. They also set loose two Level 5s that have tried to kill me. I figure they got it coming," she said with a sort of calm fury that remained quiet within her voice.

Brenden nodded, breathing out. "Revenge is a strong motivation as any, I suppose. I too have lost someone close recently . . ."

Aylen didn't need this. She just wanted to go into training. Why was this guy bothering her?

"Tell me, though . . . would revenge truly give you the satisfaction you desire? Would killing the deviant that killed your best friend truly fill the void?" Brenden asked analytically. Jared shot him a dark look that he brushed off while studying the very stiff girl. Aylen glared at Brenden, which made him curl his lip like a baboon. "Mmm, but what do I know? I'm just here to be pretty."

Deciding to ignore the drunk, Aylen turned her attention to the form that was handed to her. It asked her age, occupation, skills, past military experience, and finally listed a warning that after signing the document there was no going back. If she was accepted in, she was in. Aylen bit her lip. No going back. Those words scrambled and unscrambled themselves in her head repeatedly as she attempted to comprehend the ramifications of joining the Saint Organization. At any point during this war, it was wholly possible for her to get critically injured. It was wholly possible that she could get mauled to death, eaten alive, or die in some other horrible manner. She wasn't Jared, with any spectacular abilities that made her a warrior. She was just simply . . . her. She was nothing special. If she died, how would her mother be notified? Would they tell her mother it was just an accident of some sort? Was she truly willing to put her life on the line to battle foes that had special abilities that could easily tear her to bits? Aylen lost her breath as she looked at the daunting signature line. Memories reoccurred to her in this moment of doubt: the bloody stuffed animal in the subway, the feeling of Legion's fingers creeping down her body, the weight of Beth's dead body in her arms as she held on to her friend with hands sticky from blood. Aylen breathed in and signed the line. No going back.

"Aylen Monro?" a female voice called from out of Aylen's range of vision. Aylen looked up to see a middle-aged woman in a doctor's coat standing in a different doorway than the one Aylen had entered from. She had a fit body, long, light brown hair, and a pleasant smile on her face. Civilian clothes, unlike the uniforms of the rest of the Saints, seemed to be her choice of wear underneath her white coat. "Hi, I'm Dr. Faith Lancaster. You're here for recruitment, correct?"

Aylen nodded her head. "Yeah, I am."

"Follow me, please," Dr. Lancaster replied cheerfully, motioning for Aylen to follow her. She got up and obliged.

"Good luck, A," Jared said as Aylen began walking away.

"Don't worry, Faith doesn't bite *too* hard," Brenden jested, causing Dr. Lancaster to roll her eyes as she closed the door behind Aylen. She led Aylen down a hall that looked similar to a hospital's hallway.

"Oh that Brenden, always a character. Sauce or no sauce, he's still saucy." Faith chuckled. Suddenly a green-and-purple flash filled the room and blinded Aylen momentarily, causing her to yelp from shock and pain. She felt latex-covered fingers applying pressure on her cheek bones. Her vision returned slowly to find Dr. Lancaster staring deeply into her eyes. "Mmmhmm, looks good," the doctor muttered under her breath. She pulled away and wrote something on her clipboard. "Sorry 'bout that. Had to check to see if you were a deviant. Not to mention get your height, body mass, and measurements."

"Wh-Whoa, what? Y-you mean that machine was able to capture all of *that*?"

"Military technology has improved a lot while civilian technology has remained the same over the last several decades. Believe it or not, this machine is still a fairly older model in consideration." Dr. Lancaster smiled. "All right, now I'm going to need you to enter this room over here where I'll take your blood sample." The doctor directed Aylen into a room that, like the hallway, looked like an ordinary room taken straight from a civilian hospital. She prepped the girl's arm to get blood drawn from it.

"No fancy machine for this yet?" Aylen grimaced.

"Afraid not. Have to do this manually. Supposedly the UWF might have come up with one, but that's beyond my knowledge." Dr. Lancaster found the vein in Aylen's arm and stuck the needle inside. "Hope you're not squeamish," the doctor said pleasantly. Aylen tried not to focus on the needle as it slid under her skin. "So . . . you're friends with Jared?" Dr. Lancaster asked as she extracted the blood.

"Yeah, he, uh, saved my life a couple times," she said, tense because of the needle.

"Hmm! That's good! What'd he save you from?" the doctor asked while pulling the needle out. She transferred the blood-filled glass vial to a white machine with a red light and a green light. The green light then shone bright with a loud ding. "All right, your blood's good! Although, apparently, you're a lightweight, so if ya don't already know, you should be careful with any alcohol intake. Hand me your ID, please," the doctor directed while holding her arm out.

Aylen got out her ID and handed it to the lady. "Two Level 5 Brainless," she said, responding to Dr. Lancaster's earlier question. The doctor stopped for a second in response to Aylen's statement. "H-he saved me from two Level 5 Brainless . . ."

Dr. Lancaster looked in deep thought for a moment. "Christ, he didn't . . ." She clenched her mouth and shook her head. "Oh, Jared . . . he's supposed to *report* these kinds of things," the doctor said, exasperation showing with a raised eyebrow.

Aylen worried for a second. Crap, did she just get Jared in hot water with a superior? Dr. Lancaster looked at Aylen intensely for a second, then put the girl's ID into another fancy machine that Aylen had never seen before. The doctor sighed. "Well, if he didn't report it, he must've had his reasons. Let's keep that a secret between us three though, eh? He's not exactly a favorite around certain people."

"O-okay . . ."

Faith smiled at her. "I kind of . . . look out for younger people here. Jared is . . . *unofficially* my adopted son. I look out for him a lot, which, I can assure you, can be troublesome at times. No doubt you know how much of a handful he can be."

"Y-yeah . . . was the first thing I noticed," Aylen said shyly, briefly grinning.

"Good kid, though. Comes off like a jerk but will go to hell and back for people he cares about. I've seen him do it." Aylen thought about that. Yeah, that seemed . . . accurate. At least, from what she knew of Jared. A printer began printing Aylen's information. Dr. Lancaster grabbed the papers and began to look through them. "All right, well . . . how do I say your name?"

"AY-len."

"R-right. Aylen. Aylen Monro."

"Yeah."

Faith analyzed the papers a second. "Well, Aylen, you seem pretty healthy for a twenty-one-year-old girl. You're slightly underweight for being five-four, nothing to be concerned about, though. . . . Blood type is type O-negative. You're a fourth Apache, half German, aaaand a fourth English, roughly. In college, you have—ooooh, extremely good grades and have been majoring in medical science." At this, the doctor looked up and smiled. "If you become a Saint, I might have you help me every so often." Her attention then went back to scanning the papers. Wow, she was able to tell all of those things about Aylen? That had her a little freaked. "So, I guess all that's left to ask is this: Why do you want to become a member of the Saint Organization?" the doctor asked, looking up at Aylen. "You're on a good roll in life. You're healthy, you're pretty, you're smart. What're you doing *here* of all places?" Dr. Lancaster stared hard at her, making Aylen adjust uncomfortably in her seat. "I wouldn't wish this place on my own daughter, if I had one."

"I wanna avenge my—"

The doctor immediately put up a hand. "Your best friend, I know. Brenden went out there for a reason. But honestly, Aylen: Why are you so willing to throw your life away on this cause? Are you *sure* this is what you want?"

Aylen stared at her in disbelief, studying her as she searched for words. Her concern seemed genuine enough.

"Look, Dr. Lancaster—"

"You can call me Faith, Aylen. You're a friend of Jared's, after all," the good doctor interrupted briefly. Aylen took a moment to gather her thoughts

"Look, Faith. . . . It's *my* responsibility to avenge her. I *know* in my heart of hearts she would've done the same for me if I was the one killed. Beth . . . didn't deserve what happened. I know who her killer is," Aylen stated before nodding her head. "Her killer has to pay." There was a silence as Faith analyzed Aylen.

"Who's her killer?"

". . . A Devil's Deviant named Legion." Aylen felt the name touch her tongue like a bitter poison. It was a name that made her stomach shift and throat swell. A venomous name.

"Legion, eh? That thing's still alive?" Faith sighed. "I think I understand your reasoning, if that's the case. Very well." Faith nodded her head. "Did, uh, Legion do anything to you? It has a . . . reputation. Did it do any—"

"Did it rape me? No. It came very close, though," Aylen confirmed, looking Dr. Lancaster dead in the eye. The doctor looked deep in thought for a moment, studying Aylen before rubbing her head.

"I see." The doctor sighed. Then she got out a stamp and pressed it into an ink pad nearby. When she lifted the stamp and held it over the paperwork, she hesitated. "One last time: Are you absolutely positive you want to be a part of Saint Organization? Things can get ugly around here, and I mean *really* ugly."

Aylen nodded her head. "Yes."

"Very well, then." Dr. Lancaster brought the stamp firmly down onto the paper. The doctor then extended her hand to Aylen. "Let me be the first one, then, to welcome you into the Saint Training Initiative, Private Aylen Monro."

MORNINGSTAR

Morningstar knocked on the door of the Gilmore family's private quarters. It opened to reveal a familiar man with spectacles.

"Morningstar! Good to see you!" Mr. Gilmore exclaimed with delight.

"Hi, Mr. Gilmore, how are you doing?" she asked enthusiastically. Neither Pestilence nor her husband, Death, liked to be called their rebirth names unless they were on assignment. Mr. Gilmore was a nice man in his late thirties with messy black hair, glasses, and a darker complexion about his skin. If Morningstar had to guess his ethnicity, she'd have probably guessed Indian, though she dared not presume. He was on the scrawnier side of the spectrum, being considerably thinner than many other male deviants within the bunker under The Ninth Circle, and he often dressed in button-up shirts or polos, making him look like a suburban dad of sorts. His nose was slightly hooked and a calm, pleasant expression was almost always upon his face.

"What's that you got there, Morningstar? A kitty?"

"Yep! Was wondering if maybe Stacy wanted to see what a real cat looked like!"

"I don't think she's been around one before, so that's actually a great idea," Mr. Gilmore said before looking back. "Just, uhhh, keep your voice down when inside. Emily just got back and is sleeping in." He grinned. Mr. Gilmore then let Morningstar into the clean living space, and Morningstar saw Stacy sitting on the ground in front of a TV. She remembered when Stacy was born eight years ago. While the deviants were still roaming the wilderness outside Salutem, her birth had been a miracle to everyone back then. It gave their group a sense of hope in a dark moment within their history. Morningstar observed what Stacy looked like now: white hair, dark skin, eyes a bright magenta color, tiny little body, and the features of both her mother and her father. Stacy looked at Morningstar silently and waved hello.

"Hi, Stacy! How are you doing?"

Stacy signed in sign language that she was doing well and asked Morningstar how she was doing. "I'm doing good. Look what I've got!" the teenager said brightly, showing the kitten to the kid. The child smiled vibrantly as Morningstar carefully put the kitten in her arms. The child hugged the kitten and rubbed her face against it.

Mr. Gilmore smiled as he watched the scene taking place on his living room floor. "What's the kitten's name?"

"Jelly," Morningstar replied happily. She then turned her attention to Stacy. "Can you show me the sign for Jelly, Stacy?"

The child then put the kitten into her lap, extended her hand out, and scooped at it with her opposite pinky. "Good job!" the teenager exclaimed. She began tickling the little girl, making Stacy laugh silently.

"You really like hanging with her, don't you?" a familiar female voice chuckled behind her.

Morningstar turned around to see Pestilence, otherwise known as Emily Gilmore, standing behind her in a white bathrobe. She stared at the woman. To call her beautiful and fierce was to put it lightly. The woman was an Armenian beauty with snow-white hair, the same shade as her daughter's, and piercing light brown eyes. Despite the harsh intensity of the eyes, a calm expression lay upon her face.

"Oh! Mrs. Gilmore, did I wake you . . . ?"

"Not at all, honey, I woke up on my own. *Cute kitty!*" Mrs. Gilmore exclaimed, kneeling down to pet Jelly. For a moment, the woman with white hair waved her finger in front of the kitten, which the kitten playfully swiped, getting a chuckle out of both Gilmore parents. The older woman then turned her attention back to the teen. "You want a cup of joe or anything, Star?"

"Sure."

Mrs. Gilmore looked at her child and began signing with her fingers. "You can watch cartoons with the kitty, I gotta talk to Morningstar over coffee, okay?" she said out loud as well as through sign language to the little girl, who nodded in agreement. Mrs. Gilmore looked at Morningstar and smiled enthusiastically. "Let's go get that coffee!"

Morningstar briefly looked at Jelly and Stacy before following Mrs. Gilmore into the kitchen. Jelly squirmed while Stacy continued to hold the tiny thing. This was the first time Stacy had ever seen a cat in real life, and Morningstar couldn't help but smile at the glee on the child's face before looking toward Mrs. Gilmore. The white-haired woman hummed happily while getting together the makings for two cups of coffee. "Tell me, how have *you* been lately, Star? Any boys? Girls? Any teenage drama I can help ya out with? Tell me *everything*," the woman asked while beginning to brew a pot.

"There's not much to tell in *that* department," the teenager chuckled. "I've been good, though. Drama-free, fortunately. How was the assignment you've been on?" Morningstar took her seat patiently at the Gilmore family's dining table.

Mrs. Gilmore sighed. "Um . . . not as good as it could've been, but not too bad. Lucifer was pleased, so that's good."

"What has he been having you do?" Morningstar asked. Mrs. Gilmore looked at the teenager and twisted her mouth.

"You know how it goes. It's stuff we aren't allowed to talk about, as usual. I've been doing a lot lately, though, putting in a lot of overtime." Mrs. Gilmore poured two cups of coffee. "Whatever I can do to keep Lucifer from trying to get Paul onto missions."

"Really? He's been trying to get Mr. Gilmore to go on missions?"

"Yeah, and Paul's willing to, but you know. His ability . . ."

"Yeah, I see what you're saying," Morningstar replied as the adult sat across from her.

The white-haired woman looked into her coffee. "Yeah . . ." she said while trailing off. "How're your chores coming lately? How's Cerberus?"

"Chores are . . . boring, as usual, and Cerby . . . I don't know, he's been very moody as of late. I think maybe Lucifer has been working him too hard."

Mrs. Gilmore chuckled lightly. "That's typical. Being second in command is a tough job, though, especially when we are facing both Saints *and* the UWF."

Emily nodded. "The only lucky thing for us in this scenario is that the Saint Organization isn't well liked by the UWF, and with that being the only saving grace, there's a lot for Cerberus to juggle." Morningstar nodded while looking in her coffee. "What is it, honey?" she heard Mrs. Gilmore say. Morningstar looked up to see Stacy standing in the kitchen doorway with her eyes glowing. She clutched a sleeping Jelly within her arms. The little girl walked forward blankly, her magenta eyes glowing profusely.

"What is it, Stacy?" Morningstar asked. The girl held out her hand and put it on Morningstar's stomach. She then looked up at the teenager's face, her eyes still glowing brightly.

"It's gonna be a boy," Stacy's tiny little voice spoke out.

What? Morningstar looked at an equally puzzled Mrs. Gilmore. Stacy closed her eyes and when she reopened them, she looked sleepy, and her eyes were no longer glowing. The little girl then signed to her mother and Morningstar, asking what she was doing there.

AYLEN

Aylen walked into the building that she was specified to put her things in. It was a small and cramped little concrete building called the Female Recruit Barracks. Upon walking in she saw only three bunk beds, one with a girl lying upon the bottom bunk reading a book. As soon as Aylen saw how barren the room was, she observed the lone girl. Upon first glimpse, Aylen guessed she was Hispanic. She was a pretty girl with a sturdy-looking, athletic body and a few tattoos here and there on her arms. There was a somewhat boyish quality to her face and mannerisms, which seemed to be accentuated by the tight, *tight* bun on her head. The girl was deeply invested in her book, so deeply that she didn't seem to notice—nor care—about the bookworm's presence. Aylen looked around the room nervously. Which would be more insulting, she wondered, to take the bunk above the girl or to take one of the others, which were in a different part of the room from the girl? She observed the book the girl was reading, a collection of the many works of Friedrich Nietzsche. What a coincidence, Aylen liked reading Nietzsche. Perhaps this was to be the icebreaker with the girl.

"So, Nietzsche, huh?"

"Yep," the girl replied without looking up from her book.

Aylen thought for a moment and remembered something. A quote. Maybe it'd help break the ice. "W-we love life, not because we are used to living but because we're used to loving."

The girl looked up from her book. "You want something, man?" she asked harshly, shifting her eyes upward toward Aylen.

"T-that's a Nietzsche quote."

"Oh, I know," the girl said sharply. "Didn't answer my question, though, I *asked* did you want somethin'?"

Aylen was shocked by the hostility. "Well . . . I—I just was trying to make conversation." She felt herself shrink.

The girl lifted an eyebrow at Aylen. "My name is Marie Isabella Montoya Vasquez, I'm twenty-three years old, and no, I am not interested in being your friend. All I give a shit 'bout is killing deviants and Brainless. Making friends with some middle-class pendeja who memorizes Nietzsche quotes is kinda low on my priority list. Entienden?" Marie said bitingly.

What the hell was this girl's problem? Aylen was lost for words as she backed away. She supposed that perhaps the opposite end of the room was the best option. She put her stuff into the trunk in front of her bunk bed and lay on the top bunk. Well, this was fun. She wondered what Jared was up to. From what she could gather, she would only be seeing him sporadically throughout basic training. She felt bad about how much she had distanced herself from him since Beth's death. It wasn't Jared's fault that Beth died, yet somehow Aylen had a hard time talking to or facing Jared. She thought further about her dilemma. Maybe this time away from him would get her head straightened out enough so they could continue their friendship. She hoped that would be the case. She really valued him. He was pretty much the only one she had anymore.

BLACKWOOD

Senator Blackwood looked at the night sky of Salutem from the window in his office. Without the next bit of information Triple Six was to deliver, there was no way of knowing when or where the Devil's Deviants would strike next. The senator looked out at his beloved nation. The nation his fellow politicians had worked so hard to build. Blackwood had warned the others that there would be ramifications for dropping Project Suncloud. The council refused to believe him, though, just as they refused to believe that the deviants were an urgent matter to be dealt with. They even shirked off Commander Li's impressive proposal she presented a few years ago when she became the Commander of the Military Police. The council, in Blackwood's opinion, had become far too dependent on the Saint Organization. Though they were well experienced in handling the affairs of deviant and Brainless attacks, it was much too dangerous to get so complacent with the small militia group. If somehow they slipped up, all of Salutem's peace could easily crumble into oblivion. Then there was always the chance that the Saint Organization could turn on them. That was far too much of a chance for Blackwood to take; thus, when he stumbled onto Triple Six's proposition, he saw it as an opportunity to finally do something about the deviants. Normally, Blackwood wouldn't have trusted someone like Triple Six, but he had something that the deviant wanted very desperately.

Blackwood looked at his phone: 10:30 p.m. It was late, and the senator had been doing paperwork all day. He got up and stretched, thinking about his wife, about the pesto that she probably mixed in with ravioli, about the chicken and corn that probably went along with it. It would be waiting for him in a Tupperware at home. The senator's enlarged stomach grumbled at the mere thought of his wife's dinner. Then his phone buzzed within his pocket. Blackwood swore to himself that the text better be from his wife, or all hell would break loo—

Meet me on the rooftop, the text read. On second thought, this was better. He had been waiting for this.

Blackwood took the elevator to the roof of the skyscraper and stepped out into the night air. It was breezy and chilly up this high. He pulled his coat closer to his body in hopes of giving himself more of a semblance of warmth. Just then, a smaller, familiar figure stepped out of the shadows.

"Hey there, Blackwood," Triple Six sneered.

Blackwood rolled his eyes. "You wanted to have a meeting?" he inquired loudly as the wind picked up.

"Yeah," Triple Six answered, holding on to his beanie.

"Is it all right if we bring this meeting inside?"

"Yeah."

The senator then called the elevator to the roof and in no time, it appeared.

"After you," Blackwood offered. Like hell was he going to let Triple Six go behind him. The deviant entered the elevator and Blackwood followed. The two silently rode the elevator and made their way to the senator's office. Once they were inside, the senator sat at his desk and Triple Six observed the office around him, staring peculiarly at a particular painting. A perfectly round, red circle on a white canvas. The senator said, "So, what information did you need to—"

"Hold up, you put this shit in your office?" Triple Six asked while holding up a hand, eyes still transfixed on the art.

"Um, no, we have a designer put the picture in. You know, to liven up the offi—"

"This is complete bullshit! You're telling me that some idiot just paints a fuckin' circle and it gets called *'art'*?" Triple Six continued, interrupting the senator again. "Give me some spray cans and I'll make you fuckin *'art,'*" the deviant scoffed. He looked around, then grabbed a Sharpie from the senator's desk.

"Triple Si—" the senator tried to talk, much to his annoyance before Triple Six shushed him. The deviant drew a buck-toothed face on the red circle and gave it a stick figure body, then a penis, then another stick figure with long hair and big boobs to have sex with. He proceeded to write *ART* in big letters on the wall over the painting, then chuckled. The senator rolled his eyes.

"I think it's an improvement," Triple Six said with a disgusting smile, yellowed teeth prevalent between his chapped lips.

"You had information, Triple Six?" Blackwood said, giving the deviant a dark look.

Triple Six scratched his head. "Yeah, uh, I know which factory the Devil's Deviants will be attacking,"

"What factory?" the senator asked excitedly. Finally, the answer he had been looking for.

"Hucklegrove," the young man confirmed softly, seeming to perhaps feel guilty and uncomfortable with giving him this information. Blackwood took a small notepad out of his jacket pocket and wrote it down.

"Any idea why they're going after the factory?"

Triple Six shrugged. "I don't know, man. They never tell me nothin'." He thought for a second. "Hey, I have an idea of how to sweeten our little deal for the both of us," he said, looking deep in thought. "My brothers in Devil's Deviants are beginning to catch on to our little deal. I'm pretty positive if I go back to base, Lucifer will have me killed for dealin' with you." He grimaced a bit. "So, I figure . . . what if I give you somethin' to sweeten our deal . . . so *you* could give *me* your part of the bargain tonight. That way, I can keep my head and you can get what you want."

The senator scoffed. "Really? And what exactly could you give me that could sweeten our deal?"

"Where the DDs are hidin'."

The senator almost did a double take. He stiffened in his chair. "Really."

"Yeah, I scratch your ass an' you scratch mine. Then we both get what we want." Triple Six nodded. Senator Blackwood had already made arrangements to get the deviant what he was after; he even knew where exactly it was: the drawer of his desk. He was no fool, though. If he gave it to Triple Six now . . .

"And what promises do I have that if I give you what you want, you won't just kill me right now and be done with it?"

"You took that risk even beginning this deal, bro . . ."

"Still, I have to think it's a little too easy. I can buy that you getting into contact with me has been some sort of angle. I've been playing along and your info has been correct, but betraying your side completely? That's a new low, even for y—"

"I want out," Triple Six interrupted, staring into Blackwood's eyes. There was a sort of pitiful look within his gaze. Like a lost puppy or something. "That simple. I have been killing for Lucifer since I was *twelve years old* and I—I'm done, man. I can't do it no more." For a moment, Blackwood didn't see the infamous killer known as Triple Six, but rather . . . a boy. Was it possible he was being serious? Triple Six shook his head, his eyes looking distant. "Whatever it takes . . . I just want out, man."

Blackwood blinked. "I've seen you brutally torture an innocent man, Six."

"Dude, that's what they *made me*! That isn't—" Triple Six stared off into space. "I . . . I just need a chance. A chance to be different. I never got one."

Blackwood squinted his eyes, thinking over his next response. "Well, the info you've given has been accurate so far. . . . But you *know* even if I give it to you right this second, it'll still take time to process."

Triple Six nodded. "I know, just . . . if I could even hold it. That'd mean a lot to me."

"And if I get killed, any chance of it going through goes out the window. You will never get what you want. It'll be completely nullified."

"Of course. No funny business from me."

"All right, then. Give me the information first, and *then* I'll give you what you want."

The deviant eyed the senator with an unreadable look. "Okay, deal. I can do that." He nodded his head, then swallowed his spit. "It's a bunker underneath a nightclub called The Ninth Circle. It was built back in the Anthrodi War. If you go into the VIP Lounge of the club, you can reach an elevator that leads to it. Lucifer is down there."

Senator Blackwood smiled. "Thank you." He reached into the drawer next to him and pulled out what Triple Six wanted. "As promised, Triple Six. Or should I say: Hunter Wilson? Your identity. I'll begin processing things immediately so you can eventually rejoin society."

Wilson lit up as he saw his Identity Card handed to him. He had a sort of half-crazed and pitiful look of joy spreading across his face. "Fuckin' A . . ." he said in disbelief as he clutched his new ID. In truth, Senator Blackwood didn't mind. Hunter was a deranged psychopath and he was going to go down with the rest of his kind when the UWF made their move. Hunter wasn't *actually* going to get his identity back. The ID card was just an easy thing to track, made it that much easier to take him out in the long haul. Blackwood grinned as Hunter Wilson, the deviant known as Triple Six, pathetically mused over his ID.

After the meeting, Senator Blackwood got into his car and made his way home. He had some emails to write tonight, emails that weren't meant to be written on his work computer. He almost broke the speed limit while heading home, he was so excited. Finally! The project he had been working on for so long was near completion. Triple Six made it that much easier to bury the final nightmares of Project Suncloud once and for all. After tonight, deviants would be working their way toward extinction.

Senator Blackwood rushed into his home, feeling a wave of adrenaline following him. He looked at the food container that his wife left him on the counter, prepared the meal she made him, and devoured it. He then proceeded to make his way upstairs, where his laptop and wife were. Quietly, he entered their dark room and sat at his personal computer. He had a death sentence to write. While starting up his laptop, he heard his wife stirring in bed.

"Harry? What're you doing on your laptop, baby?" his wife said sleepily.

"Writin' something important before bed. I'll be there in a minute," Harry Blackwood replied while getting to his email. As soon as his browser got online, he surpassed the security code and proceeded to compose a new email to General Hawkings.

Dear General,

Today, I received word from my informant, Hunter Wilson (a.k.a. Triple Six), of the Devil's Deviants' main base of operations. It's a nightclub known as "The Ninth Circle." Apparently, the whole lot of them live under the nightclub in some sort of Anthrodi War bunker from back in the day. With this new information, we can put the Devil's Deviants down for good. Notify Commander Li at once. Her military prowess should be enough to launch a discrete but thorough raid on the facility. Hopefully after that we can finish them once and—

Blackwood felt his wife's hand reach down his pants and tug on him gently. "Come to bed, baby," she said delicately into his ear. The senator turned and kissed his wife on the cheek.

"Doll, I—I gotta finish this first . . ." he gently protested. His wife didn't move her hand, but rather stroked him.

"Mmm, you can finish it a little later. I have a little surprise for you."

"But, babe . . ." Blackwood tried to debate. His wife circled to the front of him and undid his zipper.

"Please? I miss you. You work so long and so often, I barely get to see you anymore," she complained. Then she went down on him.

Blackwood sighed in relief as she worked her magic. He watched her for a moment, breathing heavier by the second while occasionally meeting her eyes. "Screw it," he uttered. He pulled his wife to his mouth and passionately kissed her. She was wearing a bathrobe and nothing else. Her beautiful features glowed from the light of the laptop as Blackwood stripped her of her robe and groped her firm behind. With an equal amount of aggression, she took off his clothes as well. Blackwood turned her around and bent her over on the bed.

They made love, together and passionately. She gasped loudly and moaned moans of pleasure, then Blackwood laid her on her back, and with her help, continued the dance. Her moans slowed and slowed as she put her hands behind her head. Blackwood felt an ecstasy come over his body as he finished within—

Schlick

"Ya, know, I think she was with you for your money," Blackwood heard his wife hiss. He felt a sharp pain in the side of his throat and screamed, stumbling out of his wife and holding his throat. Warm liquid rushed over his hands.

His wife turned on a light. In her hand was a yellow-handled box cutter, stained a dark crimson from his blood. "'Cause your cock is cerrrrtainly nothing special," his wife said with a smirk on her face and a distorted voice. Her features began to fade and her body strangely contorted and twitched. Her skin faded grayish white and her eyes seemed more reflective of the light, almost glowing. Her breasts retracted into her body, her ribs became more pronounced, and her limbs became longer and skinnier. Blackwood watched in horror as she changed into something less than human. In moments, the person who was his wife became a strange, naked, sexless freak with half its head shaved and half of its head full of long, greasy hair. Blackwood continued to scream while holding his throat. "Relax, it's only a scratch. If I wanted to kill you right away, you wouldn't be screaminnn'," the sexless thing said in multiple voices to the screaming, naked senator.

Triple Six entered the room then, chuckling at the entrance. "Duuuuude! Legion, that was hella dirty!" he laughed. Blackwood's mouth dropped as Triple Six looked his way. The deviant smiled back at him. "Lookin' a little shocked there, cupcake."

"*Y-you—*"

"Yeeeeeaaah, turns out I'm a DD for life. Tossed that ID soon as I left. Good acting though, *right?*"

Blackwood thought for a moment. There was a shotgun in his closet. Maybe, just maybe, he had a chance. The senator started for the closet door as Triple Six said, "Oh, I wouldn't open that closet if I were—"

Blackwood opened the closet and out fell his wife's body, with thorny, twisted vines protruding from the orifices of her face. Blackwood screamed, horrified. "Tried to warn ya." Triple Six shrugged. Blackwood continued to scream. The sexless freak deleted the incomplete email and began writing a new one.

✉

Dear General,

Today, I received word from my informant, Hunter Wilson (a.k.a. Triple Six), that the Devil's Deviants plan to raid the Hucklegrove Factory. Be sure to tell Commander Li to tighten security to a maximum at this factory for the next couple of months. Hopefully we can stop them in their tracks before it's too late.

Sincerely,

Senator Harry Blackwood

Senator Blackwood held his dead wife in his arms and felt tears come to his eyes. It was unfair. So unfair. He had been outsmarted and betrayed.

"Annnd sent, but not sent," the sexless freak said.

"Cool, guess it's time to finish up, then," Triple Six replied. Blackwood felt a hot anger come over him.

"You . . . *monsters*. You goddamn soulless monsters!" Blackwood growled. The deviants seemed amused by the comment.

"Monsters, are we?" Triple Six scoffed. "Says the man willing to kill a fuck-ton of innocent people? Bad enough you and your buds drop Project Suncloud, now you were gonna merc everyone at our base? Men, women, *and* children? And you call *us* monsters?" He pointed his finger at Blackwood's forehead and made a shooting motion with his fingers. The beanie-wearing deviant smiled a devilish grin. "Wrap your head around *that*," he said, amused.

Triple Six snapped his fingers.

EPISODE 12

The Rook and the Pawn

AYLEN

Aylen awoke with a jolt to the sound of blaring alarms. Quickly, she hurried out of the barracks in her bed clothes while covering her ears. Outside, Marie Vasquez and two boys were all huddled together in their pajamas.

"*What's going on?*" she yelled over the alarm. One of the boys shrugged in response to the question. In the dim light of the courtyard, she studied him and the other boy quickly, but all she could see was that one had red hair and the other had messy, dirty blond hair.

A spotlight from one of the watchtowers suddenly shone on them.

"Straight lines!" a loud command echoed over the PA. The young recruits looked around in panic, still processing what was happening. "*I said straight lines!*" the PA yelled. Aylen scrambled with the others to line up.

A large man with olive-colored armor landed on the ground in front of them. Aylen gasped. How did a normal human man jump down at such a great height in front of them? Was he not human? Was he a deviant? The alarms stopped as his helmet retracted into his armor to reveal a red-faced man. "Well, well, well, what've we got here? A bottom bitch, a tree hugger, a dyke, and a midget. Ain't that cute?" the man scoffed. A midget? Did-did he just make a remark about Aylen's height? Aylen looked around; in the line, she realized she was the shortest one there. The boy with shaggy blond hair chuckled. "Did I say something funny, you piece of tree-hugging *shit*?" the man screamed into the boy's face.

"N-no—" the boy stuttered. The man backhanded him across the face and threw him to the ground. Aylen and the others jumped at the sudden violence.

"What you're gonna do is give me pushups till I'm satisfied while you say, '*I am a worthless piece of shit.*' Do you understand me, son?" the man barked at the boy. A kick from the man's armored boot connected with the blond's stomach, which knocked the air out of him. Could—could he *do* that? Aylen's awe at the man's entrance faded into horror. The boy cringed in pain while the man pulled him by the back of his shirt into position. "Do it, boy!" the man yelled at the boy. "Say I. Am. A piece of shit!"

The recruit began doing pushups while saying he was a piece of shit. "Good!" the man barked while turning his attention to the remaining three recruits. "My name is Captain Morgan Gatton. Over the next couple of weeks, I will be *destroying* you in order to turn you miserable failed abortions into the greatest killing machines that ever lived. Unlike a normal military camp, after this training you'll probably be thrust immediately into heavy combat scenarios, meaning: I'm gonna be your worst *fuckin'* nightmare." He eyed the recruits, settling on the red-headed boy. "What's your story, fairy boy? Ya look a little tired. . . . Suck too many cocks last night?" Captain Gatton joked. The boy looked offended by the comment. "I asked you a question! *Did you suck some big fat juicy ones last night?*"

"No, sir!" the boy replied, scowling, obviously trying to not let the comments get to him.

"You sure? You look like you spent *all* night at one of them bathhouses y'all people like to go to. Probably everybody's little bitch boy, ain't ya? Gettin' rammed up the ass by some old goddamn perverts, you can see it in your face. That get you off your rocks, boy, old fuckin' perverts?" Captain Gatton said, obviously getting under the boy's skin as shown by the twisted, scorned child-esque look on Adrien's face. He was turning as red as the captain.

"No, sir!"

"Yeah, whatever you say, twinkle toes," Captain Gatton said while turning to Marie, who was next to Aylen. "Well, speaking of queers. Shit, we've here got a good ol'-fashioned, motherfuckin' lesbo here, don't we?"

"Goddamn right, sir!" Marie responded. The captain looked caught off guard by this, obviously not expecting that response. He tried to say something but seemed to be stumbling on his words. There was a moment he glared at Marie and she glared right back, completely unafraid. "Got a problem with that . . . *sir*?" Marie challenged. The captain looked her up and down. "Twenty pushups. Go," he said simply. Marie obeyed and began doing pushups. The captain blinked and looked around before his eyes found Aylen. Crap.

"Oooh boy . . . the hell is *this*? I asked for *soldiers*, why did they bring me a goddamn member of the lollipop guild?" Captain Gatton smirked. Aylen stiffened, realizing she was slightly terrified as the man looked down at her. He had to be six-five or six-six in comparison to her five-four. "You look *pocket sized*, you know that? Man, I'm *really* gonna trust my life in your hands on the battlefield, Princess. Watch, we'll all be fighting the deviants and she'll be complaining about how her nails got broken or somethin'." The captain smirked. "Think you're pretty, don't you, hun?" he scoffed before spitting. He then leaned forward to look her dead in the eye. "Well, guess what? You're the ugliest little bag I've ever seen. Tits too small, eyes too big, ass too big. You look like a bulimic anorexic! If you were a whore, I wouldn't even pay any more than a few coins to have my way with you. Matter of fact, I'd make you pay to fuck *me*. . . . You are the definition of what we back home call a *sport lay*, understand?" he spouted viciously.

Aylen wilted, feeling a slight tinge of sadness and anger come over her, warring with each other as she did her best to try to not look or feel offended. This wasn't how a drill sergeant should be acting, was it? "Show me a pushup, Sport

Lay." The captain grinned. Aylen looked at the other recruits, who were staring at her as well. She shivered slightly from the embarrassment of the command. "I said *show me a pushup*!" the captain barked. Aylen got down into a pushup position and lowered herself down, then pushed up. The captain laughed. "Well, ain't that a pretty sight? Ugly li'l troll *can* do pushups. Faster, Sport Lay, faster! I want you to do a million by the time a minute goes by!" he barked. She quickened her pushups, her arms aching because they weren't used to the exercise. Suddenly, she was yanked up by the back of her shirt to her feet. "Pitiful," the captain scoffed. He walked away from her. "Now listen, fuck nuggets. Give me ten running laps around the courtyard of this here base and meet me at the classroom portion. *Do you hear me, shit-for-brains?*"

"Sir, yes, sir!" the four recruits yelled.

"Good, I'll see you there soon enough, ya piles of trash," Captain Gatton said with a sort of amusement.

They didn't waste time starting their laps. "Miserable dick," the blond boy said out loud, wincing like he was still in pain.

"Shut up," Marie replied quietly.

"He can't say that stuff, am I right? That was fucked up . . ." he continued. The sound of waves was faint in the distance. Aylen heard them, thinking that perhaps the base was close to the ocean. After all of this was over, she'd have to look into it.

"I said shut up!" Marie snapped.

"I mean, you agree with me, right?" the blond boy asked. He had to look at Aylen before she realized that he was talking to her. She studied the boy's features. In some ways, his face reminded her of a bird with a mop on the top of his head.

"Y-yeah . . ." she replied quietly.

"He's a *drill instructor*, he's supposed to say shit to get under your skin," Marie replied, annoyed.

"Yeah, but what he was saying was out of line," the redhead replied. "Especially the stuff about you," he said while looking at Aylen. Everybody looked at her while running, including Marie, who gave Aylen a sort of harsh and cold look.

"I'm Jonathan," the blond boy said, offering his hand. Aylen took it.

"Aylen."

"Did I say you could talk? Move it!" Captain Gatton barked from a distance.

"Pig," Jonathan muttered.

By the fifth lap, Aylen began to fall behind, having a hard time breathing. She was bad enough at running, but now it really worked against her that it was obvious from running beside the other three recruits.

"Oh, lordy, *look who is falling behind!* If it ain't *Sport Lay.* Tell you what, girlie, you can sit this run out. I wouldn't want a little girl like you to hurt yourself trying to keep up with the other recruits! Might mess up your toenails!" the captain laughed. At his words, Marie stopped and ran back to Aylen. "Whoa there, She-Man, I didn't say you could run back for her!" the captain barked. The angry girl grabbed Aylen by the arm and began sprinting back to the rest of the group, dragging her along.

"Hurry the fuck up!" Marie barked. Why was she helping her?

After the laps were finished, the captain went up to Marie, who looked boldly back at her drill sergeant.

Smack.

She was on the ground in no time. "I said *don't* help her, stupid bitch," the captain muttered. The recruits all looked at the captain in shock. "Go back to your barracks, your uniforms are on top of your bunks. In the meanwhile, I have a lesson to teach li'l miss dike. You have five minutes to change," Captain Gatton said to Aylen and her fellow recruits. Marie looked up defiantly at the gestapo-like drill instructor. Aylen and Marie made a small amount of eye contact before she broke away and began doing pushups on the captain's order.

Aylen continued to walk to the barracks, feeling like crap for getting Marie in trouble.

When Aylen got back to her room, she found a baby blue uniform on her bunk. It was some sort of jumpsuit that resembled something that astronauts probably wore—back when there *were* astronauts before the Anthrodi War. Space travel wasn't exactly a thing anymore. She remembered seeing people wearing these on her way in. Huh. She slipped into her jumpsuit and studied herself in a mirror. She wanted to make sure that it looked tip-top, despite not knowing how the uniform was supposed to go.

"Move yer ass!" Captain Gatton yelled from outside. Marie rushed into the barracks with a big red mark on the side of her face. She took her clothes off to put on her jumpsuit, and Aylen couldn't help looking at her body. She was very fit and muscular, with multiple tattoos in various areas. She was obviously not afraid of going to the gym or to a tattoo studio. Marie shifted, and Aylen saw multiple large scars on Marie's toned back. They almost looked like slashes from the talons of some kind of animal, and they didn't look fully healed, maybe a few months old at best. They were still shades of reddish purple with jagged skin, and each looked more painful than the next. There was also a set of scars on her trap muscles that looked like something tried to dig its jaws into her.

Marie glanced at her suddenly, and Aylen swallowed and nodded her head. "Thank you."

"Didn't do it for you, man," Marie said while putting her jumpsuit on.

"Still. Thanks."

"Come on, girlies, I don't have all day!" the captain barked from outside their barracks. The girls rushed outside to find the boys already standing up straight side by side. Captain Gatton observed them all. "Twenty pushups! All of you, now!" the captain barked. Aylen and the others dropped. "Get up!" the captain yelled roughly five pushups in. The recruits began to scramble up. "Did I say you could get up? Continue your goddamn pushups!" the captain exclaimed, clearly finding amusement in this. The recruits got back down and continued.

"Faster! Faster! Come on, shitheads! When I say faster, you better be done by the time I finish this sentence, understand me? You're all a bunch of UWF-pampered pussies! You are piles of Brainless *shit*! Your mothers *regret* the day they didn't swallow *you*!" he barked. The recruits finished and hurried to their feet. Gatton stared down at all of them, then settled on the redheaded boy on the edge of the line. "Your jumpsuit is not tucked into your boots. Give me pushups till I say otherwise, pretty boy!" the captain barked. Then he went up to Aylen. "What're the words of the Saint Organization, Sport Lay?"

"Wh-what?" Aylen asked, having no idea what the captain was asking.

"You deaf? I said what're the words!"

"I don't know, sir!"

"No, you call me 'Captain,' not 'sir', you little troll! What're the goddamn words?"

"I don't know, Captain!" Aylen yelled, attempting to not break down in front of this horrible man.

"Everybody repeat after me: Honor. Vigilance. Duty."

"Honor! Vigilance! Duty!" the recruits replied.

"Y'all say somethin'? I *said* repeat after me! Honor! Vigilance! Duty!"

"Honor! Vigilance! Duty!" the recruits screamed.

And that was how her first day of training began. The more drills they did, the more the captain yelled, Aylen felt more and more terror begin to creep in. Captain Gatton barked and barked, and Aylen began to wonder if she would even survive the day.

JARED

Jared watched the courtyard from the main building of the base through a window. Aylen was down there, getting yelled at by Morgan, being told to do pushups and all sorts of other "breaking them down" bullshit that drill instructors do. Given Morgan's personality, however, Jared had a feeling that it was particularly unpleasant. At least when Gabe was in charge of training recruits, he seemed more like he was disciplining the new recruits. Jared was certain that Morgan was bullying them, judging from the redneck's nature.

He scowled. What was he *thinking* letting Aylen get sucked into all of this? Maybe if he'd just kept her in the dark about all this stuff, the Legion thing wouldn't have happened. But then, it may have happened regardless. Legion had carefully planned this somehow and for some reason, but why? Why did it want Aylen to find the trains in the subway? Why did it stalk her and tell her to spy on Jared? What was Legion's end goal? He looked down at the book in his lap. It was some sort of old horror novel that honestly was not all that interesting five chapters in. He looked out the window to watch Aylen as she struggled to do more pushups. Jared felt an uneasy feeling in his stomach watching his friend struggle so.

"You're worried about her, aren't you?" a familiar voice said as a hand landed on his shoulder.

"She's not a soldier," he replied, shaking his head. The hand on his shoulder squeezed it softly and his unofficial stepmom sat beside him.

Faith studied him. "Try telling her that." From the corner of his eye, Jared could see her smirk. "I only talked to her for a short time and I know it would be impossible to dissuade her. She's strong-willed, that one . . ." Jared looked over at Faith, confused. "I'm good at reading people. She may appear *meek* . . ." Faith trailed off, staring out at Aylen. The doctor then turned toward her adopted son. "But I know somewhere deep in there is a girl that is unstoppable once she sets her mind to something. You can see it in her eyes." Jared looked out toward Aylen. Huh. "How'd you meet her? She said you saved her from two Level 5 Brainless, something you *neglected* to mention in your reports, by the way."

"Then you already know how I met her, Ma," he replied solemnly. Faith nodded.

"Are you two together?" she asked. Jared ignored her while watching Aylen do pushups. Faith nodded again, her smirk spreading into a full smile. "I *see*, not yet . . ." she chuckled. Jared gave her an annoyed look. "You like her, I can tell." To this, Jared rolled his eyes. Faith giggled. "Come on, I've been around the block a few times, give a woman credit."

His stepmother paused then, looking like she had a momentary thought. "Why didn't you mention her in the reports?" she asked with concern. Jared remained silent as a grave. The doctor further studied him. "Jared, that's irresponsible and you know it."

"The less people involved in this war the better."

Faith looked out the window. "And yet here she is," she responded while looking down at her lap. After a moment, she looked up at Jared.

"Yeah, well, if it weren't for Legion's involvement in things, she wouldn't be here. She wouldn't be friends with me. She'd be *safe*. If things worked out my way, she'd have thought what she saw in the subway was a dream and she never would've found out the truth. It should've been *that* way."

"I doubt that you mean that," Faith said with a deep look in her eyes. "I see that you care about her, Jared. Just think, if Legion hadn't done what it did, *she* wouldn't be a part of your life. And you wouldn't be a part of hers. I'm a firm believer that bad things happen for a good reason. For whatever reason, *she's* meant to be part of your life."

"Part of my headache."

There was a moment of silence. Even without directly looking at her, Jared could feel his stepmom analyzing him.

"Well, all I'm saying is I haven't seen you care this much about anyone since Jessica."

Jared scoffed. "Nice name drop, Mom."

"It's true," she said with a sympathetic look. "Sure, I haven't really gotten to know this girl, but I know *you* very well, Jared Griffin. And when you drove in with her by your side, you handled her more gently than someone would a bird with broken wings—"

"She's not like Jessica," Jared interrupted. "It *ain't* like that. I'm just helping her because I owe her. She wouldn't be involved in any of this if it weren't for *my* mistakes."

Faith nodded. "Fair enough," she said quietly. The doctor got up and headed for the exit. Before reaching the door, she turned around toward Jared. "Don't be afraid to open your heart, Jared. Not everyone will end up like Jessica if you allow yourself to love them," she said with an amount of sincerity only Faith could deliver. Jared huffed after hearing this, feeling something dull inside him ache. "That's all I have to say," she stated, leaving Jared alone with his thoughts.

JOSHUA

Joshua and Tara arrived on base only to be greeted by Esmeralda.

"General Quinn requests your presence at once, Josh," she said, as if ordered to. Joshua looked at Tara, who gave him a look that said, "Uh-oh."

He nodded to Esmeralda and muttered, "Thanks, Ezzy," then made his way up the steps of the main building while his girlfriend talked with Esmeralda. His footsteps trudged heavily as he moved to his father's office. It wasn't long before Joshua entered the doorway to find his father sitting at his desk with a chessboard in front of him. Oh no . . .

"You're late," Abel muttered while looking up to Joshua. "Close the door behind you and sit down," he ordered sternly. Joshua obeyed his father and sat down in front of him. He looked at the pieces: His side was white, meaning he'd make the first move. The father started a timer, and the son studied the board and moved a pawn. "So, how was the drive?" Abel asked while moving a piece of his own.

"Fine. Tara wanted to pick some flowers on the way here," Joshua responded while moving an ivory piece strategically. His father moved one of the black pieces almost immediately.

"Girls like doing things like that," Abel assured his son. There was a moment of silence as the two men studied the board. Here it came. "What date did the Battle of Red Cliffs take place?"

"The year 208," the son replied while moving another piece. Abel immediately responded with a piece of his own.

"What age did Cao Cao die?"

"It's estimated to be sixty-four or sixty-five," Joshua responded quickly after moving another piece.

"What ended the War of the Three Kingdoms?" Abel moved a black piece of his on the board, eliminating one of Joshua's pieces.

"The defeat of the Shu empire in the year 270," Joshua responded mid-moving a piece.

Abel stopped the timer.

"Wrong. It was the defeat of the *Wu* empire in the year *280*." The father gave his son a look. "It would seem someone needs to review their Chinese history," he said disapprovingly. Abel started the timer again, continuing their game "What started the conflict of the War of the Roses?"

"Richard, the Duke of York, challenged the king's right to the throne."

"And which king was it?"

"Henry VI. He was Lancastrian, so that started the war between the Yorks and Lancasters." Joshua took out one of his father's pieces. That fact was easy enough to remember, since Faith and Gail's last name was Lancaster.

"Who ultimately won the conflict?" Abel moved his queen onto the middle of the board.

"The Lancasters," Joshua said while moving a piece. His father moved his queen.

"Wrong, and checkmate," his father said firmly, now stopping the timer. Joshua felt his pulse begin to race. "The correct answer would've been the Tudors. Yes, they were descendants of Lancasters, but the correct answer was the Tudors," Abel said sternly. Joshua picked up the queen and threw it across the room, allowing his temper to get the better of him. Abel remained calm and lifted an eyebrow at his son. "Are you done yet?"

"Why the hell do we still have these stupid-ass chess games?" the son snapped. "You always end up winning 'cause you're distractin' me with those stupid questions!"

"Those questions are about the world's military history, Josh," Abel began. "And a true leader knows how to manage his people, even while distracted."

"Well maybe I'm not a true leader! Ever think of *that?*" Joshua yelled while standing up.

"Yelling at me does nothing but show immaturity and stupidity. If you are going to make a point, you talk softly and firmly, do you understand? A true leader—which, by the way, you're my son, so of course you are one—does not let his emotions get the better of him. Sit down," Abel said firmly. Joshua thought for a moment and sat in front of his father. It was times like this that made him wish his mother were still around. Somehow, she always knew how to quell the quarrels that he and his father had. "Someday, Joshua, this war will be over, and you will have to return to some sort of semblance of a normal life. What they don't tell you is that normal life and running a family is a lot like running an army. You must manage the parts of your everyday life as if you were a general in medieval times. Do your troops have enough rations to eat? Is your economy stable enough for a war? Are your troops well-trained enough to withstand the horrors of the battlefield on their own? It is questions like these that apply to both the family unit and a military unit. These same rules apply to a management position, which undoubtedly you will get into, seeing that I'm molding you into the perfect leader among men."

"If I'm supposed to be a leader among men, why haven't you promoted me yet to something higher than corporal, huh? Why? If I'm supposed to be leading people?"

The Saints Leader shook his head. "You are young. A true leader earns his rank. In order to command men to die, he must understand what it is like on the front lines. Those who earn their ranks without the proper experience in battle soon forget that they are toying with people's lives by ordering them to carry out tasks. I did not get the rank I am today without earning it through tears and blood. The Anthrodi War as well as this war have conditioned me enough for Robert Harper, God rest his soul, to be content with entrusting me as the leader of his organization. Remember that."

Joshua paused for a moment, taking in this lecture from his father. His anger still seeped through his veins, yet he understood what his father was saying. His father was an ass, but at least he was a well-meaning ass. "Why did you summon me up here?"

"Father and son bonding," Abel replied stiffly, to which Joshua scoffed. "Also, I need to ask your opinion." He sat back in his chair. Joshua caught this shift in body language and began to become interested in what his father was about to say. "Our funding as an organization is running thin, morale from the troops is dwindling at best, and we still are anticipating battles with minimal knowledge of when and where the DDs will strike next. What do you suppose we do?"

Abel sighed, obviously getting to the root of this meeting. Joshua, though, looked in awe at his father. This was the first time his father, of all people, had entrusted him with an opinion.

GABRIEL

Gabriel sat in his private quarters with a pile of files in his lap. He was determined to find which recruit he would take under his wing, because Morgan should not have been put in charge of training the new recruits. By all means, he was a monster. Gabriel scanned the first file.

Jonathan Wallace. Occupation: Unemployed. Age: 20. Reason for Joining: Glory.

No. The last thing he needed was an apprentice that wanted to be a hero. War was no place for heroes. Especially not this war. Gabriel switched to the next file.

Adrien Mahoney. Occupation: Waiter. Age: 25.

Too old. Nope. Gabriel sighed. He switched the file yet again.

Marie Vasquez. Occupation: Construction Worker. Age: 23. Reason for Joining: Revenge. Degrees/Accomplishments: Psychology Bachelors. Test Results:

They hadn't tested the recruits' strengths yet, but this seemed like possibly a worthy candidate. Construction work meant that she was probably physically fit and the psychology bachelors probably meant there was at least some semblance of brains about the girl. Revenge was a strong enough motivation as any for someone to take up arms. Marie Vasquez was seemingly promising.

Gabriel looked at the next file.

Aylen Monro. Occupation: College Student. Age: 21. Reason for Joining: Revenge. Degrees/Accomplishments: High GPA, Medical Science Major.

Faith must've enjoyed that revelation when she wrote that down, or so Gabriel figured. This candidate was still in college. High GPA obviously meant brains, but, he wondered, since she was so book smart, was she weak physically? If she was physically weak, then it most likely meant she would not persevere in the heat of battle. Most likely, she was just some little bookworm. Gabe shook his head. He knew his choice out of the four; but he would have to watch them one of these days in order to determine which would become his pupil.

AYLEN

Aylen rushed up the stairs into a classroom, where she and the other three recruits were told by Captain Gatton to sit behind a table. A shrewd lady with glasses walked into the classroom. Her hair was almost gray, her nose pointed, and sharp green eyes lay behind her spectacles. Cold green eyes. The type that wouldn't think twice about telling one of them they failed in the harshest of ways. She wore the signature blue T-shirt and green pants underneath a gray hoody she wore partially zipped up.

"Stand up for your overview instructor!" the captain barked. The recruits did as instructed.

The lady nodded. "Be seated," the shrewd lady told the recruits. "My name is Sergeant Michelle Walsh. I am your educational instructor for this week. After this week, though, I'll not be teaching you anything else and it will be Captain Gatton taking full responsibility for your instruction. My job is to teach you the fundamentals of the new technology that will be thrust into your everyday life as a Saint," the woman said coolly. She then placed notebooks in front of the recruits. "Take notes, lots of notes. We are short on time, so I shan't be repeating myself after I tell you the information I am about to entrust upon you all," the instructor told the new recruits. "We already know who the Devil's Deviants are, right?"

"Yes," all four recruits replied.

"Good. Brainless? UWF's disdain for the organization?" she asked, analyzing the recruits. The recruits proceeded to nod their heads. "I see those who informed you of our organization have done a thorough job in description, then. So let us begin." The woman turned to the board, which generated an image. All of the recruits opened the notebooks that had been placed before them and got pens ready. The image on the board was of armor similar to what Captain Gatton had on him: dark olive-green and form-fitting, not looking like it would protect one from much of anything, which was in stark contrast to the armor the UWF soldiers had worn at the outer limits of Salutem. "Can anyone tell me what this is?"

"A spacesuit?" Jonathan replied sarcastically. No one chuckled, and the teacher ignored the statement.

"Anyone?" The woman scanned the four recruits, already seeming to know the answer to her question. "Of course you don't know the technical term.

This is something that the Earth's military forces all invented shortly before the Anthrodi War. These suits of armor are called enhancer armor. Can anyone take a wild guess as to why they are called that?" the teacher asked. Quickly, Aylen thought of how Captain Gatton was able to appear out of nowhere earlier that morning. She raised her hand while writing 'Enhancer Armor' in her notebook. "Go ahead," the teacher responded.

"Because the suits enhance the abilities of the person wearing it?"

The teacher smiled briefly upon hearing this answer. "Correct. Enhancer armor is standard issue for all Saint Organization members. It's armor that enhances your physical abilities tenfold, allowing you to be ten times faster and more agile than the ordinary human. It comes very much in handy battling deviants and gives us somewhat of an equal footing against them, especially since the average deviant is ten times tougher than the average human. However, the armor we have here is of an older make and model; therefore, it does not offer much protection against anything above handgun rounds." The instructor looked at the four recruits. The tension between them rose uncomfortably after this statement. "Because of this, there is no guarantee of safety or survival in a deviant encounter. Without the armor, though, especially if going toe to toe with a more powerful deviant, certain death would be inevitable," she continued while studying the faces of the recruits. "By the end of this year, it'll be hard to say how many of you will have survived this horrible conflict. It's highly possible that you will all be dead by the time winter ends. It's hard enough to determine how long seasoned veterans will survive, let alone new recruits . . ." the instructor trailed off. She shook her head. "Anyway, moving forward." Aylen swallowed. That was reassuring. The instructor pressed a button that zoomed in on the belt of the suit. "See this right here? This is the most important feature of enhancer armor. Let me show you why," she said to the recruits. The woman pressed a button on her belt.

Aylen watched in awe as dark green wrapped itself around the instructor's body, covering it head to toe in enhancer armor.

"Whoa!" she heard Jonathan say as all four recruits looked at the sight with mouths agape. The instructor then pressed yet another button on the belt and her helmet came down.

"With the UWF breathing down our necks and the deviants infecting Salutem with their presence, being discreet has become key to our survival. The ability to be battle ready every time you walk out of your home has saved many Saint Organization members on numerous occasions. It may just save your lives too. The enhancer armor is able to do this because the armor takes a sample of your blood as well as measurements of your height, weight, build and so on. After that is entered, the belt locks in with your personal info. If there are shifts in weight, the suit will accommodate thus. Keep in mind: Belts are personalized to the individuals who own them. You can't trade enhancer armor with anyone. Activating someone else's armor can be . . . disastrous. I repeat, *never* trade armor," the instructor said gravely to the class. This detail stuck out to Aylen. There must've been people that had tried for them to feel they had to warn the new recruits. The instructor then began to lecture about the specifics and functions of the armor. Aylen listened intently to every word, attaching herself to every statement like super glue.

CERBERUS

Cerberus rode to the designated location on the back of his motorcycle: another back-alley affair. Steam rose from a vent on the ground as the cold air seeped through his bones. The hellhound cracked his neck before getting off his bike and lighting a cigar. The toxic smoke entered his lungs like a sweet vapor, soothing his heart rate as he made his way to the door of one of the buildings and knocked on it with the secret beat. Triple Six opened the door.

"'Bout time you showed up."

"He still alive?"

"Define alive." Triple Six smirked. Cerberus gave him a look. "Just kidding, all we did was rough 'im up bit. He's all yours, *Cerby*." The two deviants walked down a hall with brick walls to both sides and opened another door. Inside were a small group of deviants and a thin, balding man tied to a chair in the middle of the room. The man looked defiantly at Cerberus through patches of dried blood on his body.

Cerberus grabbed a chair and sat on it backward, studying the man. "And he hasn't talked?" he asked Triple Six.

"So far the only words we've been able to get out of him are 'go fuck yourself' . . . not very creative, to say the least."

Cerberus sighed and brushed his hand through his hair. He took off his sunglasses and looked deep into the defiant man's eyes.

"So, you want us to go fuck ourselves, eh?" Cerberus shook his head. "Truth is, friend, you're the one who just fucked yourself."

Crack.

The man screamed in pain as the tip of his right index finger twisted itself backward. The scream faded into a howl and he breathed heavily. "I can do things that make the most hardened soldier a little bitch, so I suggest you start talkin'."

"I'm not . . . gonna tell you . . . a goddamn thing . . ."

"I was kinda hoping you'd say that." Cerberus smirked. Another loud crack and scream filled the room as the man's middle finger received the same treatment as his index. "By the end of this, you will tell me the password. Make no mistake of that."

"Screw you," the man grumbled. Cerberus motioned for Triple Six, who in response headed toward him and stuck his ear next to the superior deviant.

"You know his address?" Cerberus said flatly while looking at the man in front of him. Triple Six nodded. "You know what to do."

BRENDEN

In the dead of night, Brenden walked through the base courtyard and made his way to the new recruits' barracks, attempting to be silent so as not to get himself into trouble. He knew he shouldn't be doing this, but he had to check on *him*. He went up to the men's barracks and knocked. Adrien opened the door. He looked very tired and closed the door behind him.

"Brenden? What're you doing out here?"

"I came to see you. How did training go today? I just heard about the change in instructors a few hours ago. I'm so sorry. Morgan is a dick."

"Well, he's a captain and his name is Morgan." Adrien smirked. "It's priceless."

"How bad was he, though?"

"Well . . . he keeps getting into weird homophobic rants whenever he's trying to attack me," Adrien scoffed.

"Well that sounds like him, all right," Brenden said, lifting one eyebrow.

"This one girl had it worse, though. Especially after we had classroom time. He kept insulting everything about her. It was awful."

"Probably sensed weakness in her. Especially with Morgan, I would imagine that heathen would've bled her self-esteem dry. He didn't do anything too bad to you though, did he?"

"No."

"Good," Brenden nodded his head. "I have to go now, but stay strong." He looked into the new recruit's eyes. Then he grabbed Adrien's head and kissed him. After a long moment, Brenden pulled away. "Love you."

Adrien nodded his head. "Love you too." Brenden then slipped away into the dead of night from whence he came.

AYLEN

Aylen looked for guidance in the ceiling of her barracks. Today had been a rough day. Not just physically, she could've handled that. That she had expected, but it was the verbal assault that had truly exhausted her. The captain seemed to find her pretty amusing to pick on after class. She remembered it clearly. The captain going into more detail about how she was merely a "sport lay" to him, about how ugly she was, the way he made fun of her during exercises. It was horrible. She hoped he found a different victim to pick on tomorrow. Aylen then slipped into the dark relief and comfort that was sleep.

Hoooonk.

A blaring sound awoke Aylen from her slumber and hurt her ears. She clutched them and saw Captain Gatton standing above her, holding a horn in his hand.

"Time to get up, Sport Lay!" he yelled at her. His red face was accentuated by a sea of sweat. She held on to her ears and the captain grabbed her by the hair. "You overslept, Sport Lay, get dressed on the double!" the captain barked at her while pulling. He let go and stepped back. Aylen looked and saw that the door was open, with the other recruits in uniform waiting, wearing horrified expressions on their faces. She got down from her bunk . . . and hesitated when she saw the recruits and the captain were just standing there . . .watching.

Aylen then realized. "W-wait . . . get dressed right here?" she asked, slightly horrified.

"Did I stutter?"

"You—you can't be serious . . ." At least the other recruits looked uneasy as Aylen looked to them, horrified.

"Move it, Sport Lay!" Captain Gatton yelled. No way. N-no way! Aylen breathed hard, then swallowed. This was crazy. She looked uneasily at the recruits and began to take off her shirt while attempting to cover herself. *"Too slow!"* Captain Gatton yelled. He tangled his hand in her shirt and ripped it off, then pulled down Aylen's pants before grabbing her by the hair and throwing her onto the cold ground outside. Aylen lifted herself slightly. The shock of what happened overcame her as she found herself in her underwear with her pants around her ankles and on the ground, being watched by everyone. Tears gathered in her eyes and her breaths shortened. Captain Gatton put his foot on Aylen's back and shoved her back down. "Start doing pushups, and repeat after me: *I am an ugly whore,*" the captain commanded.

Aylen began to tremble, tears pouring out involuntarily. She looked up to see Marie looking at her with an uncharacteristically sympathetic look. *"Aw, Sport Lay is crying. Do your goddamn pushups!"* the captain yelled, clearly enjoying himself. She began doing the pushups with Morgan's foot on her back. "I don't hear ya sayin' it. Repeat after me: *I. Am. An. Ugly. Whore!"* But Aylen pinched her mouth shut as tears of humiliation streamed down her face. "Say it!" the captain barked. The captain then grabbed her by the hair and tugged it. *"Say it!"*

Suddenly, Aylen felt the weight pushed off of her back, recognizing the sound of footsteps only after she was pulled up into an embrace.

"Morgan! *What the hell do you think you're doing?"* Aylen heard the woman embracing her shout. She recognized the woman as Dr. Faith Lancaster. Aylen lifted her head and saw Brenden in Morgan's face to protect her.

"She's a weak link! I—"

"You *what,* Morgan? You're not supposed to torture our new recruits!"

"And you're not supposed to tell me how to do my job!" Morgan barked. *"She* will never be a soldier! It's my job to make sure a weak li'l pissant like her don't make it into *our* ranks!"

"You're out of line!" the doctor yelled. Morgan began to charge toward her but Brenden held him back.

"I'm out of line? Wanna say that again?" Morgan's face was red like a lobster. "Do you have any prior military experience? *No!* I *know* what I'm talking about! That's why *I'm* in this position and you're not!" he yelled, barely being held back by the smaller Brenden. *"You're out of fuckin' line! Bleedin' heart bitch like you needs to stay out of this!"*

"Come on, let's get you some clothes," Dr. Lancaster said while putting her coat around Aylen's shoulders. Aylen sobbed profusely, utterly humiliated. She couldn't look the other recruits in the eyes as the doctor began walking her away.

"Get off me, ya fuckin' fairy!" Morgan said, pushing Brenden away. Brenden then began to follow Faith and Aylen.

"Do you want tea or hot cocoa?"

"Cocoa," Aylen mumbled, now dressed and sitting in a chair.

"Hot cocoa it is," Faith said while pressing the hot chocolate machine. Aylen focused her eyes on the ground. "I'm gonna make a fuss 'bout this whole thing. Abel has been hard to reach lately . . . but I'll definitely be making a fuss. Morgan usually gets away with murder around here but—" Faith went into a rant that Aylen zoned out of, replaying what just happened in her head. That bastard . . . he actually stripped her, didn't he? He actually put his hands on her like that . . .

Faith knelt in front of her. "Hey, are you okay?" she asked, running her hand through Aylen's hair.

"Yeah," Aylen responded, still feeling the humiliation she had suffered outside. Stripped . . . in front of her fellow recruits. Treated like some kind of animal. Treated like something less than human and tossed into the dirt.

"Sweet girl," Faith said, nodding her head and running her hand through Aylen's hair still. "You know, you don't have to continue training to be a soldier. If you want . . . I could take you on as my apprentice. You would never have to deal with Morgan aga—"

"No. No, thank you," Aylen said firmly. "That's what he wants. I refuse to give that *pig* the satisfaction." She breathed out. "I *will* be a soldier."

Faith looked at Aylen sympathetically. "Still, you should perhaps take the rest of the day off, to let the heat cool off?"

"No. I won't miss a day of training just 'cause that sexist asshole thinks he got the better of me," the girl stated firmly. There was a moment of silence as Dr. Lancaster stared at Aylen in slight disbelief. Finally, the doctor sighed.

"Very well, then. You should make your way to class. It starts in roughly twenty minutes." Faith grabbed the hot chocolate and gave it to Aylen, who nodded and got up to start toward the door. "Remember, no matter what he does, he is still a human," Faith told Aylen. She turned around to find the doctor staring back at her. The statement confused Aylen, but Faith seemed to stand by her statement as if she had just given her the most powerful weapon of all.

GABRIEL

Gabriel sat in his private quarters. Today was an anniversary of sorts: the anniversary of the reason he had entered the war in the first place. He sat on his bed and looked at the photograph in front of him. He was always miserable on this day. It was the one day the weight of everything the war had brought him came crashing down upon him. It wasn't a day he cried, though. Far from it. Rather, it was a day permanently shrouded in darkness.

There was a knock at his door. Gabriel snapped out of his gloom and got up to answer it. He opened the door to find Esmeralda standing there, looking beautiful as ever.

"Hey."

"Hi."

Her tan skin looked smooth, her dark eyes pierced Gabriel's soul with their stare, and the way she had styled her dark hair looked nice today.

"May I come in, or did I come at a bad time?"

"No, not at all, come on in." Gabriel swallowed his spit. He allowed her in and closed the door behind her. "To what do I owe the pleasure, Ezzy?" Gabriel asked, leaning against a counter.

"You know, I never noticed how you keep your private quarters until just now. Very cozy," Ezzy said to him while getting a beer from the fridge.

"Thank you." Gabriel smiled as she handed him the beer.

"I have to admit, I'm surprised to not see you around base doing the usual things you do every day," she told him. Esmeralda opened her beer and took a cute swig. "Awfully suspicious, Gabe," she lifted an eyebrow playfully.

He chuckled lightly. "Well, partially that's 'cause your boyfriend took my job."

A sour look washed over Esmeralda's face. "Yeah . . . sorry about that. . . . Morgan is the one at fault for all of that. Only just recently found out he got the job. He didn't even tell *me* what he was up to. I swear sometimes . . ." she trailed off. Gabriel looked at Esmeralda, puzzled.

"Not exactly a supportive tone when it comes to the man that you're with. You guys doing all right?" he asked her, the chuckle in his voice masking his concern. Ezzy looked at a loss for words.

"Y-yeah I guess, maybe, I don't know . . . I don't think I really wanna talk 'bout it, know what I mean?" Esmeralda said nervously, laughing it off. Gabriel folded his lip and nodded.

"Fair enough."

Esmeralda turned her attention to the bed and saw the photograph. "Oooh, what's that?" she asked cheerfully. She took the photo into her hand and looked at it. "Whose little girl is this?"

"Mine," Gabriel smiled.

"I didn't know you had a child," she smiled back. "Is she your only?" Gabriel felt a weight on his brow as he maintained a smile.

"Yes."

"How old is she? This photograph looks old . . ."

"Fifteen by now," Gabriel said, maintaining his composure.

"She's so pretty!"

"Thank you." There was brief silence as Esmeralda studied the picture.

"Where is her mother?"

"Long gone, I'm afraid. It's been just her and I for most of her life."

Esmeralda blinked for a moment and looked up at Gabriel, looking over the crevices of his face. "Must be hard for her, you being here all the time," she said, looking into his eyes. "Must be hard for you."

"It is."

The woman studied him before wincing. "One of those things you would rather not talk about?"

He smiled politely. "Yeah."

"Sorry."

"It's okay." There was a moment of awkwardness before Gabriel began to get up and pass Esmeralda. "I'm getting hungry. Want me to make you anything?"

Esmeralda then grabbed Gabriel's hand. He turned around, puzzled, only to be greeted by a pair of soft lips. "Ezzy . . ." Gabriel whispered while pulling away.

"Shhh." She planted another kiss upon Gabe's lips. He pulled away from her, his hand on her upper chest, pushing her away.

"Wh-what are you doing? You're with Morgan . . ."

"To *hell* with Morgan. . . . I know you want me. I've wanted you too," she said, her hands gliding over his chest.

Gabriel swallowed. "I-I'm not sure we should do this . . ." he said as her body crept in closer to his.

"Why not?"

"Because . . . it's wrong," he said under his breath, gazing into her eyes.

"This is *Morgan* we're talking about . . ." Esmeralda remarked quietly. She put a hand on Gabe's face. "You think *he's* loyal by choice?" she said softly. "The only reason that pig doesn't screw other women is 'cause he's too ugly to."

Gabriel breathed out. "I—I haven't been with anyone for a long time."

Esmeralda ran her fingers through his hair. "That's okay . . ." she said, in what was almost a whisper. "I want you. I've wanted you for a long time."

Esmeralda led Gabriel into another kiss. This time he did not protest; rather, he let himself be sucked into it. He had wanted this for a while now. He knew that she did too. What use was there fighting it?

Esmeralda chuckled while her face was next to his. "I promised myself I wouldn't do this. Guess I don't have good self-control." The two continued kissing.

"I promised myself I would deny you if you made any moves on me. Guess you're not alone in that boat. After all . . ." He lifted her chin. "How could I deny a face this beautiful?"

The two kissed, and the captain then laid the sergeant down on the bed. Esmeralda put her hands underneath his shirt and began to pull it upward. Morgan? Who was Morgan? Gabriel undid Esmeralda's pants and began to pull them down. Morgan? Never heard of him. As of that moment, Gabriel decided Morgan no longer existed.

CERBERUS

Cerberus rubbed his eyes as he re-entered the room that he had spent most of the evening in. It had been a long night, and the man had still not given up the password. He looked at the handywork from the previous night. After all the torture and pain, the man had still, somehow, kept his defiance. If nothing else, Cerberus had to respect the man's resolve. Time was of the essence, though, and it was time to play dirty if the man held out any longer.

"Look, I'm not sure how much longer you're willing to withhold that password from us, but you might wanna hurry up, or I may have to kill you." Cerberus sighed, gazing at the face in front of him that was deformed with welts, blood, and broken bones.

"Then I'll die with your password," the man uttered while chuckling through his broken mouth. It was obvious that the pain Cerberus had delivered him did affect him, despite his resilience. "Face it, freak, you have no power here. There's nothing you can do to me that will make me talk," the man struggled to utter. He began laughing weakly.

To this, Cerberus laughed with him. "I suppose you're right. Nothing *I* can do to *you* to make you talk. Six, bring her in!" he called out. The man's face dropped as he realized what Cerberus had done. Triple Six burst the only entrance to the room wide open as he dragged in the only thing that would perhaps make the man talk.

"Dad?" the woman who was being dragged by Triple Six called.

"Helen?" the man asked, eyes shifting quickly. "I-it's okay, baby, don't worry, everything is going to be fine."

"Not if you don't tell me the password. Six, show him what you can do," Cerberus said calmly. Triple Six pointed his finger at the woman's foot and snapped. A vine dug its way through the soft flesh of her foot and tore its way out through her skin, sending the woman to the floor, screaming. The man watched in horror as his daughter lay on the floor, crying in pain. He turned to Cerberus.

"If you think that by hurting my daughter you're gonna get anything from me, you have another thing coming!"

The deviant smiled. "Doubt it." He gave Triple Six another nod and the young man snapped his fingers yet again, sending another vine shooting out of the woman's leg. Triple Six snapped again, and a vine protruded from the woman's back. The woman squealed in pain, much to the father's dismay. Again and again and again, and another vine came out, then another, then another. He lifted the woman by the hair and held his finger to her head.

"Last chance old man," Triple Six said threateningly. The old man held back the tears in his eyes while looking at his child. "Say goodbye." Triple Six positioned himself to kill the woman.

"*Stop!*" the father cried out, clearly unable to take any more. "I'll tell you . . . I'll tell you . . ." the man sobbed, choking on his tears.

"Go on," Cerberus demanded coldly.

"It's . . . Artemis . . . 56673. A-R-T-E-M-I-S. 56673. Capital A, no spacing," the man said through sobs. Cerberus wrote the password down on his phone.

"All right, let them go. Get them out of my sight," he sighed. The sounds of the sobs filled the room as Triple Six untied the father and the daughter. The two embraced with pain and difficulty, then looked fearfully at Cerberus. "Go on. Get out of here. And never tell anyone of this encounter." The father then helped the daughter get up and the two limped out of the room. Cerberus closed his eyes as the silencers whispered two gunshots.

AYLEN

Aylen stood up in uniform. She had gotten up especially early to make sure Morgan couldn't torment her. It had been a week of constant harassment, and she was nervous. Today would be the last day of classes. It wasn't that she was nervous about the test that would commence on this day; this was not the case at all. She was confident that she would ace it. After this week, however, she and the other recruits would be thrust into combat training. With Captain Gatton. Oh joy.

Throughout the week she had been the captain's *favorite* target of ridicule. At least, however, nothing the captain did was as bad as the 'underwear incident' that had happened on her second day. Dr. Lancaster must've talked it over with their superiors because Morgan had considerably backed off. He was still an asshole, though. An asshole who obviously liked the power he had been granted over people.

Fully clothed, Aylen sat on her bed and waited for the sound of the wake-up call to go off. She looked across the room to see that Marie was up and ready as well. The two exchanged awkward glances.

"Ready for this test?" Aylen asked, hoping Marie wouldn't be a bitch to her.

"Yep. You, man?" Marie asked without emotion.

"Yeah, it's not too hard of a subject. I was a medical science major in college. So after that, this is a breeze."

"I, as a psych major, can relate." Marie nodded. Then she gave Aylen a bizarre facial expression, flaring her nostrils, twisting her mouth, and lifting an eyebrow before simply frowning. Aylen wasn't quite sure what to make of it. "You sure you wanna continue with this, man? I don't think anybody would blame you if you wanted to quit after today. It's only gonna get harder from here. Combat training will be hell for you. Especially with the captain being the teacher, man," Marie said firmly, catching her off guard. She stared at Marie for a second, analyzing her stoic face.

"I'm not gonna back out. . . . I'm sticking with this to the end," she said quietly. There was a momentary silence as the two girls awkwardly tried to find something to talk about. "So, um . . . you've dated other girls, right?"

Marie lifted an eyebrow. "Yeah?"

"Wh-what's it like doin' that? Like . . . how is it— How's it different?" Aylen asked awkwardly.

Marie smirked and chuckled. "Why? You interested?"

Aylen blushed a bit and blinked her eyes. Uh . . . she swallowed, not quite sure how to continue the conversation. With that, they fell to silence.

Before long, both girls were called upon by Captain Asshole to do the morning exercises. Soon after, the recruits went off to the classroom where Mrs. Walsh was already waiting for them. The teacher gave a short speech about the importance of the test, and then it began. All four recruits raised their pencils. Aylen's eyes scanned through the test and found that overall there were forty questions to be completed within two hours. Too easy. Aylen's eyes settled on the first page.

1) *What are the words of Saint Organization?*

2) *What are Tank suits?*

3) *(True or False) It is perfectly acceptable to lend someone else your enhancer armor.*

Nine questions total on the first page. After analyzing the questions, Aylen quickly put her pencil to the paper and began answering.

Aylen seemed to know every answer to every question that came up on the test. She had studied well and could remember the notes she had vigorously taken while Mrs. Walsh was speaking. Before she knew it, she had answered all forty of the questions. She double-checked all of her answers to make sure they were right. She did not want to be the first person to turn in her test, so she waited until Marie finished before bringing her test to the teacher, who gave her a sly smile. It seemed that the teacher had perhaps expected good results from Aylen.

Had the teacher been watching her while she took her test? Did the teacher secretly know that she finished her test fairly early? Aylen bit her lip a bit as the teacher accepted the papers. And thus it was finished. The recruits were allowed the rest of the day off, which Aylen was grateful for, as she felt it was necessary for the momentary break from training.

Aylen made her way outside to be greeted by a familiar face, a face she hadn't seen in a while. "How's GI Jane doing?" Jared grinned as Aylen stepped out.

"Good," she smiled. It was nice seeing Jared after what seemed like forever. It had only been a week, but after all the humiliation Aylen had suffered this week alone, it felt like it had been a millennium since she had seen a familiar, friendly face.

"How's Morgan been treating you?" he asked with concern. Aylen scrunched up her face a bit. "That well, huh?"

"Haven't you heard? I'm his favorite target."

"*Favorite target?* What kinda stuff does he do?" he asked, now obviously concerned for his friend's well-being. She smiled to herself lightly; after spending a whole week being treated like dirt, it was nice to see that someone cared for her. She thought about the underwear incident and decided not to tell Jared, uncertain of what he would do with that info.

"Would rather not get into it. I will tell you, though, that the nickname that he gave me is *Sport Lay*."

Jared immediately seemed offended by this, almost as if someone had told him his mother looked like a dead horse and smelled of cat piss. "*Sport Lay?* Th-that piece of shit calls you *Sport Lay?*" he said, cutting the air with the sharpness of words.

"Yeah, calls me an ugly whore and says if I were a prostitute I'd have to pay him to . . . you know," Aylen said solemnly. Jared tensed up, shaking his head. "Fun guy, Captain Gatton."

"You listen to me. First off, that misogynistic dickwad is *fucking* blind. You're beautiful as *fuck* and he has his head up his ass," he spat out with venom. Aylen blushed a bit at this, not expecting that.

"Th-thanks," Aylen responded quickly before Jared immediately spoke his next statement.

"Secondly, this guy is a *fucking* asshole. Abel can be a reasonable guy, Rob trusted him. If I work with Faith . . . I don't know, we'll see what maybe we could do about getting him out of the training officer position. Morgan *won't* get away with that kinda shit on my watch. Nobody was treated like that when training was under Gabriel. It was about training to survive, *not insulting the new recruits.*" Aylen had to smile a bit at how flustered Jared seemed. He breathed in and out through his nose and shook his head, then stared deep into her eyes. "Don't worry, A, that bastard won't torment you much longer. I'll see to it myself. Give me some time, though. I need to work up some kind of case against him."

She studied Jared. He was smart enough, surely. And with Faith backing him, it was hopefully possible that he would be taken seriously, despite his morbid appearance. If the leader of the Saint Organization had any sort of validity, surely he would listen to reason. Morgan *had* to be kicked out from his position, if not the Saint Organization in general. There was a piece of information Jared was missing though, one that would surely be a golden ticket of sorts.

"If you're gonna build a case on him . . . there's something I haven't told you yet."

JARED

Jared burst through the office doors of the Principal Overseer.

"Why hello, Jared, it's been a while," Abel said calmly.

"Morgan can't be in charge of training anymore," the deviant said firmly, leaning on the desk toward Abel. *"He's abusing recruits!"*

"Abuse?" Abel looked over the brim of his glasses "If you're referring to ordinary drill instruction, I assure you it's not abuse, it's discipline."

"Discipline? That fuck out there stripped a girl and forced her to do pushups in front of the other recruits! *How's that for discipline?"* Jared growled.

Abel studied him for a moment. "Those are some wild accusations, Jared. You better have some evidence to back that kinda talk. Defamation of a fellow officer is cause for demerit of rank."

"Evidence? Just talk to Faith and Brenden! Talk to the recruits! They were all there!" he snapped. "You should have *never* taken Gabriel off of training new recruits! Morgan's a fucking douchebag and he needs to be taken down! That jerkoff is—"

"Enough!" Abel shouted, interrupting him. "Shout at me any more and you're no longer a Saint, got that?" Jared shut his mouth, knowing Abel was serious. "Now about this situation, I'll look into it. Yes, Morgan is a difficult man, but that is an absurdly wild accusation, and one that will require an internal investigation. I'll get on that . . ." A dark glare came over Abel's face. Jared knew that look. Damn, he still hated him, huh? "As far as *you* go, I know you worked hard to get into this outfit and to earn trust. But if every time there's a problem you go and barge down my door accusing another soldier of foul doings, you *best believe* you will no longer be welcome among our ranks. *I'm* the Principal Overseer. You don't come in here and make demands of *me*, understand? What's done is done and Gabriel's been removed from that position. That's our business, not yours." There was a moment where Abel regained some composure, then looked back down at his paperwork. "Now, when did this incident happen?"

Jared was taken aback. He wasn't expecting to butt heads this hard with the man. Abel was a far cry from Rob. "Tuesday," he said quietly.

"Tuesday? How come I was only told of this just now if it happened Tuesday?" Abel said almost sarcastically.

"I—I don't know why. I *just* found out about it just now."

"Who did you find it out from?"

"The girl it happened to: Aylen Monro," he affirmed. Abel squinted his eyes at Jared.

"That's the girl *you* brought in, is it not?"

"Yes, sir," the deviant confirmed, titling his head in confusion.

"So tell me, being that you and Morgan already have a history of not liking each other, and you may or may not be romantically involved with this girl, what's to tell me that you two aren't just making this incident up?" Abel said skeptically. The boy with piercings nearly did a double take at this accusation.

"Excuse me?"

"You spent how many years as an assassin for Lucifer and his deviants, and mastered the craft of lying. What assurance from you do I have that anything you say is true?" the Principal Overseer asked Jared. The boy could not believe his ears.

"Wh-why would I be lying?"

"You're a deviant, it's what your kind do, you lie through the teeth."

Jared took a moment to process the insult. A cold feeling began to flow through him. A type of cold feeling that he was all to familiar with. All emotion drained out of him and a shut down of sorts occured. The deviant looked down at the floor and nodded. "Ask Brenden and Faith. You'll see I'm not lying." He began to walk out. He stopped and turned around with eyes burning a bright orange. "And if you ever accuse me of lying again just because I'm a deviant . . . Principal Overseer or not, I will rip your fucking heart out."

Abel's eyes widened and he fell silent. The color in his face drained and his mouth dropped uneasily. Jared kept his gaze a moment and could feel the man's terror as he gazed deep within his soul.

Then he stomped out. Abel still hated him, even after all these years of him proving himself. Egotistical prick. Jared had successfully completed mission after mission from the Saints, and the new Principal Overseer still wanted to treat him like an enemy? Typical. Jared sighed, worried about how much Aylen would actually be helped. If Abel wouldn't help, he'd have to think of some other way to get Morgan out of the position of Aylen's drill instructor, and the boy in black was not above taking more drastic measures to ensure that.

ESMERALDA

"R-remember that mission on Oakley Street?" Esmeralda asked through laughter. The ocean crashed outside as the woman and Gabriel lay naked on the bed. It was midday, and even though she knew Morgan would be free because of the recruit testing, she had managed a decent enough lie to get away from him for a few hours. "Covert Saint business, directly from General Quinn" seemed to do it. It was hard to describe just how happy she was at this moment.

"Oh God," Gabriel laughed, shaking his head.

"Wh-what was that guy's DD name? I can't remember . . ."

"He wasn't a deviant, he was a member of Los Lobos Muertos, one of the DDs' black market contacts."

"Right, right. Man, I will never forget that day. Chasing him down, everything's all serious, we're holding him at gunpoint then all of a sudden this big long—" The woman then blew a raspberry, getting a rise out of the man she lay with.

"I remember. You had a hard time keeping a straight face after that," Gabriel chuckled.

"Well how am I supposed to? Here I am, holding up this scary gangbanger-looking dude, had to use enhancer armor to chase him down, then all of a sudden he lets out this long, loud fart! It was disgusting and hilarious at the same time! Like a freaking comedy movie. Like, how could someone even do that, you know? Didn't even seem real."

Gabriel rubbed his eyes. "Well, I remember detaining that guy. The cleanup proved he did more than pass gas . . ."

"Uggggh nasty." Ezzy twisted her face. "Whatever happened to that guy?"

"Well, we let him go after getting information out of him, and the next thing I heard was his family was mailed his severed face."

"DD kill?"

"No, that was a signature Los Lobos Muertos move. I have a feeling the DDs didn't catch wind of that one or worse would've been done."

"Oof, Los Lobos Muertos. . . . How come I haven't heard their name in a while?"

"Rumor has it, the UWF sicced their Serious 2 Unit on them and they've been wiped out since. They weren't a large gang, easy pickings for the UWF, unlike the DDs." Gabe's hand stroked Ezzy's back. "Good thing they got taken out too. They were the DDs' main gun supplier for a long time."

Esmeralda stared off into space, thinking.

"How long ago *was* that?"

"Oooh, 'bout three years ago. It was somewhere between Jessica's death and Candace's murder–suicide," Gabriel responded grimly.

"2054, yeah, that wasn't a good year . . ." Ezzy sighed. "January that year was when Caleb . . ." With this, she trailed off, not wanting to remember. Gabriel solemnly nodded.

"Yeah . . . bad year for the Saints," he said with a sigh. Esmeralda grimaced. That was the same year she officially wound up with Morgan, so it was bad for more than a few good reasons. She snuggled into Gabe's chest. "So I have to know . . ." Gabe started as she closed her eyes.

"Yeah?"

"What is that bruise on your abdomen from?" Esmeralda opened her eyes immediately and looked toward Gabriel's inquisitive face. It looked deeply concerned. She swallowed.

"I, um . . . I slipped into my kitchen counter a few days ago," she said before placing her head back onto his chest. "I'm clumsy sometimes." She chuckled, hiding the bruises on her arm with her hand as discreetly as possible.

"Hmm," Gabriel expressed with a tightlipped look on his face. Oh no . . . she couldn't let him think too hard about it.

"You know what's also a funny story?" she asked, trying to distract him.

"Mmm?" the captain responded, staring hard at the bruise on her ribs.

"That time Brenden showed up drunk to drills," she chuckled. His gaze eased a little and a smile grew on his face

"Ah, yeah, I remember. The first group of recruits. You were in the first group I ever trained," he said with a light chuckle.

"Yep. The first civilians that were let into the Saints," Ezzy added.

"Let's see, it was you, Brenden, George, Gail . . . God, who else?"

"Mark . . . uhhh, few others, Faith weirdly enough."

"Wow . . . time flies." There was a moment of quiet as they both recounted memories.

"You know, back then, I knew somehow . . ."

"Knew?"

"Yeah . . . that'd we be here, someday. Even though Caleb and I started dating after I made corporal, I somehow just . . . *knew*. I've had a crush on you since I've met you, Gabe." Gabriel smiled at this.

"Really?"

"Yes."

"Mmm . . ."

Esmeralda now looked up. "What about you? Did you know?" The man shook his head.

"I've always found you attractive but didn't think you'd be interested in someone like me," the captain confessed. "Plus . . . I haven't seen myself as able to even have any sort of relationship since my wife passed some time ago." Esmeralda sat up slightly, looking deep into the older man's eyes.

"What'd she die of? I-if I can ask . . . I know you don't like talking about your daughter, so—"

"Cancer," he responded firmly. "Regular ol' lung cancer. Matilda was a smoker since she was fifteen. It caught up to her early in life."

Ezzy twisted her face at hearing this. "Sorry."

Gabriel shook his head. "No apologies necessary. It's been a long time." Gabriel grinned. "'Course that means it's been a long time since I've done . . . well, *this*."

Esmeralda smiled, leaning on her arm. "Well, if it's any consolation, you're still very, very . . ." Gabriel let out a chuckle at this. "*Very* . . . good at it. I haven't been this satisfied in years."

"Years, huh?"

"Oh yeah."

Gabriel nodded his head. "Can't imagine Morgan is any good," he stated, scrunching his face slightly. Esmeralda sighed, quieting. "Ezzy, I think everyone here wonders the same question: *Why* are you with him?"

At this she shook her head. "It's complicated . . ." she said with disdain. "I don't even know why myself, sometimes . . ." Gabriel seemed to comprehend this. For a moment, he stared at the bruise on her ribs again. She knew she wasn't fooling him. "Th-there was a moment there. A brief moment where I thought I was in love with him," she added. "At first, I started screwing around with him 'cause . . . believe it or not . . . he can actually be a charmer when he wants to be." Ezzy thought for a moment. "He had this real devil-may-care attitude. Caleb and I were going through problems . . . I, um . . . aborted a pregnancy we had." Esmeralda then breathed out and shook her head. "I wasn't—wasn't ready for that level of commitment. Church bells were already ringing in Caleb's head and I just couldn't hear them. Then, when he found out about Morgan and I's affair, he . . ." Esmeralda stopped herself here and shook her head. Gabriel caressed her shoulder softly. "After he did what he did, I fell into this deep, dark depression. That's when Morgan swept me off my feet. He treated me so sweetly. So gently . . . I fell for him eventually." Esmeralda thought for a moment. "I . . . I don't know *why* I stay. Scared, I guess . . . scared that if I leave . . ." She cut herself off, shaking her head. "It's—it's stupid . . ."

The conversation about Morgan ended. Neither mentioned his name for the rest of their time together.

AYLEN

After dark, Aylen lay awake in her cot, dreading what the next day would hold for her. Combat training. The main thing she came to camp to learn. With Captain Gatton, though, her chances of surviving it seemed slim to none. She was going to drive herself crazy with questions. What if she got kicked out from the Saint Organization? What would she do then? Where would she have to turn? What purpose would her life have if she couldn't avenge the death of her best friend? What would she do? Would she just go to college? Continue the path that she had already started on? All while pretending none of what she knew existed? Could she live like that? One day marry someone who knew nothing of the truth of Salutem?

The very ideas shook Aylen to the core. As she pondered her future, she heard a soft knock on the barrack's door. She opened it to find Jared standing in the doorway.

"Can I come in?"

"Actually, it might be better for us to go outside," she said, thinking of Marie's intense hatred of deviants. Aylen went through the doorway and quietly closed the door behind her. "Did you go to the Principal Overseer?"

"Yep."

"And?"

The young man shook his head. "Asshole won't help us. Not unless he asks Faith or Brenden. Apparently, he's one of the many people here who don't like me." Jared grimaced.

"So what? Am I supposed to even try to attempt to work under that sexist asshole?" Aylen felt hot anger come over her. "Jared, if I do combat training under that prick, I'm gonna be kicked out for sure!"

"Hold on there, A. This is just a minor setback. Maybe, if somehow we can convince Faith or Brenden to validate what I told him, we might still be able to get Morgan out of that position," he said, attempting to comfort her. She closed her eyes and felt the night air brush up against her body. The cold gripped her the way her sense of helplessness did. It disturbed her frail frame and unsettled her stomach, sending a sharp feeling to her spine and weighing her brow down like an anvil in a cartoon. With this sensation, she took a deep breath in. Jared turned her around and she opened her eyes. His hands warmed her shoulders, as if the fires he could control dwindled through his veins. "Everything will be fine, A, trust me." Aylen looked into Jared's eyes to see them beginning to glow orange. "Even if we can't get Morgan out of there right away, just hang in there. I believe that you can do it." His reassuring voice felt like soothing milk and honey for Aylen's ears. His beautiful, glowing amber eyes looked straight into hers and pierced her soul as she felt her heart pound against the confines of her chest.

"Thank you," she said shyly. The two stood looking at each other in the moonlight for a few moments before awkwardly turning away from one another. Even through the moonlight, Aylen could tell that Jared was blushing.

"I should get going, you're gonna need rest for tomorrow," he murmured while beginning to walk away.

"Wait," Aylen said through instinct. Jared turned back around to meet her gaze.

"Thank you . . . for everything," the girl said with a hopeful heart. Her faithful friend then nodded to her and continued on his way. Aylen took comfort in the fact that at least somebody believed in her.

The next morning, roll call went as usual, with the same humiliating remarks from Captain Gatton. Aylen was slowly becoming conditioned to the torment, a fact that she wasn't sure she should feel glad or frightened about. After the usual pushups, Morgan scanned all of the recruits with his eyes. He seemed to be sizing them up while walking past them.

"Jog three laps around the courtyard and then meet me in the training area! *Now!*" he barked. By this point, all four recruits knew better than to dillydally, so they hustled as fast as they could.

"What do you think we'll go over today?" Jonathan asked the group.

"Does it matter?" Adrien responded.

"I'll tell ya, if he picks on Aylen, I'll clock him," Jonathan smirked.

"Do you *ever* shut up, man?" Marie spewed venomously.

"Seriously, he pulls any of the shit he did like the second day of training, he's goin' down," Jonathan smiled. Aylen looked at him silently. "Don't worry, Aylen, I got your back," he said, and she realized: He was trying to flirt. She just looked at him and continued to run.

"I do, too, man," Marie muttered. Aylen was caught off guard by this, though she supposed by now she shouldn't be.

"Me too," Adrien confirmed additionally. Aylen then smiled a small smile.

"Thanks, guys," she in a hushed voice.

After the run, all four recruits went to the training area as instructed. Aylen surveyed the space. It seemed like it was only a mere closed-off sand pit with balconies on the buildings surrounding it. In front of the four recruits was a table with four belts, each with their names labeled below them.

"Put your enhancer armor on, Shitheads," Morgan growled. The four recruits looked at the belts in front of them with caution and picked them up warily. "I *said* suit up!" he barked. The four recruits put the belts on. Aylen glanced up and noticed a man she had never seen before appear on the balconies with Brenden, Faith, and Jared. She also saw the Black couple that was in Jared's photograph appear up there. Oh dear, what was this? The man she had never seen before studied her and the others like a hawk, like a farmer trying to find the ripest of fruit. He was obviously somewhere in middle age, grayish blond hair, and a handsome face slightly worn from battles, perhaps.

Morgan pressed a button on his suit, which enveloped him in armor. "Okay, y'all. Remember how to activate your suits?" Morgan's voice said electronically through his helmet, the visor of the helmet hiding his pink-skinned face.

"Sir, yes, sir!" all four recruits said in unison.

"The hell you waiting for, then? Do it," Morgan said firmly. "Your belts already have y'all's blood samples and measurements. They won't crush ya," the captain stated. The four recruits looked at each other. Marie, without hesitation, pushed the button and became covered in the dark green armor. The boys looked at each other and followed. Aylen watched them with unease. "Move it, Sport Lay," Morgan said sharply. Aylen looked up and her eyes met with Jared's. He nodded to her, giving a slight bit of comfort to her uneasiness. Out of anybody, he believed in her. It was up to her to prove that she was worth believing in.

Aylen looked down at her belt. It was metallic and uncomfortable, weighing on her hips like an anaconda squeezing the life out of its prey. She remembered the button on the belt that was supposed to be pressed and pressed it. A tingling sensation came over her as the suit wove its way around every curve and crevice of her body. Any parts of her that were cold from the fall air now warmed due to the suit's internal heating system. Aylen looked up to the sky as a faceplate covered her field of vision, tinting everything she could see in slight green. This armor made her body feel comfortable and warm, not how she would have suspected it would feel at all.

"Took y'all long enough," Morgan's voice uttered from behind his helmet. He grabbed a remote of sorts and pressed it. The sand pit lowered into the ground, and a few platforms and pillars in the pit rose. Without fear, Morgan jumped into the descending pit and looked up. When the pit was roughly twenty feet below the ground, the pit stopped. "Here's your first test in combat skill level. Whoever can land a blow on me passes." Even through the helmet, Aylen could hear the smug self-righteousness in Morgan's voice. "Sport Lay!" the captain commanded. Crap. "Since you were last to suit up, you're first. Get your ass down here!" He laughed through his helmet. She uneasily made her way to the edge of the pit.

"You got this, Aylen," Jonathan assured her through his helmet. God, why was the distance from the edge to the ground so high up? Aylen disliked the height from which this was to take place.

"Go on, Aylen, just jump," Adrien assured her from behind. A knot developed in Aylen's stomach and she felt her hands shake a bit from the pressure. She took in a deep breath and jumped from the ledge. She felt weightless for a second as the ground drew closer.

Bam.

Aylen's gut ran into Morgan's foot and she flew in a different direction. She heard the armor skid across the sand as rocks swooshed past her visor. She struggled to get up and catch her breath as Morgan's suit of armor came racing at her like a locomotive, eventually delivering another blow to her solar plexus. Aylen rolled on the ground from the blow and found her footing. The captain then grabbed ahold of her armor and threw her into a pillar. Even despite the armor, Aylen could feel the stone bang into her spine. On instinct, her legs pushed off the pillar and she went flying the other direction. Morgan's fist headed for her face midair and she leaned away from the punch, successfully dodging the blow. The inertia of the jump sent her skidding across the sand.

Aylen stopped herself and faced her seemingly gigantic opponent. The two faced off for a second before Morgan began toward her like a raging bull. In this moment of peril, she focused on a gap between his legs and decided to go for it. Pretending she was back in high school PE playing baseball, Aylen slid between the legs of the man, effectively avoiding his attack. In a moment of pride, she then saw a platform next to her. Keeping in mind the agility aspect of the enhancer armor, she jumped for it and climbed atop it. On instinct she jumped toward the big man—

Morgan caught Aylen in midair and before she knew it, she plunged face-first into the ground. He turned her around and pressed a button on her belt, revealing her face to him.

Whack.

Aylen, for a brief moment, lost all bearings on where she was, feeling herself get tossed through what felt like stone. Her vision blurred and her ears rang as she felt a wet stickiness on her face. As her vision cleared she saw Morgan walk away.

"Guess we got our first failure of the day."

She heard him laugh. He cheated. He frickin' cheated. Aylen lifted herself, still dozy from the smack to the face, her eye swollen shut.

"Ladies and gentlemen, Sport Lay is the *definition* of the type of person we shouldn't have in this outfit. She's absolutely fuckin' pathetic!" the asshole boasted to the blurry crowd. "An absolute waste of time, energy, and resources. We should be trying to recruit the finest and fittest for the Saints. I can't make a soldier out of *this!*"

She felt something cold and fist-sized under her hand and clenched it as she lifted herself from the ground.

"Find me some worthy recruits to train, 'cause *this* ain't it."

She'd had enough of his bullcrap. The douchebag had played his last cruel hand against her. Silently, as he pointed to the next recruit, she crept toward the man.

"All right, Treehugger, you're next," Morgan commanded.

As soon as she got two feet into range, Aylen felt something bottled up inside her let out an ungodly yell as she bashed the rock into the back of Morgan's head. A thunk sounded as the rock collided with the armor and he yelped in confusion. Before he could turn around, she pulled him down to the ground by the shoulders and found the helmet button on his armor. His stupid face looked pale and bug-eyed as it became unveiled.

Thwack—Thwack—Thwack

Aylen's fists, as if in slow motion before her, deformed Morgan's face with punch after punch. Bruises began to cover the man, cuts, blood. His lip split, a tooth flew, his nose crunched. In that moment, she became a wild animal. She grunted and screamed with every punch, letting out something deep and angry from within her soul. All the pain from Beth's death, the near rape at the hands of Legion, the incident on the subway, the underwear incident under Morgan's hand—they culminated in a frenzy of rage that had been bottled up inside her for far too long.

"Aylen, stop!" Aylen felt Jared pull her away from the now bloodied and unconscious Morgan. She found herself looking into his eyes, breathing hard, eyes wet. "Aylen, enough," he said, his eyes wide and brow furrowed. She felt herself shake, crying involuntarily as Jared pulled her into a hug. "It's okay, it's okay," he comforted her.

Aylen looked up to watch the spectators. All of them wore looks of shock or concern. All except for one person: The man she had never seen before seemed to be studying Aylen eagerly, with a pleasantly surprised grin. In whatever he was deciding before, it seemed he had made his choice.

EPISODE 13

The Seeds of Knowledge

AYLEN

Aylen lay on the hospital bed as the pain of her black eye and on the back of her head made her wallow in torment. The ice pack Faith gave her barely helped at all. After the incident, she and Morgan were rushed to the medical quarters to treat their head wounds. While Faith analyzed and treated Aylen's wounds with an intense focus before going off to treat Morgan, Aylen noted that both she and Morgan were handcuffed to their beds before being separated into different rooms in the sick bay. He had remained unconscious after her attack: She definitely broke his nose, took out some teeth, and welted up his face. He had to have suffered *at least* a mild concussion after being hit in the head with punches from enhancer armor. She probably fractured his skull.

Good.

But now what? Taking a shot at Morgan like that was a risky move. Beating him like that was riskier. If what Jared said about how Abel treated the situation was true, she could be facing the serious consequence of being thrown out of this place in shame. Or worse.

Still, the prick deserved everything he had gotten. Even if she was kicked out of the Saint Organization, she was proud she went out with a bang. How many people could actually say that they had punched their bosses in the face? That was pretty cool, she guessed. If nothing else she had that, she supposed. But . . . how would she ever get revenge on Legion now?

Aylen felt the tender flesh of her black eye with her finger. Not only did she have a black eye, but certain parts of the skin around the eye were cut from Morgan's armored glove. Dr. Lancaster had given her some stitches to seal the cuts around the eye, and when Aylen brushed her fingers along the stitches, they stung, causing her to immediately pull her fingers away from her face. She thought about that cheap shot that gave her the black eye. She'd most likely also suffered a light concussion, due to her head hitting the ground from the punch. That would explain why she'd lost touch with where she was for that moment.

There was a knock at her door. Odd. Was it Jared? No, it couldn't have been. Faith had kept him away so she could heal from her injuries. Wary, Aylen decided to greet the mysterious knock.

"Who is it?"

"A friend, possibly," a man's voice said from behind the door. She took to this statement with caution. If it was anyone familiar, she would've recognized their voice, in theory, and if it wasn't she had only one way to find out who was on the other side of that door. Even if it happened to be Legion with a knife ready to slit Aylen's throat, she figured it was best to take her chances.

"Come in," she uttered with caution. Soon after her invitation, the mysterious middle-aged, grayish-blond man who had watched her fight from above the pit entered the room. The two stared at each other for a moment, sizing each other up. Then the man pulled a mint from his pocket and held it out before him.

"Mint?" he offered.

Aylen shook her head softly. "No, thank you." Her voice was little more than a whisper. The man shrugged and put the mint into his own mouth, chewing it and taking a seat next to her.

"Brave move out there. Brave and stupid," the man said firmly. "A reason why respect matters? If you had done that to *me*, your bags would be packed by now. No one would argue, no one would blink. I've earned respect around here and there would be no question about putting you on the chopping block. Morgan is not respected. He probably more than had it coming and everyone knows it, hence why *you* haven't been thrown into the brig. A little lesson to be learned here. There was no way for you to know any of this, though, being a new recruit. You're just lucky." He spoke with a sort of cocksure attitude, and adjusted in his seat before continuing. "I heard about the incident with the stripping, so I guess Morgan more than deserved it. And that cheap shot during the combat test? Well, that idiot has always been trouble, since day one." He thought for a second as Aylen observed him. "Still . . . doesn't change the fact that *you* are in a lot of trouble. Morgan may have been a prick, but unfortunately he's *our* side's prick, which means you're up for expulsion, possibly worse." Aylen stared the man down. "Where are my manners? I'm Captain Gabriel Webster, the *former* trainer of new recruits." He smiled, holding out a hand.

Aylen looked warily at the hand and slowly reached out with her own. "I'm—"

"Aylen Monro. Twenty-one. Medical science major in college. Best friend killed by Legion. I read your file." The captain nodded while shaking her free hand. She wasn't sure what to be more impressed by, that he got her name right the first try or that he even read her file. "You're a fascinating girl, Aylen. Your grades are top-notch and Faith tells me you've survived multiple encounters with Legion as well as two Level 5 Brainless, even helping take one of them out. Quite frankly, I'm impressed. And then your stunt today absolutely blew me away. A mousy girl such as yourself having the courage to beat the snot out of a man you're half the size of?" He chuckled, finding amusement in this. There was another moment where he sat, thinking. Then his grin vanished.

"Despite the cheap shot, you're likely to be facing some major consequences. At least, if Morgan gets his way. It's highly possible he could too. Abel wouldn't want to admit he's wrong about the man he ordered to take my position. Damn fool has always been too stubborn and proud. You also happen to be in the unfortunate position of being Jared Griffin's lover," Gabriel affirmed. Aylen was about to protest when he put up his finger. "Speculation and rumor, not necessarily true. True enough, though, for the odds to not be in your favor with Abel. He, like others in the Saints, has discriminatory feelings regarding the deviants." Gabriel paused for a moment, studying her. "There are three things that *do* work in your favor, however: First, there have been witnesses to the attacks on you from Morgan, meaning when there is an internal investigation, you will have some support. Secondly, Morgan is out cold. Faith speculates he might be that way for at least a week, which buys you some safety from his retaliation."

"And what's the third thing?"

"You might just have a way out of those major consequences." Gabriel gave her a sly grin. She stared at him, waiting. "Let me explain. You and I, we both have a common enemy: Morgan Gatton. We are both facing less than favorable odds, and we both have something to be gained from one another. Abel has given me a deal to earn myself back into a training position. He has allowed me to choose a pupil from the recruits—"

"So you want me to be your pupil to earn back your rank," Aylen interrupted dryly. She didn't like the thought of being used for the inner politics of the Saint Organization.

He smiled. "Clever girl."

"I-I'll pass," she stated in response. The captain was struck by this for an instant. He tilted his head and licked his lips.

"I don't think you understand how much hot water you're in. Without my support, you *will* be at the very least expelled from the Saint Organization, and that's if Abel is feeling generous. Quite frankly, it would be Jared's word and yours against Morgan's, and given Abel's feelings for deviants, those odds don't work in your favor at all . . ."

Aylen remained silent, thinking about what the man was saying.

"Come on, *be smart*. You obviously have some brains in there . . ." Gabriel's eyes kept calm yet had the fierceness of a hawk. There was something understated but commanding about his presence. "If I take you under my wing, you at least have a chance of staying in. Morgan will probably try a defense like you being too emotionally unstable and unfit to be a soldier. Faith will do her damnedest to try to fight for you, but Abel already thinks she's a basket case anyway, so that wouldn't work. Brenden has never been known to fight for anyone. The words of recruits would fall upon deaf ears simply because of their rank. You *need* someone like me. I may no longer be seen as fit to be an instructor in Abel's eyes, but I still hold a huge sway with him when it comes to decisions. In a way, you could say I'm his right hand. With my support you will stay in the Saints," he affirmed. He then studied Aylen. She was surprised at how in-depth Gabriel was able to go about the politics of her situation. Frankly, he was right too. If she was going to stay in the Saints, she would need his support.

"Thought you wanted to avenge your best friend?" he said. "Don't you want to be given the techniques to learn how to kill your enemies? You can only do that if you stay with the Saints, and you can only do *that* if you agree to become my pupil. Besides, I'm no Morgan. Under my tutelage you would efficiently learn to actually be a soldier. I want to help you achieve your goals, so let me help you do what you need to do by doing what I do best," Gabriel insisted.

Aylen thought for a moment. Jared always vouched for this guy and how he was a great teacher. Even if she was to be used as a political pawn, she *would* be learning exactly what she needed to learn. Not to mention, having a personal teacher focusing solely on her could be even more beneficial for her. The better soldier she was, the better the chance of Gabriel earning his rank as an instructor was, and the better chance of her getting revenge. It was a win-win.

Aylen looked Gabriel in the eye. "You'll train me to efficiently kill Devil's Deviants?"

"You'll be among the best with my help."

"And with those skills, I'd be able to kill Legion?"

"Legion wouldn't stand a chance."

Aylen breathed out and thought for a moment. "Fine. You've got yourself a deal," she said, holding out her hand. He grasped it.

"Not a deal . . . a *partnership*."

With that they shook. The captain began to exit the room. "I'll let you heal, because as soon as you do, we've got work to do," he said as he left Aylen alone in the hospital room. Hope began to fill her. With Gabriel's help, she might just actually be able to become a soldier for the Saint Organization after all.

PESTILENCE

Emily Gilmore was holding a white plastic horse while sitting on the floor with her daughter. Stacy's little hand held another horse and had it galloping across the play set Emily had bought her last Christmas. God, it was getting close to that time of year again. Stacy's birthday was the same month as Christmas, and Emily loved spoiling her rotten. She got toys for both her birthday and the holiday. Sure, she could've just given her gifts on one or the other, but Stacy was a good girl, she deserved it. Plus, it was one of the few ways Emily could make sure she was a constant in her daughter's life, since she was always gone on missions.

Just as she was about to have her horse interact with Stacy's, a knock came from her front door. Emily frowned. Paul was home . . . Morningstar was probably busy at this time. . . . It was someone else, which meant it was probably work-related. She signed to her daughter to "hold on" before getting up. Stacy could hear perfectly well, but Emily thought it best to use sign language to talk to her when it was just the two of them to help the girl practice and learn new signs. Upon opening the front door, Emily didn't even attempt to hide her disappointment when she saw who had knocked.

"Need to talk to you," Cerberus said coldly. After a momentary sigh, Emily nodded and motioned for him to follow her inside. The large, Viking-like man followed behind her and didn't even look at her daughter as they passed.

Upon entering the safety of the kitchen, Emily folded her arms and leaned against her counter. "What is it?" she responded rather harshly. Cerberus looked out toward Stacy for a moment then back at the white-haired woman.

"Duty calls again," he grumbled. "Legion delivered us one of its spies to sacrifice. Going to use the whole angle that the spy's information is something that nearly got you killed on your last mission. You know Lucifer loves selling the people a good narrative."

Emily scrunched up her face. Shit. "An execution . . . when? Tonight?"

Cerberus shook his head. "The morning after tomorrow. You'll be suppos-edly 'getting your revenge.' Really, it's just something to stir the crowd, get them excited for our next major attack. You'll be running point on it, after all."

Emily was caught off guard by this. "The next attack?" she then asked, shooting a look toward her daughter. Cerberus nodded.

"We'll be launching it soon. I'll be running everyone through the plan of attack tomorrow."

Emily sighed and nodded before looking at her daughter. "If that's the case, I wanna make a request to Lucifer."

MORNINGSTAR

Morningstar returned to her living quarters to find that Jelly had knocked a basket of her personal items onto the floor. "Jelly!" she exclaimed as she rushed to pick everything up; the items were strewn all over. She cleaned and saw the kitten peeking from around a corner. Jelly then pounced on her hands and began to roll around in the items and ran off with a piece of paper in her mouth. "Hey!"

While running away, the kitten dropped the paper and leaped onto a coffee table. The teenage girl sighed. Jelly was cute and all, but the kitten was simply *a lot* of work to take care of. She took the uncomfortable bandages off her deformed eye and felt the scarred and altered skin as she looked in a mirror, being careful to not poke herself in the eye that she no longer felt—a tad bit of a nervous habit she'd had ever since Project Suncloud—then covered it back up with the bandages, ashamed to look at it, and went to pick up the paper the kitten dropped. She unraveled it to find a pleasant sight, one she wished the kitten hadn't chewed up. It was a picture Stacy had drawn of the two of them together. Jelly was in the picture too. She smiled at sloppily disproportionate figures holding hands, with rectangular bodies and circular happy faces. Stacy had been so happy seeing a cat for the first time the other day.

The other day . . . Morningstar's smile faded and she licked her lips. What did Stacy mean? For years, Stacy had remained dormant, without any abilities, as most deviant children did. Was her ability to see the future? Surely it must've been—

"Cute cat," a voice said behind her. Morningstar turned around to see Triple Six standing in the doorway. She froze.

"Wh-what are you doing here?"

"Sorry, I heard you yelling and saw the door was open . . . so I thought I'd see if you were all right," he said. Morningstar looked Triple Six over. It seemed like the concern on his face was real enough. She didn't know him as well as she knew other deviants in the fallout shelter underneath the Ninth Circle; she only knew him by reputation. He was supposed to be a cold-blooded killer. The look he gave her, though, it looked innocent. His eyes were pretty and blue, and his face looked young. Almost her age. "Your name is Morningstar, right? The healer?"

"Yeah . . ."

"Shit, hear 'bout you all the time but I never get nothin' more than a tooth-ache so I've never been around ya. How old are you? You look young."

"Seventeen." Part of her was surprised that he didn't ask about her bandaged-covered eye. Then again, physical deformities were common among the deviants.

"That's dope. I'm twenty-one." The young man smiled. Whatever kind of killer he was, all Morningstar saw before her was a boy.

"Yeah, you're roughly 'bout Azrael's age, right? Weren't you guys friends?" she asked politely. He thought for a second, as if he was reliving some old memories.

"Yep. 'Bout a couple months off, but yeah, he and I were buddies back in the day. That was before he turned fuckin' traitor, though. I don't really like talking about it," he said while slightly squinting his right eye.

"I'm sorry."

He smiled kindly. "Don't worry 'bout it." Triple Six walked toward the kitten and held out his hand. The kitten leaned in to smell his fingers. After a moment, he lifted the kitten and held her like a baby. "And what's this little guy's name?"

"Her name's Jelly," Morningstar stated, starting to warm up to the supposed killer. He let out a little chuckle.

"That's cute," the boy said with a smirk. The killer waved his finger in front of the kitten. The kitten pawed at it playfully, which caused the young man to chuckle. Morningstar bit her lip nervously. Wasn't his ability based on his fingers? Was he going to hurt Jelly? Everyone had told her that Triple Six was perhaps one of the most insane of Lucifer's soldiers. . . . What if—

Triple Six kissed the kitten on the head and put her down gently, surprising Morningstar with the kind gesture. He smiled at the kitten as she went off somewhere into the living quarters, then he turned his attention back to her. "Why'd you yell earlier?"

"Kitten was being naughty. Knocked stuff over."

Triple Six laughed. "Kittens do that," he stated. "If you want, I can give you pointers on taking care of a cat." He smiled. She observed the boy. "Used to have a cat back in Neolympus, called him Puppydog . . ."

"You called your cat Puppydog?" she asked with a slight smile.

"Yea, I was kinda a dumb kid," he responded pleasantly. There was no hint of malice in his face. No hint of a killer, just a sweet, nice boy. Like the ones Momma used to always tell her about. She did not doubt Cerberus's statements about him, but maybe, just maybe, there was more to Triple Six than that stuff. The view of Triple Six was that of a mad-dog killer. Azrael had been like that too, when in reality he was a good person. The other deviants believed Azrael had betrayed them, but Morningstar couldn't bring herself to believe that he could've done anything that he didn't think was right. If he *did* betray them, there had to be more to the story. She never doubted his heart. He was sweet on a level that most Devil's Deviants weren't. She had seen the lengths Azrael would go for others and she'd never forgotten that. If Triple Six was *his* friend, maybe he had a side to him like that too. Maybe there was more to him than what everyone saw.

Morningstar smiled. "Sure, I could use some tips." The nice boy grinned pleasantly at her. It was hard to see him as the violent boy everyone said he was.

AYLEN

Aylen sat next to Gabriel in the waiting room outside the Principal Overseer's office. She looked up when she heard voices talking in the other room, her stomach turning while sitting next to the man she barely knew. This meeting would be *the* meeting. The meeting that would determine whether or not she would remain a member of the Saint Organization. She hoped, prayed even, that Gabriel would help her case rather than harm it. These days, Aylen couldn't help but be suspicious of everything.

"Don't be nervous," Gabriel said without looking at her.

"I'm not," Aylen lied. He shot her a sideways glance and lifted an eyebrow, then proceeded to look at his watch.

"Abel and I spent many years fighting side by side as the Principal Overseer's two most trusted officers. We were also part of the same unit in the Anthrodi War. If he'll listen to *anybody*, he'll listen to me," he said firmly while looking at the watch on his wrist again. The door to the office opened and out walked an all too familiar face with blond hair.

A catlike grin grew on his face when he saw Aylen. Uh oh. She shrank back in awe as the boy walked out.

"Hey, A. Sorry to hear 'bout Beth. Good luck on your big meeting." Eric grinned slyly, then walked off, leaving her flustered.

"You know him?" Gabriel asked.

"Yeah . . ." Aylen answered. Her stomach did somersaults. Gabriel analyzed her. "What is *he* doing here?" she asked. Gabriel watched as Abel headed for the open door.

"His suspension was lifted last week," the captain said while standing up, pulling Aylen up with him. "Greetings, General Quinn," he said to the Principal Overseer as they shook hands.

"Hello, Captain. Is this the girl?" General Quinn asked, looking Aylen up and down, particularly at her black eye and stitches. "Come in. Both of you," he commanded. The two followed his orders and went into the office. Gabriel closed the door behind them as Abel sat behind his desk and Aylen sat in front. Abel wrote something down on a notepad in front of him. Then he stared at her eyes. "Tell me what happened, girl. I have heard everyone else's version . . . except for Morgan's, of course. Now I want to hear yours. Tell me everything."

Aylen looked at Gabriel, who nodded his head. Then she looked down and took a breath in.

"Well, um . . ." Aylen swallowed for a moment and nodded. "Where to begin . . . I came to the Saints after the death of my best friend. All I've ever wanted since her death was to be a member here." Aylen looked at Abel's face to see it unmoved. She swallowed, then continued, her face aching. "I was willing to do just about whatever it took to avenge her. Whatever the training needed me to do, I was gonna do it. Beth was . . . well, she was the sister I never had. I was willing to put up with almost anything. Almost . . ." Aylen studied Abel's face. It remained unflinched. There was a sort of bias she could feel in his gaze, and she breathed in through her nose to dispel it. "For all of this week, I have undergone sexual harassment as well as physical *and* verbal abuse from Captain Morgan Gatton. An absurd amount, in fact. So I guess when he played dirty in the combat test and undid my helmet to take a cheap shot, I just got sick of the abuse and let my emotions get the better of me, sir."

Abel sat back in his chair and twisted his face with a light scoff. "Sexual harassment? Physical and verbal abuse? You sure you weren't just being subjected to ordinary drill instruction?" He chuckled slightly in disbelief. Aylen merely glared at him.

"Is being forced to strip, then having your clothes ripped off part of drill instruction? Being thrown to cold, dirty ground in your underwear while being forced to do push-ups and say that you're an *ugly whore* . . . is that all a part of drill instruction, sir?"

Abel cleared his throat and adjusted in his seat, not looking her in the eye. "Right, well—"

Aylen wasn't done and overrode him. "*Is it written* in the *drill instruction manual* that you have the right to call a girl Sport Lay and tell her that if she was a prostitute you'd make her pay to have sex with you? Is that standard protocol, sir?" Aylen said calmly, hellfire behind her gaze and words.

Abel blinked repeatedly at this information and turned his attention to Gabriel, his mouth agape.

"This is all true, sir," Gabriel said. "Faith, Brenden, Jared, and each of the recruits can all testify to this. I am also a good friend of Esmeralda, Morgan's significant other, and she has told me that he has been on a personal mission to destroy Aylen's path to becoming a soldier. Morgan has, in particular, been singling her out this week for humiliation. It is apparent that perhaps you should rethink the position, perhaps give it to Brenden or Esmeralda. If nothing else, you might divide responsibilities and have Morgan exclusively train male recruits only, seeing as he is capable of sexually harassing a young woman like Miss Monro over here," Gabriel suggested.

"We'll discuss that later," Abel confirmed. He then looked toward Aylen. "Now as far as *you* are concerned, you understand why I can't let you be a part of the Saints, right?"

Aylen blinked her eyes. "Sir, I—"

"You almost bludgeoned a *superior officer* to *death*. Were this a true military installation you'd be detained and facing a prison sentence. If we were a gang, you would be dead. You're lucky this is the Saint Organization you're dealing with and I'm the leader, understand? Anywhere else, you'd *really* not have a good time."

"With all due respect, sir, that's not fair at all," Aylen retorted, giving a look to Gabriel, who kept quiet and looked like he was watching. Not Abel, but her.

"Fair? It's *more* than fair. What you did is a serious crime, Miss Monro, and I'm letting you leave in one piece. I'm *only* doing that because there *is* evidence that Captain Gatton abused his power."

Aylen swallowed hard while Abel adjusted his glasses. What about Morgan? Was he even going to be punished? Abel cleared his throat. "I hereby declare, as Principal Overseer of the Saint Organization, your immediate expulsion. You have an hour to pack your things before our soldiers escort you out."

Aylen's stomach dropped and she felt speechless. Oh god . . . was that it? Was that to be the end of her stay with the Saints?

"Actually, sir," Gabriel interjected with an uncharacteristic grin. "That's precisely why *I'm* here. To talk to you." Aylen breathed out hard. Man, that was intense.

It took General Quinn a moment to process what he was implying. "*No. Absolutely not, that's out of the question!*"

"You *said* I could take any recruit of my choosing."

"Do you want to have your brains bashed in if you anger her? She's a possible loose cannon. You know protocol."

"I may know protocol, but I also know this girl has survived two Level 5 Brainless attacks as well as an encounter from Legion. She even assisted in the extermination of a Level 5. She got one hundred percent on the written exam, and I believe her when she says she's willing to do just about anything to avenge her friend. To throw her out of this outfit would mean we're losing a great soldier." Gabriel paused there, letting his words sink in. "Unlike what Morgan was trying to prove, professionally speaking, I don't think you could ask for a better Saint recruit."

Abel stared at Aylen for a long time, and she stared back defiantly. After everything she had experienced up to this point, this asshole didn't scare her.

He scoffed. "You want responsibility for this girl? *This* is the candidate you want?" Abel indicated her with his head.

"Yes."

The leader sighed. "Very well, she's all *yours*, Gabe." Aylen's heart leaped for joy as she felt a boost of adrenaline hit her harder than Morgan's punch to her face. "Just don't come cryin' to me if she attacks you too."

She was going to be able to stay and train! She couldn't believe it! It was hard for her to not smile.

"Thank you, sir," Gabriel said with a nod. The Principal Overseer dismissed them and the two hurried out of the office. Aylen took a moment to process things as she and Gabriel walked through the halls. Gabriel then opened his mouth. "I've made arrangements. You'll be staying in Jared's private quarters so you don't interfere with the other recruits' training. We'll be meeting in the forest on the northeast wall of the base for training every morning at the crack of dawn. No pointless drills. No more child's play. I'm giving you the rest of the day to move your things into Jared's quarters and heal your wounds, so I'll see you tomorrow morning."

With that, the two parted ways and Aylen began her way toward the girls' bunks. She was going to be a soldier. That was the only thought in her mind at that moment.

She was going to be a soldier.

BRENDEN

In Salutem's nightlife, in the Rainbow District, a bar named Xtasy was the life of the town. Brenden had spent many a drunken night here. Hell, it was here that he had met Adrien, his current boy toy. Brenden didn't want to think about him, though. He was . . . preoccupied at the moment.

Brenden felt his heart pound as he pinned the stranger to the alley wall and stuck his tongue down his throat. The man was Asian, seemed fit enough, and after a drink or two the man was easy to talk into going into the alley with him. His face was a little pudgy, but to be honest Brenden didn't care what he looked like. The haze of booze running through his veins would make him forget what the man looked like, anyway. The two men played tonsil tennis passionately until the Asian man pulled away.

"What's your name?" he asked in a flamboyant, feminine voice.

"Names aren't important, baby," Brenden said as he viciously went on the attack again. The man's vulnerability definitely indicated that he was a bottom, and in all honesty he was perhaps a little too pretentious and feminine for Brenden's taste. Nevertheless, here he was, about to get lucky tonight. He was hardly ever sober anymore. And why should he be? All that waited for him when he was sober were the wicked memories of seeing George's corpse. George, who had been mangled at the warehouse, an arm and a chunk of his head missing. It was clear that the deviants—

Brenden refocused his efforts and reached for his current partner's genitals on instinct. Being with a man would take the pain away. Drinking would take the pain away. Life was beginning to blur to a sweet, sweet numbness.

The man he had seduced was obviously somewhat young and inexperienced. He awkwardly put his hand on Brenden's face as they kissed. The darkness hid him as he committed more sins than he could even recognize. Not that he should care about sins. It's not like most religious figures thought of homosexuals as anything but abominations anyway. The Saint had become disillusioned with the aspects of religion at a very young age: If there was a God, why did prejudice exist? Why did rape? Why did war? Why was Caleb killed by that Brainless? What merciful God allowed Brenden's little brother to get slaughtered? On account of some whore, no less? Then there was that question of if there was a God, why was he so prejudiced against his own creations? Why were homosexuals and other outcasts of society labeled as sinners for something that was inherently written into their genetic code, their nature even? Why should Brenden follow such a big hypocrite? George had always puzzled Brenden, how he could always keep his faith even if—

There was that name again. Brenden felt bitterness toward it. Felt himself shudder from it, the way a demon would shudder if struck by holy water. He hated the name. He hated that he loved the name. He didn't need George. How dare that piece of shit leave him by himself in this world? It was bad enough that Caleb had died, and Caleb died because of that slut Ezzy. If she would have kept that filthy gap between her legs closed, none of this would've happened. Caleb would still be alive. That cheating—

A cold realization came over Brenden. *He* was a cheating slut. He was in a relationship with Adrien. What the hell was he doing here with this—

The whiskey floating in Brenden's head made him feel out-of-body as he undid the stranger's belt buckle. Then he heard a sound behind him.

"Look, Jerry, what have we got here? A couple of *fucking homos.*" There was a sound of something scraping against a wall.

"Yep, just what we were looking for. Look at how they're making out. Fuckin' disgusting," another voice said behind him.

"Heads up!" a man yelled. A brick smashed into the wall next to Brenden, making both him and the other gay man jump. Brenden turned around and looked at the source of the voices. Five preppy college douchebags stood in the alley in front of them, laughing like idiots. Brenden felt anger arise in him. The man he had pinned against the wall took one look at the five men before muttering, "Shit," and running off into the night.

"Oh no, the boyfriend ran off, queer boy is *all alone,*" one of them laughed as they began to close in.

Brenden stood his ground and smirked. "Trying a little hard there, don't ya think?"

"The hell?" one of the men laughed. The five stood around him like a pack of jackals around a cornered zebra, drunken looks on all of their faces.

"Five men in a *dark* alley in the middle of the *Rainbow District*? Who do you think you're kidding? It's 2057!" Brenden then scratched his chin, looking the men over. He began pointing at each of them. "Let's see . . . *he* is in love with *him*, but *those two* are definitely hooking up when no one is looking, and that one . . . *he* has the look of a man who knows what a penis tastes like. Do I have that right?"

The buffoons looked at each other with vacant expressions and furrowed brows. "The fuck he say?"

"I mean, clearly you're not actually here, grown men, *in the middle of the Rainbow District,* to just harass queer people right? No way you're actually *that* pathetic? Just five young men looking for a little action, yeah that's gotta be it," Brenden spouted off, getting a rise out of the drunk men who all held beer bottles in their hands. "Shit, if you just wanted your dicks sucked, why didn't you just come out of the closet and ask? I mean, *I* discern but I'm sure one of the boys in the bar would be more than happy to oblige yo—"

Something came at Brenden's field of vision and hit him in the face, shattering shards that sliced into his skin. Brenden yelped, putting his hand to his bleeding face. He lost vision in one of his eyes and felt his feet go out from under him as someone dragged him to the ground. Shoes pounded into him from all directions.

"Fucking homo!" he heard one of the men shout as they beat him. Brenden felt the wind get knocked out of him. Gasping for air, he reached for a small item in his pocket, but when he pulled it out he felt it fly away from his hand. He dishearteningly watched it roll from his grip and out of sight in between the assailants' feet. Shit. Was he done for? After all the shit he had seen, all the foes he fell, all the life he lived, was this to be its climax and conclusion?

Brenden detested the thought. As if driven by primal instinct, he tugged on one of the blank-faced men's legs and bit through flesh until blood seeped into his mouth. The iron taste of the man's blood filled Brenden's taste buds as the man to whom the calf belonged screamed in pain. He then lunged into the man's groin, sending the man to the ground.

The Saint climbed atop the man on the ground and began pounding his fists into his face. A foot smacked Brenden's head, sending the warrior to the ground again. Blinded by the sudden change of scenery and alcohol, Brenden felt his head spin as he lifted himself to his feet. As his eye focused on the ground, he saw the item he had lost earlier in the fray. In desperation, he grabbed it and pressed the button on it. Without seeing his attackers, he swung his arm wildly. A chain extended from the item and wrapped itself around one of the throats of his enemies. He momentarily observed the face that was being suffocated by the chain. Just some boy. A damn boy. Brenden pulled the chain and sent the boy face-first to the ground, unwrapped the chain, and swung it at his other attackers.

"*Shit!*" one of the young men exclaimed as the chain smacked the face of one of his buddies. Brenden felt his heart race as he slammed the metal chain into his attackers' bodies. Capitalizing on a moment of perceived fear, he pushed the button on his belt and felt his enhancer armor cover him completely. As the face shield came on, Brenden watched as the preppy assholes had their worlds forever changed.

"Let's get out of here, man!" one of them said from the ground.

"Holy shit . . ." another muttered.

"*Go, dude! Run!*" another exclaimed. The men scurried off into the night like rats at the sight of a feline. Brenden was thankful that the armor was intimidating.

"*Pussies!*" he yelled after the men. As he soon found, however, the armor was uncomfortable and made his ribs and face hurt. He pressed the button again and the armor retracted into the belt. His ribs were sore and blood trickled from where the glass bottle had hit his face. He bent over in pain, coughing as he wiped blood trickling from his lip. "Damn it," he whispered in agony as his breaths pushed their way out of his lungs. Brenden reached into his pocket and pulled out his cell phone, wiping his bloody hands on his clothes before touching the touch screen.

"Gail . . . never mind that swan-eating bullshit, it's Brenden, l-look, can you tell Faith that I need medical attention? I-I've been jumped. . . . No, no, by assholes, behind my favorite bar. . . . Then wake her up or something! . . . Look, c-can you just send someone down here? I'm in real bad shape. . . . Yeah, send him, he's a night owl. . . . Yeah, get someone down here, Gail, please."

Brenden hung up and laid his back against the brick wall of the alley. Then he closed his eyes and let himself slip into unconsciousness.

ESMERALDA

Esmeralda lay awake next to Gabriel as she caressed his naked body. The woman had millions of thoughts on her mind that night, none of which she dared wake him to discuss. Morgan was unconscious for now, but for how long? Had anyone put two and two together about their affair yet? Was it such a good idea to cheat on *Morgan*? What was she going to do about this situation? If he found out about the affair, he'd probably do worse than hit her. The best idea would be to leave him. Maybe, just maybe, it would be the more peaceful route out of this scenario. Not that anything was ever entirely peaceful with Morgan, but the least Ezzy could do was make sure that she didn't get another Caleb scenario on her hands. She owed that to the man she had been with for four years.

Esmeralda remembered Caleb. He was a good man and didn't deserve the hand that he had been dealt. Brenden was right: Their breakup led the man to his death. Everything she and Caleb had built had been destroyed with the revelation that she had been cheating on him with Morgan. The craziness of the war was bad enough without adding that into the mix. To this day, Ezzy was unsure of why she had set out to hurt that man so. He wasn't abusive like Morgan. If anything, his temperament resembled Gabriel's more. She looked back on what had happened: She had loved him but . . . she had also been afraid. Afraid of the commitment. Afraid of permanent change. *Afraid.* Despite her fear, though, when she'd witnessed the Brainless overpower her former lover, she'd felt something inside of her get destroyed. She could still see it very vividly in her head: Caleb torn limb from limb, the final look of betrayal he shot her right before his throat was ripped out. At that point, as his internal organs were shredded from his torso, she could never take what she did back. She could never regain all that she had thrown away due to fear. This was perhaps Esmeralda's biggest regret: She could never make up for her selfish mistake. Caleb was never coming back. Morgan was a huge mistake. No wonder Brenden hated her.

Ezzy felt herself shake at the memory as tears formed in her eyes. Desperately attempting to not wake Gabriel up, she held her breath as emotions flowed out of her. This time would not be like last time. She wouldn't allow it to be that way. She wouldn't—

Gabriel silently put his arm around her. Without speaking, he seemed to know what was on her mind and comforted her with his embrace. He was always an insightful man; sometimes it frightened her how insightful. It was almost like he always knew what she was thinking. Perhaps that's why she had feelings for him. He always seemed to understand. He knew everything about her without saying a single word. In this, Gabriel thrilled her and made her fearful. He knew everything about her, but she knew so little about him. Gabe's stoic nature kept him as quiet as a grave at times. All she knew about him was that he was filled with a deep sadness that hid behind his blue eyes. Maybe one day Esmeralda would discover what troubled him. And maybe one day she could ease his pain. Maybe. Just maybe.

With this comforting thought, she drifted off to sleep.

JARED

Jared watched Aylen as she brushed her teeth in his bathroom. This was . . . odd. He wasn't used to having company in his private quarters on base. He remembered how much she'd mused that the main building of the Saint base was bigger than it looked up front, which was accurate. From the front, the building looked only four stories high. The truth was, on the other end of the cliff the base descended down five more levels, allowing such living quarters to exist in the building. He wasn't lucky enough to have a room that faced the ocean, but the ones that did? Man, did he envy them.

"So Gabe is a good teacher?" Aylen called out, apparently between spits. She began brushing her teeth again after asking the question.

"Not if you call him *that*." He chuckled. "When you're under him, you have to call him Captain Webster. Respect kinda thing, you know?"

Aylen spit again. "Well, *duh*."

"He's a good teacher, though. He's no Morgan. Part of why I'm so efficient with my scythe is due to his training. He's the best teacher anyone could ask for. He's an expert in all weapons, even swords." He smiled, Aylen finished brushing and turned off the sink, now peeking her head out of the bathroom.

"Swords? We use swords here?" Aylen blinked for a moment before giggling; it was a very dorky sound. "That's crazy! Is he, like, the best swordsman in the Saint Organization?"

"No."

"Who is?"

Jared breathed in and tilted his head. "You're not gonna like the answer."

"Who? Morgan? Me? 'Cause if it's me, the Saints are *screwed*."

". . . Eric."

Aylen paused. Her goofy smile faded a little. "No crap?"

"No shit. He's the best swordsman in all of the Saint Organization. That's why he only had suspension for a short time. Our side needs him. He and I, we're kind of the trump cards that the Saints heavily depend on. With me, it's 'cause of my deviant abilities. With him, it's 'cause he's *really* fucking good. He's the best swordsman I've ever seen,"

Aylen leaned on a nearby wall and looked him over. "You almost sound like you respect him."

"Only in that sense. Hate that dick, otherwise,"

She tilted her head a bit. "So, uh . . . why *do* you guys hate each other? I mean, I get he's a jerk, but I get the feeling it's deeper than that."

Jared thought for a moment before responding. He looked forward and twisted his mouth. "Uh, let's just say that he and I have personal reasons for hating each other. He hates me more 'cause I'm a deviant . . . I took something from him once . . ." An image of Jessica popped up in his head. The two of them on a snowy beach in front of a house. A memory of kissing her, a memory of throwing snowballs, a memory of walking side by side, laughing. "And eventually I royally fucked up. Lost the thing forever . . . for the both of us. So he hates me now and I, uh, deal with the brunt of it."

Aylen nodded, looking serious for a moment, then her cheeks turned red as she sucked in her lips and snorted. "What?" Jared asked, puzzled.

"You make it sound like you took his virginity!" Aylen busted out with laughter.

Jared's mouth dropped as he found himself having a hard time not laughing too. "Oh *fuck* you!"

"Well, I mean, you took something of his you can never give back . . ."

"You— That shit is *not* even funny!"

"I *thought* there was some sexual chemistry between you two! I mean, every time all three of us are around each other, I *do* always feel like a third wheel!"

"Oh whatever, leave me out of your yaoi fantasies, fuckin' nerd." He shook his head, still laughing.

"*Oh my God,* a yaoi of you two would be *so sexy!*"

"Fuckin' A—" Jared started. His ringtone sounded out above Aylen's roar of laughter. She plopped herself on the couch as he answered. "'Sup?"

"Jared, you have an immediate assignment, top priority," Gail's familiar shrill voice said.

"*Right now?* Christ, Gail, can't it wait? It's late at nig—"

"Jared, I swear to *god* I will write you up for insubordination if you keep talking back to me. How dare you even—"

"Okay, okay, *fuckin' hell,* calm down. I'll do it, don't have an aneurysm. . . . What is it?"

". . . Brenden's been attacked. We need you to get him to the base at once for medical assistance," Gail stated sternly.

Jared took a moment to process this. "Attacked? By who? Deviants? Brainless?"

"No, he's been attacked by some civilians in an alley . . . didn't sound like he's doin' too well on the phone."

Jared blinked somberly and sighed. Shit. "Got it. I'll get him."

"I'll send you coordinates on your phone."

"Thank you, Gail," he said mockingly before hanging up. As he pulled the phone away from his ear, he heard Gail say "fucking deviant" quietly.

Aylen's brow was furrowed. "Everything okay, Jared?"

"Yeah, just gotta do something real quick. Quick errand. I'll be back. Feel free to sleep on the bed. I'll sleep on the couch," Jared told her. Aylen began to protest but he put his hand up. "I insist," he said while grabbing his jacket. Jared put the jacket on and went out the door before running into the night.

While running through the woods, he saw a small pack of wild Brainless lurking nearby. All Level 4s, nothing too crazy. They were close to base but not close enough to be an immediate problem. Patrols would probably exterminate them in the morning.

CERBERUS

Cerberus walked into Lucifer's room to see his leader pouring himself a glass of brandy. "Ah, Cerberus! Just the man I wanted to see! Drink?"

"No thanks," Cerberus objected.

Lucifer tilted his head. "Ya know . . . all these years and you still won't have a drink with me. I have to ask, were you an alcoholic at one point? You avoid alcohol like the plague."

"I was. Once upon a time," Cerberus said unflinchingly.

Lucifer took in this information for a moment and nodded. "I see. Well, if you want, I have plenty of other refreshments in the fridge. As always, you're more than welcome to help yourself,"

Cerberus nodded. "Thank you, sir."

The deviant leader smiled momentarily, then offered his right-hand man a seat. "Go on, sit down, we have much to discuss." He motioned with his hand toward the chair and Cerberus planted himself in it. "So, we were able to extract the necessary info from Mr. Regis . . ."

"Yeah. He was a tough nut to crack, but after some necessary convincing from his daughter we were able to get the password."

"A father and daughter's love. Shame that they both had to come to such a grisly end. That's life, though, I suppose. Who knows what they would have said if we actually turned them loose?" Lucifer shrugged before sipping his brandy. Cerberus stared at the drinking man. To some degree, his leader enjoyed the fact the two had to be killed, didn't he? What had this war done to them? Cerberus pondered this as Lucifer swallowed his drink and said, "Does everyone know their position in the attack?"

"Yeah, but Pestilence *did* ask for some time off after this assignment. Stacy's birthday is coming up, after all."

"And she's agreed to carry out the execution tomorrow?"

"Yes."

"Done, then," the leader smiled. "She does a lot for us, it's the least we can do for her. When's her little girl's birthday?"

"A few Tuesdays from now, I think."

"How old will she be?"

"Eight, I think."

"Eight! They grow fast, don't they?" Lucifer took a sip and leaned in with a grin. "Any sign of an ability?"

Cerberus twisted his face slightly, uncomfortable at the amount of interest Lucifer showed in the question. "No, I don't think so."

Lucifer sighed and tilted his head. "Shame . . . well, she's still young and her mother is a *dynamo* with her abilities. A very effective killer. It ought to be interesting to see what Stacy's ability will be." He took another sip of his brandy. "You know, after this attack, we'll be one step closer to completing our goal, my friend." He smiled. "The Saints are dwindling. We've cut off their gun supply line, I doubt anyone in the black market would dare sell to them or ally with them at this point, and that embarrassing stunt by the UWF has weakened their resolve, I'm sure. They're likely anticipating a move from us, but I'm almost certain that internally they're crumbling right about now. Being quiet for a moment is working in our favor. One of two things is likely to happen in the near future: Either the Saints will merge with the UWF or the Saints will crumble into nothing. If the first happens, that could either be bad or good for us. On one hand, it makes two enemies one. On the other hand, we will have the full forces of the UWF on us, which was always inevitable. I'm a firm believer in our strength, but my thought is this: After we launch this next attack, we *need* to launch a finishing blow on the Saints before they have a chance to team up with the UWF. We already have an advantage on them, but we need to finish them once and for all while we have the opportunity."

Cerberus nodded. "The only problem is . . . we have no idea where they're stationed."

"Well, perhaps we'll capture one of them and extract the info from them the way you do so well. That is, if you can capture one before they take their cyanide pill." Lucifer chuckled. "If you were able to, I bet you'd make them sing like a canary. I hear Rob Harper's cries of torment were . . . legendary." Lucifer appeared amused, but Cerberus felt slightly uncomfortable at this remark. It wasn't something to take pride in, being skilled at torture. Lucifer's eyes scanned Cerberus, grin dying on his face, and lifted his eyebrow. "Cerberus . . ." he began with a sigh. "I want to discuss something with you . . ." Cerberus didn't say anything but rather remained quiet. "I've noticed . . . the killing of General Harper didn't sit too well with you, did it?"

"I did as I was told without question."

"Yes, but you didn't *like* doing it, did you? The deception of the move and all, it was not a move that you take pride in. You killed the *enemy leader* and yet you do nothing but go silent at the mention of it," Lucifer discerned. "Why is that? You can be honest, not like saying why will bring Rob Harper back to life. Go ahead, my friend, speak your mind," he said while tilting his head.

Cerberus looked around at the floor. "It wasn't the way I would've preferred to kill him. Even though he was our enemy . . . he was an honorable one. Gave us trouble for seven years. Guess it's easy to demonize the man, but not once did he throw around moves like the one we pulled." He looked up at his leader. "Just seemed he was more deserving of an honorable death. Something more . . . dignified."

Lucifer nodded his head. "You're a noble man. Honorable. Strong moral compass. I understand your viewpoint. I was once that way myself. I was a *man of God* once, as you know. I'm certain that maybe he did deserve a better death. But what about the lives we lost in Project Suncloud? They deserved to die of old age. Instead, a lot of them died either being mutated or being eaten."

"Not the same thing. Harper never sideswiped us at any point."

"And now he's dead," Lucifer jumped in, obviously disapproving of Cerberus's statements. "You know what your problem is, Cerberus? You have a conscience. Rob Harper had a conscience. I had a conscience. I was a Catholic priest, *God* did I have a conscience. But you know what a conscience gets you in the end? Do you know what being an honest, moral individual gets you in the end? Ask Rob Harper. Ask the Saint Organization, built on morals and princi-ples. But where are they now? Imploding from traits that go against everything the Organization was built upon. Good and evil? It's a *lie*, a lie that religious figureheads made up years ago to give people an excuse to say they were better than each other. They set up rules and principles we're all supposed to follow."

Cerberus looked down as Lucifer licked his lips, clearly not finished.

"Do you know what life is truly about? Survival. Does anybody truly call a lion in the wild evil because it eats the gazelle? No, because it eats the gazelle for survival. In this world, no one is good or evil. We are all just merely fulfilling the needs that are written in our DNA for our own survival. The food chain cut off at humans, so we had to classify ourselves into two categories: wolves and sheep. The wolves prey on others for survival, while the sheep blindly follow a moral code because they would rather pretend that life is dictated by a sense of right and wrong. Rob was a sheep. I am a wolf. He was my enemy, so I decided to prey on him. For *our* survival. All of the Saints are sheep, the UWF is another wolf. We were sheep before Project Suncloud, we were preyed on by the UWF, but they made us something stronger than a wolf and now *that* wolf is our prey. The UWF's made us something at the top of the food chain, and now humans are our prey. I'm speaking metaphorically of course, it's not like we're Brainless or anything." Lucifer chuckled.

"My point is, Cerberus, our fight against the humans is a battle of nature. We're the new evolved breed, and like other new breeds of animal, we have to fight for our survival, we have to make our place in the world and distinguish ourselves from lesser species. Honor means nothing in a fight for survival. Our deception to Rob Harper was a move out of necessity, and because of our move we're back on top in this war. Now it's *our* job to stay on top, which is what we *will* do if we can somehow manage to take the Saints out," Lucifer confirmed.

The speech didn't sit well with Cerberus, but he knew his leader was right. Honor had gone out the window long ago, when the UWF dropped Project Suncloud. Ever since then, this war had been a fight for survival, and a fight for revenge. Lucifer was right: In order to win this war, everything had to be cold and calculated. No remorse. No honor. Every dirty trick necessary.

"Understood, sir."

JARED

Jared walked up to Brenden carefully, making sure there wasn't anyone around who might try to jump him. Brenden was leaning up against the wall with his head down. As Jared got closer, the wounded soldier looked up and chuckled weakly. "Took you long enough."

"Gimme a break. Never been to this, uh . . . area of town," Jared said while lighting one of his black cigarettes.

"Not too many straight people have."

Jared winced, glancing at the part of Brenden's face cut by the bottle. "Jesus, dude, what'd they do to you?"

"You should see the other guys." Brenden laughed before coughing and clenching his ribs.

"Come on, man, let's get you some medical attention," Jared said, carefully putting the man over his shoulder in a fireman's carry.

"Oh, this is totally the way I wanna be carried, darling. Ass up, face down, going thousands of miles an hour . . ."

Jared lifted an eyebrow. "Got any better ideas? We'll be back in a matter of minutes."

In the blink of an eye, they were out of the alley.

When Jared arrived at the base, he found Faith already waiting for them near the entrance. She rushed to them.

"How bad is his condition?"

"He's been better," Jared replied.

"I think I lost my lunch a few miles back . . ." Brenden said, hanging upside down from Jared's shoulder.

"Let's get him to a room," Faith insisted. They hurried through the halls of the base to the infirmary. Faith showed him to a room she'd already prepped, and Jared placed Brenden carefully onto the cold metal slab waiting for them.

"Ah! That hurts!" Brenden complained, his eyes scrunched closed. Faith got out a pair of scissors and began to cut Brenden's shirt open. Jared watched as shades of black and blue were revealed beneath.

"Damn, dude, what'd you do to piss somebody off?"

"I merely suggested they go fuck themselves," Brenden said with a bitter chuckle. "More accurately, I told them they should fuck each other. Somehow, they didn't find it *absolutely hilarious* . . ."

"Jesus . . ." Jared muttered under his breath. Whoever the punks that beat Brenden were, they beat him good. Bruises, most likely a broken rib or two, the welts on Brenden's face, the glass shards in his skin so close to his eye. Hopefully one of those shards didn't get into it. He looked closer at Brenden's left eye. It hadn't opened. "I'm kinda worried about that eye, Faith. It hasn't opened, and there's glass shards all around that side of his face."

"Some guy threw a glass bottle at my face," Brenden said, wincing. The alcohol must have been wearing off.

"That'll be first on my list of things to look at," Faith said hurriedly while dragging a lamp toward the table. "You should go to bed, Jared. It'll be a long night as far as this goes."

"Right. You take care, Brenden," Jared said.

"A little fuckin' late for that!" Brenden called out as he left.

AYLEN

Aylen laid in the dark in Jared's bed. It wasn't the most comfortable, but it was considerably more comfortable than the cots in the barracks. What was better was it had Jared's smell on it. It wasn't a smell that one would expect. It was a unique scent, a warm and comforting smell that she found hard to describe.

Perhaps it was the deodorant that he wore, or maybe it was his natural phero-mones, but there was something she really liked about the way he smelled: It was a nice smell, not the harsh and bitter smell of a smoker. She felt a sort of safety and comfort in it, perhaps due to the experiences that they had shared. Jared, on multiple occasions, had stuck his neck out for Aylen. Through all the hard and horrible things she had gone through over the last few months, he had been there by her side as a sort of guardian angel. Going down the list: He saved her from the Blob and Stretcher Brainless; he told her the truth about Eric and the world they lived in; he rushed to her side when Beth died, and stopped her from killing Morgan; upon finding out what Morgan had done, he barged down the door of the Principal Overseer, possibly risking his position in the Organization; and now she was sleeping on his bed so she could continue to train at the Saints. Jared was perhaps her truest friend, and at this point, her best.

Aylen was slightly anxious, though. Tomorrow, she would be truly learning what it meant to be a soldier. If Gabriel was half the man Jared praised him to be, he was already miles ahead of Morgan. Still, there was the question: Was the student worthy of the teacher? Ultimately, the way it sounded to Aylen, Gabriel was one of the best soldiers in the Saint Organization. What could he have possibly seen in her to want her to be his pupil? Did he think that she was the most hopeless case out of the group? Why her out of the other three?

These questions were wandering Aylen's mind when she heard the front door opening. She pretended to be asleep as Jared entered sloppily and closed the door. She listened as the footsteps made their way into the restroom, and she identified the clanging of a belt being undone and what sounded like clothes being changed. The footsteps, now softer without boots, made gentle pitter-patters on the carpet right before the sound of a body dropping onto the couch boomed.

Aylen opened her eyes to see the light of Jared's phone illuminate his face in the dark. It wasn't long before the light went out and Jared turned toward the cushions of the couch. Aylen watched for a bit and soon, Jared was out like a light. She thought for a second. He must tire himself out whenever he used that superspeed of his. After all, he did just run for miles and miles in hardly any time, a fact that could easily be forgotten with someone so fast. Despite his tough demeanor, he was a real sweetheart. She got up and silently made her way over to the sleeping deviant, far away somewhere in dreamland. He looked troubled when he slept, as if sleep tormented him in some way that was so horrible it made his face remain stuck in a grimace, like a lonely gargoyle. She ran her fingers through his hair lightly.

Jared jolted and turned around, half-awake, to see Aylen. "What are you doing?"

Aylen continued to run her fingers through his hair. "Just thinking. That couch looks uncomfortable, maybe you should take the bed?"

Jared was barely awake as he looked at her "No, A, *you* keep the bed. You need it for tomorrow."

"We can share if you want."

Jared awoke a little more at this. A familiar look of concern crossed his face. "Are you serious?"

Aylen shrugged. "Yeah. Not in a sexual way or anything, I just . . . figure that running fast everywhere has gotta make you super tired. You should sleep in the bed, we'll both sleep in it. It's big enough."

Jared thought for a moment. "Okay," he agreed. He got up sleepily and moved to the bed, climbing atop it and lying on the right side. Aylen laid next to him as he closed his eyes. She thought for a moment, and then put her arm around him.

"Hey, Jared?"

"Mmm?"

"I . . . I just wanted to say . . . thank you for being so good to me. Letting me stay here and all. Helping me through the whole Legion thing and whatnot.

You're a really great friend. I just want you to know I'm *really* grateful for you," she said. He opened his eyes slightly.

"Thank you for not being like everyone else," he said. "Thank you for not treating me like a freak."

Aylen smiled. "Don't mention it."

"Go to sleep. You're really gonna need rest for tomorrow," he said, closing his eyes and re-adjusting himself in the bed. Aylen cuddled up against Jared, feeling his warmth and smelling his sweet scent. For a moment she lay awake, clutching him tightly and draping her body over his. She pressed her face against his back before drifting off to sleep. It was easier to sleep with her guardian angel around.

She woke at dawn to the sounds of birds chirping. The blue light of the morning painted the sleeping Jared and the sheets in dark blue. She dressed in her uniform quietly and got herself a breakfast bar before brushing her teeth and heading out. As she walked through the courtyard, she saw the other recruits doing drills that were led by a Hispanic woman Aylen didn't recognize. For a moment, she saw the recruits give her what looked like either a gleam of jealousy or a nod of silent respect. Even the woman in charge of the recruits stared at her for a moment, as if sizing her up. Oh great. Another one.

Aylen proceeded toward the gate and nodded to the guard, who opened the front gate for her. The woods were cool, with a light fog and fresh mist that heavily elaborated the smell of rainfall that must have happened barely even an hour ago. Aylen headed over to the area that Gabriel had designated. He wasn't there waiting for her, though. Perhaps he was getting a late start, Aylen thought. At least she could enjoy the forest while she waited.

Slurp.

Aylen paused for a second after hearing the strange sound, the location of which she couldn't pinpoint. "Captain Webster?" she called. She tensed while searching for the source.

Slurp. Slurp. Slurp. Slurp—

Aylen went dead silent as she heard the slurping commence. It was a little deeper in the woods, slightly farther in. The naïve her of yesterday would've safely assumed that it was simply . . . Captain Webster, perhaps, sucking on clams? . . . *Clams?* Really? Out of all the hopeful fantasies she could come up with. Aylen clenched her fists as she silently moved toward the sounds of ominous gurgling and slurping. Those dreadful sounds grew louder and louder with each near-silent crunch of her footsteps on the forest ground.

Gurg slurp gulp slurrg slurp slurp glug—

Aylen traced the sound behind a bush. She reached her hand out silently toward the plant as she felt her heartbeat fill her ears. An uneasy feeling crept into her pit of her stomach. She had heard similar sounds before, the night the subway was attacked. She moved the brush out of the way and saw a pale and skinny naked figure sitting with its back toward her. A dead stench rose to her nose as she watched the figure's ribcage pull in and out with each breath. She looked down at the thing it was chomping on to see it was a similar disfigured creature, one with three eyes and missing a jaw. The first creature used the six-fingered hands on both wrists to tear the flesh from the naked corpse into the direction of its mouth. For a second, the pale, naked creature reminded her of Legion, almost looking non-distinct in its sex as well. The creature then perked its ear and turned its head. On instinct, Aylen began backing away.

Yellowed eyes glanced at her and began to take interest in her. The creature gurgled and dropped the bit of flesh that it was sucking off the bones. The creature then stood up, possibly spanning up to roughly seven feet in height once it fully unraveled, and Aylen quickened her steps backward before hitting a root or a rock with her ankle and falling, hurting her backside. The creature had no lips, two noses stacked atop each other, two smaller arms, and what looked to be a dead child's face at its stomach. She felt like gagging and transfixed her eyes on the dead child's face, which appeared to have been carved or embedded into the creature's stomach with half-open eyes, a tiny nose, baby cheeks, and lips that were apart. God, it was horrible. So horrible. The creature made an ungodly sound as it started limping toward her. Aylen looked at its leg and saw what looked like two deep cuts in the creature's calf. Blood trickled from its mouth. It was getting closer.

She crawled a few inches before getting up and running. The horrible thing limped after her and made a nasty, pained roar. Aylen stepped into muddy earth and her foot stopped, momentarily prohibiting movement. She looked back at the advancing creature, coming up quickly despite the obvious limp. Then she pressed the button on her belt and armor covered her body.

Bam.

Aylen hit the ground with a hard thud. The creature wasted no time in attempting to rip through the armor with its elongated fingernails. She heard the scratches against her armor, then the creature yelled in frustration and lunged for her face with its mouth. Aylen lifted her arm and put it into the path of the creature's blood-soaked jaws. The metal of the armor screeched as Aylen began to feel the pressure of the bite, and the pain compressing on her armor as the jaws worked their way through, pressing into her skin, as if a woman with long nails was digging them into her arm. She grunted in pain and punched the creature off with her free arm. The enhancer armor knocked the creature to the side easily, and she rolled out from under it and climbed to her feet. Despite the mud, and the creature lifted itself off the ground and growled at her. Aylen looked around and saw a sturdy branch jutting out from a tree. Maybe, with the enhancer armor's strength, she might be able to pull it out—

The creature started for her again. She rushed for the tree and felt herself get knocked forward onto her face as the creature went to work on her back. Claws pierced through the armor on her back, and she tried to lift herself up before the creature knocked her down again. But this wasn't how Aylen was gonna go. She refused for this to be the end of her.

She set her knees on the ground and pushed herself up, using the strength of the armor to elevate her, momentarily pushing the creature off her back. Then she jumped toward the tree, jumping higher than she initially anticipated, and crashed through the tree branch, rolling along the ground from the inertia of the impact. She lifted herself up and saw the creature heading toward her, and she grabbed the tree branch and began to try to lift it. In the armor, it felt like thirty pounds, but she heard the mechanical armor make a struggling sound, which must've meant it weighed a lot more. As the creature came closer, she threw her body weight into a swing, and before she knew it the creature flew five feet, landing with a hard thud that cracked the tree branch. As the creature rolled on the ground, Aylen felt the suit struggle to continue holding the tree branch, so she put one end on the ground and kicked the cracked end, causing the branch to snap into a roughly baseball bat-sized stick. Her heart raced as she began toward the creature, who struggled to get up this time, letting out heavy, troubled breaths. It looked up at her and roared a much more airy roar. To Aylen, it sounded like she might have broken the creature's ribs. Then she clutched the branch and swung the branch at its face, knocking it back to the ground and out of commission. But the impact of the blow revealed the stomach.

Aylen looked at the child's face in the creature's stomach. It was still and asleep-looking, but only for a moment. The child's eyes opened and the small arms began to move. Its yellowed and bloodshot eyes looked up at Aylen.

"*Aha aaaaaaaa aha aha aha aaaaaa!*" the child's wails began, revealing sharp, tiny teeth in its little mouth.

At that moment, Aylen almost lost all incentive to live. That creature was once a human, it was once *two* humans. It was living, breathing, suffering, still struggling to find its next meal. Project Suncloud had melded these two together into one abominable creature.

Tears came to her eyes and her hand began to shake. She looked at the wooden piece in her hand and saw that the end she broke earlier in the fray was sharp. Amid the child's wail, she looked at the larger version of the creature as it opened its eyes to look at her. It started to lift itself off the ground. The child's tiny arms began to reach for her, and though Aylen felt emotion come over her, she lifted the sharp branch above her head. Struggling with what she had to do, she screamed as she brought the branch down onto the stomach, into the child's face. A gush of red liquid splashed onto her visor as she plunged the wooden branch through bone and tissue, feeling the creature reach up with all four arms and attempt to stop her. Then, almost as suddenly as the arms had come up, they fell to the ground, dead. Aylen breathed hard and wiped the blood off her visor.

Then another sound behind her started. It sounded like a growl.

Boom.

A gunshot as loud as a cannon rang through the woods as a body fell to the ground. Aylen looked behind her to see another misshapen and dead Brainless. Through the fog, she saw a figure lift itself from the ground with a rifle in hand. From the shadow it gave off, it looked to be covered in shrubbery and moss. As it approached, Aylen realized it was enhancer armor wrapped in a cloak with leaves and shrubbery attached to it.

"Good. Very good. Impressive," the mechanical voice from the armor said. The enhancer armor's helmet retracted into the suit to reveal Gabriel, wearing the armor and holding the sniper rifle. "I now know what we have to work on."

Aylen undid her helmet and looked at him in horror, completely out of breath. "*What?*"

"Your survival instincts are good, but you need to be more aware of your surroundings. If that was a Level 5, you'd be dead."

"This—this was all—*this was all a training exercise?*"

"In all fairness, it wasn't planned, but after seeing the small herd of Brainless this morning, I thought it might be a good idea for you to show me what you can do. I'm afraid the incident with Morgan wasn't enough. He may be as dumb as a Brainless, but nowhere near as dangerous. I give you a five out of ten on how you handled the scenario. If it were more than one Brainless, you'd be dead. True, you did kill this one without weapons, and I commend your quick thinking as far as using the branch. Single-mindedly heading for it, though, as the Brainless was ripping through your armor? Very careless, indeed."

Aylen was still stuck on the first thing. "*This was all a test? That thing could've killed me!*" she screamed.

"I was watching the whole time," he said calmly. "That wouldn't have happened. That Brainless killed the others over its mate, which is the one that's dead behind you. Notice the belly on it, as well as the breasts and genitalia." Aylen looked behind her at the grotesque, naked figure on the ground. A belly protruded as if it was pregnant, and its breasts and genitalia were definitely female. She looked up at Gabriel as he continued. "Your fighting skills show you have zero to no training. That I can help with. But you have to be much more aware of your surroundings. You should have put the armor on as soon as you saw the Brainless. If that Brainless hadn't been wounded, you would've been killed. They can be very fast, the Level 4s. You also should've landed the killing blow as soon as you had the chance. One more moment and its mate would've killed you."

Aylen scowled, still catching her breath. "I killed the damn thing, yet I got five out of ten?"

Gabriel grinned ever so slightly. "If it's any consolation, you scored higher than your fellow recruits would have." He handed her a water bottle. "Catch your breath and then follow me."

Aylen reached for the water bottle slowly and looked up at him uneasily, but he was already walking away with rifle in hand. One of the best soldiers in the Saints, huh? Aylen attempted to catch her breath, all while thinking over the entire event that had just taken place.

PESTILENCE

A crowd of deviants viciously cheered from above as Lucifer stood in the center of the bunker under the Ninth Circle.

"Brothers and sisters!" he called out, a somber look on his face. "We have been successful in our efforts as of late . . . but only just recently one of our most valued members *almost lost her life!*" Recognizing her cue, Pestilence stepped forward. Lucifer held out his hand and closed his eyes hard. "Our beloved white-haired beauty, Pestilence, was on a mission for me, when none other than the *Bastard Saint* appeared and tried to take her *life!*" To this, the crowd gasped. "The Bastard Saint, who we did not think would be at the exchange, nearly plunged his blade *through her heart!*" he said, pointing at her. A sly grin spread across his face. "But . . . he underestimated the might of our mighty Pestilence. In one-on-one combat, she successfully came out of the fight unscathed, and made him and his fellow Saints run back to whatever rock they crawled out from under!"

The crowd cheered. Pestilence looked up at her fellow deviants. It was amazing how willing they were to buy almost anything that came from his mouth. Lucifer lifted his finger and the crowd quieted. "But even though our Pestilence was successful and victorious, there is still an issue . . . somehow, our resources failed to alert us of the Bastard Saint's impending presence in this mission. Someone must pay for that close call."

Just then, War and Triple Six dragged out a woman in her forties. Her makeup was running down her face and her hair was a tangled mess. "Legion has personally informed me that this was the spy that was supposed to monitor the Bastard Saint. She was supposed to keep tabs on his movements! Yet somehow, she failed to let us know the Bastard Saint was active again!" Pestilence quickly looked over to where Cerberus was watching and exchanged glances with him. He understood how she felt, even if he'd never admit it. Then she looked up above and saw Morningstar watching, looking concerned. The white-haired woman turned her attention to the spy.

"P-please don't . . ." the woman spy sobbed, pleading with her. Triple Six and War made her get on her knees.

"Pestilence has confided in me that before she goes on her next great mission for the cause, before she goes into battle yet again for us, she wants this human woman's blood!" The crowd cheered. "*What say you?*" Lucifer screamed to the crowd, whose cheers were all but deafening. Pestilence closed her eyes hard and sighed. The woman's death warrant had just been approved.

The white-haired woman breathed in and out through her nose. The spy sobbed hard as she was forced to lean forward. Pestilence twisted her face. Goddamnit, she hated these. She turned her hand into a blade and stared at the back of the woman's neck.

Schlick.

The woman's head hung on by only a small strip of skin before Pestilence kicked it completely off. Blood had splattered her face and the crowd was deafening. Without emotion, she extended her fingers, turning each into its own individual spike, and jabbed them into the top of the skull. She lifted the head to show to the deviants above.

"*Pest-i-lence!*" the crowd chanted. "*Pest-i-lence!*"

Times like this, she hated everything about the Devil's Deviants.

EPISODE 14

GHOSTS

JARED

Jared opened his eyes and saw Aylen getting out of bed. "Hey, did I wake you?" she asked sweetly in the bright light emanating from the window. It was sunny. His eyes strained as the light glinted in his vision. Jared stared at Aylen. For a moment, the sunlight hit her face in a way that made her look like an angelic creature, graceful and beautiful. He was at home with her. He rubbed her arm and her face glowed in the sunlight. This morning she wore an oversized shirt and shorts, making her look very comfortable and adorable and at ease.

"Nah. You didn't."

"Did you have any dreams?" she asked, staring right into his eyes. Her brown eyes turned to shades of amber when the light refracted in them.

He smiled. "No."

Aylen planted a soft kiss on his lips. "First time in a while."

"Yeah."

She returned his smile before leaning in, and they kissed each other more aggressively. Aylen pulled away and looked at Jared's lips with a grin before climbing off him "Want me to make breakfast?"

"Sure." It was all he could say. He was speechless as he watched her move to the kitchen of his private quarters. She started digging through the cabinets and drawers and grabbed tools for making pancakes. "So, uh, how was your training with Gabriel yesterday?" he asked across the room, watching her prance about the kitchen like a graceful doe.

"It was goooood," she drawled out. "Yesterday we started on gun logistics and rifle training. Really interesting stuff!"

Jared watched her mix the batter, then as she poured it over a hot pan on the stove. He was smiling again. A real, and genuine smile. He was the luckiest guy in the world. How did he get this lucky? How did he get a girl like Aylen? Girls like Aylen only ever came once in a lifetime.

"Did you hear? Because of what he did, Morgan didn't just get kicked out of his position, he's out for good."

"Wow! Really?"

"Yep, shame Brenden isn't alive to see it, though." She grimaced. He felt his happy mood take a nosedive.

"Yeah, real shame, he loved that man," Jared heard himself say. Wait, what? Loved? Jared looked out the window and saw Faith golfing out on the golf course. It was a really reliable tool for the Saints, that golf course. A really good idea. Helped the Saints really let out some tension when they weren't fighting the UWF.

He turned his attention back to the lovely pixie dancing around his kitchen. She turned her back to him to get a spatula out of the cupboard. Jared climbed off the bed and rushed behind her, embracing her from behind and kissing her neck. Aylen let out a chuckle as she leaned into him and the two almost kissed again, lips mere inches from each other. Jared reached between her legs. She smiled and moaned. "I thought you wanted breakfast . . ."

"Fuck breakfast. It can wait." He smiled between kisses. She turned around and kissed him passionately, allowing him to lift her up in his arms. He moved them both back to the bed and placed her on it, pulling off her shorts and panties, letting Aylen help him out of his drawers.

They began making love. And he—he wanted this. He wanted this so bad. They clutched each other desperately, Aylen with that sweet tenderness that he had come to know. Her skin tasted sweet as he planted kisses on her cheek. He had missed this. He had missed it so much. Heavy, labored breaths filled their chests and mouths as a flow of ecstasy flushed through their veins. He lifted Aylen's shirt to reveal her breasts while keeping their movement going. Her lips tasted of candy. He stole another kiss and then turned her onto her belly, face-down on the bed, revealing her nice, firm buttocks to him. For a moment, her hair looked straighter and her skin looked considerably paler, but both quickly reverted back to Aylen's features. He blinked, and when they remained, the two continued the dance of flesh. Her skin felt warm and soft under his fingertips as he resumed thrusting. He heard a sound and looked out the window to the evening stage that the Saints had set up outside, where Eric was finishing up his clarinet solo.

"I fucking hate jazz," Jared muttered under his breath.

"What?"

"Nothing."

The two broke away for a second and he laid on his back while she placed herself on top of him, taking her shirt completely off in the process. As the rhythmic motion continued, Jared blinked his eyes and suddenly it was Jessica on top of him, instead of Aylen. He blinked again and she was Aylen again, moaning and breathing hard.

"Don't stop! Don't stop!" she cried out. He reached up to scratch her back, peeling away flesh that lodged beneath his nails. "*Yes, yes, yes, yes!*" she screamed. His heart racing, he scratched at her face, tearing it off to reveal a bloody, charbroiled skull. "*Yes, yes, yes, yes—*"

Deersmouth

Jared woke as suddenly as if someone had used a defibrillator on him. Cold sweat drenched him all over as he felt his stomach turn in knots. *Aylen!* His eyes adjusted to the dark as he realized he had woken up in his room, alone. His heart beat against his chest like a bongo drum, and it hurt. It was an overcast day, which was normal. He looked out his window and saw Esmeralda training the new recruits. All except Aylen, who went off to train with Gabriel for the first time today. Right . . . Aylen was still alive.

He breathed heavy and clutched his bed, wanting to cry tears that would never find their way out of his eyes. A nightmare. A strange and horrible nightmare. Letting Aylen sleep in the same bed as him wasn't a good idea. It wasn't— He couldn't know— He didn't want her to— Jared looked at his bedside counter and took one of the pills Faith had prescribed him, heart beating in his ears. The nightmares remained a constant even with his pills. A constant hell that made sleep unpleasant almost every night. Aylen. She—she was . . . she was . . . He felt his heart slow as he swallowed the pill, taking deep breaths. He thought about the dream. Aylen died in the dream. Died because of him, died—

No . . . no he couldn't think like that. He shouldn't . . . but he couldn't help it.

Was he getting too close to Aylen? Jared's lips trembled. She was too close. He couldn't let that happen. Not again. Not ever again. He let Jessica in too close and they *took* her to get back at him for joining the Saints. They— Jared remembered. Jared remembered the mangled, half-alive girl he'd carried in his arms. Her malnourished, half-naked body, the bruises, the cuts, the amputations. Then Cerberus—

Tears filled his eyes and Jared felt his throat swell like he was going to vomit, overwhelmed by memory. His body shook and twitched. In Jared's mind, he had already begun to make parallels. Both girls were brunettes, both treated him kindly, both were romantically linked with Eric. *Eric.* Was that why he was in the dream? Was that—

Jared put his hands on his face and rubbed it before letting his fingers slip into his hair, shivering. Aylen was too close. She needed to be distanced. She needed to be far away from him. He couldn't . . . he couldn't allow another Deersmouth to happen.

MORGAN

A redneck with a barely recognizable face marched through the halls of the main Saint building like a steaming locomotive. His head rang and stung, but he'd forced himself out of bed upon hearing the news. His nose made a squeaky wheezing noise as he breathed in and out through it, and one of his eyes could barely open. Various Saints moved out of the way as the man, whose face was swollen with shades of black and blue, trudged forward like an angry six-foot-six train. In no time, he was at his intended destination, and Morgan burst through Abel's door, anger fueling his veins.

"Ah, Morgan, I wasn't aware you were awake," Abel said very calmly while signing some paperwork.

"*You let her stay in the Saints?*" the red-faced man barked at his leader.

"Let who?"

"That *bitch* that did *this* to me!" Morgan pointed at his face. The Principal Overseer took a moment to look over his mangled features. Morgan's face still ached from the welts, bruises, and stitches. "Not to mention, I hear that this Alien chick, or whatever the hell her name is, is now Gabe's student? *You told me Gabe wasn't allowed to teach!*" the captain growled, pointing a finger at his superior.

"Did you undo her helmet during the combat exercise?" Abel asked calmly before taking a sip from a water bottle.

"*What?*"

"You heard my question, Captain. Did you undo her helmet and punch her in the eye during a training exercise?"

Morgan was caught off guard slightly. "Yeah? So? It was a training exercise. Thought you wanted soldiers, not babes sucking off their mama's tit. Gotta toughen 'em up."

"Yeah . . . that's intentional sabotage of a recruit." Abel adjusted in his seat and squinted his eyes. "I also hear of this incident where you stripped her to her underwear, forced her to do push-ups, and tried to get her to yell she was an ugly whore?"

Morgan paused for a moment and shifted his weight, licking his lips. "Uh, yeah . . . standard drill sergeant stuff. She got up late and needed to be punished. It's hazing!"

"No. No, it's not. I know you know it's not," the Principal Overseer immediately interjected, clutching the bridge of his nose. Abel sighed. "I don't know how they did things in *your* unit back in the Army, but that isn't disciplinary action. That is *sexual assault* here. Now, I wanna be on your side. I really do. But you doing *those kind of things* shows me that I made a mistake making you a drill instructor."

"*A mistake?* The hell, Abe? Thought you wanted me to make soldiers. I was *doing my job!*"

"*By harassing recruits?*"

"By doing what's necessary to train—"

"*Necessary?* Everyone I've heard has said you've been intentionally singling out Aylen Monro out for public humiliation—"

"She's not fit for this outfit! I was doing our side a favor by trying to get her out!"

"You don't have that authority!" Abel yelled, lifting himself from the desk and startling Morgan. "For your misdeeds, I relieve you of your position as drill instructor for the new recruits. The position will now officially be split into two divisions, and Esmeralda and Brenden will now be the drill instructors."

"E-Ezzy? You're gonna replace me with *Ezzy?* She can't fuckin' teach—"

"That is my ruling as Principal Overseer, Morgan. You still will lead the tank suit unit, but don't make me take that away too." Abel's face tightened and his mouth twisted in disgust. "It is *only* due to your rank and because we need to look like a united front at this time that I am sweeping this under the rug and don't discharge you altogether. I have bigger fish to fry and you're *goddamn lucky* with your timing. Now get out before I change my mind, I have official business to attend to."

"Oh, don't you worry. I'm going. I see how it is."

"Good. And don't you forget it."

Morgan gave one last scowl to Abel, then burst out the doors. This . . . *fucker.* Him? Almost discharged? Taken off training the recruits? The most decorated veteran in the Saints, and Abel really considered discharging him? Over trying to get rid of an unworthy recruit? If *Morgan* was in charge, he'd have taken the side of the drill instructor, piece of shit. This place would be entirely different if he were in—

A thought occurred to him. Ezzy was going to replace him. She . . . *she* had a hand in this. Those secret meetings she'd been having with Abel lately. She screwed him over. *Dumb bitch* screwed him over and stabbed him in the back. Clenching his fists, Morgan decided to go back to their shared quarters . . . and wait.

AYLEN

Birds sang in the Forest of Sorrows as Aylen began her ascent, muscles aching and shivering. "Come on! Keep going!" Gabriel beckoned from down below. Aylen clutched the rope tightly against her wet body and looked down. She was barely four feet up on the rope. "Come on, Aylen, you're almost there!" Aylen struggled as she attempted to pull herself up on the rope. Suddenly, her grip slipped and she fell backward with a hard thud. Her head spun after hitting the ground. Gabriel rushed to her side. "You were very close to completing the course this time. We need to work on your upper body strength, though, if you're ever going to climb that rope. Take five and we'll move on to gun logistics."

"Wait, I can try one more time," Aylen protested from the ground, still feeling cold and damp.

"It's no good now, your arms are jelly. Take five and then we'll move on."

"But—"

"Take five. That's an order, soldier. Here, take this towel," he commanded while handing her a towel. There was no denying that this man was different from Morgan. She picked herself off the muddy ground while watching him as he paced back and forth like a wildcat waiting to strike. She then looked at the training course; it was a long obstacle course that even included a part she was supposed to swim through. She was actually amazed that she got as far as she did on it. Multiple times, even. Soaking wet from the part with the lake, Aylen turned back to the rope she was unable to climb. It was at least thirty feet long, if not more. With the rope, she was supposed to climb up to a wooden platform, or at least fifteen feet up before coming down. That was to be the end of the obstacle course. Why the end of the course, though? Why was it placed smack-dab at the end? Aylen was not to wear enhancer armor while doing it, so putting it at the end just didn't make sense. It was the hardest part of the obstacle course. Was it even physically possible to do that at the end?

"Question, sir," Aylen said while catching her breath.

"Yes?"

"Out of curiosity, why's the hardest part of the obstacle course at the end? You'd think something that would require that amount of endurance would be more in the middle of the course than the end, right?"

Gabriel looked at the rope and grinned. "The hardest parts of life are usually at the end of a slew of personal obstacles. It's up to us, though, to figure out how to work our way around it. Not too many people have completed this course in its entirety. But there are those that have, and the ones that have found a way within themselves to climb that rope. Those that have, they've become some of the strongest soldiers in the Saint Organization." Gabriel studied Aylen for a moment with squinted eyes.

"It can be done. There was a girl once . . . a little younger than you. Best student I've ever taught. *She* climbed to the top of that rope. She didn't have military training prior, but she was much like you, just had guts . . . willpower. You could almost say it was her superpower. She went on to become one of the greatest soldiers we ever had." Gabriel sighed, then grimaced, staring at the rope. Aylen noticed the key word "had."

"What happened to her?" Aylen asked. There was a brief moment of silence as it looked like Gabriel was lost in thought.

"Not even the strongest can survive the horrors of war sometimes," he said finally, shaking his head. He then looked back at Aylen. "She did, however, help us win a hell of a lot of victories. Come now, time for gun logistics." Aylen wrapped the towel around her shoulders. For some reason, that one phrase Captain Webster said stuck with her: Not even the strongest can survive the horrors of war sometimes. It was not just Legion she'd be fighting, but all of the Devil's Deviants. She was a soldier now. A soldier at war.

She followed Gabriel to the gun training area, where he began his introduction to guns. Aylen, for a moment, looked back at the obstacle course and at the thirty-foot rope. It hung there like the gallows of an old execution ground. Only the best in the Saints had been able to best that rope climb, and it was all too clear to her what she must do. In order to conquer Legion and get revenge for Beth, she had to become the best, and the best mastered that dangling menace. She would conquer that rope one day. She would be the best.

PESTILENCE

Pestilence stepped out of the car she had driven and squinted her eyes as Cerberus arrived on his motorcycle and parked right beside her. The two briefly exchanged glances before continuing forward, accompanied by fellow deviants who exited their cars. This whole affair was ridiculous. Almost as soon as Pestilence had gotten cleaned up after the execution, she found out about the current situation. She knew Dupont was an idiot, but she had no idea that he was this much of a moron. They were in an abandoned lot deep in the industrial section of Salutem, and the gray skies overhead cast the day in a dreary light. Ahead of them were men dressed in tan enhancer armor with rifles, as well as Dupont and an even smaller, more pathetic-looking man beside him who seemed to be trying his damnedest to look tough. He had intense blue eyes and an annoyingly stupid haircut, some kind of undercut–mullet thing with a rat tail.

"Ahhh, Pestilence, lovely as ever, and this man, I'm assuming, is the great and powerful Lucifer?" Dupont said in his heavily accented voice, offering his hand. Cerberus was easily almost an entire foot taller. He stared down the man's hand then looked back at his face.

"Cerberus. I'm Lucifer's number two."

"His—his number two?" Dupont scoffed slightly. "I requested a meeting with Lucifer himself," he said, maintaining a fake smile, putting his hand down.

"I'm afraid Lucifer doesn't get out much. I handle every major transaction," Cerberus said with an equally fake smile. Pestilence turned her attention to the scrawnier man next to Dupont. He seemed to be either checking her out or trying to intimidate her, but he shifted his weight so eagerly she could tell he was nervous. Pestilence stared back, unimpressed, before looking back at Cerberus and Dupont.

The Frenchman nodded his head. "Qui . . . all right, then."

"And who's this . . . *handsome* young man giving me the death glare?" Pestilence asked. At this, Dupont seemed to light up and he put his arm around the younger man.

"Ah, this my little brother. I brought him to show how business is done! He is just a little excited," the man said proudly, rubbing his brother's head vigorously and ruffling his mangy hair. The younger man smiled politely, looking as if he was embarrassed his brother was ruining his tough-guy facade.

"I see," Pestilence muttered, unimpressed.

Cerberus briefly exchanged glances with Pestilence before turning toward the smaller men. "Speaking of business, where's the rest of the supplies you promised us, Dupont?"

Dupont bit his lip and let go of his brother. "I have found . . . that I've needed to bump up the price for my goods." Pestilence blinked and turned her eyes to Dupont's brother, who was eagerly looking at the two deviants. "Rome wasn't built in a day, after all, as they say," the older Dupont then stated. "The first two shipments were the price we agreed . . . but as my brother has pointed out to me, that's a fairly generous price for the amount of goods. Empires aren't necessarily built on being generous."

"Y-yeah, market value for some of those guns is twice what we've sold them to you for!" the brother said.

"He speaks," Cerberus commented calmly, getting out a cigar.

Dupont sighed. "I'm sure you understand, I can't give you the equipment for that price anymore."

Cerberus lit his cigar. "That's not what was agreed upon."

"It may not be, but that's just lucrative business," Dupont stated. Cerberus and Pestilence exchanged glances.

Cerberus tilted his head. "You know, you throw that word around a lot, but I'm not sure you know what it means . . ."

"Non, it means when we ask for more money, you be *good little boys* and give it to us," the brother said, tilting his head and moving in slightly. Dupont put his hand in front of his brother and breathed out.

"Forgive my brother, he has yet to understand the *intricacies* of business," Dupont said with a smile.

Cerberus paused and blinked his eyes, giving the younger man a brief, annoyed glance before looking at Dupont. "I don't see how that price change affects our arrangement. When you make a deal with the Devil's Deviants, you keep that deal. We aren't exactly your average customers—"

"Just a couple of *freaks* trying to get out of paying their dues," the younger brother said cockily, interrupting him. Cerberus shot Pestilence a look. The white-haired woman stepped forward, closing the distance between herself and the young man.

Swish.

In seconds, the younger Dupont brother's throat was split open by both of her metallic hands. The young man gurgled as red liquid spilled from his neck, spraying onto his brother's face. Cerberus used his ability to yank the guns out of the hands of the men in enhancer armor, and the DDs behind the pair aimed their own weapons at the men. Dupont froze as his brother fell to his knees, still gurgling, and slowly fell onto his side.

Cerberus calmly moved in toward him. "I don't like being interrupted . . ." he said calmly, then sighed. Cerberus was toe to toe with the Frenchman, staring him down as he breathed out cigar smoke. "You have till midnight to give us the rest of the shipment. Unless you wanna join your brother, I suggest you honor our deal from now on, hmmm?" He patted his large hand on the tinier Frenchman's shoulder. "Look on the bright side. Now he'll never try to usurp your empire." He walked away from the lost-looking Frenchman, who watched as his brother let out his final breath.

Pestilence walked alongside Cerberus toward the cars. "You sure it was a good idea to do that to Dupont?"

"We're hardly hurting for supplies. If he ever gets a bright idea like the one he just had, we'll just kill him and replace him with one of his goons. Shouldn't be too hard. Doubt his men care for the weasel that much."

COMMANDER LI

Commander Li brushed her hair back with her hand as she hummed a David Bowie tune and walked down the halls of the UWF Department of Justice building. Her stiletto heels drove into the tile floor as the sun shone in through the windows ahead of her. Other UWF officials walked by quietly and nodded to her as she made her way down, showing respect to the right hand of the one and only General of Salutem. Melyssa Li had worked hard to get to her position. She was an accomplished veteran of the Anthrodi War, with at least three Medals of Valor and Honor against the enemy. After the war, she sought out a government position, which was made possible through her connections and friends in high places. Originally, she had started as a low-ranking police lieutenant, but through the grace of her mentor she wound up as the *commander* of the military police. Many in the UWF High Council were very impressed with Li's track record and her efficiency in high-stress situations. Li was even getting praise that she was better at the position than her predecessor. That was fine and everything, but she had her eyes set on a bigger prize at the end, a position not even her predecessor and mentor had reached. *General.* The High Chairman, otherwise known as Prime Minister, was a figurehead. A sock puppet. After years among the High Council, Li had made a keen observation: Whoever was general ruled the world, more or less. The things she would be able to do as general? The sky was the limit. *One day* she would get there. One day . . .

Commander Li turned the attention of her mind to the task at hand. General Hawkings wanted to see her. She had a feeling as to what the meeting was going to be about but decided to keep an open mind. Usually if General Hawkings contacted her it was a matter of national security. This meant it was likely to be deviant related.

Deviants. Fucking freaks. Li would burn them all if she could and if the chairmen of UWF would allow her. But alas, if she were to make an actual move on the deviants, it would result in national outcry. If the knowledge of deviant existence came out to Salutem, who knew what would happen. The knowledge of another war to be fought would send people rioting in the street, and perhaps worse. The only people who would not be complaining would be the soldiers, the surviving units from the Anthrodi War that had somehow lost purpose when the war ended. The taste of battle was almost as enticing as the promise of good sex. At least, that's the way Commander Li saw it. The rush of adrenaline and ache for action. Ever since the Anthrodi War ended, Melyssa Li had missed true action. She never felt more alive than in the heat of battle. Because of this she had an ulterior motive for being such an active commander, more than just to keep the peace of their now "peaceful" world. In truth, she envied the Saints, despite all of them being a bunch of fucking morons. She wanted to rid the world of deviants once and for all. If only the council had approved her proposition some years back, to make the Saints permanently inactive and wipe out the deviants in one fell swoop, things might be much different. Of course, the spineless council didn't have the stomach for such a move. Pity.

When they thought back to the Anthrodi War some soldiers probably thought of how the enemy's advanced weaponry wiped out so many at a time. They probably thought about how horrible the enemy looked, maybe had nightmarish flashbacks of how their friends were killed. For Li, it was the proudest time of her life, like when she was known as "The Hero of White Falls." For three solid days, the Anthrodi had unleashed an onslaught onto her forces, yet despite all odds, *she* led her side to victory. It was a defining achievement. It woke a part in her that she had only truly begun to understand long after the battle had ended. For her, war wasn't hell, it was home. As it stood at the moment, she was a goldfish at the bottom of a mostly drained fishbowl. She had felt that way for quite some time now. There was a war to fight, yet she was forbidden from fighting it. The only thing she could even possibly think of doing to remain sane was to enjoy the power that being commander granted her. The position had allowed her a certain level of freedom and wealth that she had never experienced in her life before she had gotten the position. It didn't fill the void, though. It didn't quench the ache.

Commander Li entered the doors of the General Hawkings's office, immediately setting her eyes on her least favorite person in the world. There she was, the general's blonde secretary. A dumb, pretty thing that, quite honestly, probably only kept her position based on how much literal dick she sucked. Not that Li could judge on that front. Girl's gotta earn somehow. The blonde girl looked up at her with the most dopey smile Li had ever seen.

"Commander Li! Wassup, homegirl!"

"Hello, Jean," Li responded with fake pleasantry. "The general summoned me?"

"Yep, yep, I gotchu. I'll let the general know you're here, he's still with his previous appointment right now, so if you wanna sit down, he'll call you in shortly."

"Thank you . . . *Jean*," Commander Li smiled back. This cunt would be the first to die if there was ever a war.

Commander Li sat on the couch in the waiting room patiently, watching the blonde carry on about her business, a vacant smile on her face that showed the lights were on but no one was home. Commander Li utterly hated Jean. Maybe it was her youth, maybe it was how close she was to General Hawkings, maybe it was that *god-awful* fake hair color. Not even porn stars had hair dyed *that* blonde. There was no denial that Li absolutely hated her. So happy-go-lucky, so non-aware of the world. It was *sickening*. She probably never knew a hard day's work in her life, probably never had her dad beat her ass with a belt, probably got *everything* she ever wanted all throughout life. Her tanning-salon tan was just right on that perfect little body that age hadn't touched. She was humming some pop song that was a Top 40 single on the radio, chewing on gum. It was bad enough the commander had to hear the shitty song on the radio (it was definitely no Bowie tune) but now she had to hear this tone-deaf bitch hum it. And the chewing! Oh, the chewing, like some sort of large dog chewing with their mouth open. It was revolting. Li had seen torn-up corpses and all manner of debauchery, but the way this bitch chewed was one of the most revolting things she'd ever seen in her life. Her jaw just moved up and down, up and down, a large clamping machine of perfect white teeth relentlessly squishing into her probably fruit-flavored gum.

Li continued glaring viciously at the oblivious girl until General Hawkings finally opened his office door and let out a man in a suit. Couldn't be soon enough. On instinct, Commander Li stood up and saluted her superior. General Hawkings was a man in his late fifties with a large nose and gray lining his hair. His weathered face had a mole on it as well, one that reminded Commander Li of that *Godfather* actor Robert DeNiro.

"At ease, Commander," General Hawkings said in a thick accent. If the commander had to guess what it was, she would've said pre-Salutem New Jersey or New York, perhaps. Definitely Eastern United States.

"You needed to see me, General?"

"Come on in, we have some things to discuss."

As Li entered, she noticed the small collection of vintage car miniatures on the general's desk and lifted an eyebrow. Cars. The hell was it with men and cars? She could understand her son's fascination, but grown men? "Please, have a seat." The general directed her to the chair.

"Thank you, sir," the commander acknowledged as she sat across from the man.

There was a moment of awkward silence as the general studied her. "I hear the streets have been peaceful lately."

Commander Li sighed. "All except for the latest two homicides, things have been relatively peaceful. The shameful part about the homicides, though, is we know who did it without really being able to pursue them for conviction."

"Deviant activity?"

"Afraid so. The latest two victims were tortured and shot, then their bodies were burned beyond recognition. We can't even identify the bodies due to the teeth having been individually plucked out."

"Jesus . . . goddamn DDs, eh? Well, given that they were tortured, they were probably pumped for info. Have you checked the databases for any missing employees lately?"

"Way ahead of you sir. Unfortunately, it seems that there has been a slow and steady rise in kidnappings from the Devil's Deviants. Especially since Senator Blackwood disappeared."

"Actually, that's part of why I've called you in today. When running diagnostics on Blackwood's computer to look for clues, our guys found this . . ." General Hawkings handed Commander Li a printed sheet.

"It's an email that failed to send from Blackwood."

Commander Li read the email:

Dear General,

Today I received word from my informant, Hunter Wilson (a.k.a. Triple Six), of the Devil's Deviants' plan to raid the Hucklegrove Factory. Be sure to tell Commander Li to tighten security to a maximum at this factory for the next couple of months.

Sincerely,

Senator Harry Blackwood

Li twisted her face. "Hucklegrove? Why Hucklegrove?"

"It's a testing facility, they work on the latest technology there. Weapons, transports, you name it." Li blinked in annoyance. She *knew* that but Hawkings took a certain joy in treating her like an idiot. He continued and Li did her best to not glare at him. "It's one of five major testing sites. There's also Eastend, Westbrook, Shadowhill, and Worshire—"

Li cleared her throat, looking at him and forcing her lips into a fake grin. Hawkings and Li exchanged glares. If looks could kill, one of them would be in a body bag. "Okay, but *why* Hucklegrove? Out of the five factories, why that one?" she asked dryly. Hawkings shrugged.

"Tactically, Hucklegrove does make the most sense. Worshire is in the city, we'd have reinforcements there in no time, Shadowhill is so far outside of Salutem that it's even farther than the Condemned City. Eastend and Westbrook are too heavily fortified. Hucklegrove is the smallest facility, and perhaps the least protected of the five. It'd make sense that they would attack that one out of all the factories," General Hawkings said while studying Li. "So my thoughts are this: The DDs got to Blackwood right as he was sending this and intercepted the email. Betcha anything that he was on it like a fly on shit as soon as he found out and they—"

"Or at least that's what we're led to believe," Commander Li interrupted, unable to listen to the old fool any longer. "The Devil's Deviants are usually very good about covering their tracks. If we happened to find this, it was probably meant to be found."

"Interesting point," the general concurred, and he thought over the note. "But what about the bases? Hucklegrove does make the most sense."

"Maybe . . . unless they know something that we don't."

"Eastend and Westbrook are the most heavily fortified of the bases. Do you really think they'd have the gall to attack Worshire or the time to attack Shadowhill?"

Li shrugged. "If there is one thing that I've learned after covering up deviant attacks all this time, it's to never underestimate the Devil's Deviants. If I *may* make a suggestion, sir?" Commander Li asked.

The general nodded. "Go ahead."

"Tighten up security on *all five* bases. That would probably be your safest bet. And that's banking on if the factories even are their actual target. There's a good chance it's all subterfuge."

"Suggestion noted." He nodded his head while his eyes searched the room. "There's another matter I wish to discuss with you, about the Saint Organization." The general turned to face the commander, studying her.

At this, Commander Li scoffed and chuckled. "What about them?"

The general now pointed a finger at her. "First off, that little demonstration that you did a while ago in disciplining the Saints, Ronald Brown? That was too extreme. Way too fuckin' extreme. You had no authority to pull that."

"If I may sir, the Saints had overstepped their boundaries—"

"And you overstepped yours. You *know* you should have consulted me before sending that boy to his death. I don't care if you are the council's golden child, Melyssa. Don't do that again," General Hawkings commanded. There was a moment of silence and Commander Li crinkled her face while nodding, swallowing some pride. This was typical with this asshole.

"Understood. I apologize. It will not happen ag—"

"It better not. Salutem is not a fascist regime, nor is the UWF a fascist government. Don't you *dare* turn it into one. Do anything like that again and you'll be relieved of command. Got it?"

"Yes, sir," Commander Li said sheepishly. The general then wiggled deeper into his chair, getting comfier, and leaned on his desk. Self-righteous prick.

"Now then, there is another matter that we need to discuss involving the Saints, and I'm going to want your honest opinion on it. A proposition has come up."

At this, Melyssa Li's ears perked. What sort of proposition involved the Saints?

MORNINGSTAR

"—and you just have to pay attention to their meows. They'll tell you different stuff," Triple Six told Morningstar while handling Jelly. She watched him as he held Jelly in his arms like a baby. "They'll tell you when they're hungry, when they're hurt, when they're scared. They'll let you know when they wanna play. You just have to listen to them. They'll tell you what's up."

"Wow, you're really good with cats!" she said while chuckling. Morningstar was honestly surprised that Triple Six had come back, just like he said he would. He had spent all day teaching her all about how to take care of a kitten. Honestly, given how the stories around camp were about Triple Six, she thought that by now he would've eaten the kitty, or something. Yet, here he was. All Morningstar saw was a nice and charming boy, not some sadistic killer that everyone made him out to be. He seemed sweeter than that, gentle even, kind. In many ways, Triple Six reminded her of Azrael. Azrael was a gentle soul too.

"See, if you raise your kitty right, she can be a real charmer. Hell, even if you end up dating some guy who's not a cat person, he'll end up liking Jelly 'cause she'll be more chatty."

"Date . . . ?" she repeated, rubbing her fingers on her eyepatch.

"Yeah, any boyfriend you end up getting one day will fall in love with this li'l baby." He grinned, continuing to rub Jelly on the belly.

"Not likely . . . but thanks! Who knows, though? Maybe Cerby will end up liking her." Morningstar chuckled, carefully taking Jelly into her arms from Triple Six's.

"Not likely? What, are you a, uhhhh—"

She put up her hands. "N-nothing like that . . . I just, uhh . . . I'm not very dateable."

Triple Six scoffed. "What? Says who? Nice girl like you, I'd be surprised if every guy in this bunker wasn't lining up for the chance to get ya,"

"Well, it's just . . . I'm not very . . . attractive."

At this, Triple Six stood up and looked at her, up and down. "You look fine to me."

"Look, I know you're just being nice to me. I-if you saw under my eye-patch, you probably wouldn't—" Morningstar started. The boy put his finger on her mouth.

"Shhhh."

Morningstar's heart raced faster the closer Triple Six got to her. His blue eyes studied her face as his hand touched her skin slightly. She was mesmerized for a moment and then felt embarrassed and ashamed.

"Don't!" Morningstar backed away and turned around. There was a beat where she had her back to him. Her heart sounded off like a drum.

"Turn around," he muttered calmly. She took a breath in as she analyzed whether she should or shouldn't. "Please?" he asked sweetly. Morningstar turned around slowly and looked up at Triple Six's blue eyes, which twinkled like blue topaz stones as he stared at her. His hand felt her face again and her breath shuddered. Cool sweat came over her as he put his fingers under the eye patch and began to take it off.

Morningstar felt naked and exposed as her disgusting, deformed eye was revealed to the boy. She felt shame come over her, and humiliation. She hated her eye, she absolutely hated i—

"That's it?" He chuckled softly. "That's what you think makes you unattractive? We have a guy on our side with five arms and purple skin!" he said, obviously finding it amusing. Morningstar looked into his eyes; they were sweet and nonjudgmental. She knew the look of someone being cruel, and he was not. She swallowed.

"You . . . you don't think it makes me unattractive?"

"Heeeell no! I ought to punch any asshole who says anything like that! You're beautiful."

Morningstar was astonished "You—you really think so?"

"Of course. And guess what?" He took off his beanie and lifted his blond bangs to reveal his forehead, right as another eye opened and looked down at Morningstar, who stared in awe at the sight. "You're not the only one with eye problems," Triple Six said sweetly. She then smiled back at her three-eyed friend. He was like her. Just like her.

Triple Six pulled out his phone and looked at the time. "Shit, I better get going," he muttered as he began to walk away. "Hey, I'll come back tomorrow with some gifts for the cat. Cats need toys," he said to Morningstar as he began to get through the door. "See ya!"

"Uh . . . b-bye!" she called after. She had connected with Triple Six. He saw her deformed eye and didn't judge her or make fun. He was like her. Just like her. Morningstar smiled to herself as she closed her door. It seemed that she had found a new friend. Someone just. Like. Her.

BRENDEN

The medical room was cold as the doctor turned toward her patient. "So I have good news and I have bad news about your eye," Faith told Brenden.

"What's the good news?" Brenden asked while lying on a bed in the infirmary.

"Good news is, you still will be able to somewhat see out of that eye."

"Huh . . . and the bad news?"

Faith waited for a second to find the best way to couch it. "Well, that eye has changed color from the trauma . . . and some of the scarring is permanent."

"Whoa, seriously?" Brenden asked while sitting up, struggling due to his rib injuries. "Hand me a mirror!" he demanded. Faith obliged him and he took a look at his face. His eye was the first thing he noticed. There was a small scar on the eyelid, and a cloudy blue eye where his normal brown eye should have been. Brenden let that sink in. His eye would never be brown again; it would always be that light, discolored blue. Brenden then looked at the area around the eye; jagged scars twisted this way and that over almost that entire side of his face. "And I thought you said it was bad news."

"This is a sign, Brenden," Faith started. He chuckled to himself. Here it comes. "A sign that it's time for you to *stop*. Stop drinking yourself silly, stop hooking up with random guys at the club, stop any of that. You're honestly lucky to be alive. If these guys beat you any longer, they'd have beat you to death. You've had your time to grieve George. It was hard, yes, but it's time to be a big boy and move on. God knows you're not the only Saint who's lost somebody."

"Gee, I admire your positivity and optimism, truly inspiring."

"Look, I just told you to act like a grown-up. Saints got enough issues without you destroying yourself. All I'm speaking is some hard truth, either you take the medicine or don't. Those are just my suggestions as your friend, though," Faith said sternly. The scarred man thought for a moment. She was right. If anybody knew anything about losing people it was her, and she was absolutely right. The drinking had gotten out of control. The partying had gotten out of control. It had become a beast that he no longer had power over. It had consumed his life. He *did* get off lucky.

Brenden looked at his friend for a second and then at his face in the mirror. "Thanks, Mom."

AYLEN

Dusk fell over the Forest of Sorrows. Aylen had finished the cardio exercise Captain Webster made her do, and returned to find him in front of a make-shift campfire near the obstacle course. Her muscles ached and she shivered slightly, still feeling like her clothes were soggy from swimming in the lake. As she trudged forward, her instructor noticed her arrival. "Come . . . you must be cold," he said, placing two blankets onto the ground. He handed her a third blanket that she immediately wrapped around her shoulders. Aylen's breath shuddered slightly as she clutched herself, getting closer to the campfire.

"Oooh," she expressed, her voice shaking. She put her hands out in front of her and stood next to the fire as Gabriel sat on one of the blankets. "That feels so good."

"I'm sure. Soggy clothes and cold weather don't make for a good combo."

"S-so that's it for today?"

Gabriel smirked at her. "Why? Did you want more?"

"I-I'm good," she said with a smile. Today was actually a pretty good day. Today, for the first time, she had begun to feel like a soldier. Gabriel didn't demean her or humiliate her. The difference in instructors was shocking. With Gabriel, she actually felt she was learning something now.

"C-Captain Webster?"

Gabriel looked up with a kind glance. "Private Monro?" he asked in a jok-ing tone.

"What made you choose me?" Aylen breathed a shuddering breath. "To be your recruit, I mean?"

The captain stared at her for a moment, then chuckled to himself, turning his attention to the fire. "Why did I choose to save your career in the Saints you mean?" His face glowed in the orange light as he stared into the flames. Aylen sat on the other available blanket on the ground and looked at him. "I suppose it *was* a risk. Especially with you pulling a move as impulsive as you did," the captain said thoughtfully. The man scrunched his face slightly. "When you've been doing this awhile, you can sniff out a good soldier from the rest. That girl, Marie Vasquez? Not a doubt in my mind she'll be an excellent soldier. The others in your group? Well, they don't have *it*." Gabriel sniffed in and curled his lips. "Sure, there's a chance they could survive this war a long time . . . but I wouldn't put my money on either of the boys."

"And . . . you think I'd make a good soldier?" Aylen asked. To this, her instructor turned to her, a stoic look on his face.

"No," he stated firmly. Aylen blinked in surprise, almost offended.

"Uh . . . I don't—I don't understand."

Gabriel nodded. "You're not a soldier. I don't sense it about you," he answered honestly. "You aren't the type that's made to live and die by orders. When someone says 'jump,' you don't say 'how high,'" he continued. Aylen was puzzled. "You're something better than a soldier," Captain Webster said while staring at the fire. "A survivor." Aylen's ear twitched at this. "Someone that adapts and overcomes."

Aylen looked at Captain Webster as his battle-hardened face stared grimly at the fire. "You think for yourself, and no one, not even me, can convince you to do otherwise." Captain Webster breathed out through his nose. "I'm tired of training good soldiers. They can't think for themselves, usually wind up dying. You're resourceful, though. No matter what happens in this war, if I train you, I *know* you will most likely survive," he said, looking toward her. Aylen blinked, feeling the smoke from the fire make her eyes sting. "You're smart, Aylen . . . and you follow your instincts. *That* is why I chose you." A smirk spread on the older man's face. "I'm babbling. Guess I just like the cut of your jib."

Aylen breathed out, looking now to the fire. "A lot of people die in this war, huh?" she asked. Gabriel nodded his head.

"Part of being a Saint is watching your friends die," the captain said bluntly. "And everybody here has a sad story. If they don't, they will." There was a moment of silence between the two where it was just the crackle of flames and the sounds of birds. Suddenly, Gabriel turned toward his student. "You should get some rest, big day tomorrow."

Aylen left the campfire, her mind reeling. A survivor, huh? Aylen didn't know what to make of tonight's conversation. Oddly grim note to end a good day on.

When Aylen got back inside the base she took a shower, changed out of her dirty training clothes, and made her way to the private quarters area. She had a bit of an accomplished feeling about the day. During gun logistics, she seemed to do well with the rifle trial, much to Captain Webster's approval. The blade training, however, could've gone a little better. She tried hard enough but it was clear she was no shogun assassin. Still, all things considered, she seemed to fare well. A small part of her was even proud about how she'd bested the Level 4 Brainless, though she would never say it.

But thoughts of Gabriel's speech at the end of the day roamed her mind. Not a soldier, but rather . . . a *survivor*? Wasn't sure what she was supposed to make of that.

She was excited to tell Jared about her day. She wondered what he might've been doing all day. What kind of thoughts were on his mind. What kind of dreams he dreamed in that deep sleep he was in. When she came back to the private quarters, though, she found Jared putting on his boots. He didn't look up as she stood in the doorway, not seeming to notice her as she came in through the door.

"Hey!"

"Hey," Jared replied coolly, still not looking at her. Aylen was admittedly a little put off by him ignoring her.

"What's up?"

"Going out," he replied stiffly, still ignoring her. Immediately something seemed . . . off. Aylen didn't like this attitude, and she was briefly reminded of Jared's similar attitude around the time she first met him, before he'd told her the truth about Salutem. Something was up, she was sure.

"That's cool . . ." Aylen trailed off. "Trained pretty hard today with Captain Webster. You were right, he *is* an amazing teacher."

"That's great, A. I gotta get going," Jared said quickly, standing up while putting on his jacket and beginning to pass her, looking around for something.

"W-well . . . where are you going?"

"Already told ya. Out. Where the fuck I put the keys?"

"Okay . . . and the non-sarcastic answer is?"

His eyes flashed orange in an instant. "I'm *going out.* The fuck is this, A? An interrogation? Jesus," he replied sharply before turning away.

Aylen scoffed. "Jeez, somebody woke up on the wrong side of the bed this morning." Jared stopped and glared at her, a dark look in his eyes growing visibly more tense. "It's just . . . an expression?" she replied, caught off guard by the look. Jared continued to stare at her with a vicious glare that puzzled her. Aylen squinted her eyes.

"You okay? What's gotten into you?"

Jared paused for a moment, then scoffed and twisted his mouth. "Into me? Dunno, what's gotten into *you*? One moment we're friends, next thing you're snuggling up to me in bed and shit, running your fingers through my hair—"

"Whoa, okay, I—I didn't *mean* anything by—"

"Didn't mean anything by it? *Didn't mean anything by it?* So what, you spoon all your friends? Don't give me that bullshit, A. People who are *just friends* don't—"

"Jared, what are you—"

"I mean, who the fuck you think you are, my girlfriend or somethin'—"

"Okay, wait . . ." Aylen chuckled slightly, confused. "All I did was invite you to sleep in the bed with me. I—I was just trying to be a good friend."

"Yeah, I bet that's all that was on your mind."

"What're you—"

"Friends, yeah, the kind of friends you were with Eric when you almost fucked him? That kinda friend?"

At this, she felt her cheeks burn as if he slapped her, and immediately she felt like biting his head off. "*Eric?* What the *fuck* does that have to do with *anything?*"

"Yeah, well, all I know is inviting a guy into your bed says a lot about where you think our friendship is—"

"What? You think I was trying to *screw you?* Are you for rea—"

"I don't know what the fuck you were thinking! 'Just friends' was clearly not it, though!" Jared shook his head and looked away from her. "You crossed a line, A. It wasn't cool."

"Jared—Jared, come on . . ."

"Lay off. Not in the mood."

Aylen froze, unsure what to say as Jared walked past her. She thought she heard him mutter, "There's the keys," before hearing the jingle of metal. Her breath came hard as her chest squeezed; she wasn't completely sure what she was feeling.

"Fine! Fine, maybe we're not *just friends*, okay?"

Jared stopped dead in his tracks. Aylen's face twitched and her heart raced. "Maybe you—maybe you mean something to me! Is that a problem? *You saved my life!* You're my *best friend*, I care about you!" Aylen yelled back. Jared shook his head, slowly turning around and facing her, his pale face oddly filled with a little color. Aylen moved in closer. "I knew you probably ran for however many miles? I knew you had to be tired, so I figured I'd let you get some rest! And me putting my fingers through your hair? Fine, I'll admit, maybe I was out of line to be so intimate, but you mean *so* much to me. I *care* about you. I really, really care about you."

"Yeah, well who says I give a fuck about you?" Jared mouthed off sharply. Aylen's eyes widened. He looked at her for a moment, losing the anger in his face as he and Aylen stared at each other in silence. Then his brow wrinkled as he looked down, as if he was ashamed of what he said.

Aylen swallowed. "You don't mean that. . . . You can't . . ." Jared sniffed, but kept silent, glaring at her. She shook her head in disbelief. "Wh-why are you saying these things?" Aylen asked, her world shattering in seconds. Tears began forming in her eyes. "This—this isn't you. I know—I know this isn't you—"

"*And what the fuck do you know about me?*" he finally yelled, making her jump. He came in closer to her, eyes burning the brightest orange she'd ever seen them burn. A rage in him she had never seen before. Aylen backed up, terrified. "Do you know how many people I've killed? The innocent people I've butchered? I've killed entire families, I've killed friends, almost everyone that's ever been close to me I've betrayed, murdered, or failed! *Everything I touch dies!*" he yelled in her face. "*I'm a curse! A fucking monster! I* was one of those Devil's Deviants you're so dead set on stopping! What? You want to be close to me now? I sound *fucking ideal* now?"

Aylen backed up to the nearest wall, face crumpling and tears beginning to fall. Jared's face was mere inches away from hers. He breathed in through his nose with a glimmer, Aylen thought, of regret in his eyes.

"I—I don't care about any of that . . ." Aylen said with her voice shaking, looking him up and down, tears streaming down her face. Her hands went to his face and he closed his eyes hard. They were almost forehead to forehead as he put his head down. "I just—I don't wanna lose you . . . please, Jared, please . . . I—I need yo—"

"*Don't you get it? You never had me,*" he said through his teeth, firmly pulling her hands from his face. His eyes were cold as he backed away and he stared harshly at her, breathing heavy. "What makes you think . . . I ever gave a shit about some *stupid* little nerd like you?"

Aylen stared in horror, lost for words. Jared blinked, shock crossing his face, then he looked around, possibly horrified at what he had just said, seeming to sober up slightly. "I-I'm goin' out for smokes," he said, sending his glance to the ground and adjusting his jacket. He spared her a small look, as if he wanted to say "I'm sorry," before turning around and leaving.

As soon as he left, Aylen sobbed. His words pierced her heart like ten thousand spears with jagged blades that were thrown by ancient warriors. After everything the two of them had been through. Was she wrong with what she did the previous night? Was she so wicked? So evil? Didn't care about her? Ever? No. She refused to believe it. Absolutely refused to believe it. There had to be more to this. Did Jared feel like she was playing with his heart? Was Jared . . . playing with her heart? She didn't know. Other than a few experiences in high school and those experiences with Eric, she had no frame of reference.

And she had no reason to cry. There was literally no real reason why she should've been crying. She'd faced certain death at the hands of that Brainless and didn't cry. This wasn't Morgan humiliating her, this wasn't Legion mind-screwing her, this wasn't Beth dying in her arms. It was Jared having a tizzy over nothing. Literally nothing. Why should this low-life piece of crap telling her she means nothing to him be more upsetting to her as those other things? Why did this hurt so bad?

Aylen clutched her chest as she wailed alone in the room.

JARED

Jared stormed out of his room breathing hard. This was for the best. This was for the—

He immediately punched the nearest wall as hard as he could.

"*Fuck!*" he yelled, breathing hard and eyes stinging. The way Aylen cried . . . Jared noticed a bloody mark on the wall as he pulled his fist away. His fist was bleeding, and he had left a crack in the wall. He observed the blood on his hand a moment and closed his eyes hard before looking back to his room. His face dropped, remembering Aylen's brown eyes leaking tears he had caused. He was a piece of shit. An absolute fucking piece of shit. But it was better this way. A part of him wanted to vomit. He did that to Aylen. . . . He *actually* did that. . . . He swallowed, and after a moment of contemplation he continued on his way, shaking his head. It was for the best. No matter how much he hated himself for doing that, it was for the best. He would only get her killed.

ESMERALDA

Esmeralda swallowed as she opened the door to her living quarters. The smell of cigar smoke and whiskey flooded the room like that of a seedy tavern. *He* was in there. Great. Before even seeing his figure sitting in the dark of the room, she knew exactly where he was. A bright ember from the cigar glowed in the dark as Morgan's husky face breathed in the toxic air and blew the smoke out like an angry dragon. "You're home late," Morgan breathed, his swine-like eyes piercing Esmeralda's soul like two burning black coals.

"Yeah, I had a meeting with Abel," Esmeralda lied.

"Oh yeah? What does the stupid Black fuck have to say?" Morgan spouted angrily. Ezzy looked up, her mouth twisted and eyes squinted.

"Is that kind of talk really necessary?"

"What? He's a dumb Black fucker. What would a stupid spic like you care about what I call 'im?" he slurred. Ezzy sighed, this asshole—

"You're drunk and being racist. I'm not gonna talk to you when you're like this," she said sharply as she began to walk to her closet. A firm and large hand grasped her arm as she walked past Morgan.

"You didn't answer my question: The hell did he say to you?"

"It's none of your business!"

Whack.

Esmeralda's vision was forced to the floor as Morgan pulled her in closer. "You don't think I already know what he told you, *you stupid bitch*? Huh?" he yelled. "You're now the teacher of recruits? Huh? You? A stupid whore?" Morgan tossed Esmeralda into the wall. "What'd you do? You slept with him, didn't ya?"

"*No!*" she protested, water forming in her eyes.

Smack.

Blood filled Ezzy's mouth as she wallowed on the ground in pain. His firm hand grabbed and pulled her hair. "Don't lie to me, you piece of shit! Why else would he give a wormy li'l fuck like you a high-ranking position?"

"I—I don't know! He just thought I was good, I guess!"

"*Good at what? Sucking his dick?*" Morgan yelled, positioning himself to hit her again. Esmeralda broke down, wails coming out of her mouth.

"I didn't sleep with him! I didn't sleep with him . . ." she said through sobs. Morgan let go of her hair and stared at her on the ground, sobbing and scrunching up into fetal position.

"You're pathetic." Morgan shook his head and went back to the kitchen table. There was a moment of silence, filled only with Esmeralda's sobs. She then remembered something. Something that they kept in a drawer nearby. "If I were in charge," Morgan continued, "a slut like you wouldn't be training recruits. It'd be a highly trained and qualified *soldier*. If I were running this joint, this war with the deviants would be fuckin' done with," he bragged. Esmeralda picked herself up off the ground and went for the drawer. She'd had enough.

"Yeah, we'd all be dead," Esmeralda said, pulling out the item she had in the drawer.

"The hell'd you say?"

She pointed the pistol at Morgan "You heard me, you stupid . . . ignorant . . . *wh-white trash piece of shit!*" Esmeralda snapped. "*You will never be a leader, you racist, misogynistic bastard!*" she yelled. Morgan's eyes widened as the gun in her hand shook. Ezzy calmed herself down and raised the pistol to point at Morgan's head. He obviously had not anticipated this. She swallowed. "F-four years. I've put up with your bullshit. Left a good man for you. Had a good man killed because of you. Four years I have suffered, put myself under your torture 'cause I—I thought I deserved it. Well, guess what? I don't. I don't love you. I never have. I didn't even visit you in the infirmary when that girl knocked you out. As a matter of fact, I *laughed*. Must've really stung to get beat up by a *girl*." Esmeralda felt herself chuckle through the tears.

Morgan began to get up.

"*Don't move or I swear you'll get one in the head!*" she screamed before calming down and steadying the gun at her former lover. "You *won't* touch me ever again. You *won't* hit me ever again. If I even so much as catch you looking at me the wrong way, I'll kill you. You understand?" Esmeralda spoke calmly as she reached behind her to grab the doorknob. Morgan looked as if he was about to speak. "Don't talk. You don't deserve to talk to me," she said fiercely as she opened the door behind her and walked out backward, still pointing a gun to Morgan. The door creaked, and Morgan slowly disappeared from her sight.

As the door closed, Esmeralda felt every muscle in her body collapse, as she sobbed and leaned against the door, keeping her hand on the doorknob, just in case. She forced herself to lift up her gun and kept it pointed at the door as she backed away before turning around and running to Gabriel's door and banging away on it. In a mere moment, he answered the door. For a brief second, Esmeralda saw shock overcome Gabriel's face. She felt the water of her tear drops drip down her face as she stared up at her real love. "C-can I come in?"

PESTILENCE

Pestilence watched the deviant in front of her carefully as the hour grew late. The deviant in front of her had a charcoal color to his skin and orange, reptilian eyes. Sweat was pooled on his brow as he carefully handled the tool in front of him, making sure to not put too much of a rush on the process he was undertaking. Pestilence swallowed hard as she looked at the vial that the deviant in front of her was handling: glowing, light blue, and heading closer and closer to the explosive before him. Suddenly, there was a slight click, and both deviants breathed out as the vial was successfully encapsulated in the explosive.

"Any more than that, Pestilence?" the deviant asked, clearly feeling exasperated from tonight's exercise in preparation.

"No, that ought to be the last one we fill with Cherubine. Any more than that and we might risk infecting our own people," she said before tapping his shoulder. "Good work, Focalor." With that, she backed away. It was a muggy night in the underground cavern beneath the bunker. Pestilence began looking over the deviants prepping the equipment for the next mission. There were a large number of them, and enough Jeeps to make the journey through the sewers, well-armed and armored in case they ran into any trouble below the surface. Still, would it be enough to tackle the task they were commissioned to do? Dupont had been a good little boy and gave them the rest of the weapon shipment they needed, but still, was it enough?

"Pestilence!" Cerberus barked, walking toward her through the various deviants that were prepping the weapons. Pestilence began toward the larger man.

"What is it?"

"Lucifer wants to meet with you and Dagon. Quick meeting because Pluto has a new invention," he said. Pestilence swallowed. New invention? This meant yet another thing to account for in their plans. The white-haired woman nodded, then began following him. "I see Dupont did well on remembering his allegiances," Cerberus commented as the two began walking through the tunnels.

"If he didn't believe in God before meeting you, he definitely did after, Cerberus."

"Good. Think we will have any further troubles from him?"

Pestilence shook her head. "As you said before, he pulls anything like that again, we'll skewer him. I think he gets the idea." Cerberus merely nodded at this, keeping his attention forward.

As they walked out of the tunnel, they came to a large clearing in the cavern, which was significantly colder than the rest of it. A bridge was before them, surrounded by various mechanical parts. The cavern seemed to be lit blue in contrast to the well-lit tunnels. Pestilence felt her stomach turn slightly as they got closer to the bridge.

"We'll be meeting everyone up ahead," Cerberus stated firmly as they began their trek up the black mechanized bridge. Pestilence went to the side of the structure and looked down to see what she knew was down there. The drop down below was at least forty feet down. A large, illuminated block of ice filled the trench below them. Small machines with red lasers were slowly but surely melting the ice, doing so carefully, layer by layer. It wasn't the ice that unsettled the woman with white hair, rather, it was what she knew was frozen inside. Faintly, she could already see the large brown shape encased in the thick layers. She could already feel the thing's consciousness, the thing's wild spirit. She stared at the ice and breathed hard, faintly remembering how hard it had been to capture the damned thing.

"Well, well, well, if it isn't White Hair," an Australian voice said next to her. She slowly glared at who she knew had arrived. He was a smaller man, maybe an inch or two shorter than Pestilence. For being named after a water demon, the man looked more like a weasel with his strange, rodent-shaped face. It was almost as if Project Suncloud had fused the man with a rat, with his enlarged front teeth, whisker-like goatee, and large, almost completely black eyes. If the white-haired woman didn't know any better, she would've thought he and a sewer rat had become one. His dark, stringy hair was sloppily combed backward, and he ran a hand through it as he stood before her, cocking his head when he was through as if to challenge her.

"Thought I smelled rat shit in the cave, Dagon," Pestilence remarked dryly.

"Very funny, love, as usual," he replied snidely. "Almost as funny as failing to kill Abel Quinn." Pestilence was about to say something when Cerberus cleared his throat.

"Lucifer on your six," he said under his breath. Pestilence turned around and did indeed see Lucifer heading for them, a smile on his face.

"My, what a dashing group of the Devil's Deviants' finest." He motioned with his head for the others to follow him. "Pluto has a new toy to show us all," the horned leader remarked pleasantly, turning back the way he came. The group looked briefly at each other, then began following their leader.

"We got the weapons we needed?" Lucifer asked, without looking at Pestilence.

"Dupont came through on what was agreed upon," she responded as they entered yet another tunnel, which led to a flight of stairs.

Lucifer looked briefly at Pestilence. "And the creature? Do you feel it yet?"

"Yeah. . . . Faintly, but there's still some layers of ice to get through. Doesn't seem to have been in any way unconscious during its cryofreeze, though," Pestilence remarked grimly. She hated the creature; it made her feel ill to even be around the thing.

"Hmm, so the thing doesn't sleep, after all. Thank goodness we have a deviant as powerful as you controlling it, Pestilence. The creature sounds truly terrifying indeed. Any other news on your front?"

The group reentered the metallic bunker, which didn't feel nearly as muggy as the caverns. Pestilence nodded her head. "Added some Cherubine to some of the mines we'll set up around the perimeter. Figure that ought to be a nasty little surprise to anyone they send in after we make our initial assault."

"Lovely. What about you, Dagon? Your scavengers know exactly what they'll be on the lookout for?"

As Dagon answered, the white-haired woman breathed heavily. She wasn't excited to see what sort of invention Pluto had cooked up. Quite frankly, it didn't interest her in the least. She just wanted to finish the required amount of prepping that she had to do tonight and go back to her quarters.

After arriving in front of Pluto's lab and quarters, passing that pet Brainless he had with relative ease due to Pestilence's ability, the group entered the large lab. It was filled with various machines and felt vast and cramped at the same time. Pestilence briefly looked at the "machine" Pluto had been working on for the last few years. She furrowed her brow as she tried to figure out just what it was. She had vague ideas about it, but it was odd. Lots of wires were still all over, but it was beginning to look like some sort of pod. Pestilence turned her attention to the table next to it. On the table was a glass case that contained something that sickened her. The hand, though well preserved, was tiny, shriveled, and rotten, almost mummified. It was as Pestilence was staring at the decrepit thing that her attention was then turned toward her side.

"Well, Pluto, time to show us the brand-new toy," Lucifer stated dryly. The fat, round little man with the oversized brain looked caught off guard after adjusting a part of some sort of exoskeleton that was worn by a young, purple-skinned, and somewhat uneasy-looking deviant named Ifrit.

"O-oh! Yes! Well, perfect timing, perfect timing," Pluto said, seeming nervous and wearing a fake smile. Pestilence never thought any smiles from the little fat man were genuine. In a strange way, every movement of his seemed calculated and forced. Because of this, a part of her never fully trusted him. Something that seemed validated as soon as Pestilence noticed bits and pieces of tan enhancer armor torn apart across his little lab.

"Did—Did you tear apart the enhancer armor that we got as part of Dupont's shipment?" Pestilence asked in disbelief. The rest of the deviants seemed to notice what she was looking at. "We could've used those!"

Pluto looked visibly shaken before smiling a nervous smile. "Y-yes. Yes, I did tear it apart, but—"

"That armor could've put us on equal footing with any of our enemies!"

"Well, you see—"

"Those things weren't cheap!"

Lucifer cleared his throat, causing both to silence. "Pestilence, let him explain. Though, I do have to ask . . . Pluto, why the waste of resources?"

Pluto licked his lips and nodded his head. "A-a simple demonstration will suffice . . ." He grabbed an assault rifle off his work bench and pointed it at the pile of armor parts. Each deviant covered their ears as he fired at the armor. After firing a few shots, he put down his rifle and walked over to the parts. Lucifer and company uncovered their ears. "While enhancer armor is impressive in enhancing speed and agility . . ." Pluto began as he picked up a chest plate from the pile. Large holes glared back at the group as they observed. "There's a fundamental design flaw." Pestilence lifted her eyebrows at this. "It doesn't take much to pierce this quality of armor. If it were current UWF armor, it'd be better suited to our needs, but Saint-quality armor is, to put in a word, unreliable," the fat man explained. "So given that it'd be hard to get the resources to efficiently get us a tougher brand of armor, I figured I'd repurpose the armor we have . . ." Pluto trailed off.

Lucifer nodded. "Hmm. That, and because we are *deviants*, after all, there isn't much need for us to wear armor. We aren't as fragile as humans," he boasted. Pestilence twisted her face. Still would've been nice for an extra layer of protection. "Show us what your new version of the armor can do," Lucifer commanded.

Pluto nodded, then looked at the young deviant wearing the exoskeleton armor. "Ifrit, would you do the honors?" the fat man asked. The young deviant nodded and pressed a button. Pestilence immediately widened her eyes. He— he just— In moments, Ifrit had disappeared and then reappeared in front of them where he was before.

Lucifer heartily chuckled. "Brilliant! Absolutely brilliant! Well done, Pluto!" Even Pestilence had to admit, she was thoroughly impressed.

"Only have limited resources to make armor like this, though. Can only make a limited amount," Pluto remarked. Lucifer eyed the exoskeleton-wearing deviant in front of him hungrily.

"Make as many as you can. The UWF won't stand a chance," he said. Pestilence's fears about the upcoming mission completely dissolved. With armor like that, the mission would undoubtedly succeed.

EPISODE 15

The Rope and the Girl

ABEL

It was late at night when Gail entered Abel's office. The Saint leader's eyes strained as he struggled to keep them open. Gail and who she had been meeting with must've had trouble scheduling, because she looked like something the cat had dragged in. He breathed out hard as the two met eyes.

"It's all set?" he asked.

"The meeting is a go."

Gail took a seat in front of him at his desk. As it if it had been a signal, he let out a sigh. Whether it was of relief or despair, he wasn't sure. He closed his eyes hard. He had no choice. Any benefactors of the Saints had long abandoned them, there weren't any black market contacts they could do odd jobs for anymore, and the remaining Saints, including himself, didn't have the resources to save the Saints financially. His son had suggested what was probably their only alternative now, other than disbanding the Saints altogether. He clutched the bridge of his nose as the two sat in silence.

"You must think I'm weak . . . or a coward," Abel finally said, breaking up the silence. He looked up at Gail, who was frowning between the tousled strands of her mouse-brown hair. She shook her head.

"No, not at all. I think, considering everything, it's the smartest play you could possibly do."

Abel bit his lip and stared at the ceiling. "She won't be easy to deal with . . ." Gail sighed and nodded her head. Abel shifted in his seat. "She's always been hard to deal with, but this will just make it harder on us. What really rubs salt in this is that she has dirt on a good majority of the high-ranking officers."

Gail twisted her mouth. "Dirt?"

Abel nodded his head solemnly. "Dirt. On me specifically too." Abel breathed out through his nose. "She'll probably use it to manipulate me in the future." Gail swallowed and frowned at the desk briefly before looking back up.

"Wh-what does she have on you?"

Abel shook his head. "When I was a teenager . . . I had a breakdown of sorts. It was around the time that my mom died, I just . . . lost touch with reality for a while there . . . stopped sleeping, got violent toward myself and others. Some of it I remember, most I don't. Apparently broke an orderly's jaw at one point." Gail's eyes widened. "I was just . . . gone for a bit. Doctors treated me, and after a while I became functional again. But not a day goes by since that I worry it might happen again. I stopped taking the meds long ago . . . and even through the battles and everything I've suffered since I don't seem to need them. Still . . ."

"A-Abe, oh my god . . . that's terrible! I-if the rest of the council knew—"

"I know. They'd vote me out of this position. Li has made the threat before that if I don't comply with her demands, she'll reveal my secret." Abel sighed.

Gail shook her head. "That fucking bitch . . ." she said under her breath. "You're sure it won't happen again, though?"

Abel firmly shook his head. "There were other factors at play at the time. I haven't had anything like that since I was sixteen. Still, though, if the council gets word . . ."

Gail nodded. "Yeah, they'd try to vote you out or something. Especially that prick Morgan. It'd be one thing if it was just a depressive episode, the fact you got violent during it though? Legitimately hurt someone? People would exploit that. People that don't want you as Principal Overseer. Try to say something like you're mentally unfit for the position, anything they can cling on to. It'd hurt your image with the Saints overall." Gail twisted her mouth. "Well, I guess we keep your secret then, at all costs."

Abel lifted his eyebrows and weakly smiled. "I wasn't sure how you would've reacted to this revelation."

Gail shrugged. "So you lost your mind once, everybody in the Saints has. And everyone in the Saints has secrets. Hell, if it makes you feel any better, I've secretly been quite the little slut since Manolo died. Even fucked Greenfield a few times," she admitted. There was a moment when the two stared at each other, then they both laughed. Abel got out some liquor and two shot glasses from his desk drawer.

Abel cleared his throat. "I think *that* deserves a drink." Gail nodded, still laughing. "*You* and Greenfield?"

Gail shrugged. "Hey, he's good-looking, in his twenties, and knows what he's doing,"

Abel winced. "I don't—I don't like thinking about that," he remarked between chuckles. "Though I do think Corporal Greenfield has proven himself the real slut in this scenario. That kid gets around. Jesus."

Gail laughed. "He is quite infamous for it."

Abel poured the liquor into the shot glasses and handed Gail one before raising his own to toast. "To secrets, may they not prove our undoing," he said. Gail raised her glass.

"To secrets."

The two drank their shots.

Yet another moment of silence overcame the pair as they sat thoughtfully. Then Gail said, "You know, I'm glad you trusted me with your secret." Abel lifted his eyebrow at this. "I consider you very, very near and dear to me. I'm— I'm glad you could trust me with such sensitive information."

Abel sighed and nodded. "I'm not sure I feel I can trust too many people these days. Admittedly, you're one of the few people I can trust anymore."

Gail smiled. "Well, your secret is safe with me." Abel smiled back, but then his face became troubled. Gail must've picked up on it because her expression changed as well. "What is it?"

Abel sighed and shook his head. "This . . . new thing . . . with the UWF. Not sure how our resident deviant is going to fit in with it." Gail's face dropped, and she breathed out.

"Hmmm," she merely uttered in response.

AYLEN

Aylen sat in bed staring at the wall in the corner of Jared's room through the darkness of night. It curved inward in an odd way that the corner of a room wouldn't ordinarily curve. She wondered: What the *crap* was the architect thinking, curving that particular corner like that? She understood the base was an old military base from the Anthrodi War, but honestly, why the hell was it shaped that way? Aylen continued to stare at the corner and ask herself meaningless questions in an attempt to force herself to go to sleep, something she had been trying to do for hours but was ultimately unable to do. Maybe it was because some not-so-meaningless questions crept their way in occasionally. Questions like: Why did Jared snap the way he did? What could she have possibly done to make him turn on her so quickly? It didn't make sense to her. She had always treated Jared like a person. Had always treated him with care. There was that four-letter word again, the word he so spitefully threw back into her face. Didn't care about her? *Didn't care?* Bullcrap. It had to be bullcrap. Jared wouldn't have done everything he did if that was true. Still, it hurt. It hurt that he would even let that slip out of his mouth. How dare he? How freaking dare he?

The door opened and closed, and footsteps stomped into the room as Jared's silhouette walked in. Where had he been all this time? What made him have the balls to come back? Of course, these were his private quarters, not hers. He could easily kick *her* out if he wanted. That didn't stop Aylen from glaring at him, though. Jared noticed her looking at him and looked away immediately, going about his business and grabbing pajamas. He stomped into the bathroom and turned on the light after closing the door. There the sound of a rustling belt and the movement of cloth, followed by the sound of water and teeth being brushed. In the dark, it was difficult to tell what kind of look Jared had given her. As best she could tell, it was an "Oh, you're still here?" look. Was he still mad at her? Did he regret what he had said? Did he care?

Aylen remained seated as Jared exited the bathroom and plopped himself on the couch. Immediately, he retreated to his phone, deliberately ignoring her. Should she say something? Should she even try to interrupt what Jared was doing? Aylen wasn't sure. He remained on his phone for the next ten minutes, then the white glow of his screen disappeared and Jared's shadowy figure lay back on the couch and faced away from her. She dared not approach him as he quickly drifted off to sleep. Or, at least what Aylen perceived was him drifting off to sleep. After a minute of staring at the sleeping goth, she laid back on the bed. The cold night air swept over her and made her pull the covers over her body. Within moments, she drifted into a dreamless sleep.

ESMERALDA

Esmeralda sat on the bed, tears still falling from her eyes as Gabriel cleaned her busted lip. He kept silent as he worked, his face somber and sympathetic. When he finished he gave her a bag of ice for the welt on her cheek and breathed out softly, then licked his lips. "Can I get you anything?"

Esmeralda looked down and nodded. "Water, please," she croaked. Her throat hurt from yelling at Morgan. Gabriel nodded and got up, fetching her a glass of water. After he brought it back she graciously thanked him and sipped it. "Um . . . how was training the Monro girl today?"

Gabriel studied her, then lifted his eyebrows. "Good. She's a high-spirited student. You can tell she really wants to be here. Believe it or not, she's actually not a bad shot, despite never firing a gun before today."

Ezzy smiled weakly at this. "That's good. Morgan was very wrong about her, I guess." She sniffled.

Gabriel looked like he wanted to make a comment but refrained. "How is training the other recruits so far?"

Esmeralda smiled the best she could. "Tough, 'cause Brenden is still out of commission. But I think I'm doing fine by myself. I'm not *you*, though." Gabriel nodded, eyes turned away from her. He was obviously thinking about something other than what she said because he had a far-off look in his eyes. "Marie is the best of the bunch, no question. Good all-around so far. Jonathan is a decent shot. Unfortunately, Adrien doesn't seem particularly good at anything yet, but time will tell, I guess."

Gabriel breathed out through his nose. "Ezzy . . . we need to talk about the bruises and welts. This is too far—"

"Gabe, no—"

"I've kept quiet, but now I can't. We need to bring Morgan's abuse to the council." Gabriel nodded, a glint of menace in his eyes. "And if that doesn't work, we could always get rid of him the old-fashioned way—"

"Gabe!" Esmeralda shook her head. "It's done." She breathed out, shuddering. "He will never hurt me again. Not after tonight. He's stupid, but not *that* stupid. He knows I will shoot him dead if he ever so much as looks at me again. Bringing it to the council will just embarrass me, and you killing him . . ." There was a momentary pause, then she shook her head. "Just . . . no."

Gabriel sighed. "I want to after seeing you like this." He nodded and his face seemed to curl. "I want to throttle the miserable coward. I want to go over there with my pistol and—"

Esmeralda put her hand on his face, catching him off guard. "If he ever tries anything ever again, I'll fill him up with bullets myself. I don't need you to save me."

The older man studied her for a second and breathed out. "Why didn't you let me step in? Why didn't you tell me what was going on? I had an idea, but I wasn't sure."

"I can fight my own battles, Gabe. I'm not some helpless little girl. I'm a woman of the Saints." Esmeralda let her hand drop. Gabriel nodded, his mouth still twisted. He looked deep in thought, and she couldn't help but smile at him. He had a real, genuine concern for her well-being. She'd almost forgotten what that felt like. "I'm gonna need to probably stay here for a bit . . . if that's okay with you."

Gabriel smiled softly. "Of course." He studied her for a moment and brushed the hair out of her face. "You can stay here as long as you need."

Esmeralda leaned in and softly kissed him, despite her busted lip. It hurt her, but she didn't care. When they pulled away, staring deep into each other's eyes, Esmeralda felt her lips tremble. "I, um, have a confession. . . . I—I wasn't sure if it was too early to say it. But, but after tonight . . . I don't think I care," she said, breathing out. "I love you." Gabriel blinked, breathing in and out through his nose. A smile creaked onto his worn face. A bigger one than she had ever seen before.

"I haven't said that to anyone romantically in the longest time. . . . And it probably *is* a little early, but . . . I love you too."

The two then shared yet another soft kiss. Ezzy, for the first time in a long time, felt like she was at home.

AYLEN

With some trouble, Aylen got up at the same time she had the previous morning and got ready in the same fashion. Jared remained asleep on the couch as she left the lonely living quarters, not wishing to stay in the room with him a moment longer. What a prick. He didn't even apologize for what he said, and it seemed he had no intention of doing so. Of course, there was always the chance that *she* was in the wrong . . . but how could that be right? All she did was let him sleep in the same bed as her. Once. She didn't touch him inappropriately, and she didn't make a move on him, and he never said anything to suggest otherwise. And what if she did? There was no way Aylen could believe that Jared would've refused her if she did make a pass at him. For a moment, she realized what the ramifications of that might've been. Would they have become a thing? Would they have slept together? Maybe . . . just maybe, Jared wanted her to make a move? Maybe he was so mad at her because she didn't? Maybe she should have—

Wait, what?

Maybe she needed to get Faith to look at her. Maybe she got a concussion from the previous day's Brainless fight. Her worry pervaded her as she approached Gabriel, who was waiting for her next to the obstacle course.

"Good, you're here. Let's get started with those stretches we did yesterday," he told her. As Gabriel led Aylen through preliminary stretches, she thought about the obstacle course. More specifically, she thought about the rope. The damned rope. It loomed in the corner of her eye like a thin, gaunt giant. Already, by the stretching Gabriel had her do, Aylen knew the obstacle course wasn't going to be an easy one today. The forest ground was moist and muddy, and soon enough she would have to drag herself through it. No enhancer armor. Just her and some training clothes that Gabriel gave her the day before. Goody.

"All right," Gabriel said, the stretches finished before she was even fully aware, "now get into position for the course, and I'll get the timer set up." Here went nothing.

There were two wooden posts on the ground to indicate the starting position of the course. Aylen's heart began to race as she started toward the starting position. Upon arriving, she felt a tinge of nervousness come over her, not being sure how much of the course she might be able to complete. "All right . . . go!" Gabriel shouted.

She began running through the mud and felt the uneasiness of the ground under her feet. Upon coming up to the trenches, Aylen threw herself into the dirt to crawl under the barbed wire. The mud immediately seeped through her shirt, cold and sticky, and even got on her face among other uncomfortable places. Aylen tried to keep her mind off it as she dragged herself through the terrain. Upon getting up, she threw herself at the next obstacle, carefully stepping into each tire. Then came the balance beam, which made her slow her movements so as to not fall down. She stepped up and carefully calculated her weight distribution with each step.

"Come on, Private Monro, let's go! Double-time, double-time!" Gabriel called out as she approached the end of the balance beam. "Move, move, move, move, move!"

Aylen came to the wall she had to climb and took it aggressively, pulling herself up and over and jumping over the hurdles that came next. It was coming up. She climbed the taller, netted wall and got to the top.

"Step on it, Monro!"

Aylen looked down at the lake below. From yesterday, she already knew the water was freezing, and that memory made her hesitate. At Gabe's beckoning, though, she flung herself into the icy water, feeling the cold grip on every inch of her body. She pushed herself up to the surface and gasped from the shock to her system. "Come on, Monro, you can do it!" Gabriel called. Aylen shook her head and paddled through the water as fast as she could, before the cold could seize her muscles, then pulled herself to shore on the other side. She breathed heavily. She had covered the course so far within a relatively short time.

Then she looked up at her current obstacle. The last obstacle. Towering above Aylen for what looked like miles was the menacing rope. The entwined fibers looked soggy, hard, and uncomfortable to touch, and when Aylen grabbed the rope, she found she was not wrong. "Wrap your leg the way I showed you!" Gabriel encouraged her. She obeyed his suggestion and began to attempt climbing the rope, but soon stepped back to the ground. For a moment, Aylen could imagine Jared making condescending remarks about her failure; instead, she only heard Gabriel: "Come on, Monro, clock is ticking! Try again!"

She tried again, this time attempting to jump onto the rope to start higher up. It did get her higher . . . a *foot* higher. Aylen clung to the rope to stay on and attempted to pull herself up. Her arms shook before they finally gave in, nearly causing her fall. Aylen could practically see Jared, standing on the ground below her, laughing at her and how she couldn't even pull herself up. She could imagine his words. *Fucking loser.*

"Come on, Monro, you can do it!" the captain called, a world away from Aylen's self-torment. The truth was, Jared didn't give a crap if Aylen conquered this rope. If she believed him, he didn't give a crap about her at all. She could break her neck and he wouldn't care.

No.

She would show him. She would overcome this rope, and that would show him. *That would show him.* As anger pressed through her, she felt a surge of adrenaline come with it. Slowly, she pulled. The next thing she knew, she was a little higher than before, then a little higher than that. She was beginning to do it, she was beginning to—

Aylen slammed to the ground before she even knew she let go. Imaginary Jared's laughter drowned her thoughts. She was a loser. She was a wimp. She couldn't climb the rope. Gabriel rushed to her side. "Monro! Are you hurt?"

"No," Aylen lied. Her ego was hurt . . . and her tailbone and parts of her lower back. She was a failure.

Gabriel observed her quietly. "What were you thinking about on that rope?"

"Climbing the rope."

Gabriel blinked for a moment and smirked. "My mom used to have an old saying," he said. "It's been around for years. You don't hear it much anymore these days, but it's true. Rob used to say it a lot too, and it's this: Don't shit a shitter. If you were just thinking about climbing the rope, you would've climbed it." Aylen felt herself shiver from the cold water. Her teacher handed her a towel and she began to dry herself off. "Ya know, that rope is not as scary as you think it is. The fact that you think it's scary is what makes it hard to climb. It allows doubt to enter your head, mess with your mind. Once you allow that in, the rope wins."

Aylen observed Gabriel and blinked as he glanced back up at the rope.

"Story time, something that happened to me. There was a deviant once. His name was Behemoth. Scariest-looking SOB you'd ever seen. Almost seven feet tall, purple skin, mutations so bad he looked more creature than human. Word around camp was that he was one of the scariest and most ruthless deviants alive, other than Cerberus, Triple Six, and War, of course. Ability was rumored, or I guess more assumed, to be one of the deadliest. Anyway, one day I'm on a mission and suddenly I found myself trapped in a room with him. Just the two of us. I pull out my hatchets and start waving them around a bit, ready and willing for a battle to the death with Behemoth, and you know what he does?" There was a pause and Aylen gave Captain Webster a look that told him she had no clue. "Sumbitch tries to run away. Apparently his big, bad superpower was the ability to control small gusts of wind that barely did anything, and he knew it. See, he was hyped up because he was physically strong and looked terrifying, but as far as being a deviant, he was weak. Pretty dumb too. So I knocked him around for a bit and then got out of there alive, against the apparent big, bad deviant. He turned out to be a coward. He didn't even really fight me when

I beat him up a little, just kept trying to get away 'cause I had hatchets and all he had was his power. My point is, Aylen, just because something seems scary and impossible to overcome, doesn't mean it's as bad as you think it is."

Aylen nodded and thought for a moment. "Whatever happened to Behemoth?"

Gabriel chuckled. "Well . . . Devil's Deviants don't take too well to cowardice. Needless to say that was pretty much the last time we heard from big, bad Behemoth."

Aylen thought for a second and looked at the rope, and she understood what Gabriel was trying to say. She'd let herself think that the rope was too high, which allowed her to doubt herself. The thing with Jared didn't help. Up until now, Jared had been her biggest support; if she had him behind her, she could do anything. Now that he hated her, Aylen didn't feel any sort of support from anyone. Her world felt lonelier. It was a smaller place.

They ran the obstacle course again, and she failed again. After bruising her ego the second time, Gabriel had mercy on her and they went over gun logistics. Upon entering the gun range, he handed her the same training rifle as before rather than the pistol he'd started with the previous day. Aylen looked at Gabriel with question in her eyes, but Gabriel was busy pressing a button that made the target almost disappear out of sight. She began to panic. The gun range was maybe a mile long. Someone would have to be a really good rifleman to hit the target all the way over there.

"Hit the target," Gabriel said. She looked worriedly at him. "We're burning daylight, Private Monro. Let's go."

"B-but, sir, I can barely *see* the target!"

"Try anyway. The machine will let you know if you hit it."

Aylen looked out at the target, her body still slightly shaking from the cold of her wet clothes. From this far, with its body-shaped outline and all, the target almost looked like a real person. She swallowed as she positioned herself onto the buffer in front of her that separated her from the target.

"Like this?"

Captain Webster helped her reposition correctly. Aylen took a deep breath and pulled the trigger. Nothing. Nothing happened. Anxiety crept over her as she inspected the weapon.

"Before you fire your weapon, what must be the first thing you check?" Gabriel asked Aylen. Crap. She completely forgot the first rule. He put a carton of bullets next to her on the buffer. "Always check to see if your weapon is loaded," he said firmly. She undid the magazine of the rifle—*that* she remembered at least—but when she attempted to put bullets into the magazine, she struggled and found herself unable to do it. "No, no, watch me." Gabriel took the magazine from her hand. "You slip it in like this and push it down." And just like that, the first bullet was in the magazine. Gabriel then put in the second bullet, going slowly to make sure Aylen could see how he did it. He handed the magazine to her. "You try." She tried and found herself successful, much to her own delight. "Good. Now get about two more in there and you'll have a full magazine." Gabriel smiled. Aylen did as her teacher told her, put the magazine back in the rifle, and positioned herself the way Gabriel had just shown her. Then she aimed at the target.

Bam.

Nothing. The machine that was supposed to let her know if she hit the target didn't go off. Crap. She ejected the bullet casing via the bolt action and aimed again.

Bam.

Nothing again. Frustrated, she did the bolt action and fired again. The machine still didn't indicate that she hit anything. "It's too far! There's no way I can—"

"No, it's not too far. Relax, Monro. You're getting too worked up. You *can* hit the target. You have two more shots left, make 'em count." Captain Webster stood close to Aylen and looked toward the target. "Take a deep breath in. Hold it and exhale when you squeeze the trigger. Old sniper trick."

Aylen looked at the target and felt her nerves tense. She took a deep breath in, carefully aimed her rifle, and squeezed the trigger.

Bam—ding!

Her eyes widened when she heard the machine indicate that she had hit her target. A boost of confidence flooded her with warmth. The first thing she had done right all day. "Finish 'em off, Private. Last bullet," Gabriel encouraged. Aylen took another deep breath and squeezed the trigger.

Bam—ding!

A smile crossed her face after hearing that second ding from the machine, indicating she had hit her target. Gabriel pushed a button, and within seconds the target was right in front of them. In the human cutout were two gunshots: one in the shoulder and one in the leg. He pointed to the shoulder injury. "Shoulder injury means the target, at best, would be knocked over and in pain, maybe have their arm taken out of commission. Bleed out over time if not attended to, but otherwise a survivable injury. *This* one, though"—Gabriel pointed to the leg—"is the—"

"—femoral artery," Aylen said. "If not treated quickly, they can die from blood loss within minutes." The captain looked at her with surprise. She chuckled. "Med school student, remember?"

Gabriel thought for a moment and pushed a button that sent the target back to where it was. "Again."

The rest of the training day went well, although blade training revealed yet again where her weaknesses lay. At the end of the day, though, she couldn't complain. She entered the showers and sighed as the warm water ran over her body. She washed the dirt off herself, which admittedly took longer than she would've liked, and her mind turned to Jared. She would have to return to the room after the shower, and Aylen dreaded that thought beyond belief. She didn't care if he'd said what he had just to spite her; telling her that he didn't give a damn about her hurt her in more ways than one. After everything they had been through, that's all he had to say? Nice. Really nice. She left the warm, womblike shower and put on some fresh clothes. The comfort of the transition were oddly surprising. Perhaps it was the high she was riding from her success at the gun range earlier. Screw Jared. Who gave a crap about that prick? She exited the women's shower area to then be greeted by an unwelcome sight.

"Miss me?" Eric grinned. Great. This was the last thing Aylen needed.

"No."

"Ooooh, harsh." Eric gave her a cocky smile as he caught up with her. "Does that mean I can't invite you to dinner?"

Aylen chuckled without humor. "I'd sooner have dinner with a cannibal."

"Who says I'm not one?" Eric said with a smile. Aylen sighed and looked him over. Same Eric, just wearing Saint clothes. What was with this jovial attitude, though?

"Look, I don't really wanna have dinner with an ex. I'm in no mood."

"Then how's about with an old friend?" At this, Aylen stopped and lifted her eyebrow. Eric shrugged. "Come on, Monro, we were friends before we dated, and two dates hardly qualifies me as an ex, don't ya think?" Aylen stared at him blankly, waiting for him to provide another reason this was a good idea. "Just wanna catch up is all. Plus, I noticed you could use someone other than that old hack to teach you 'bout swords."

Aylen looked at Eric with a question in her eyes. "I watched you train," he confessed. That only made Aylen feel a little uneasy.

She stepped forward, glaring at Eric. "What makes you think that I'd wanna have dinner with a guy who lied to me and tried to use me for sex? And what makes you think I'd want *you* to train me?"

Eric grinned devilishly "'Cause you and Jared are fighting and you have *nothing* better to do than to eat with me in the cafeteria."

Aylen was caught off guard. "How did y—"

"Let's just say I'm highly observant and I have eyes and ears all over the place. Ones that keep tabs on everybody in this shithole. Money goes far," he said. "Dinner?" Eric lifted an eyebrow. Aylen thought for a moment. He was right. She didn't have anything better to do.

She sighed. "Fine. Why not? You pull any funny business, I'll just stab you with a fork."

Eric chuckled. "Don't threaten me with a good time."

When they entered the cafeteria, Aylen couldn't help but think of what a step down this dinner was from their first date. Between crappy food service, the rowdy clientele, and the mush being served, the Saint cafeteria was a far cry from the fancy restaurant he had taken to her what seemed eons ago. Still, somehow this felt much more honest and more reflective of Eric's personality. They got their food and then sat across from each other. Eric started munching into a burger and watched her intently as she stared at him instead of touching her food. He grinned while chewing. "So, sweet li'l Aylen Monro decided to join the big, bad Saints. Beth's death have anything to do with that?"

Aylen hated him. Aylen hated Eric. She already regretted this dinner. "Yeah, something like that."

"Nah, it's either like that or it's not. Word on the street says Legion killed her. That's one nasty fucker."

Beth's name-drop didn't make her feel very giving. "Yep."

"Tough. Sorry to hear. Knowing Legion, it probably wasn't pretty. Probably theatrical and twisted." Eric took another bite of the burger. "Probably made a show of it."

Aylen glared at Eric, feeling her cheek twitch. "It slit her throat, put an ax into her boyfriend's head, and then wrote a message to me in their blood in big letters all across the wall. How's that for pretty?"

Eric chuckled. "Nah, it didn't do that."

"Yeah, it did."

"Afraid not, Monro. Ya know how *hard* it is to write big letters in blood? On *drywall?* How much blood that takes? Don't even get me started on the nightmares of coagulation and how it would turn brown and look like shit.

Probably more likely some sorta dark red paint." Eric shrugged. "More theatrical that way. You can make it look like blood, but you can usually see it better 'cause it's thicker. Plus, given Legion's tendency to not leave fingerprints at its crime scenes, for it to suddenly stick its finger in someone's wound and finger paint on the wall doesn't fit its MO. Not saying it's not possible, just highly unlikely. You should know that, you're a med student."

Aylen bit her lip to prevent herself from causing a scene in the cafeteria. Who gave a crap about what Legion used to write the message? Beth was dead. She was dead and never coming back.

"You do wanna shank that bitch, though. Am I right?"

Aylen breathed out, her lip curling in anger. "Of course."

Eric leaned in, a predatory look in his eyes. "Then let me show you some pointers on how to do it. Lemme show you how to kill that eely fuck once and for all with a good old-fashioned blade." Eric smirked. "Kill someone with a gun? Sure, it's effective, gets the job done. But to stab someone? To drive that blade in, feel their blood rush over your fingers, watch the light go out of their eyes as they look at you, knowing you're the last face they'll ever see?" Eric's smirk died down as he nodded. "Man, blades are the perfect weapon for revenge. They send a message. A message they picked the wrong person to fuck with. You kill Legion with a blade? Well, the revenge will be that much juicier."

Aylen nodded. A part of her didn't want to admit it, but what Eric had to say was appealing. A part of her wanted to rip Legion to shreds, tear it limb from limb. She wanted to see Legion in pain. She sniffed in, gathering her thoughts. "And what's in it for you, teaching me how to do that?"

Eric shrugged. "I'm just doin' it out of the kindness of my heart. Liked Beth as a person."

"Bullcrap." Aylen leaned in, studying Eric. "I don't buy it. What's your *real* endgame here? What do *you* have to gain from teaching me anything?"

Eric chuckled and nodded, leaning his head. "Honestly? Amusement." Eric licked his lips and cracked his neck. "Saw the bang-up job you did on Morgan.

Not gonna lie, you kicking his ass is the *funniest* shit I've heard in a bit. I'm just wondering if you got any more surprises in ya. Clearly, you're not who I thought you were, so I'm just wondering what other kinda damage you can do."

Aylen squinted her eyes and huffed. Eric leaned in. "I can teach you things about swords even Gabe doesn't know. I've been training since I could hold one, and I'm *really* fucking good at what I do." Eric leaned back and tilted his head. "Besides, with you and Jared having a li'l tizzy, what have you got to lose?"

Aylen studied the boy across from her for a moment. He was a complete and utter stranger to her. She twisted her mouth and nodded, staring Eric dead in the eyes. "Tell me . . . what did Jared take away from you that you'll never be able to get back?" she asked, realizing as she said it that she was jeering.

Thwack.

The sound through the room. Aylen looked down at the table and saw Eric clenching a hunting knife that was buried in the apple on her tray. She didn't even see Eric pull it out or anything. It happened faster than Aylen could blink her eye. She looked up at Eric, who was glaring at her. Chills ran through her at the icy look in his eyes. Then he softened and twitched his cheek slightly. "It's not a loss if it wasn't worth keeping in the first place," he replied calmly, before lifting the knife and taking a bite out of her apple. "You want my help or not?" he said around the chunks of fruit. No, she didn't like him, but she *did* need his help. If Eric had just shown her anything, it was how handy he was with a blade. With Eric's help, maybe she could become an even better soldier.

"All right, you can teach me," Aylen said, sighing. "I trust you as far as I can throw you, but I *do* need to get better with blades. . . . We're on. But the *moment* I sense something funny going on, deal's off."

"And the newbie accepts the master's offer. Your smartest move yet." Eric grinned. "Sounds like we got a deal, Monro. Gimme a week to sort some stuff I got going on. In exactly one week, though, after your training and before you take a shower, meet me in the blade training area. Be ready."

Eric stood and grabbed his tray. Aylen stared at his catlike grin as he stared back at her, his once warm eyes now icicles piercing her soul. "Live long and prosper, young padawan," he said mockingly as he walked away. What the hell did she just get herself into?

Aylen's mind was completely occupied with the possibility of Eric training her as she made her way back to the main building where she lived with Jared. It was . . . surreal to think about. The guy she'd had a crush on for the longest time and briefly dated was going to train her to use *swords*. Swords. As in the sharp, metal, pointy things that were around in medieval times. The world of the Saints was very different from the world she was used to, where Eric was a rich, ex-jock, pretty-boy, med student. In this world, he was an unnerving killer, good with a blade. It was surreal to even think that the man she had just had a conversation with was the same Eric. He almost seemed like a completely different person.

One thing was certain: Whatever happened, she had to be careful. Eric wasn't trustworthy, he had proven that to her. Aylen felt uneasy as she reached Jared's door. An entire week. All right . . . she had time to get ready.

Upon opening the door, she immediately noticed that Jared's quarters were empty. Everything was still there, but Jared himself wasn't. Whoa . . . Aylen looked into the quarters, dark from not having any lights on save for the light coming in from the hallway. She turned on the light switch next to the door. When the room lit up, she noticed an envelope on the bed. Aylen sighed and twisted her mouth, closing the door behind her. What now? Aylen grabbed the letter and read what was written on the envelope.

To Aylen.

TARA

Joshua and Tara lay in bed looking at the ceiling after the most dissatisfying sex that they had ever had. Tara grimaced while attempting to not show that to Joshua. His ego could be so fragile that if she said anything that was the least bit negative, he had a tendency to either clam up or get huffy and puffy about it. Of those two modes, she wasn't sure which was worse. It wasn't anything that was horrible, the sex; just something had been lost over their time of being with each other. Everything felt like routine, like a perfectly mastered, synchronized dance that they rehearsed over and over again. Even when they tried new things, it still felt more or less the same. Was there something *wrong* with them? Were they so used to each other, so used to being with each other, that sex had ultimately just lost its appeal? Joshua rolled over and checked his phone quietly as Tara lay in bed thinking about their sex life together. She hadn't even been finishing the last few times they had been intimate; she had just pretended so she didn't hurt his pride.

"So it looks like Dad is following my suggestion 'bout the funding."

Tara sat up and smiled. "Yeah? Look at that! Old man Quinn's coming around."

"Yeah," Joshua scoffed. "Now if only he'll just make me a position higher than corporal."

Tara sighed. Here they went again. "Give it time. You know how your father is, you just gotta prove to 'im you're fit to be sergeant."

"Yeah. . . . How much longer I gotta prove myself to him, though? How many missions I gotta survive to get promoted? Been in this outfit for a while now . . . I deserve some respect from people. I *deserve* to be sergeant by now. I'm his *son*, for fuck's sake."

"Babe, I love you, but think about it this way: Would you want a rank that you didn't earn?"

Joshua gave Tara a look. "You saying I haven't earned a new rank?" he asked, obviously starting to work up his own temper.

"Josh, you know that's not what I said."

"Nah, enlighten me, Tara. What haven't I done to earn a higher rank? Have I not survived or killed enough? Have I not kissed somebody's ass that I should've?"

"That isn't what I meant at all. Damn."

"What'd you mean then?"

"What I meant, *Josh*, was that just because your daddy is the leader, it doesn't mean you get special treatment! I've been in the Saints just as long as you have, but you don't see me complaining!" Tara snapped back. He shook his head and scoffed. He didn't have anything on that argument, so he decided to pout. She sighed and snuggled up with him, hating to see him like this. "Babe, look I'm not saying that you don't deserve to get a promotion. Look at Jared and Eric; they're two of the best, but they haven't risen above corporal. It's obviously nothing personal if not even *those two* are any ranks higher. This isn't exactly a normal army structure. There are only so many levels of command."

Josh only responded with silence. At this, Tara resigned and laid back into bed. She was far too tired to deal with his bullshit tonight.

GAIL

The slapping of skin permeated the room as two nude figures moved frantically. Gail breathed hard as the man behind her thrust his hips forward repeatedly, slamming into hers. She was bent over her bedside table and accidentally pushed her alarm clock and lamp to the floor with her arms. "Oooh, yes, yes, yes!" she squealed in delight. The rhythmic motion didn't cease for a second, even as she squirmed. "Don't . . . fucking . . . stop!"

A large, firm hand clasped her shoulder while the other one slapped her bottom, causing her to chuckle. The hand on her shoulder moved to her throat, pulling her up slightly and choking her. She smiled at this.

"Somebody missed me," Eric whispered into her ear before kissing it.

Gail giggled. "Mmm, parts of you . . ."

Eric forced her to the bed roughly, causing her to squeal in delight. She began to crawl away, but he pulled her to him before he positioned his muscular body behind her again and pushed her head down into her sheets. She gripped the sheets as hard as she could as he moved roughly behind her, into her. He pulled out momentarily to turn her onto her back, so the two faced each other, then slid back inside. Eric's cold blue eyes looked down at her, no sympathy whatsoever for how rough he was treating her. There was a moment where his body tensed and her body arched and she moaned. Silence came over them as the two caught their breaths before chuckling and kissing. Eric stood and threw away the condom, and Gail lit herself a blunt.

"Holy shit, I needed that," Gail said after taking the first puff.

Eric shrugged, heading back to the bed. "I live to serve." He plopped himself down beside her. She offered the joint to him and he accepted it and took a puff.

"*Nobody* on this base fucks like you, Greenfield." This got a chuckle from Eric before he took another puff of the joint.

"Why thank you." He handed her the blunt.

"Jesus . . . and it really doesn't weird you out I look just like my sister? I know she's the mother you younger Saints never had."

Eric scoffed. "Faith isn't my mother." Eric briefly looked away then looked at Gail with a wicked grin and felt her hip. "I *have* two mothers . . . and I hate both of them equally."

Gail smiled. "Lucky me, then."

Eric shrugged. "Plus, after how much she supported that deviant and Jessica's relationship, you are definitely my favorite of the Lancaster twins."

"Well, you *are* fucking me."

Eric smiled at this. "True."

Gail twisted her face. "You shouldn't have been suspended. Nobody decent to screw for months. So you killed a deviant kid, who gives a shit? World is better off without 'em, anyway."

Eric nodded as they traded the blunt yet again. "Rob was always soft on 'em. Luckily it doesn't seem your boy Abel has that problem."

"He doesn't. He's hated deviants since they put Denise in the hospital some years back. Never has forgiven them since. It only worsened after they killed her at Widow's Mountain."

"Yeah, about that . . . I wonder what you're doing here with *me* now that she's gone."

Gail did a double take. "'Scuse you?"

Eric grinned deviously. "Everyone sees how you hover over him. Unrequited feelings, perhaps?"

Gail rolled her eyes. "Don't be stupid. I don't have feelings for Abel. Not like that."

"*Not like that?*"

"No. He saved my life a few years back. I've considered him a close friend ever since. Not everybody wants to fuck each other the way you like to, Eric."

Eric chuckled. "I do believe I've hit a nerve."

Gail thought for a moment, taking a puff of her blunt. "What about you? I saw you hanging out with Jared's latest squeeze in the cafeteria."

Eric sighed at this. "You're more observant than I give you credit for."

"Well? You falling in love with *that* slut?"

Quite suddenly, Eric's hand wrapped around her throat. "She's not a slut."

"Now I think *I've* hit a nerve." There was the ringing of a blade as Eric put a knife at her throat, getting on top of her and leaning in toward her.

"No, she's not a slut. Not like you . . ." the boy said, biting her ear.

Gail chuckled. "Oooh?"

"She's a prude. A fact I'm counting on 'cause it's gonna make everything so. Much. Worse." Eric moved the blade away from Gail's throat and eased his grip.

"So . . . it's revenge on *him* finally, after all this time," Gail said, watching the knife as Eric twirled the blade with his fingers. He could kill her instantly if he wanted. Part of her liked that.

"More of a Plan B scenario." He grinned. "Kill two birds with one stone. Whatever happens with Emo Bitch, I'mma fuck over Monro either way. She's earned it."

"So confident you can get into every girl's pants, aren't you?" Gail smiled. Eric matched it, still twirling his blade.

"Got into yours, didn't I?"

"Poor girl. She has no idea how much of a manipulative bastard you are, does she?"

Eric stopped suddenly, looking like he was keeping himself from throwing the blade at the wall. Instead, he put the knife on the bedside table. "Would I be any good at it if she did?" Gail lifted an eyebrow. If he threw that knife and ruined her wall, she'd be livid. After some thought, Eric tilted his head. "Where is Emo Bitch, anyway? After their little spat he hasn't been around base."

Gail scoffed. "Is that the only reason you fuck me? Information?"

"If I were only fucking you for information, I'd fuck a better informant." Eric was annoyed by the question; she could tell by his tone.

Gail smiled. "The university. He's been there since he left. What are you gonna do, Eric? Kill him?"

Eric grinned slightly and licked his lips. "When the time is right, which will be when I see an opportunity."

"Good," Gail said calmly. Eric seemed slightly surprised at this reaction. "I hope you kill that little bastard once and for all. Hate his fucking guts."

Eric blinked for a second before chuckling. "Tell me how you really feel, Gail."

"It's about damn time." Gail shrugged. "A deviant doesn't belong in our ranks, doesn't matter how many successful missions he's done. If you're gonna kill him, I'll gladly look the other way,"

Eric smiled. "Such a cold-hearted bitch. I love it." He put his mouth to her breast, his hand between her thighs.

"Then get down there and *prove it*, little man," she said seductively. Eric chuckled and began kissing down her body.

"I'll break your hip, old woman," he said before putting his face down.

She laughed. "You're such an asshole!"

PESTILENCE

A clock ticked somewhere in the dark, whispering the hours away in a family home. It was more morning than night, a time most people weren't awake. A warm light was on in only one room in the otherwise dark, cell-like quarters, in the room of a little girl as her mother sat on the edge of her bed. There was a dreary stillness in the night as Emily Gilmore looked at her sleeping angel, Stacy. The little white-haired girl lay in bed holding her favorite stuffed animal. It was somewhere near 2:25 a.m. and drowsiness was finally creeping over Emily as she moved her long white hair out of her face. She couldn't sleep, though. Soon enough, Emily would be sent away from her daughter, all in the name of protecting her daughter's future.

Stacy was already almost eight. Eight, and she had never really seen the world outside the bunker. It was probably for the best, all things considered. The world outside was violent and cruel. Hell, even this bunker was violent and cruel. But eight years and locked in a cage, never knowing what it was like to live a normal life? That was the real crime of it all. Stacy would never go to school like a normal kid, play outside, have soccer games, go to school dances. Stacy would just be down here. The grim possibility of Stacy growing up to be a Devil's Deviant haunted Emily. The possibility that sooner or later, she would see the Rituals, see blood and death. It was hard to stomach. Emily continued running her fingers through Stacy's white hair. How much longer would she be able to protect her baby?

"You should come back to bed," a familiar voice behind her said in a hushed tone. She turned to see her husband standing in the doorway. "You look tired," Paul added. She sighed and stared at him, frowning.

"Sometimes I think to myself: Do I honestly think this war is gonna end soon? Before Stacy has to fight?" Emily briefly looked at her husband before turning her attention back to Stacy. "Sometimes I think . . . I ask . . . is—is it even worth fighting anymore?" She looked at her daughter. Paul came up behind Emily and rubbed her shoulders.

"Of course, it is, Em. How else are we gonna return to a normal life? How else is Stacy gonna be safe when she grows up?" Paul planted a kiss on Emily's cheek.

"Y-you aren't out there, Paul. . . . You don't feel it. We've been fighting *so* long . . . I—I hardly even know what we're even fighting for anymore. These back-alley deals, the constant back and forth with the Saints, it all just feels pointless." Emily sighed in despair. "I'm . . . getting tired. I just want our old lives back. The us *before* Project Suncloud . . . before we were even deviants . . ." Emily turned her attention to her husband. "I wish I could just erase it all, 'cept for Stacy."

"I get it." Paul nodded, being the sweetheart he was. "I know you don't think I do but, I get it."

Emily sighed, then laid her head on his chest. "The truth is, even if we win this war . . . I don't think we can ever go back to how things used to be, Paul," she said. "I'm scared this nightmare will never end. I'm scared I'll never be a normal person again after all this . . . if it ever ends."

Paul hugged Emily in silence. "It'll end. Deviants *will* be able to live normal lives again, and one day you and I will get that suburban house we talked about when we were kids." Emily smiled sadly and clutched her husband tighter, closer. "White picket fence, normal jobs, everything. Stacy will attend a good school, you'll be a soccer mom, I'll mow the lawn, we'll have barbecues in our yard . . ." Paul's warm voice told her. Emily couldn't help but let loose some tears from her eyes. "And every morning we'll wake up in a sun-filled room, and we'll be happy." Paul ran his fingers through her hair. Emily sniffled as she hugged her husband. "You're overworked. You need time off, Em." She nodded, still keeping it close to his chest.

"I know . . ."

"Maybe I should start doing more for the cause."

Emily was caught off guard by his statement and lifted her head from his chest. "Like what?"

"I don't know. Start going on missions in your place? *Something*, you know?"

Emily sobered up from her sadness at the thought. "Paul—"

"No, I'm serious. I think I should get more involved in the cause."

"Paul, you *know* you can't control your ability. Suppose you hurt somebody on our side, or end up getting yourself in some sort of trouble, or wind up *dead?*"

"Em—"

"No, I'm serious, Paul. I don't want you to get hurt."

"I can learn to control it."

"It's been *ten years* and you're still not able to control it. What makes you think you'll be able to control it now?"

"Em, there's a *reason* I'm called Death. The least I can do is somehow do my part for our side," Paul whispered. Emily pouted and pulled away. "You're getting overworked, and I'm the man of the house. Out there, I'm a joke, a weakling who can't protect his family. All because I don't go on missions. People never look at the reasons why, all they see is me not doing my part. They think I'm about as useful as a Brainless that can't move."

Emily looked at Paul, scrunching up her face. She didn't like that analogy.

"I *need* to help out in some way." Paul frowned. A part of Emily knew he was right. It couldn't have been easy for him among the others, especially with the majority of them being so calloused to the horrors of this war. But with how dangerous and uncontrollable Paul's power was, it just simply didn't make sense for him to join the fighting. The unpredictability of battle was scary enough, but the unpredictability of his power in the midst of battle was even scarier. The question of his involvement in the war was a double-edged sword.

Emily sighed. "I'll think about it."

Paul took a moment to register this and then sighed. "Wanna go to bed?"

"Yeah." Emily got up and went with her husband to the bedroom. "I love you."

"I love you too," Paul responded. The two shared a tender kiss. Emily briefly frowned as they pulled away. That was going to be one of her last kisses from her husband for a while. She would probably leave for the mission before he woke up.

AYLEN

Aylen jumped into the icy water and felt the cold rush through her as fast as red wine through a paper towel. For a moment, she stayed submerged and felt her hair swirl wildly in the deafening silence of the lake. After a couple of days of doing this, the ice water was more of a welcome, soothing rather than a burden. While submerged, she thought briefly of Jared. It had been a few days since her encounter with Eric and going back to her room to find the note in Jared's room that told her he was staying at the college temporarily, rather than the Saints' base. He had run away from her, she supposed. Not that it mattered anymore. Jared had very quickly put himself on her list of least favorite people within a very short span of time. He wasn't even answering her texts anymore. She was done with the bullcrap. The next time she saw him, she was determined to give him a piece of her mind.

She rose to the top of the water and kept swimming.

"Come on, Monro, let's go! Move, move, move, move!" Gabriel yelled. She finished swimming out of the lake and came up to dry land. Here it came, the part she constantly failed. "Come on, Monro, let's do it!"

Aylen looked up at the rope. No matter how many times she tried to climb it, the damn thing was still intimidating. She jumped as energetically as she could and began to pull herself up it very slowly. Each time her arms pulled at the rope, they trembled with exhaustion. Aylen wasn't exactly a muscular girl, but after this training, there wasn't any doubt in her mind that she would end up looking like Brunhilda the warrior woman. Keeping all of her thoughts in line, she focused on climbing, pulling herself higher. By this point, she wasn't sure how high she had gone, only that she had higher to go.

"Keep going, Monro! You can do it!" a familiar voice called from below. It wasn't Gabriel's voice. Aylen looked down to see Eric down below, right next to the captain, and in her surprise she lost her grip. Aylen panicked for a moment and felt herself slide down the rope. *No!*

Aylen clenched her fists and stopped her fall, regaining her foothold on the rope and then looking up at the remaining length she had to go. What the hell was Eric doing here? That creep. He probably just said that to make her fall, huh? Evil son of a bitch. She measured in her mind just how much more she had to travel. It looked like maybe she lost two feet in that brief fall. No matter, though; she would conquer this rope. She would! She would show Jared *and* Eric that they picked the wrong girl to mess with. She would show them. She began climbing again, her arms beginning to feel like noodles; they felt like they could give in at any second. She was too high, though, way too high to fall now. If she fell now, she could break bones. If she fell now, she could die. At the thought, an instinct came over her. One not much different from what she felt during every Brainless encounter she'd had. Adrenaline filled her as she kept climbing. Sweat dripped from every pore and the fire within her began to roar.

"Come on . . . mothertrucker," Aylen gritted through her teeth. "You're my . . . Behemoth, huh?" she continued. "Pretending you're a . . . badass . . . when you're just a . . . big wuss, huh?" She was almost at the top where the wooden ledge was. Almost there. In the back of her mind, she couldn't help but laugh. She was beginning to sound like Jared. "A big . . . wuss . . . ass . . . crap."

"Way to go, Monro!" Gabriel yelled happily from the ground as Aylen swung herself over the wooden ledge. When she let go of the rope, she collapsed. She had never worked that hard in her life to do anything. Her body was numb and her lungs burned as she rested her head against the railing on the platform. Then she turned around and looked through the railing bars toward the ground. Holy crap! Good thing she didn't stop. Aylen's eyes widened as she looked at the height she had conquered. It was at least thirty feet off the ground, but from here she felt like it was much higher. A smile came over her face. She beat her Behemoth.

She pulled herself up and looked up at the trees surrounding her. Through the tall forest trees, she could see the Saint Organization's base in its entirety. She could see the ocean on the horizon.

She did it. She actually did it.

Aylen was now not just going to be a soldier, but she was going to be one of the best. She was going to have the adventure of her lifetime. Aylen giggled to herself from the happiness and realization of the moment. From the beginning, she was never destined to have the boring life of a doctor; instead, she was always meant to have *this* life. A life of adventure, excitement, and thrills. She was going to be like the heroes in all those books she used to read. This was *her* story, and *she* was going to beat the bad guys in the end. It was her destiny.

After a moment of basking in her newfound glory, Aylen lowered herself down via the nearby stairs to find Gabriel and Eric waiting for her below.

"What's *he* doing here?" Aylen asked her instructor while indicating Eric with her head.

"Captain Webster's been summoned by General Quinn to discuss the intel on the latest DD movements," Eric said, sounding official instead of his usual mocking.

She looked at Gabriel, who nodded. "Get dressed in some clean clothes and meet me in front of General Quinn's office. We'll continue training another time."

Aylen nodded and proceeded to do as he told her while giving Eric a look. He glanced back at her with a mischievous grin as she passed him. They hadn't started their training yet, but a brief thought slipped into Aylen's mind: Why had Eric wanted to wait a week before teaching her how to use a sword? Was he up to something? She shook the thought off as she went to the showers and changed. By the time she finished and made her way to General Quinn's waiting room, she found Captain Webster waiting patiently. There was the sound of muffled voices in the office. Aylen couldn't quite make out what was being said, only that it sounded like a female and a male talking. Suddenly, the door opened.

"It's been a pleasure doing business with you, Mr. Quinn," the woman standing in the doorway said. Then she closed the door and looked forward, giving Aylen a good view of her features. The woman was Asian and wore a woman's business suit, her long, thin black hair draping down her back. Captain Webster looked like someone had just slapped his mother across the face as he watched her cross the room. "*Captain* Webster, I presume," the woman said to Gabriel, as if it was part of an inside joke.

The woman then looked at Aylen, who stared right back at her. In a brief glancing moment as they observed each other face-to-face, time seemed to slow. She didn't know this woman, but something didn't feel right. Something about her was . . . *rotten*, to the core. The woman's black eyes seemed like they were picking Aylen apart piece by piece. There was a familiarity between the two, though they had never met. A feeling like they knew each other all too well. A spider staring at a fly, a sun taunting a black hole. The woman and Aylen briefly sized each other up before the Asian woman politely smiled and nodded her head, her gaze like ice piercing into Aylen's soul, freezing her veins and sending a chill down her spine. It was like staring into the face of death itself.

"Come in, Gabriel," General Quinn called from inside the office. Gabriel and Aylen walked into the office. Aylen sat down in the back chair while Gabriel sat in front. "You're probably wondering why I—"

"What the hell was *Commander Li* doing here?" the captain interrupted, obviously feeling fire in his veins. The general took a moment to process the blunt question before calmly opening his mouth.

"She was discussing the terms of the new agreement the Saints have with the UWF."

"Which is?" Gabriel asked sharply.

Abel paused for a moment and nodded his head. "Now, Gabe, before I explain this, I need to put things into perspective for you as far as how the situation looks these days. We're low on supplies, our funds almost nonexisten—"

"Oh Jesus, Abe, tell me you didn't!"

"There was no way we were going to last with our own money. All of our benefactors are long gone, we don't have any more friends in the black market, and we've taken a lot of hard hits. I've merely done what is right."

"What's the exact deal?" Captain Webster said quickly, his tone sharper than Aylen had ever heard before and his breaths shallow.

"That we work with them to bring down the deviants and they'll handle the funding."

"Great, so basically not only do we kiss their ass now, we bend over when they tell us to?"

"We don't have enough money to keep going on our own!" Abel yelled. "It's either this or the Saint Organization loses the war by forfeit!"

"Yeah, well. By getting in bed with the UWF, we aren't exactly winning either." Gabriel breathed out and leaned in "Abel . . . don't you realize they only need the slightest reason now to take complete control of our organization? To *destroy* everything we've built?" Gabriel shook his head. "Why didn't you consult me about this? Hell, the whole counsel should've been consulted about thi—"

"*Because it wasn't your choice, Webster,*" Abel said forcefully. "It was *mine. I'm* the leader here, not *you!* I had to make a decision for the good of everyone—"

"*You made it because you lost your spine—*"

"Rob trusted *me* with the Saints! *Not you!*" General Quinn yelled. Gabriel's face dropped. "Fall in line, soldier," Abel added. The tension between the two men lingered as they stared at each other. Aylen wasn't sure, but this looked and felt like the final nail in the coffin of a camaraderie that had lasted for ages. In the eyes of both men, the last bits of friendship seemed to crumble as they looked at each other disapprovingly.

"All right. Come on, Aylen, we're leaving," Gabriel said while standing and heading for the door. Aylen hesitantly stood up, feeling the thick tension in the room.

"Wh-where are you going?" General Quinn asked gruffly. "We still need to discuss the deviants'—"

"Like you said, you're the leader," Gabe said, turning around to glare at him. "You can handle it." He walked out of the general's office, and Aylen rushed to follow.

"*If y-you leave now, you'll never get your old position back!*" Abel yelled as they walked away. Aylen looked back at the general, who was staring at Gabriel's back. At that moment, Aylen did not see a powerful man; she saw a lonely and worried man. Considering that he was to lead her, that concept frightened her.

ERIC

Eric Greenfield walked into the Forest of Sorrows. The dying light of day illuminated the trees in a purplish-blue color as his shoes crunched on fallen leaves. After walking consistently straight past the training grounds with the rope that Gabriel liked to put new recruits through, Eric arrived at the creek, and he stared at the water for a moment, remembering. He closed his eyes, then looked up at the dusk sky, listening to the sounds of the rushing water.

"I don't know why I still come here," he said out loud, with the same bitter smile that he always wore. He looked around at the forest. "How many times have I come to this spot? Long after everything with you happened. *Our* spot . . ." Eric looked down at the creek. "Still remember all the picnics we used to have out here. Your funny li'l—god, what'd you call 'em? The *chippies* you used to make. Tasted like shit but I ate 'em anyway." Eric laughed a little. Then he scoffed and shook his head. He thought for a moment before sitting down, looking at the familiar trees, breathing in the pine air tinged with sea salt. "Ya know, I've fucked other girls out here. Wonder if you ever saw any of that . . . even fucked *Gail* out here once." He chuckled softly, then he sniffed in the air and felt his smile wear down. "Didn't really work, though. Still come out here . . . like it'll change a goddamn thing . . ." He frowned. "I don't love you anymore. Not even sure I hate you anymore either . . . dunno what I feel about you these days."

Eric sighed, folding his lip. "I *will* tell you who I do hate, though. Your *precious* . . . little deviant bitch, Jared." His smile started to return. "It's like every time I try to forget about what happened, his *face* just reminds me of you. . . . It's *his* fault you're dead . . . and I don't think I'll ever get past it. Not till I get my revenge on that sorry sack of shit." His breath shuddered slightly, his eyes moving frantically as he rocked back and forth a little. His breath came heavier and he shook his head, his smile widening, eyes beginning to strain. "I-it's not like I even care about you anymore. Just—I can't feel *anything* since I saw you *die in his arms.* It's been years and *I've been numb!*" The smile disappeared from his face completely. He licked his lips, then shut his eyes tight. "I just want . . . to *feel* something again . . . other than resentment . . . and hate." He swallowed and felt his energy drop. His face trembled. Tears threatened to come out, but it was rare they ever did. "I've turned into this—this *thing* I don't recognize since . . . I'm so lost without you—I don't— Everything's just gotten so *fucking* dark and . . ." Eric wanted to sob but couldn't quite do it. Everything in him wanted to cry his eyes out, but he couldn't. His body never allowed him that kind of emotion. Not anymore. He was frozen.

"I can't see . . ." Eric stopped himself, finding the words caught in his throat. Memories of the only person he ever loved flooded his head. His body sore and covered in blood to only find her already dead, her limp body in Jared's arms, her head leaning the wrong way, Jared crying over her corpse. The things the deviants did to her, they . . .

Eric felt a part of himself deaden. "I've become my *mother's* son." He glared at the sky, a tear beginning to drop down his cheek and his lips trembling slightly. "And I'm telling you like you care." Eric thought for a moment, then wiped the tear away. What a joke. All that for a single tear. He sniffed in and cracked his neck before nodding. "I'll be waiting for the right time, but when I get my revenge . . . I hope you watch. I hope it breaks your heart."

He stood. "Think this is the last time I'll ever come out here. Goodbye, Jessica." With that, he left the picnic area near the creek, never to return.

THE MANAGER

The Westbrook factory manager filled out paperwork while humming a happy little tune. He was a thin man with greased-back hair and drooping earlobes that often got compared to Dumbo. He was a man that enjoyed the simple pleasures of life: He was a father on his way to becoming a grandfather. His other child was just finishing high school and was expected to get himself into university soon enough. The man looked for a moment through his thick glasses at an older picture of his family, taken when the kids were still kids and his wife still had the vibrancy of her early thirties about her. A time when both he and his wife didn't have wrinkles and didn't have to worry about aches and pains in the middle of the night. The picture was of the four of them at the park, where they had enjoyed a lovely picnic with peanut butter and jelly sandwiches and fresh watermelon that melted in their mouths. That was a good day.

The manager looked over the numbers detailing the production of the new weapons the factory workers were working on. The eggheads at the lab were coming up with some truly strange and terrifying things, things the factory manager hoped in the back of his mind would never be used on other human beings. Things that rivaled the enemy's weapons in the Anthrodi War. The manager turned back to his family and wife. At the end of every work week, UWF transports took him and select others home to Salutem for their weekend. He needed it. It would be a relief from the crazy week it had been. Security had been tightened lately, something about fears of a DD attack on one of the factories. The manager disliked a lot of the new protocols that were put into place due to this slight bit of panic from UWF headquarters. Westbrook was a desolate place in the middle of a snowy mountain range. The Devil's Deviants would have to be either desperate or ballsy to venture all the way out here. The manager just wanted to see his wife again. With all the paranoia around this place lately, the entire environment was uncom—

A low rumble shook the building and all the items on the manager's desk began to rattle toward the edge, then fall off. Suddenly, files began to drop from the shelves and the lights flickered on and off.

Boom!

A sound as loud as a cannon burst. It made the ground shake. Screams that almost sounded like people on a rollercoaster rushed through the building. There was something terrible about the screams, shrill and perfectly synchronized.

They pierced the ears even as they traveled farther away. Terrified, the manager looked out his window onto the factory floor to see what was going on. A large object protruded from the ground and slithered out of sight, deeper into the factory, at a terrifying speed. Whatever it was, it was the size of some of the largest machines they had. Machine gun fire ensued and the manager looked at the source of the noise. Freakish-looking men and women were climbing out of the hole and opening fire on the factory workers, gunning down every person they saw. Impossible! What were the deviants doing *here*? Why was *this* the factory they were attacking?

He heard a sound behind him and turned to see a beautiful woman with snow-colored hair. She wore a black tank top and military pants and boots. Menacing tattoos danced up her arms, and she wore an equally menacing facial expression.

"*Wh-wha-what do you want?*" The manager cowered, backing away from the woman. Her skin faded into something metallic and chrome, and her arm morphed into what looked to be a blade. She stepped toward him.

"Your life," the woman said simply. He had to get away, he had to—

The woman rushed to him and stabbed him in the gut. Iron-tasting liquid filled his mouth as he stared at the woman's cold, metallic face. She pulled her arm out of his gut and the man fell to his knees, but not before the woman spun and decapitated him in one fell motion.

EPISODE 16

Red Snow Part I

COMMANDER LI

It happened. The attack they were anticipating finally happened. Commander Li's heels clacked through the lonely hallways of the Department of Justice building at the UWF headquarters. It was surprising, the factory that the Devil's Deviants chose: the Westbrook factory. While it wasn't the farthest from Salutem, it certainly wasn't around the corner either. It seemed the security measures the UWF took to secure the five factories weren't enough, though. What the hell happened? The commander sighed as she entered her destination. The room was dark aside from the blue light emanating from computer screens. Men and women sat at their desks monitoring the flashing data, and facing the largest screen was a familiar silhouette. Here went nothing. Commander Li hesitantly headed toward General Hawkings.

"Looks like you were right . . ." General Hawkings said, looking at the screen ahead of him. Commander Li followed his gaze. Her eyes widened. Green dots all over the facility's satellite image. *Green* dots. Not a single blue dot. "It's worse than we thought." How . . . how were the DDs able to amass such a force so quickly up there?

"Any communications? Do we know what they're looking for up there?"

"None yet. It would seem they've killed every human at the factory, so I'm guessing they're not looking to negotiate." General Hawkings sighed. "You have less than forty-eight hours, Commander."

Commander Li looked over quickly. "*Less than?*"

"To fix this . . . before I drag Serious 2 into this mess. The DDs have gone too far this time."

Commander Li swallowed and nodded her head. "Yes, sir." With that, Hawkings left the surveillance room. Serious 2? Not a chance she'd let those clowns get ahold of this. Breathing in nervously, Melyssa Li turned back toward the screen. Less than forty-eight hours . . . and she had some ideas.

AYLEN

Aylen awoke with a stuffy nose and felt a chill seep through her covers. It was darker and mistier than usual outside and there were puddles of ice strewn out on the ground. Winter was upon them. Luckily, Gabriel had stopped having her run the obstacle course, which she was grateful for. At this point, that lake part would have been torture. She packed on the layers and went to train, all of which consisted of weapon logistics and hand-to-hand combat. The day moved quickly, but that was perhaps because of the fact that today was the day she was to meet with Eric, and that made her nervous.

Training with Gabriel went by so fast she could barely remember what they had gone over if someone had asked her. When the captain dismissed her, she made her way to the blade training area. The sun peeked out more at this time of day as it began to set on the forest. Aylen saw her breath puff out from her mouth in a cloud as she walked through the cold landscape. For a brief moment, she wondered if there would be snow soon.

When Aylen arrived at the blade training area, she found Eric sitting on the railing of the barrier. Despite the fact that she wasn't very good at blades, this area of the base was her favorite. It was outside the main base and very close to the cliff that dropped into the ocean, so the smell of sea salt filled the air and a light blue tennis court-like material covered the ground—and it was even slightly larger than a tennis court. On either side were six dummies on poles that were torn from people slicing into them this week. A large white circle in the middle indicated where Saints could practice sparring with training blades. There was a protective railing on the back of the course and on its left side. On the latter side, where Eric was sitting, the trees crouched in low, and not too far behind was a fallen trunk. Eric sat in the beautiful sunlight, wearing that cocksure grin of his while keeping his sea-green eyes squinted. Suddenly, he sent something flying toward her, which she awkwardly caught between her chest and her forearms: It was a training sword.

"Let's see what the old hack taught you so far."

Eric jumped off the railing and onto the ground. He grabbed a training sword for himself and whirled it around as he settled into the attack position. "You ready?" A very different sort of smirk spread across his face. This one frightened Aylen more than his usual. With this one, his eyes widened like a cat about to pounce on a mouse. There was bloodlust in his eyes that shook Aylen deeply. She assumed the position that Captain Webster had taught her.

Thwack.

The swords sounded as Eric knocked hers down and put his sword right to her neck, stopping before he hit her throat. "Dead. Now try to attack me," Eric said. There was an odd intensity and seriousness about him. That bloodthirsty grin was still strewn on his face as he pulled his sword into position. Aylen matched him, and they twisted around in a circle. She thought she saw an opportunity and went in for a stab. Immediately, Eric parried the strike and put his sword at her belly. "Dead. Try again." Eric flashed that grin as he turned his back to her and then turned back around in position. She tried to strike again, and Eric knocked the blade out of her hand and backhanded her across the face with his free hand. Aylen went down and looked up angrily at Eric, who twisted his sword around as he got back into position.

"*What the hell was that for?*" she snapped, channeling her inner Jared. Eric put his training sword on his shoulder and stood up straight.

"First rule of modern sword fighting: There are no rules."

That douche. That colossal douche. Aylen would show him. She picked up her training blade and Eric put one arm behind his back. With the fury of the hounds of hell, she lunged at him. The blond boy easily stepped out of the way of her attack. "Whoa," Eric chuckled. Aylen then came in for a side swipe, which he blocked. She continued the assault with the different sword strikes Gabriel taught her as fast as she humanly could. The sound of the training swords clashing turned from a slow drumbeat to a fast-paced snare as she grew angrier.

"Not bad. Footing is a little off, though." Eric was enjoying this, wasn't he? Aylen growled from frustration, giving it her all. "Try to keep me from anticipating when your next attack will be!" he shouted over the clashing of the training blades. She went in for a stab and he tripped her in a barely visible movement. Before she could get her bearings and realize what happened, Eric's wooden sword was pointed at her neck.

"What'd we learn?"

"That you think very highly of yourself?"

"No, you knew that already," he said, leaning down toward her. Instead of offering a hand, he tapped her nose. "Don't get angry in a fight, it'll kill you." He smirked before standing upright and throwing his training sword aside. "Lesson's done for the day. You're pretty worn out," he said while walking away. With that, his back was turned, and Aylen saw her opportunity to get back at him for that sucker slap. She grabbed her training sword and charged for him.

Swish.

In a moment, Eric had a real sword at Aylen's neck. Somewhere in the distance, she heard half of her training sword hit the ground. The look on Eric's face was different from the smug look that he usually wore. Instead of a smile strewn across his lips, he was stone-faced, unfaltering. His eyes pierced her soul, flashing in the dying light as if turning from a nice shade of green to one of ice blue. She felt the cold steel of the blade and how sharp it was. He breathed in from his nose as the two stared each other down. Aylen wasn't sure if Eric would slice her throat. At this very moment, she did not doubt it.

"If you want me to keep teaching you, I suggest you *don't* do that again."

There was an iciness to the statement as Eric stared at Aylen, lightly pressing the blade into her skin. A cold wind picked up and blew through their hair. A cool sweat dripped from Aylen's brow. He could lop her head off if he wanted to. One fell swoop and she knew she'd be history. There was a reason he was considered the best swordsman in the Saint Organization. His speed perhaps even rivaled Jared's, and Eric was a normal human being.

Eric turned around suddenly with his sword on his shoulder and walked away. "If you still want to learn, be back here tomorrow, same time. I'll be waiting," he said while walking. Aylen took a deep breath in and felt herself shudder. *That* was scary.

As Aylen made her way to the cafeteria for dinner, she still felt the same sense of terror as when Eric pointed that sword at her. He could've seriously killed her, couldn't he? She gave all she had in that little mock sword fight and Eric just toyed with her the whole time, getting amusement from the experience. Aylen walked into the cafeteria, got her food, and sat down by herself, thinking. Eric kicked her ass. Granted, that wasn't hard considering her skills at swordsmanship. Still, though, he *kicked her ass*. There was no contest there. It did sound, however, like he was trying to give her some pointers on how to train. Who knows? Maybe he actually was trying to teach her how to wield a sword. Aylen thought about it for a second. Even though the sucker slap probably was enjoyable for that piece of crap, he had a point. In real life, no fighting was fair. Was she expecting the deviants to play nice in a fight to the death? No. Why should Eric practice with her like someone who would? He also had another good point: Fighting angry could get her killed. Still . . . messed up ways to show that to Aylen. Maybe, though, that was how those lessons needed to be taught. Aylen decided. Even if Eric was an asshole, she would go back the next day.

"Hey, Aylen!" she heard a familiar voice call. Aylen turned her head out of curiosity to find her three former classmates sitting at the table next to her. Jonathan was the one who called her, his hand still in the air and a dumb smile on his crooked face. She was wondering how those three were doing. After surviving the relentless onslaught of Morgan's harassment, and even after training alone with Gabriel, she felt a sort of camaraderie with the three. She studied their faces: All of them were smiling at her, although Marie's smile was more one of tolerance. "Get over here, homegirl! We haven't seen you in forever!" Jonathan beckoned.

"Yeah! Sit here!" Adrien added. Aylen grinned and went to sit with them. It was nice to know that she had other friends in the Saints than Jared. *Jared.* That was a name that crept back into the forefront of her mind. She hadn't seen him in a while. Even if last she saw him they were fighting, she still wondered how he was doing, or for crying out loud *what* exactly he was doing. They hadn't spoken at all and she had begun to worry.

Jonathan chuckled. "Yo, think I speak for everyone when I say: Mad props on what you did to Morgan, dude. We *still* can't get over it."

Aylen uneasily laughed in response. "Thanks?"

"It was awesome! You made his face into *ground beef!* Literally, nobody saw that coming," Adrien said, chuckling while chewing his food.

Marie tapped Aylen's back, an oddly soft look about her eyes with the ghost of a smile on her face. "Good job, man."

"Thanks, I guess."

Adrien leaned in. "By the way . . . who was that guy who came in to hug you afterward?"

"Guy?" Aylen swallowed, blanking out for an instant.

"You know, the guy with all the piercings and tattoos? You guys hugged pretty tight there. Is he your boyfriend?"

Jared wishes, Aylen thought in the back of her mind.

"Nah. Can't be. Gotta be her gay best friend or something," Jonathan blurted out. Adrien gave him a look.

"His *name* is Jared Griffin. He's the resident *deviant* at the base here. She and him are best friends, man," Marie said almost mockingly while glancing at Aylen. She immediately stuffed food into her mouth. *Oh yeah*, Aylen thought, *Marie hates deviants.*

"Whoa, what? *That* guy's a deviant? I always thought they were supposed to look . . . freakier."

"Some do look freakier. He just looks normal, if that's what you can call it," Marie said spitefully. Aylen shot her a look.

Jonathan's eyes darted between them. "But he's, like, just a best friend, right? Y-you guys aren't dating or nothing, are you?" Adrien chuckled and rolled his eyes.

"No," Aylen smiled shyly while giggling. Jonathan was about as transparent as an open window.

Marie cleared her throat before giving Jonathan a look that could scare the spots off a dalmatian. She gave Aylen a softer look. "Anyway, how's training with Captain Webster? He treatin' ya right?"

Aylen nodded. "It's good, he's a really good teacher."

"That's good. Yeah, Esmeralda ain't so bad herself," Marie said before taking a sip of her drink. "Like her as a teacher. You can tell she gives a shit 'bout her students."

Jonathan seemed to light up. "Oh, you know what I heard? Captain Webster and her are a thing, I think."

Adrien put down his burger. "*What?*"

"Yeah, yeah, you seen those bruises and welts? Well from what I've heard, get this: Morgan and her used to be a thing first, right? But they broke up and Esmeralda has welts on her face now, supposedly 'cause of him, right? Word is that it's 'cause she was cheating on him with Captain Webster."

"Where'd you hear that load of stupid shit?" Marie asked.

"Dunno. Word just gets around, ya know?"

Adrien picked his burger back up and began chewing thoughtfully. "Wonder if it's true."

"Hell no," Aylen said. She shook her head, not liking that rumor at all. "Captain Webster is a *respectful* and *honorable* man, he wouldn't do that. I refuse to believe it. Even if it *was* Morgan, I don't think Captain Webster would do something like that."

Adrien's eyes then looked over to somewhere. "Ya never know with some people." Aylen looked in the direction he was looking to see that he was eyeing Brenden as he walked across the room. For a moment, the exchange of glances between the two men made things slightly awkward. Adrien's face darkened and intensified, and Brenden's glance looked like one of resentment or embarrassment. Then Aylen noticed something different about Brenden: his eye. What the hell happened to his eye? The scar tissue surrounding it looked pretty bad and the eye itself had become discolored and cloudy.

Jonathan looked around at the other recruits, seemingly unaware of Adrien's distraction. "So, uh . . . I found a *guy* here at the base." The awkward silence being disrupted caught the other three off guard.

"What?" Aylen asked stupidly.

"I found a *guy*, guys," Jonathan said, lowering his voice.

Marie chuckled. "Didn't know you swung that way."

Jonathan rolled his eyes. "No, guys, I *found* a *guy*."

Adrien bit into a fry and shook his head "Saying it a different way isn't gonna make us figure out what you're saying, Jon."

At this, Jonathan dug into his pocket and pulled out a bag that looked like it was filled with dead brussels sprouts while trying to keep it hidden in his pocket. Marie and Adrien shook their heads and laughed, but Aylen squinted her eyes. Was that what she thought it was?

Marie snorted. "Weed? You kidding me? What you think this is, man? Grade school?"

"Keep your voice down, dude!" Jonathan muttered through his teeth.

"Where'd you get it?" Aylen asked out of curiosity.

"Like I said, I found a guy! Reasonably priced too. It's not the highest qual-ity, but hey, it isn't super dank or anything. Not gonna be killin' anyone with the smell," he said quietly. "You guys wanna light up?"

Marie scoffed. "With you? Nah, man, I'll pass. You'll probably *drool* all over the fuckin' thing."

Adrien and Marie both laughed. Aylen tilted her head. That seemed like an inside joke she wasn't in on. Jonathan barely blinked an eye before turning to the laughing redhead nearby. "What about you, Adrien? You down?"

Adrien shook his head, easing up on laughter. "N-no, no thanks dude, I'm not really all that into pot."

"I'll do it," Aylen blurted.

At this, the entire table looked her way. Adrien laughed a little and shook his head, and Marie looked like she smelled a skunk. "*Really?* With *him?* You kiddin', mamacita?" Marie asked, lifting an eyebrow and pointing to Jon.

Aylen shrugged. "I've never done it before. I figure why not?" All four recruits looked at each other. Marie, in particular, looked like she was still pro-cessing things. Jonathan, though, donned a huge grin, nodding his head.

"Sick. Wanna go right now?"

"Yeah, sure."

Jonathan got up excitedly, and Aylen began to wonder what she had gotten herself into yet again.

Marie chuckled. "Hey, Aylen . . . he flashes his tiny shit at ya, I'll do to him what you did to Morgan, man. En mi madre, no mercy, man. I got yo back."

Aylen blushed a little. "Thanks, Marie."

She followed Jonathan to the roof of the main building of the base, and they sat on the edge that overlooked the ocean. The moon was round and the air was chilly, making the night a sort of magical one in a strange way. Her thoughts turned to Jared again. What was he doing at this very moment? Would he care that Aylen was about to smoke weed for the first time? Probably not. Something was nice about that thought, though. How much did she care about him? To always think about him with every chance her mind wandered. It was somewhat painful to think about, how she was desperately and constantly wondering about what he was doing when he was probably doing other girls or something. How pathetic was she? He wasn't even interested in her, and here she was constantly drooling over him.

Jonathan crushed the weed into a pipe he had on him and lit it. He took a puff of it and blew the smoke out, then handed the pipe to Aylen, who looked at it like a strange foreign object. What the hell was she gonna do with this?

"Man, you weren't kidding when you said you've never smoked pot before, huh?" Jonathan laughed. "Here, lemme show you. Put your hand like this. On the pipe." The boy smiled while showing Aylen the proper hand positioning. She put the pipe to her mouth and Jonathan put the lighter into the bowl. "All right, when I light this, take a deep breath in." Aylen obeyed his directions, and Jonathan lit it. In moments, the smoke viciously attacked her throat. She coughed heavily. "*Yeeeeaaah!* That's how ya do it!"

While struggling with the burn in her throat, Aylen looked out at the ocean. It was so peaceful, so quiet as the waves crashed onto the rocks down below.

Aylen breathed in the salty air mixed with weed smoke before disrupting the quiet moment. "You sure we should be doing this up here?"

"Oh, yeah," Jonathan said after a puff. "At around this time, about nine o'clock-ish, the cameras on this roof always turn off for an hour. Some sorta glitch in the system that nobody has been able to figure out for a while now."

Aylen looked over at a nearby camera. "How do you know that?"

"I've heard stories."

Aylen turned her head to the boy. "Stories?"

"You know . . . *stories*." Jonathan began making crude gestures.

Aylen twisted her mouth. "Oh, I get it."

"This is a favorite spot of people our age here. I bet if you got a black light up here you'd find all sorts of nasty stuff." He chuckled. Aylen ignored that thought and looked out toward the sea. To think . . . out there used to be an entire world's worth of people, and now it was just the people in Salutem. To think that one big, stupid war could do that to the population of the world. How sad.

Jonathan took another hit from his pipe. "So, uh, I don't see you around the barracks anymore. Where they got you nowadays?"

"With Jared, at his quarters," Aylen replied.

The awkward boy looked panicked for a second. "Oh, uh, is he, uh, okay with us being out here like this?"

She chuckled. "No, not like that. He and I aren't together. I mean . . ." she sighed. "It's not like that."

"But I take it you wish it was?"

Aylen flinched. "*What?*" she asked in shock. "I—I never said that."

He shrugged and handed her the pipe silently. "Tell me more about him." Jonathan's smile was kind as he looked out toward the ocean. Aylen sighed. This boy could see right through her, couldn't he?

"W-well, he saved my life. Twice. And . . . and he's been there for me for a while," she said. She took a hit off the pipe and began to cough.

Jonathan patted her back and let out a hearty chuckle. "I get ya. He saved ya, and now you got feelings for him, right?"

"I mean . . ." Aylen began, but found herself at a loss for words. This kid had her pegged, didn't he? There was silence.

"What's he like?"

"He's just . . .different. He isn't like other guys. He's got a very peculiar view of the world. He's funny. He's smart. Without the piercings, he's pretty handsome. But *no one* gives him the time of day. No one gives him the chances he deserves. Everyone just sees this intimidating goth, or punk, or whatever. He's someone that's been crapped on a lot, ya know? And . . ." Aylen thought for a moment. About how he said he was a fucking monster. "I sense his pain. It's a pain I wanna soothe. I wanna make him smile. I don't know anyone more than him that deserves to smile. H-he saved my life. I owe him that much, ya know?"

"So . . . you relate to his pain in some sort of way, and you feel obligated to help him. And in helping him, you might relieve some of your own." Jon took another puff of the pipe, looking over at her. Aylen was embarrassed. Jonathan shrugged, taking another hit. "Or maybe it's just the weed talking." He offered Aylen the pipe. Why was she telling this boy so much? What was it about him that made it seem so normal and comforting to reveal such private info? Was weed that powerful of a drug? "So, if you dig this guy this much, why haven't you told him?"

Aylen took a hit and felt slightly lightheaded. "I kinda did . . ."

"Kinda?"

"I—I don't know, I told him I care about him. I—I . . ." Aylen trailed off and sighed. "I guess I didn't really. I don't know, we had a fight over nothing not too long back and I'm not even sure if he feels anything for me, honestly. If anything . . . it feels like he hates my guts." She sighed. She was spilling her secrets in a way she didn't even know she had in her. Maybe Jonathan said the right thing about her wanting to soothe Jared's pain to ease her own. Jared obviously had some issues, but admittedly so did Aylen. She knew she couldn't fix Jared or change him, but she felt like he needed someone. Someone to help him sleep at night without a troubled look on his face. Someone to help him smile. Maybe Aylen tried too hard to be that person and that's why Jared pushed her away so viciously. She wasn't about to pretend that Jared's negative attributes were attractive. If anything, Aylen detested his negative attributes. He was rude, sarcastic to a fault, moody, temperamental. All of this, coupled with the fact that he carried whatever baggage Project Suncloud and his former lover had brought upon him, made for one messed-up guy.

Yet, somehow, she couldn't help but care for him. Maybe *that* was part of a negative attribute of hers. Maybe, somehow, along similar lines as Jared, Aylen was just as screwed up as he was. No, she didn't quite know everything he had been through, but that wasn't the point, was it? There was something . . . *broken* in her that felt called to what was broken in him. Something not even she could fully recognize.

"So, uh, I have a confession." Jonathan smiled a paper-thin smile that could barely hide how awkward he must've felt. "I actually kinda brought you up here for another reason than to just smoke pot."

"I figured," Aylen admitted gently while chuckling. This response made Jon raise his shoulders and look down.

"Well, I was gonna ask a question . . . but now that you told me all about this guy . . . I—I don't know if I can." He chuckled nervously.

"Well, go ahead and ask." Aylen smiled kindly; the boy was struggling enough. Jonathan looked at her for a moment and took a deep breath.

"Okay, here it goes. Uhhh, do you think maybe, after training, I don't know, we could go out sometime?"

"On a *date*?" she asked bluntly, lightly busting the guy's chops. He nodded. Aylen thought for a moment and shrugged. "After training? Sure."

Jonathan's face lit up. "Whoa, seriously?"

"Yeah. Not like I have any plans after training. And Jared . . . well, like I said, he doesn't really seem to feel the same way. Might as well."

Jonathan looked like he did a double take before his face spread out into a wider grin. "F-for sure! Sweet! That's—wow. That's awesome!"

Aylen figured, why not? Not like Jared gave a crap anyway. Ultimately, Aylen didn't see anything going anywhere with Jonathan, but she figured a date was harmless enough. Besides, what'd she have to lose? Not like Jared would get jealous of Jonathan, of all people. He didn't even wanna be anywhere near her these days. He said he didn't care about her so . . . yeah, why not?

Shortly after their conversation, Aylen made her way downstairs to Jared's private quarters. The weed made her feel lightheaded at best, maybe a little sleepy, but that was it. It wasn't all that stoner movies made it out to be. Aylen did feel tired, though. She closed the door and plopped herself onto the bed. Sleep came easily as her head hit the pillow.

COMMANDER LI

Commander Li sighed impatiently as she sat back in her chair in the surveillance room. The air was tense as the men and women behind the computers kept vigilant watch over their screens. Nothing yet. Her people weren't in position. The commander sent a flirty text to her latest boy toy to distract herself from the tense situation. If there was one thing she didn't miss about action, it was the wait. The calm before the storm. The type of calm when you're waiting for the other shoe to drop. The calm when you know shit is about to be tossed at the fan and get all over the living room. She breathed in through her nose as her latest fling sent a dick pic she had to make sure to keep hidden. With a roll of her eyes, she sent a bored "Yummy" back. One more time hitting it and this one was done. Fucking boring assh—

"They're in position," one of the men behind the computers announced. Commander Li quickly deleted the dick pic and looked up.

"Put them through," Li said, putting away her phone. In moments, the big screen ahead of her lit up hazily, and a somewhat blurry image began coming through of men in a snowy ditch wearing thin black enhancer armor. The screen was dark but still highly visible with the color correcting filter. If it was that dark on camera, it was darker than shit in real life. The wind howled and snow blew fiercely on the screen. The shape of the camera looked to be the shape of a visor inside a helmet.

Static sounded on the huge speakers in the room before a voice spoke. "Sergeant Sommerset to Commander Li. Do you have a visual?"

"Affirmative, Sommerset. Let's go ahead, take a look around,"

Sommerset's helmet camera began turning around before eventually settling on a familiar set of buildings in the distance, partially lit by lights. "Wait, hold the camera steady," Li commanded. Sommerset obeyed. "Bannan, go ahead and zoom the image." The camera zoomed in on the buildings in the distance. On one of the front buildings was the familiar insignia of the Devil's Deviants: the infamous orange pentagram. The entire room shuddered as they stared at the building. Hanging from the top of the building were mangled, skinless corpses, looking as if they had been torn up by animals. Headless corpses hung by their feet, the top halves of skinned bodies hung by their necks, and disembodied limbs hung by themselves. The commander swallowed and closed her eyes hard. Shit. She sighed and folded her lip.

"Commence operation."

Sommerset's hands appeared in the frame, signaling to the others to proceed forward. Then Sommerset lifted his rifle and began leading the recon squad through the snow toward the lit-up the factory. The air was still as they crept through the snowstorm, the sound of harsh wind blowing just outside of Sommerset's helmet. "Getting in range . . . no sign of tangos so far," Sommerset whispered calmly. Commander Li watched the screen intensely as the group crept closer and closer to the chain-link gate on the edge of the factory. A thermal scan appeared on the screen.

"No visible traps on the other side . . ." Sommerset took his place alongside the line of black armored figures. "Go, go, go!" the man whispered to his men. One by one, the men silently and swiftly used their enhancer armor to jump over the gate, with Sommerset being the last to clear the jump. "Okay, past exterior gate."

"Careful, Sergeant. Stay radio silent from now on."

"Copy that. Commencing radio silence." With that, the only sound that could be heard in the room was Sommerset's breathing.

"Do another thermal scan. Wanna be sure the recon squad doesn't get hit with anything un . . ." Commander Li trailed off.

What the . . .

"Commander?" one of the men behind the surveillance computers asked. She thought she saw something move on the screen. Something in the blizzard.

"Thermal scan. Now, please."

Li stared intensely at the spot on the screen she thought moved. Suddenly, the screen changed colors and revealed the heat signatures of the surroundings. Nothing out of the ordinary. Just the men in enhancer armor and the lights that emitted heat signatures. "Back to normal." Li stood up and walked toward the screen, searching. Something was off. She couldn't place it, but . . . "Sergeant Sommerset, look to your left."

The screen began looking to the left when a loud sound suddenly echoed in the speakers. Sommerset's helmet looked to the other side, where the sound came from. A white-haired woman, dimly lit by the overhead lights of the facility, began marching toward the men, who immediately raised their weapons. The woman's skin became metal as she slowly stomped her way forward.

The sounds of blades and machine gun fire rattled through the air. Sommerset's helmet looked toward the gunfire to see one of his men being lifted slightly from behind, something unidentifiable piercing through the man's chest. Commander Li's eyes searched in shock as Sommerset looked to the side to see another getting his throat slit by something not visible to the camera. Li's eyes dashed this way and that, trying to catch what she was missing. "Th-thermal scan! Thermal scan right now!"

"Signal's jammed!" one of the surveillance men said. Li looked behind her, wide-eyed, then turned back toward the screen. Sommerset's unit was being butchered by unseen opponents. Sommerset then turned and was face-to-face with the white-haired woman.

Slich.

Sommerset's visor began to roll. "Oh, nonono—" Li put her hands on her head, watching the image on the screen drop and roll onto the snowy ground. A boot appeared and came toward the screen.

Crack.

Fizzzzzzzzzzzzzzzz . . .

Static appeared on the screen. "*Fuck!*" the commander yelled, putting her hands on her hips.

"Signal lost . . ."

"No shit." Li breathed out in frustration. She stared at the ground a moment, processing everything before chuckling in disbelief and shaking her head.

"Shall we ready a strike force to reclaim the factory?"

Commander Li breathed out and forced a smile on her face. "Course not . . . we won't be wasting any more of *our* men trying to retake Westbrook." The commander chuckled, shaking her head. Her face dropped slightly as she looked at the screen hungrily. "Ready my convoy. We're gonna pay our new best friends a little visit."

ABEL

Knock, knock, knock. There it was again, the disturbance of Abel's sleep in the dead of night. He looked at the clock. The bright red numbers read back to him: 3:05 a.m. Abel heard the harsh, hurried knocking on his door again. "G-General Quinn! Abel! Get up!" Gail's familiar voice called outside his quarters. Gail? What the hell? Abel rubbed his temples for a moment.

"Hold on a second, I'm coming . . ."

Abel stood up, cracking his neck and feeling his bones ache. The Saint leader then opened his door. Gail was in her pajamas with a too-familiar worried look on her makeup-less face. Her eyes were wide and her brow furrowed, and her mouth was doing that strange twisty thing it did. "What is it, Gail?"

"It's Commander Li. She's here! Says it's an urgent matter!"

"Commander Li? Wh-what kind of urgent matter?"

"The kind where I ain't gonna wait for ya to get out of your jammies to tell you 'bout . . ." a familiar voice said from deeper in the hall. Abel turned to the voice and found Commander Li standing there, surrounded by a small group of men in black enhancer armor. Abel looked in confusion at Gail, who breathed out uneasily. He couldn't exactly scold her for letting non-Saint personnel into the hallways of the quarters of the Saints. Commander Li probably came in like a bull seeing red. She shifted in slight annoyance. "Time is of the essence, Mr. Quinn. Ya gonna let me in?"

Abel swallowed briefly. "Y-yes. Come in, Commander . . ." The Principal Overseer moved to the side and turned on the light in his quarters. Commander Li gave the guard to her right a look and the men stationed themselves outside the door. Gail, knowing better than to be in the middle of the formation, backed away as Commander Li headed inside. Gail and Abel exchanged glances as he closed the door, soldiers standing directly in front of it.

"Mmm, neat place. Nice and tidy. Guess that's what I should expect from you, though." The commander pulled out a cigarette. "Hope you don't mind if I smoke." Before Abel had the chance to object, she lit her cigarette. Abel exhaled in disapproval but bit his tongue, heading over to his kitchen and pulling out a small bowl. The commander sat at his dining table and looked around at his quarters. "You and my son both have things for cars. They're cool and fun and all, sure . . . buuut I don't entirely get the obsessio—"

"If I may be so blunt, Commander, what in God's name is the urgent reason you barged into my room at three in the morning?" Abel asked sharply, placing the bowl on the table in front of the commander.

"Ah!" Commander Li flicked her ashes into the bowl. Abel sat across from her with disdain. "*Somebody* is grumpy this time in the morning." Li chuckled slightly, digging into her inner coat pocket. In moments, she pulled out a small stack of photographs and slid it across the table toward Abel. The Saint leader immediately began looking through them. What the hell?

"Approximately around three or four yesterday morning, the Devil's Deviants took over the Westbrook factory and killed every single person that worked there." Commander Li sat back in her chair. "Wanna know how *I* spent today? Well, I spent today gathering up some of my best surveillance operatives into a recon squad, sending them out *all* the way to Westbrook at a moment's notice . . . and they just went dark about two or three hours ago." Abel recognized the blurry figure of Pestilence in one of the photos before him. Jesus. . . . It was a lot to process. "Oh, and the DDs are still there, by the way. Gettin' their hands on as many of our secrets as they can, no doubt. If something isn't done within the next few hours, there's no telling what may happen." Commander Li's face dropped without any pretense and looked serious. Abel squinted his eyes.

"I don't understand. If it's that urgent and that dire, why aren't you sending out a strike force to retake the factory?"

Commander Li's face then slinked into a smile. "Ah, but I am." She licked her lips, and it took a moment for Abel to register what she was saying. His stomach began to clench.

"W-wait a minute . . ."

Li chuckled. "Not a morning person, are you, Mr. Quinn?"

"Th-this is a major military operation! This—"

"Is exactly the kind of thing you train Saints to handle, is it not?" Commander Li took a puff of her cigarette and tilted her head. "Saints . . . always talking about fighting the war of good versus evil. Always talking about fighting some noble war against the deviants . . . Well, now is your chance to prove it. A *real* battle." Li smirked. Like a cat with a live rodent in its mouth, wriggling and squeaking in agony, helpless in the smug cat's jaws.

Abel swallowed hard. "With the number of enemy combatants, how . . . how much help would we be getting from the UWF?"

Li chuckled at the back of her throat. "Help?" she coyly remarked. "You *are* the help. You're UWF now, or at least UWF property. I'm trusting the extermination of DD forces completely to the Saint Organization."

Abel looked at Li in disbelief. No help? For a force that size . . . no help? Abel's mouth hung low.

"Don't tell me you forgot the recent deal already," Li said.

Abel breathed out uneasily. "W-we won't be getting any help? Of any sort?"

Commander Li shrugged. "We in the UWF want to spare as many resources as possible making this little situation on our hands go away. And the Saint Organization are professional deviant killers, are they not?" Her brow overextended itself and her mouth formed an "O" shape while she tilted her head. "Or was I wrong?" Commander Li put out her cigarette into the bowl in front of her. Abel swallowed and thought for a moment. This . . . this bitch . . .

"This is a suicide mission." Abel stared at Li's unmoving, blank face. "You are *trying* to get us killed, aren't you?"

The commander chuckled. "That's awfully dramatic of you to say, Mr. Quinn."

"*That* number of enemy combatants? No external help? That would require—"

"Require all active and inactive members of the Saint Organization to join the battle? Yep." Commander Li sniffed and tilted her head the other way. "All recruits, all people on leave, even your son, who you coddle, has to go." Abel squinted. Even Joshua? "Come now, don't give me that look. I know you protect your son from action as much as you possibly can, keep him away from all the *major* assignments. I'd do the same if he were my kid. But everyone, and I do mean just about everyone, has to clear out Westbrook. We have to exterminate every last deviant in that place. Who knows, maybe your son will bump up his kill count."

Abel scoffed. "Rob was right, you're a downright evil bitch, aren't you?"

Commander Li sighed in annoyance. "Course, we *could* just completely cut off the deal, cut the Saints out of our funds, our charity . . . hunt you down as traitors. That's always an option. . . . Hey, we've scratched your back with that latest little pay bump. It's your turn. Earn that money we just funneled to you."

Abel grimaced, then looked down at the photographs. Shit . . . he couldn't get the Saints out of this if he tried, could he? "I suppose by everyone, you mean I should dust off my enhancer armor, then?"

Commander Li twisted her face. "Heavens, no. Everyone but you and the doctor. You are the one who brokered the deal with us, and the doctor is rather useless in a fight, isn't she? Besides, I'm sure you're going to need her for all the injured that come back, right?" Abel's stomach swirled slightly. Everyone . . . including recruits and Josh . . . it made him sick.

In defeat, Abel looked down. "All right. We'll do the job."

Commander Li grinned. "Good! I'll let you get dressed, then, and you can start planning your method for attack. Your Saints leave as soon as possible." The woman stood up. "On that note, I'mma find me some coffee! Maybe get recon girl out there to make me some. She's cute, in a . . . menopausal sorta way." With that, Commander Li left Abel's quarters, leaving the Saint leader alone to ponder. For one last moment, he stared at the photos Li had handed

him. A full-blown military operation, with no outside help from the UWF. . . .
What had he done?

AYLEN

Aylen opened her eyes to find herself in an open field. The sky was a vibrant
blue and the air felt warm and sweet as if it were the middle of spring. She
turned her head and found a sight she did not expect to see: Lying right next
to her was Jared, with his arm under her. She smiled and closed her eyes again,
snuggling into his strong chest. The sun shone brightly on them, their eyes
closed against the glare. Aylen gently opened her eyes and saw white flowers
bobbing up and down in the wind. She turned over to face Jared, whose eyes
were half open. Aylen stared into them, those beautiful brown eyes of his. The
two lightly pecked each other on the lips.

"I miss you," Aylen heard herself say. Jared stroked her face lightly and
smiled with a hint of sadness in his eyes.

"I know."

Aylen looked into the deep pools of his eyes. She always loved looking into
his eyes.

"Hey! Aylen!" a familiar voice called from out of view. Aylen saw Beth in
the distance waving to her, and Aylen's father behind Beth. They were both
smiling. They were alive. Beth and her father were alive! She felt tears come to
her eyes as she watched Beth and her dad. Then the two turned around.

"Wait . . ."

They began walking away. "*Wait! Don't go!*" Aylen screamed. She ran after them. "*Don't leave me!*" Yet the two kept on walking, like they didn't hear
her . . . they just kept walking. Jared grabbed her from behind and lifted her up,
preventing her from running after them. "*Lemme go!*" Jared didn't say a word

while he held her. She watched Beth and her father walk out of sight. "Beth! Dad!" Aylen called out, attempting to fight Jared's grip. "*Daddy!*"

Everything is connected.

Aylen awoke at the touch of a hand. She opened her eyes slightly and began sobbing immediately. Why did she dream that? Aylen cursed her mind for dreaming up that nasty little dream. Daddy. Beth. They were gone. Gone forever, and they were never going to come back. Whoever had woken her put a box of tissues to her face. Aylen looked up and saw Jared standing over her, a cold, unreadable expression across his face. How long had he been standing there? Aylen sniffled while looking at him, confused, her face wet from the tears she had cried.

"Everyone has been ordered for debriefing downstairs," he said simply, no sign of any emotion on his face.

Aylen sniffed while getting a tissue out of the box. "Debriefing?"

"DD attack." Jared's face remained stone. "Everyone is going to be involved in this mission. Get dressed, and I'll take ya to the debriefing room." He turned his back to Aylen and headed to the bathroom while lighting a cigarette. As soon as the door closed, she changed into the appropriate clothes. A Devil's Deviants attack? Why were the recruits getting involved? Was this going to be a battle? Was Aylen going to have to *fight* in a *battle*? Her stomach tightened at the thought of having to finally live up to what she had been planning on doing. In battle, she'd have to kill. She'd have to survive.

Shortly after Aylen got dressed, Jared silently led her to the debriefing room. The room was large enough to fit the entirety of the Saint Organization. She looked through the sea of faces to see if there were any familiar people that she recognized. Save for a few, many of the members were unrecognizable. In front of the Saint underlings was a stage that held General Quinn, Captain Webster, Morgan, the Hispanic woman with bruises that Aylen guessed was Sergeant Esmeralda Rodriguez, Faith, her twin Sergeant Lancaster, and Brenden. On stage along with them was the icy woman in the business suit from before, whose name Aylen didn't know. The Saints seemed uneasy in the presence of the Asian woman, who seemed to notice Aylen from across the room and watched her with intent. Jared sat Aylen down, then sat down next to her.

Suddenly, the lights dimmed and the room hushed. Sergeant Lancaster went to the front of the stage and behind the podium. "Good morning, members of the Saint Organization. As I'm sure you have all now been informed, this is an emergency briefing, as the enemy has taken a vital outpost belonging to the United World Federation. Here to inform us of the mission is Commander Melyssa Li of the UWF Military Police, as we will be working with the UWF on this particular mission."

Right, that's who that woman is, Aylen thought. *Commander Li, the person Captain Webster freaked out about.*

Commander Li went to the podium and easily took charge in front of the Saints. "Hello. Most of you probably remember me from the execution of Private Ronald Brown." The tension in the room began to rise, which Aylen could see the commander got a rise out of. "Hell, I recognize most of your faces from that day." The commander then shot a glance at Aylen. "Save for a few new faces. . . . Anyway, I'm sure that I'm not exactly a fan favorite after that unfortunate little incident. This is not about that, though. I wanna clear the air and tell you that today I come to you as an ally, not an enemy. Today, I come to you because Salutem needs you, now more than ever."

Commander Li nodded and parts of the walls around them came down to reveal gargantuan computer monitors. The screens showed the outside of a factory. On the side of the factory looked to be a pentagram with five dots surrounding each arm of the upside-down star, then surrounded by a circle that seemed to be made with the same reddish-orange spray paint that the entire insignia seemed to be made up of. Aylen's stomach turned slightly when she recognized the shapes of severed body parts hanging from the building. That . . . was that normal?

"At three a.m. yesterday morning, the Westbrook factory was compromised. They went dark, and judging by the insignia it's pretty obvious who's done it. We sent in a recon party, but as of last night the recon party went dark as well. That being said, we were able to get some photos as well as satellite feed." A picture appeared on the monitors. It seemed to be a heat signature camera of sorts. Green dots littered the area that was shown on the screen. "The funny thing about deviants and Brainless is that their signatures appear as green rather than the normal blue of humans in our satellite feeds. Each one of those green dots is an enemy combatant," Commander Li said smoothly. Aylen swallowed. She now understood why all the Saints were called. That was a scary amount of combatants in the picture. She had never felt so underprepared for anything in her life.

"The Devil's Deviants, from what we can survey from our satellite info, have made something of a residence in the factory. That factory is one of the five essential weapons and research facilities that the UWF has. If the deviants make it out of there, you can probably kiss all of Salutem goodbye. Your mission, as per the new deal between the UWF and the Saint Organization, is to exterminate all enemy soldiers. Their main mission is extraction. We cannot allow a single deviant out of there alive, and the factory is too valuable a resource to simply destroy. Quinn, if you will please go over the plan of attack with your troops." Commander Li then offered the podium to General Quinn. The picture switched to a blueprint of the factory. The general took a breath of what seemed to be momentary embarrassment and then went on to explain the plan.

"Essentially, the plan of attack is simple. Since the object of the game is extermination, we hit them from all sides. Captain Gatton will strike from the south with the Tank Suit Unit and additional ground support, toward the biggest access point, the easiest to move heavy firepower into. Sergeant Rodriguez will lead the majority of our infantry to the east of the factory, to an access point that hasn't been tried yet and is probably where they'd least be expecting us to hit. There's another access point to the west, where the UWF tried to breach. Sergeant Schumacher and Corporal Greenfield will hit there with a smaller unit, maybe try to figure out what the hell went on over there and provide an attack from that angle. Now, to the north there are some cliffs that overlook the factory, so that's where we'll station Captain Webster's sharpshooters. They'll be our eyes overhead. Finally, Corporal Griffin will take an expedition through the sewer tunnels, as we believe the enemy's entry point may have come from there and that may be the way they will attempt to escape once they know the shitstorm they're in."

"Goddamnit," Aylen heard Jared mutter next to her, obviously less than pleased about his assignment.

"First the corporal will be dispatched, then the infantry forces, and finally, once the enemy is out in the open, the tank suits will move in and clean up the remainder of the forces while keeping stragglers from leaving the battlefield, which is also a duty we'll be expecting from the sharpshooting unit as well. We will have three Troop Transports at the ready for medical evac near the different entry points, and when ya need to get the hell outta there the airships will pick you up. Any questions? No? Good. You have thirty minutes to suit up and meet with your units. For those of you unclear, the units and names will be on the screens, and you'll be able to find your unit leaders on the stage. Give 'em hell, people. Fight for honor, vigilance, and duty. You're dismissed."

The lights shone bright and the computer screens showed who belonged in each unit. Aylen found herself in the sharpshooting unit and sighed with relief. She wouldn't be too deep in the action.

Jared quickly left her side without a sound and went to Gabriel. The two began discussing something hurriedly, and Aylen might consider them almost panicked. The two briefly looked at Aylen, and then continued talking. Uh-oh.

They were talking about her. She made her way toward them, but Jared walked off. She paused and looked at the computers again for the other three recruits from her class and found Jonathan was in the same unit as her. The other two wouldn't be so lucky. Marie was in the Tank Suit Unit with Morgan, and Adrien was in the infantry unit with Sergeant Rodriguez. At least, if anything, the Sharpshooter Unit wouldn't be too close to the fighting. Still, as Aylen stared at the screen a sinking feeling enveloped her gut. She was going to be in a battle today. She was going to have her first taste of war.

PESTILENCE

Pestilence looked out onto the snowy landscape from the balcony of one of the control towers. The wind blew through her white hair, gripping her body in a cold embrace. The factory was out in the middle of some snowy mountain, and the pine trees surrounding the fortress were caked with white snow that looked almost like whipped cream. The sky was filled with clouds and snow dropped onto the thick white canvas, making it even thicker.

Seeing nothing to note, she walked back into the watchtower where her comrade, Dagon, and a few others discussed the plans to extract the equipment that Pluto needed to finish building his project. Dagon looked as if he was contemplating something, stroking his thin little goatee.

Pestilence huffed. "I don't understand what the fucking problem is, Dagon."

"The problem, *Pestilence*, is figuring out how to handle the sheer size of Pluto's equipment as well as maybe snatchin' some of the other weapons in this factory. Not to mention, as Abraxas has said, the downloadin' of the files is going to take a tick due to the amount of projects they been workin' on here," Dagon said in his pre-Salutem Australian accent.

"We don't *need* those other weapons, though! Weren't Lucifer and Pluto's instructions only for the equipment, not anything else?"

Dagon sneered at her response. "What would you know 'bout that part of the mission, love? Lucifer trusted me and my scavengers to collect, an' that's what we're doin'. Collectin'."

"Well tell your people to hurry up. We don't have much—"

"I'm sorry, you tellin' me what to do, Pesty? See, I'm the leader on this part of the operation, and what *I* say goes."

"Now is not the time to be waving dicks and arguing," Pestilence said with a growl, letting her annoyance show a little. "We *just* killed a recon squad a couple hours ago. You don't think they'll be sending a force up here to take us out? They're probably monitoring us as we speak! The longer we spend here, the longer we're giving them to organize and—"

"We got the creature, don't we?"

"Yes, but—"

"And we got *you*, don't we? The great Pestilence?"

Pestilence felt her face grow dark. "The hell you implying?" Dagon smirked at this, his self-righteous, rat-like face getting under Pestilence's skin.

"I'm implyin' that as long as we got you and our creepy li'l friends, we're good, ain't we? UWF can fuck around all they want, but they ain't prepared for our friend the creature. *Nobody* we come across will be. Worst case scenario, the creature gets a nice li'l snack. Now, you did *your* job an' set up the security measures, didn' ya?" He grinned, revealing his crooked teeth.

Pestilence breathed out hotly. "The security measures are set up. But, Dagon, unless you want me to tell Lucifer how *you* didn't trust my judgment enough and put the *entire* mission at risk for everyone involved, I suggest you and your goddamn scavengers put a pep in your step. Got it?"

Dagon looked at the other deviants and scoffed.

"*Got it?*"

"Fine, fine. Step pepped. Keep ya panties on, love."

"Thank you." Pestilence shook her head and headed back out to the balcony.

"No wonder her husband is her bitch," she heard Dagon laugh as the door closed. Any other day, she'd threaten to chop off his balls and feed them to Brainless, possibly even going as far as grabbing them and putting a blade to his throat. Today, however, was not one of those days. Not with this much at stake. Not when the dreams of the deviants were so close to reality. Pestilence continued to observe the landscape and where she had carefully plotted out the traps. She didn't like what Dagon had implied, a force coming and having to sic that . . . that thing onto the enemy? The truth was, if they did that she wasn't sure she'd be able to control it. It had been hard enough to stop it from tearing the whole factory apart! If she let that *thing* feed on large groups of people or the machines they might bring . . . no. They would not rely on that thing. That *abomination* contained below the factory was going to stay there, for better or worse, and they would all return to the DD's base at the end of all of this. Then, hopefully, they'd put it back on the ice for good. She hated that thing.

Pestilence felt her stomach turn as she felt its presence. Always hungry . . . always angry. And what was worse? If it did get out of line, out of her control, she had no idea how they'd even approach killing it. It was the most dangerous creature she'd ever dealt with. A weapon that felt like playing with fire.

All of that being said, were the DDs enough to take on a fully trained UWF force on their own? Pestilence stared out toward the white horizon. Dagon better hurry.

JARED

In the armory, Jared put on his enhancer armor for the first time in several months. It felt awkward, restricting, and uncomfortable. Didn't help that it was winter armor too, which meant it was just a little thicker with a light snow camouflage programmed into the settings. Yet Jared would be damned if he wasn't going to wear armor as he traveled through sewers. Of all the shit jobs they could've given him, this was literally the shittiest. Fucking sewer duty? He knew he wasn't exactly Abel's favorite, but this was absurd. Let alone the fact that it would just be him down there—alone. Jared was pissed. He dug out a black cigarette and lit it, hoping maybe that it would relax him a little.

"Wow," he heard a familiar voice to the side of him say. Jared looked to see Aylen in enhancer armor too. Her smile was weak, and he could tell she was just trying to make conversation. "I think this is the first time I've seen you in enhancer armor."

"Ya want something?" Jared avoided eye contact, pretending to be pissed at her. He hated it, but this was the only way, the only way to keep her away. It was for her own good, Jared kept telling himself. For her own good . . .

"Just, you know, wanted to wish you good luck on this battle. Plus . . ." Aylen stopped herself midsentence.

"Plus?"

"Plus, I don't know if this is the last time I'll ever see you." He looked at her for a second. She looked vulnerable and uneasy. He knew her well enough by now to know that she was scared out of her mind. Oh man, how could he be a dick to that? Jared looked around, lost for a second on how to respond, and decided that perhaps he didn't need to be a dick with this answer.

"Gabriel will keep you safe. Don't be dramatic." Jared looked away and focused on his cigarette. In the silence, Aylen took a seat beside him. A rather close seat. Even though only their armor made contact, Jared couldn't help but feel his heart begin to pound as nervous sweat slicked his palms.

Keep your cool, Jared, he thought in the back of his mind. *Keep it cool.*

"Yeah, but what about you? You're going into the sewers all alone, by yourself."

"I'll be fine. I can handle myself." Jared took a puff from his cigarette while tightening some straps. He blew the smoke out into the air.

"Yeah, but still—"

"How 'bout you just worry about yourself and I'll just worry 'bout me. How 'bout that, A?"

It's for her own good, he kept thinking. *For her own good.*

"Jared . . . you gotta help me out here. I really, *really* don't understand why you're so mad at me. I mean, running my fingers through your hair isn't a good enough reason for all this. What's really wrong? Why . . . why do you hate me so much all the sudden?" Aylen said with a furrowed brow. To this, Jared blew cigarette smoke into her face; maybe that would get her to back off.

As the smoke hit her face, Aylen's expression visibly soured. She nodded her head slowly. "Know what? I changed my mind. Go *die* in that sewer. I don't give a crap."

Jared had to blink twice. Damn. He would've never expected *that* reaction from her. That was . . . different. Ow. He deserved that, but . . . *ow.*

Aylen got up quickly and walked away. Immediately, Jared felt like an even bigger piece of shit. He wanted to go after her and apologize for his behavior. Apologize to her for being a dick. But this was the only way that he could keep her safe. He couldn't be her guardian angel. He didn't want her to die on his watch, like Jessica. Caring about him would only get her killed. It was for her own good.

Jared watched Aylen look back at him with obvious hurt in her eyes and then quickly turn away as she continued walking away from him. It was for her own good.

AYLEN

Aylen walked back to her unit enraged. Screw him. Screw that emo piece of crap. He could rot in hell. She stomped to her unit, roughly twenty people not including Jonathan, Gabe, and herself. Other than the Tank Suit Unit, it was the smallest. Everyone was preparing themselves for battle, loading and prepping highly advanced sniper rifles, far cries from the training rifles that Gabriel had trained her on. Luckily, they didn't seem so different that Aylen wouldn't know how to work them. She grabbed a rifle and began to load it angrily. Out of the corner of her eye, she saw someone approaching her.

Jonathan let out a goofy chuckle. "Hey, A, same unit. Who'd have thunk, eh?"

Aylen continued to load her weapon, still pissed at her encounter with Jared. She looked back down at what she was doing. "Yeah."

"Whoa, A, are you okay?"

"I'm fine. Just a run-in with an asshole."

"My, my, my." A familiar voice interceded in the conversation. Aylen looked over and saw Eric with that devilish grin on his face. "I wonder who you're talking about there." Aylen and Eric had a brief staring contest where Aylen tried to direct all her fury at him before he shrugged. "I guess we won't have a lesson today after all, Monro."

Aylen stared at Eric like she was going to punch him again. "Yeah."

"Shame. Was really lookin' forward to it." Eric licked his lips then looked over Jonathan up and down and chuckled. "Psh, who's your friend?"

Jonathan looked offended by the chuckle and pointed to himself. "*Me?*"

"Who else would I be talking 'bout, palooka?" Eric grinned. He then stared down at Jonathan and made his way to his unit.

Aylen shook her head. "Day's just filling up with assholes."

Then Captain Webster yelled out, "All right Sharpshooter Unit, let's move out!"

JARED

Jared listened to Gabriel's command that he and Gail followed Gabe's unit. The unit piled into a land vehicle that looked something similar to a long box with wheels. It was a Troop Transport, as the people around the camp called it. Jared was sure that it wasn't the official name of the vehicle, but he never bothered to find out what the official one was. It was rare he was ever put in one. The idea was that the airships would take them so far, and then the Troop Transports would creep the soldiers into position, so as to not alert the enemy of their presence.

All the troops huddled into the car and sat side by side. The vehicle shook as it headed to the airship that would take them to Westbrook. This type of airship—known as a SAPA, technically, but was referred to by Anthrodi War veterans as a "Meat Delivery Drone"—was a nifty-looking aircraft with two helicopter blades on top and five smaller ones connected by arms at the sides, rear, and contained in the wings of the vehicle like fans. A loud mechanical noise filled the air as the transport lifted itself from the ground and attached itself magnetically to the car. Before any of the troops sitting in the car knew it, they were off the ground and soaring through the air.

Jared looked deeper into the car to see Aylen, who seemed to be holding her breath throughout the ride. She looked scared, like a tiny mouse. He wondered if he should've done what he had done. It was a real asshole move. How else would he get her to stop caring, though? And why the hell were *recruits* going on this mission, anyway? This was a bad idea. Regardless of Jared's involvement, Aylen could get seriously hurt, or worse. He spoke to Gabriel, though. The captain would keep her safe, it's part of why she was in his unit. Out of all four units, it was the safest. She'd be far away from the actual fighting.

He looked out of the window of the Troop Transport and saw how the ground glimmered. They were going farther north. Westbrook was stationed in the snowy mountains past the Forest of Sorrows and Widow's Mountain. *Widow's Mountain.* Based on the intel that asshole Commander Li gave, Westbrook was likely gonna be an even worse bloodbath than Widow's Mountain. Oh, joy.

Jared turned his attention to the possibilities of who might be involved in the taking of the factory. Westbrook factory was supposed to be one of the more secure factories in the UWF's possession. What could the Devil's Deviants possibly have that could have allowed them to cut through the UWF's defenses so easily? Westbrook was no slouch in fortification. Did the DDs get a new member perhaps? Some deviant kid with even scarier abilities than he knew were possible? Lucifer often cherry-picked preteens from the deviant colonies that the DDs looked out for to get new members. Child soldiers. If that was the case, a new member with a scary ability, Jared might have to put down a kid today. He knew from experience that kid soldiers came in two kinds: the scared and the radicalized. One could be reasoned with and talked to, the other couldn't. He knew that better than anyone. There had been no reasoning with *him* until his late teens. Jared lit another cigarette and began puffing away at the new one, thinking about the battle. He really hoped it wasn't a new member.

"Put that cigarette out," Gail said sharply from across from him. He turned his head and found her hateful gaze. This shit again.

Jared took another puff of his cigarette. "Why?" he asked.

"Because I said so, that's why. I hate the smell. Put it out."

Jared grinned. This petty bitch. "A please would be nice."

"Jared, as your superior officer I command you to put the *fucking* thing out."

Jared looked at Gail, grinning even bigger to intentionally be an asshole. He made the ember die down to almost nothing just by looking at it.

"All right, all right, I'll obey. See? It's out."

Gail stared at him for a second, and then Jared made the cigarette spark. The tip burned as bright as if he were taking a puff.

"Ah *shit*, guess it relit itself. Oh well, what can ya do?"

Jared began taking another puff of his cigarette, but she snatched it out of his mouth and threw it on the ground before giving it a resounding stomp that made the entire car look at the two of them. He shrugged at the others while keeping the smirk on his face. Aylen looked disapprovingly at him, as if knowing he was causing trouble. Gabriel watched in silence, his head pressed against the wall of the car.

What Jared couldn't believe was that he had to work with Gail. Dr. Lancaster was one of the sweetest women that he had ever known. Sweet enough that he could call her Ma and it felt more right than it ever did with his real mom. Her twin sister, though, was two steps away from being Satan. Sure, they had worked together many times before, and Gail often was the one who informed him of his missions, but it was always clear that they never liked each other. She didn't like Jared due to her prejudice toward deviants, and he disliked her because he saw no reason in respecting someone who didn't respect him. The same went with many a Saint Organization member. He had often thought that if it weren't for people like Faith, Brenden, Joshua, and Tara, he would've left the Saint Organization after Rob's death. Maybe that would've kept Aylen safe. Then again, if he ever did quit, he had no doubt in his mind that Eric, among others, would hunt him down and probably try to kill him. That aspect of it almost made it worth doing. Then he would have nothing holding him back from ripping out that fucker's throat.

Jared looked out the window, their descent beginning with the factory still out of sight. This was their stop. The car landed on the ground and there was mechanical whirring as the Troop Transport released itself from the SAPA. The driver of the transport, who sat to Jared's left, started up the vehicle with a low rumble.

The ride was anything but luxurious or comfortable, with the transport shaking as it hit every bump and crevice underneath the snow. Considerably, though, it was fast. Faster than the air transport seemed to be as it rushed past trees and rode along the top of the mountains. Jared could see his non-smoke-filled breath in front of him as the temperature dropped.

The car slowed to a stop as they reached what looked like a bomb shelter vault in the snow. This was the stop. The back hatch of the Troop Transport opened as the sun began to peek through gloomy clouds. Snow dropped through the air as Jared and the Sharpshooter Unit began to get out of the car.

"All right, Sharpshooter Unit!" Gabriel yelled. "Except for the recruits, come with me! Privates, observe how Sergeant Lancaster uses the radar to track Corporal Griffin's movements!" Jared looked back to Aylen, who watched him with a furrowed brow and quick breaths. So *that* was how Gabriel was going to keep her safe. Not a bad plan. He grabbed his assault rifle and held it tight as he stepped out of the Troop Transport. Gabriel and the Sharpshooter Unit began their journey to the edge of the mountain, where they'd be able to do the job they were assigned. Jared began toward the vault door and entered the security clearance onto the panel.

"Remember, Jared, no fire," Gail called to him before he went inside. "Gas lines are supposed to be down there." Jared turned around and gave Gail a look. No fire? The fuck? Great. Jared looked at her for a while and then at Aylen, who stood behind Gail within the Troop Transport as she began to set up the radar inside and put on her headset. He pressed a button on his armor, letting the visor cover his face. Then he walked into the sewer and shut the door behind him.

Darkness. Darkness filled the tunnel. Jared exhaled as he turned on his helmet lights. Before him, about ten to twelve feet away, was a wall. Before that wall, though, there was a hole in the metallic ground before him. A hole with a ladder. Jared walked his way to the edge of the hole and looked down. In the dim light, he could vaguely make out what looked to be the true sewer. For a moment, he was thankful for his helmet. To be trapped in this disgusting steel dungeon and have to endure its smell would have been too much. He spotted a stone and kicked it off the edge with his foot, not hearing a sound for a couple of seconds. His stomach turned when he heard it hit the water with a foul sound that made his stomach turn. How the hell did he get stuck with this literal shit job? He grabbed onto the ladder and began his way down. Each step clamored through the seemingly never-ending abyss as Jared ventured farther and farther down into the sewer.

"Got a visual on anything in there?" he heard Gail ask, her voice echoing in his helmet.

"Pretty sure I stepped in shit."

"Anything or anyone down there?"

"Oh yeah, there's an Italian plumber. Says he's looking for a princess. I think he's on shrooms."

"I'm serious, Jared."

"You know what I see, Gail? Not a goddamn th—"

Jared's foot slipped and soon he found himself falling down *"Shit!"* With a hard thud he hit a metallic ground face-first. Then there was darkness again, and he lost track of his assault rifle. He heard a monstrous clump in a body of water next to him, which very quickly solved that mystery. "Ow."

"Jared? Jared? Do you copy?"

He felt his head spin as he looked around in the darkness. No light. It was pitch-black. "Y-yeah." Jared's head spun as he tried to regain his bearings. He felt woozy. "I'm good. Think the flashlight in my helmet got busted, though. Took a fall down a ladder. I think I'll try my lighter."

"Negative. Gas lines down there, remember? You can't use any fire."

"Gail, I can control it. Even wi—"

"No fire, Jared. Direct order."

Bitch lived to torture him, didn't she? Jared got out the next best thing, something which he needed now that the assault rifle was gone. Gas lines? He had excellent control of fire even with gas around. Gail was just being a bitch. Well, what she didn't know didn't hurt her. Jared pulled out the rod from his utility belt and pressed the button, extending his glowing scythe out in front of him like a torch. At best, it offered him a minimal amount of light as he staggered onto his feet. He then looked behind him at the ladder he had fallen from. One of the stilts was severely bent in the middle. Jared turned toward the rest of the tunnel. In front of him was a long, foreboding hallway that stretched out from what little he could make out in the dim light.

AYLEN

"Gail, I'm gonna need you to be my eyes," Aylen heard Jared say through the radio. She observed the screen as Gail watched it.

Gail breathed out. "Okay, I got visual on your position. Charlie Mike, Jared."

"If you say so. I'm pretty blind in here."

Aylen watched Jared's dot move slowly through the sewers.

"All right, you've still got quite a bit to go before you reach the factory. I need you to go super speed on us."

"You nuts? I can barely see a thing."

"That's an order, Jared. I'll be your eyes."

"Fine."

The dialogue between Gail and Jared seemed even more hostile at every end. There was clearly no love lost between these two. Aylen supposed that wasn't hard, especially with Jared's attitude. His dot began moving at an incredibly fast speed.

"Keep going. Keep going. Keep going."

Jonathan looked over at Aylen. "So his deviant ability is super speed?"

Aylen briefly looked at him before turning her attention back to the screen. "Yeah, one of them."

"All right, Jared, now bank left," Gail said over the intercom.

"Got it."

Jared turned left down the tunnel and the dot continued its hurried pace. Gail licked her lips. "Okay, it's going to be a right . . . right about now." The dot turned right, showing Aylen that he had obeyed Gail's command. Then Jared's dot started heading for an extremely sharp left turn that bordered some kind of empty space. "Keep going." The dot moved closer to the edge. "Keep going." Aylen looked over at Gail. The sergeant seemed to be sweating. Her eyes were transfixed, and she breathed shallow breaths, a look of excitement glowing on Gail's face as her mouth twisted into a grin. What was she—

Aylen looked at the radar screen. The dot was getting closer and closer to the edge. She pulled off the headset, ignoring the obscenities Gail began yelling at her.

JARED

"*Jared, stop!*" A voice that didn't sound like Gail's sounded in his ears. Jared halted in his tracks found himself standing at the edge of the walkway. *Shit!* That was close. He took a sharp breath as he looked down. Even despite the dim light, what was before him looked like an endless abyss. Jared thought for a second. The voice that screamed had sounded like Aylen's.

Jared breathed hard, bewildered at the fact he had almost fell into seemingly bottomless darkness. "Aylen?"

"Yeah, it's a sharp left. Turn left." Jared looked to the side of him and saw that the path continued.

Gail cleared her throat on the intercom. "Thank you, Private Monro. Keep going straight, Jared, for a long while. There will be momentary radio silence." Jared took another look at the abyss. If he fell in, he would've probably been a goner. Did Aylen just save his life?

AYLEN

Aylen saw Gail turn red as she turned around to look at her. Her eyes were wide and her nostrils flared, making her look like a demon from hell. The sergeant grit her teeth. "Go."

Aylen lifted an eyebrow. "Go?"

"Go to Captain Webster and join the rest of the Sharpshooter Unit. *Now*."

Gail stared daggers at Aylen. Aylen looked at the driver of the Troop Transport, who simply stared back calmly. Aylen was flabbergasted. Gail was the anti-Faith. Was she trying to get Jared killed?

"Are you *fucking* deaf? I said move it, soldier!"

Without any other options, Aylen began to back away.

Jonathan looked dumbfounded and his mouth moved like fish. "H-hey, Sarge, she was just trying to help ou—"

"*Both of you go, now!*" Gail snapped. Aylen and Jonathan hurried out of the Troop Transport, whose back door compartment closed almost as suddenly as it had opened, with a mean-looking Gail supervising the whole thing.

Jonathan clutched his rifle like a teddy bear. "I think we're in trouble."

"Yeah, probably . . ."

The two went off in the direction they last saw Gabriel and the sharpshooters head. It didn't take long to catch up as they continued to make their way to the cliff's edge. Gabriel noticed Aylen and Jonathan coming up behind them and stopped momentarily, his face scrunched.

"What is it, Privates?"

"Sergeant Lancaster asked us to accompany you rather than continue observing her, sir," Aylen replied with the charm of a robot.

Gabriel thought for a moment, sighing, and then nodded his head. "All right, then, follow me. We're almost there." The Sharpshooter Unit kept trudging forward, digging their heels into the snow. Aylen looked toward the horizon and saw what looked to be the outline of the factory. It was gargantuan in size and stout in nature, standing low with tall pipes reaching the heavens. Aylen gulped as they approached the edge of the cliff. This was it.

They were about five feet away from the edge when Gabriel told them to crawl the rest of the way to get into position. As soon as Aylen got to the edge and readied her rifle, she looked through the scope. Everything seemed so peaceful. Could a battle really happen here? Today? "We wait till the sergeants draw 'em out to the kill zone," Gabriel said, "then we start our portion of the assault."

JARED

Jared walked fast through the sewers rather than taking a run. Running had almost gotten him killed, so when Gail beckoned him to run again after the brief radio silence, he refused. His steps echoed through the tunnel as he walked carefully, using the orange light from his scythe to guide the way. There was a drip somewhere in the distance, and he carefully planted his steps to avoid falling into the muck below. He noticed crevices along the walls, like something bigger than the tunnel had pushed its way through. "Whoa . . ." Jared said silently, his eyes widening as he noticed more and more. Something big had burrowed through these tunnels. Something inhuman. An unsettling feeling began to rise in him as he looked at the walls. "Gail, you would not believe what's down here—"

"Mayday, Jared! Withdraw! *Now.*"

"'Sup, Gail?"

"You're completely surrounded! Brainless! Go now!"

Suddenly, water from below began to slosh about, and figures shrouded in darkness appeared in Jared's dim light.

Jared sighed. Of course. Just what he needed. "Shit."

ESMERALDA

Helmetless, Esmeralda and her soldiers moved silently toward the enemy base after exiting the Troop Transport. The Saint veteran's eyes scanned what she could see of the factory. It looked lifeless and empty as she and her unit moved forward. Against the main building ahead were human body parts hanging by chains from the roof. Typical DD bullshit.

Clutching her assault rifle tightly, she saw Joshua and Tara head out before her. Using only hand signals, Ezzy's unit positioned itself in front of the factory gate. It was a chain-link fence, nothing too awkward or special about it. Joshua and Tara worked as a team to quickly cut a hole through it with specialized equipment; Esmeralda breathed hard as she and her unit huddled together in the courtyard to wait.

Something similar to the smell of burning rubber pervaded her nose as they ventured into the silence. A jungle gym of metallic poles filled the airspace between buildings overhead. Broken windows were scattered across the factory's face, the result of the missiles, tanks of god knew what, and war machinery that stood like snow-covered statues within the courtyard. No sign of the enemy yet. Esmeralda tried to look at all possible vantage points the DDs could strike from, yet it was difficult: The factory was filled with far too many blind spots to count on just one possible vantage point. As Esmeralda watched over the vantage points, she pointed to one direction and then the opposite. Joshua and his part of the unit went in the first direction, and Tara and her part of the unit went in the second direction. Everything was too peaceful. Everything was too—

Boom.

Esmeralda's ears rang as she watched Joshua's body disconnect from his legs and right arm while sending members of his unit backward. Joshua, flying through the air, looked dumbfounded right before his face was engulfed in flames from the mine he stepped on. On her other side, Ezzy saw Tara's mouth stretch into a scream as she began to run toward her fallen lover.

"Wait, Tara—" Esmeralda started. Suddenly, heavy machine gun fire filled the air from the windows. Within seconds, the Saints present began to be cut down as the bullets riddled their bodies. Tara went down to the ground and clutched her leg. Another explosion roared nearby, sending bits and pieces of Saints flying through the air. "Find cover! Return suppressive fire!" Esmeralda yelled while jumping behind a pile of machinery parts on the ground. Struggling to look up, she saw a gun turret in the window with a disfigured bald man wielding it. In other windows of the factory, hails of bullets came from similarly dressed combat assailants, all wearing pre-Anthrodi war military winter gear and the symbol of the Devil's Deviants.

Another mine nearby exploded. Bullets whizzed by as Esmeralda watched Tara drag Joshua's body to safety. "*Tara*, he's gone! Leave him!" she attempted to yell but was drowned out by the sounds of heavy artillery and the dying yelps of her unit. Nearby, a Saints' head exploded, splattering her face with blood. She peeked over her cover, laying suppressive fire in the general direction of the DDs before crouching down again, hearing bullets bounce off the metal she hid behind. She looked to her side when she realized someone was here with her, and she found the redhead newbie, Private Adrien Mahoney. The two looked at each other and had a silent nod of acknowledgment. He indicated with his head toward his gun that he was was going to cover her, to which she nodded. With that, he began to spray covering fire. Ezzy then got up again and laid some suppressive fire of her own, her rifle's automatic recoil making the assault rifle tremble in her grip. Running as fast as she could, Esmeralda made her way to Tara, who had managed to get Joshua and herself behind a piece of machinery that served as cover. When close, she jumped behind Tara's cover and lifted herself off the ground slightly while putting her back to the machine. "Tara! You okay?" Esmeralda yelled while reloading. Tara breathed hard and whimpered while clutching her leg, tears rolling down her face as she kept her other hand on Joshua.

Tara winced in pain. "I—I got shot . . ."

"Lemme take a look." Esmeralda moved Tara's hand away from her wound. She was bleeding heavily, but it luckily was just a flesh wound. Blood spurted as Ezzy stared at the mangled flesh. "Oooh, you need to get that treated. It's a bad graze. If ya actually got shot by that turret, your leg would be gone." Esmeralda prepared to call the Troop Transport.

"Him first, not me."

Tara indicated Joshua with a nod of her head. The boy was a charbroiled stump. His face was badly burnt, and his arm and legs were gone. Joshua's body looked lifeless. She then looked woefully at the younger woman. "Tara, he's gone—"

"*Check his fucking pulse!* He's breathing!"

Ezzy put her ear to Joshua's mouth and felt a small breeze on her ear. He was alive. She wasn't sure how much longer he had, but given that this was General Quinn's son, she had to try to save him.

Esmeralda then put her radio to her mouth. "Troop Transport 7, Troop Transport 7, mandatory extraction at ground zero! We have high-priority medical evacs and possible expectants. I repeat, high-priority medical evacs, possible expectants!" Esmeralda took another look at the young couple as Tara cried over what little of Joshua there was left. Hopefully, the transport would get there in time.

AYLEN

Aylen stared through the scope of her rifle and watched the chaos commence. Holy crap. *Holy crap, holy crap, holy crap.* She watched as Saints got gunned down in the courtyard. Gabriel and the other sharpshooters began to fire their rifles, but Aylen froze. She couldn't find the strength to pull the trigger. Instead, she could only watch. She watched as whoever was wielding the gun turret got his head turned into an explosion of red jelly. She watched as a girl her age with green skin shouted something while shooting, before having the lower half of her jaw fly off shortly before more red holes tore apart her body. People were dying . . . they were really dying. An arm blew off a Saint. Another Saint was crying over a missing leg, mangled bits of red-covered flesh sticking out of the stump. Aylen forgot what they were fighting for. It didn't make sense. Why was everybody killing each other? Why was she here? How did she get here? Aylen's chest tightened as she stared at the carnage down below. Pools of blood stained the snow and bits and pieces of people were scattered everywhere while the fighting continued. She couldn't breathe. This was really happening. This was—

Just then, a low rumble filled the mountainside and shook the sight on Aylen's rifle. The Sharpshooter Unit stopped their firing and looked backward. Gabriel's face turned white as the rumbling got louder, and closer. He lifted his rifle and looked through the scope.

"Everybody jump down to the factory," he said calmly, despite his look of bewilderment. Aylen lifted her rifle and looked at what was headed for them. A seemingly endless wave of Level 4 Brainless seemed to be charging toward the Sharpshooter Unit, flooding into view at the speed of a sports car. The twisted, naked figures with limbs in the wrong places charged toward them, kicking up snow like dust. "*Go now!*" Gabriel yelled while firing his rifle, then turning around to jump off the cliff.

Aylen watched as various Brainless in the front went down only to get trampled by the ones behind. Gabriel landed on the roof of one of the buildings below, continuing his fire at the Brainless. "*Jump!*" Gabriel commanded. Aylen blindly followed her captain's command, with Jonathan shortly behind her. The wind pushed through her hair as the enhancer armor catapulted her off the cliff from a height she didn't even want to think about. She desperately clutched her rifle before her feet hit the ground with a heavy sound, turning around to see some of the Sharpshooter Unit following them. Other members were not quite so lucky, jumping only to be Brainless food within minutes. Some were pushed off the cliff to their deaths by the charging Brainless. The Brainless clearly didn't care if they died; they spilled off the cliff of their own volition. Some made it onto the rooftops where Aylen and the others had jumped, and they continued their charge after the soldiers.

"Fuck!" she heard Jonathan yell, seemingly a world away. Without Gabriel even having to tell her, she made a run for it, letting her rifle hang loosely from its strap around her shoulder. She was not alone; the other remaining sharpshooters around her did the same. Up ahead, there was a higher building that maybe, if they jumped to the roof, would keep them safe. Captain Webster apparently saw it too. Aylen heard screams behind her that she knew belonged to the other sharpshooters, getting torn apart and eaten alive. She focused her eyes straight ahead.

Gabriel jumped to the taller building, which rose above them by fifteen feet. Other sharpshooters followed, and soon Aylen felt herself dragging behind even despite the enhancer armor. Brainless snarls filled her ears as her heart pounded in her chest. Gunfire began to fill Aylen's ears as the people on the taller rooftop became entangled in a firefight with DDs while covering behind a small barricade. The sounds of what might have been a thousand angry creatures nipped at her heels as she jumped up to the taller building, feeling her chest take the brunt of the impact as she slammed into her landing and pulled herself up, keeping her head down because of the nearby firefight.

"Aylen!"

Aylen turned to see Jonathan running from the remainder of the Brainless that weren't already feasting on the corpses of the dead. He was the last one. The very last one. He was running, but seemed to have trouble, and the Brainless were catching up to him. "Go, Jon, go!" Aylen yelled at the top of her lungs.

He must have hurt his leg when they all jumped from the cliff. He was going at a fast limp at best. Bullets buzzed nearby as Aylen watched him get closer, and she put her rifle on the ground next to her. "Jump, Jon! Come on!" Aylen urged, frantically motioning with her hands. Jonathan jumped up and caught the ledge, but failed to pull himself up before he lost his grip. Aylen dove forward and caught his hand. The two dangled off the side, Aylen barely still on the ledge, lying on her belly with both arms fully extended as she held on to

Jonathan's hand. "Come on, I'll help pull you up! Grab onto the wall!" Jonathan attempted to reach up, but his other arm fell short of the ledge.

"I—I can't!"

"Use your legs to climb the wall!" Aylen grunted through her teeth as she attempted to pull him up. He was heavy, even despite the fact she had enhancer armor.

"M-my leg! I can't—"

"You have to try!"

But in moments, the Brainless horde were jumping toward them, and one or two caught him and began to tug at his legs. Jonathan screamed and twisted in terror. Aylen felt the struggle as she tried to pull him up, almost getting pulled down herself. One or two Brainless quickly turned into more as they began nipping and reaching up like baby birds in a nest trying to get a worm from their mother. They were climbing on top of each other, nearly in biting range. Jonathan looked up at Aylen, eyes round like a scared little boy.

"Help me!" he screamed in terror as one of the Brainless began tearing through his enhancer armor. It bit into his flesh. Aylen began to get up to her knees but felt a tug on her arm that almost pulled her forward into the horde completely. Aylen couldn't do it; she was having a hard time pulling Jonathan up. She had to try, though, right? She grit her teeth as she pulled again and tried to get to her knees.

"*Please!*" Jonathan kept screaming helplessly as the tendons of his leg became exposed. He looked to be in pain, so much pain. Aylen tried to pull him up with a sharp tug but felt a pop as she pulled his arm, almost like she dislocated his shoulder. Tears came to his red eyes as he screamed in agony, words decaying into soundless yells. The Brainless horde was bigger now. They ripped and tore away at his midsection. Streaks of red flew through the air as Aylen continued to try to pull him up.

"*Ayyyyleeeeen!*"

Someone stronger and bigger than her came up behind her and helped pull her up. A larger arm then grabbed a hold of her arm.

Thwack.

A hatchet came down onto Jonathan's wrist. The boy was screaming at the top of his lungs now, as the hatchet rose again and prepared to fall. Aylen looked up; it was Gabriel holding the axe. She watched in horror as he slammed his hatchet down on Jonathan's wrist again.

Thwack. Thwack. Thwack.

Jonathan and his hand separated, and he and a few Brainless quickly fell into the horde below. From there, it was like watching a human paper shredder. They dug their claws into Jonathan's body and tore him open, revealing his innards and organs to her. Some of the Brainless began eating the Brainless that fell, but Jonathan was clearly the main course. His eyes stayed on Aylen through it all, teardrops welling up in his near-lifeless eyes as his screams stopped when his throat was ripped out. Two of the Brainless fought over his arm after pulling it off. Another Brainless began to tear the skin off his cheek with its jaws. Jonathan's blood stained the snow a deep crimson red as he became a mess of body parts in under a minute.

Gabriel pulled Aylen away from the sight. On instinct, she pushed him away. "*Why would you do that?*" she screamed. Gabriel still held Jonathan's severed hand. *He was still holding Jon's severed hand.* She pushed against the captain's chest. Gunfire rattled off in the distance. Some zips that sounded like angry bees passed nearby. "*You fucker!*" Aylen yelled, sobs coming out around the words. She grabbed Gabriel's armor and tried to shake him. "*We could've saved him! You didn't have to kill— You didn't have to—*"

Slap.

Aylen landed on the ground with blood coming from her lip. Gabriel knelt down and grabbed her by her armor. "*Wake up, girl, we're in a war!*" he yelled into her face, wide-eyed. "Listen to me! This isn't some little game that you play in the backyard when you're a kid! People *die.* Your friend was going to get you *killed.* He would've dragged you down as the Brainless devoured him! *I saved your life! You understand?*"

A sharpshooter nearby got shot in the head and fell over, their head leaking blood. Aylen and Gabriel both looked at the body before looking at each other. Gabriel sighed then threw Jonathan's severed hand into the pile of Brainless below. He looked at Aylen sternly, taking a deep breath. She stared at him dumbfounded, feeling her lip sting from the hit she took. Tears clouded her eyes and wet her cheeks as she stared at her mentor.

"Welcome to war, Aylen," he said to her before turning away and readying his gun. Gunfire sounded all around, coupled with the sounds of dying and Brainless devouring corpses. Uneasy and shaking, Aylen picked up her rifle from the ground. *Welcome to war,* she repeated in her head as she huddled against the small barrier that protected the sharpshooters from the oncoming gunfire. She hugged her gun like a stuffed animal, swallowing and trying to get a handle on just where she was.

Welcome to war.

EPISODE 17

The Red Snow Part II

BRENDEN

Brenden kept his helmet off as he led his unit toward the west end of the factory. It was completely silent, quiet enough to hear snow hitting the ground or the thumping of another's heart, making the air thick with tension. Brenden hated how quiet it was. It made his stomach quiver with dread and anticipation as he and his troops moved forward.

Within seconds, his unit passed the fence and began roaming through the exterior of the large facility. This section of Westbrook was far from the central courtyard and resembled a field more than any part of a factory, with a long stretch of metallic, plantlike objects in the snow that stuck straight up into the air roughly ten feet. Eric walked next to Brenden confidently, his rifle ready. There had yet to be any sign of the enemy. Sweat accumulated on Brenden's forehead despite the cold. Obviously the other units had yet to run into any trouble, as there had been little to no sign of DDs anywhere so far. A small wind blew past Brenden's ears, the mountain chill making his head cold.

"Stop," Eric called out. Brenden looked at the younger man, who pointed to the side. The grotesque display almost made Brenden jump. A severed head with missing eyes was impaled onto an assault rifle that stood upright in the snow. Eric turned Brenden's attention to more of the same display.

"Is—is that the UWF Reco—"

"Shhh." Eric looked backward. "We're missing two men—"

Boom.

A large explosion sounded off in the distance. No doubt Ezzy's group, Brenden thought. In moments the whisper of distant gunfire echoed through the wind. The fighting had officially begun.

Eric and Brenden exchanged glances. Brenden shook his head before speaking. "We'll worry about them later. Right now, we need to get into posi—"

Swish.

A warm spray of red landed in one of his eyes and splashed over his scarred face. The spray had an iron taste in it, and his heart skipped a beat when he realized what it was. Blood? He looked to his right to see the Saint next to him, a woman in her midthirties who was staring at him in bewilderment. For a brief moment, Brenden wondered what was so odd that the woman had to stare at him like that.

Suddenly, the woman's head began to lean, as if he had said something questionable. Her gaze rolled sideways as her head left her body and landed in the snow in front of him, blood seeping its way from the severed neck and into the snow. The body soon followed.

Brenden watched, stunned. His heart began to race.

"W-we're under attack!" Brenden yelled. The group panicked, frantically looking with dumb expressions on their faces as they began to search for the assailant. A scream in the back sounded as something Brenden could not see burst through a man's chest. The Saints fired their guns frantically, but they began getting picked off by unseen enemies. One's throat was slit; a hole appeared through another's eye—all by something they couldn't see.

And they were dropping like flies.

Gunfire rattled, zipping by at random as Saints fired at unseen enemies. One of the Saints slammed into the snow, taken down by stray gunfire, as Brenden tried to make sense of the chaos. "Huddle together! B formatio—"

Something tugged at his hair.

Glush.

He felt another spray of blood on the back of his head. The grip of whoever had tugged his hair loosened. Brenden turned around to see Eric holding one end of a red-splattered sword. An orange-skinned man began fading into view, bug-eyed and with the other end of the sword sticking out of his mouth. Eric pulled the sword out and huddled his back to Brenden's. Two other Saints, a man and a woman, joined them, blades at the ready.

"Something's cloaking them!" Eric yelled, readying his sword. Brenden slung his assault rifle to his back and pulled out his chain.

"What the hell is this?" the female Saint screamed through her helmet. Just as Brenden turned, another Saint was disemboweled in front of him. Only he, Eric, and the two other Saints were left alive out of their unit. Anger filled him. He swung his chain in circles, prepping it for an attack. "Bastards! Show yourselves!"

"He asked so politely." A disembodied voice chuckled.

A moment passed, and then roughly eighteen deviant soldiers that weren't there before surrounded them, swords in their hands. Brenden's eyes widened. *What the hell?*

The deviants looked at each other as if to mock the small group. Then one yelled and charged toward Eric. With the grace of a dove, Eric parried the attack and slashed through the man while moving past him, then he stabbed the same deviant without looking and pulled out the sword, readying it in an attack stance.

The deviant group all closed the distance between them and the four Saints with swords ready. Brenden pressed a button on the grip of the chain and spikes protruded from the links in an instant. He parried a sword attack and swiped his chain into the face of his opponent, slashing off the skin on the man's jaw and inviting a flurry of attacks.

Exchanges between the remaining four Saints and sixteen deviants became heated as swords and Brendan's chain clashed, singing the song of an old battlefield with every metallic clang. One of the Saints was stabbed in the back by one deviant while fighting off another with his ax. Brenden did his best to fend off multiple attackers at once, barely avoiding the swinging blades. He looked to his side and saw the Saint that had been stabbed was on his knees—then one of the deviants took off his head. Brenden backed away as the deviant who had been the most aggressive in his attack charged toward him and swung.

Brenden stumbled back over what felt like two logs, barely avoiding the blade meant for his neck. He had tripped on enhancer armor-covered legs. The female Saint that had been huddled with them was leaking blood from her neck like a leaky faucet, writhing on the ground like a fish out of water. It was her legs he had tripped over. He stared in horror as she twisted, clutching her throat and trying to breathe before a sword stabbed straight into her head. Brenden looked up. Both his initial attacker and the deviant that had killed the female Saint were staring at him. He struggled to get up but immediately felt a pressure on his shoulder, like someone had used him as a springboard. Before Brenden could comprehend what happened, Eric sliced through the head of one of his attackers, then stabbed the other through his chest, cleaving the deviant's head with his knife for good measure.

"That's the Bastard Saint!" one of the remaining deviants called out as Eric helped Brenden to his feet. In moments, the deviants disappeared again.

"Shit!" Brenden breathed heavily while swinging his chain.

"Watch the snow!" Eric called to him as they huddled their backs to each other again. "You can see their footprints!" There was silence for a moment as footprints tracked through the snow. It was hard to tell how many sets there were, as they overlapped each other. The footprints began to encircle the two men.

"Get down," Brenden said under his breath.

"What?"

"I don't feel like dying today. Do it."

"Brenden, I can't hear you," Eric growled while watching the footprints tighten the circle around them. This was unnerving.

Brenden pushed Eric to the ground and swung his spiked chain. Red liquid spurted around them as lines of blood became visible in the vacant air. Brenden kept swinging like a madman, until a loud spurt sounded and one deviant faded into existence, half of his head missing. His blood splashed onto a few formerly invisible figures, making their outlines clear.

"My turn." Eric jumped toward one of the vague figures and stabbed, revealing the deviant. He spun his sword around and stabbed another combatant, who appeared out of thin air. An unsettling grin formed on Eric's face was as he quickly dispatched another formerly invisible deviant, then another, and another. Somehow, he knew where they all were. He leaped through the air and dodged invisible attacks as if he was dancing, and Brenden watched in awe as the young man made dead deviants appear out of thin air like some sort of strange magician with a sword.

The six remaining deviants showed themselves and readied their weapons, to no avail. Eric threw his knife into the forehead of one and disemboweled another that tried to strike him from behind. Brenden wrapped his chain around the throat of one and pulled, beheading the man while Eric regained his knife and used it to slash the throat of another that attacked from behind. He swiped down one more as Brenden swung his chain into another's head.

They were done.

There was only a brief moment of silence before a sound near one of the large plantlike objects caught the Saints' attention. Eric stomped toward the sound hungrily. A young, disembodied voice began to plead, "N-no, God, please! N—"

Eric immediately stabbed downward, and a shriek sounded. A teenage boy with purple skin faded into view, leaning against the large machine with Eric's sword in his gut. He couldn't have been more than seventeen. Blood was pouring out of his mouth. His eyes were red and his lips trembled, as if he was about to cry, all while Eric's face remained cold.

"Hurts, huh?" he said, no emotion in his voice.

"I—I was just following orders. Just following orders, just following . . ." The deviant whimpered, clutching Eric and staring wide-eyed at the blade in his gut. Eric twisted the sword. The deviant boy gritted his teeth in agony.

"Aren't we all?" Eric said.

"P-please . . ."

Brenden exhaled. "Just finish it," he said solemnly. Eric briefly looked at Brenden before pulling out the blade and beheading the deviant boy in one fluid motion. Brenden looked at the head on the ground. The mouth was agape and the eyes were dead. It was a boy, just a scared boy. Probably a greenhorn, judging from his cowardice. Maybe he didn't go on too many missions beforehand, maybe it was his first taste of the rougher stuff. Then again, seeing Eric in action for the first time might make any opponent rethink their allegiances. But cowards never lasted long in the DDs. It was just how they were.

Eric stared at the head for a moment before looking up. The two Saints caught their breath, then looked at all the carnage that surrounded them. Everyone around them was dead. Without Eric, Brenden would've been one of the dead today, too, a couple times over. Brenden shifted his gaze, and he froze when he saw Brainless in the distance, jumping off the cliff to the north. What were they to do now? They couldn't exactly be very helpful as reinforcements at this point, not with there only being two of them. They stood in silence while ghosts of gunfire and screams filled their ears just under that damned soft breeze.

Eric chuckled at nothing and looked at Brenden. "Hey, Sarge, I've got a wild idea."

JARED

"Gail, you see a way out for me?"

Jared tightened his grip on his scythe as he backed away from the figures shrouded in darkness. To the side, he could see Brainless creeping in toward him. Then he heard the snarls behind him.

"Come in, Gail? Gail!" Jared called again. He hugged the wall with his back. He really was surrounded. The only reason they probably hadn't pounced on him yet was because of his deviant smell, but they were creeping in on him with a sort of curiosity, sniffing. It'd only be seconds until they started lunging to kill.

"*Gail!*" he yelled. No response. He was on his own. She had abandoned him. Figures. Jared looked at the walkways. There was probably no way he'd be able to fight them on those. He looked at the water in front of him and grimaced. Oh, *come on!* The sewage appeared to be knee-high at this point, and it would be a wide enough space for Jared to fight his way through and escape. Shit. He was grossed out, but it was his only chance for survival.

He jumped off the walkway and into the sewer water, making a huge splash as he landed between the Level 4 Brainless at the bottom. The moment he landed, the rest dove for him. On instinct he moved his scythe and lopped the head off one, and before the other Brainless even knew what was going on, he began cutting through them as fast as he possibly could.

"This shit is pissing me off!" Jared yelled as he cut through them, trying to make a path out. A Brainless tried to pounce on him; he sidestepped it and planted the tip of his scythe into its skull. The rest surrounded him and began to tear away at his armor. They jumped on him only for him to immediately knock them off. They scratched, clawed, and bit. Jared swiped his scythe around, splitting the ones closest in half.

Jared realized one fault with this fight: He could barely see. He had no idea where he was going or how to get out of this predicament. The Brainless on the walkway were beginning to jump into the water with him. He slashed through them in seconds, but the array was endless. He had to use his fire—there was no other choice. That "no fire 'cause of gas" rule Gail was so worried about was ridiculous. Even with gas, he could control the impact and direction of the flame. Gail was just being a prick by putting that limitation on him anyway, wasn't she? And she was nowhere to be found on the intercom? She was *trying* to get him killed, huh? Probably led him here on purpose before telling him he was surrounded, knowing he was coming upon an entire pack. Jared grit his teeth.

"Gail, you fucking asshole!"

He sliced through another Brainless. He focused on the orange parts of his scythe and they became engulfed in flames, lighting up the tunnel for him. Jared's eyes widened as he looked into the distance. Brainless filled the entire sewer as far as he could see. "Today's just not my day," he muttered to himself. He was boned.

Jared waved the fire in front of the Brainless, fending off their attacks and keeping them at bay. He looked desperately around. If there was a gas line around here, why couldn't he find it? Jared was almost ready to give up on the search when something caught his eye. A small, thin pipe near the top of the tunnel glimmered in the light from his burning scythe. There it was.

He cut through a Brainless in front of him, then began running. When he hit the right speed, he changed his footing and began running up the wall. It was a thin pipe, so one good swipe should do. He narrowly dodged a Brainless that jumped for him, twisting his body to try to get the damn thing. One good swipe, that's it. *One good swipe.* With a lightning-fast swing, he severed the pipe.

In seconds, Jared felt fire surround him, and with his will, it filled the tunnel, blowing straight through the roof. Brainless disintegrated around Jared as he fell backward midair. Time stood still. Jared watched his power light the entire tunnel with fire.

Brainless burned to ash, squealing in agony. It was familiar, like a movie he had seen over and over again. It was strange and it was beautiful, the fire. The flames always kept him safe. Just like they did at his childhood home, just like they did more times than he could count throughout his life. Chunks of his armor disintegrated from the intense heat as the blaze engulfed him, but the flame left him unburned and unaffected. It was a warm blanket for him, a hot shower, a heat that cleansed.

Jared landed on the floor, where the water was being pushed back by the inferno. He closed his eyes as he the fire cradled his body like a wet nurse would a baby. Then he looked up at the hole in the top of the tunnel that his power had made. The fire faded until it was just the flame surrounding him. The water that had been pushed back rushed around his knees. Parts of Jared's enhancer armor were still simmering from the heat. He ripped those pieces of the armor off his body and then removed his helmet and dropped it into the water, finding he barely had any armor left. He looked up to the sky as the remaining fire evaporated into black smoke that exited the tunnel amid the burnt Brainless bodies. The sky above him was a pretty shade of blue.

ESMERALDA

Esmeralda and Tara stared at the huge explosion that sounded outside the factory, just beyond the buildings. A large black smokestack rose in the distance. *What the hell was that?* Esmeralda wondered. Gunfire continued to roar all around. Brenden's unit had yet to show up, and there were too few signs of the Sharpshooter Unit nearby. They were more or less on their own in the courtyard.

Suddenly, she heard an engine in the distance. The Troop Transport. Esmeralda stared hopefully at the black vehicle as it burst through the gates. General Quinn's son and Tara would be saved after all. Esmeralda smiled at this. The Troop Transport was bulletproof and even had a gun turret. Hopefully, it could carry out General Quinn's son and—

A loud explosion stole away her dreams of getting Joshua from the battle almost immediately. The transport lifted up and turned over, skidding on its roof while engulfed in flames. No.

No, no, no. Shit, shit, *shit.*

A white-haired woman stood on top of the tall main building of the factory. For a second, Esmeralda did not recognize her. The woman's hair looked like the snow, she wore winter military gear, and she stood tall like some sort of goddess among the clouds. On her shoulder was a rocket launcher and upon her face was an icy, emotionless gaze. The firing ceased as she threw the rocket launcher down beside her. Saints and DDs alike seemed to be in awe of the woman's presence as she glared down into the courtyard.

"Brothers and sisters!" the white-haired woman yelled. "Why waste our bullets when we have something *better* at our disposal?"

The woman lifted her arms and a rumble began from inside the factory buildings. Then Esmeralda realized that none of the DDs were on the ground fighting, it was only the Saints. In that moment, she recognized who the woman standing on the building was.

"Pestilence," she muttered to herself. "Everybody huddle together! Now!"

Almost to punctuate her command, waves of Level 4 Brainless began to burst through the windows of the buildings. Saints huddled in terror as some dropped out of the sky from the higher windows, while others charged on the ground from garage-like doors. The Saint operatives fired into them, releasing a barrage of automatic fire, but the Brainless were circling them all around. They seemed endless, like ants in an anthill. Esmeralda looked on helplessly as the white-haired woman and deviants retreated into the main building. She had no choice but to call in help; they could only hold off this big of a Brainless swarm for so long.

Swallowing any pride, Esmeralda called on the intercom.

"Tank Suit Unit, come in. I repeat, Tank Suit Unit, come in! Need an assist! It's kinetic out here and we can't tactically retrograde! Tank Suit Unit, please assist! We're getting slaughtered!"

AYLEN

Aylen watched as the Brainless on the rooftop suddenly turned their attention toward the courtyard and began jumping off the roof. The woman's voice had come from somewhere she couldn't see, but after hearing it the Brainless began pouring in from everywhere conceivable. In the middle of the courtyard, the remaining Saints huddled together as the waves of Brainless came toward them. Her heart pounded for the Saints below.

On instinct, Aylen lifted her rifle and pointed it toward the Saints. She looked through the scope and began firing at the Brainless, attempting to protect the group in the center. The other sharpshooters attempted to do the same, but it became clear that it was impossible. The Saints in the center fired upon the Brainless valiantly while attempting to protect their own wounded. The sound of machine gun fire filled the air as Brainless snarled and jumped upon the soldiers below.

Aylen watched helplessly as Brainless devoured the Saints as they attempted to maintain their ground. Gabriel looked into the middle of the battlefield with horror in his eyes. He seemed to be watching the sergeant in charge intensely as she yelled into her intercom while protecting two wounded soldiers. The captain then threw his rifle to the ground.

Puzzled, Aylen said, "Captain Webster?"

Gabriel looked around at his troops, squinting. "Keep firing at the Brainless! Protect the group in the center!" Then he pulled out his hatchet and extended another one in his other hand.

That was when Aylen started to figure out what he was doing. Her eyes widened. "Captain Webster?"

Gabriel smiled at her softly as he climbed atop the barrier. "You're the best student I ever had, Aylen. Remember, you're a survivor. Stay alive."

"Captain?" Aylen watched in shock as he jumped into the fray with hatchets ready. As Gabriel landed, he dug a hatchet into the skull of one Brainless and hit another one in the face with his other. Aylen watched him through her scope. He rushed through the battlefield on his way to the center where the Saints had formed their circle, keeping the Brainless at bay with their suppressive fire.

"*Ezzy!*" Gabriel yelled.

Sergeant Rodriguez turned around, but as she did so a Brainless tackled her to the ground. Gabriel quickened his pace as the Brainless began to claw at the armor at her back. Aylen could hear her screams even from the roof.

Gabriel readied his hatchet and planted it into the back of the creature's neck, which made it roll over in reaction to the sudden pain. The captain climbed on top of it and began hacking away at it mercilessly while the sergeant got back up, bloody scratches visible on her back.

A Brainless turned its attention to Gabriel. Immediately, Aylen looked through the scope of her rifle and fired, hitting the creature in the head. Gabriel saw the creature hit the ground and looked up toward Aylen.

Okay, she had to get her crap together. She could be scared later; now, she had a job to do. She wasn't about to let her captain get killed so easily.

MARIE

The Tank Suit Unit sat outside the factory and watched the smoke in the distance. Marie twisted uncomfortably in her seat, feeling the cold slip through her gray flight suit. She briefly looked over at the other tank suits, all standing in a row next to hers, each with two mechanical legs that attached to a cockpit that jutted out perhaps a little more than Marie liked. Two large cannons sat on top of each cockpit, spread evenly apart, and on either side of the death machines were two large machine guns, looking more like arms than actual weapons.

Each tank suit was a different color. Marie's was navy blue. She had been training in this one and normally felt quite comfortable in it, but even with the heaters on, it was freezing. She didn't envy the reserve forces with them outside as they shuddered in only enhancer armor, waiting. They looked like they were doing their best to stay warm.

Marie focused again on the smoke ahead. Shouldn't they be doing something right now? From the smokestacks and sound of gunfire, it sounded like all hell was breaking loose.

Just then, their intercom channel turned on.

"Tank Suit Unit, come in. I repeat, Tank Suit Unit, come in! Need an assist! It's kinetic out here and we can't tactically retrograde! Tank Suit Unit, please assist! We're getting slaughtered!"

Marie looked over at the other three tank suits, who proceeded to all look at Captain Gatton for a command of what to do. Morgan's tank suit was just like the others. Nothing impressive, quite a bit like the man inside.

"Sir, what should we do?" one of the tank suit pilots asked.

Captain Gatton continued to sit back and watch as Brainless attacked the forces inside. His face looked carved from stone as he lit a cigar.

"Hold your position," he said finally. "It ain't time yet."

"Sir, if we let them hold out much longer, they could die!"

"What you got between your legs boy? A pencildick? I *said* hold fire. Won't say it again."

Ezzy's voice came on again. "Tank Suit Unit, *please*! There's too many Brainless! Need an assist! We can't hold them. *Tank Suit Unit, we're dying out here!*"

This time the intercom did not shut off. Sounds of Brainless roars, gunfire, and screaming sounded in the cockpits. The soldiers in the outpost looked uneasy at the sounds of the dying screams.

"*Morgan!*" Esmeralda's voice screamed again. The sounds of multiple Brainless growling and gurgling filled the air. Morgan continued to watch the battle, seemingly unmoved by the horrors they could hear.

The pilots and ground forces all looked tense. Despite the enhancer armor and advanced weaponry, at that moment none of them looked like soldiers. They stood there, horrified faces frozen. None of them looked like they wanted to go anywhere near the fighting.

Marie thought for a second about Morgan's motivations. Could this be because Esmeralda had been the one who called in? Were the rumors true? Was Morgan willing to allow the deaths of all the Saints trapped in that mess just because of what happened between him and Esmeralda? Marie looked again at Morgan, frightened by the possibilities, by what this meant. Was he so selfish of a human being that he wouldn't lift a finger to save those men and women?

Marie heard the dying cries of people being devoured by Brainless. The gurgles and familiar roars. She breathed hard, remembering her own run-in with Brainless and a deviant, before joining the Saints. The claws, the gnawing, the bites. Her scarred back ached at the thought. Piles of bodies . . . like the one she had been left for dead on. Her brow slicked with sweat while gunfire rattled through the air. The pilots of the other tank suits looked nervous, listening as people they loved and knew died after crying for their help. The soldiers with helmets off outside had no color on their faces; one was dry heaving. They all looked two seconds from shitting themselves.

As Morgan sat back and did nothing, Marie felt an anger rise within her.

"Fuck this," she grumbled as she pushed the stick in the cockpit forward and began her way toward the battlefield.

"The hell do you think you're doing, Private?" Morgan yelled over the intercom.

"What's right: Helping our people."

"I said hold your position!"

"We do nothin', they gonna die, man."

"I'm in fucking charge and you're gonna fall in line! You're gonna stay in position till I say so. *Understand me, Private?*"

Marie continued on her way in her navy-blue tank suit, ignoring him.

"Hey! Keep walking and *I will end you!*"

Marie turned her tank suit slightly. She saw the angry red man turn pinker and pinker. More importantly, she saw the guns on his tank suit were pointed at her. The other Saints merely watched, terrified expressions on their faces. Marie looked back at Morgan and stared at him. He really didn't want her to go help them? The fuck was this? She sniffed in and licked her lips.

"You really gonna use those on me?"

"You don't get back here I will, swear to God. I don't take people goin' AWOL lightly. Fall back, Private. I *won't* repeat that order."

Marie glared at him with her head tilted back. "Go 'head, pendejo, *do it* . . . if you got the balls."

Marie and Morgan stared each other down. It only lasted five seconds. He was bluffing. Marie could see it in his face. All that big talk, but he was scared. Decorated war veteran her ass. He looked like a scared little boy trying to be tough. All that talk . . . and he wasn't about to do jack shit.

She briefly looked back at the other soldiers, who didn't speak up or lift a finger in any way. All of them resembled scared mice. Then she turned around and began her way toward the battlefield again.

"Let me know when you pussies grow a spine."

Morgan began yelling something, and Marie shut off the intercom.

TARA

Tara breathed hard as her vision blurred. She had to stop the bleeding. She reached into the emergency kit on her belt and pulled out the incinerator, a black rod that resembled a baton and had an orange, burning tip at the end. She whimpered at the pain of her open wound.

Joshua was probably dead by now. The Troop Transport failed to come. It *failed*. Tara jammed the incinerator into her leg wound and screamed as the flesh in her leg sizzled, the incinerator cauterizing the wound. Tears fled from her eyes as the smell of burning flesh seeped into her nostrils. She looked at Joshua, who lay in front of her lifeless and limbless. The tears came in an onslaught at the sight. His burnt body was grotesque shades of red and black. He was probably dead by now. Now, she had no one. No parents. No family. And now Josh was gone too. The only thing she had left in this world . . . gone. Tara had no one left.

Tara looked around at the Saints getting torn to ribbons by Brainless. A woman with a pretty face lay on the ground nearby, her torso torn open. Her eyes were open. She looked like she was staring at Tara. She looked so peaceful, so accepting of her fate. The snow fell on her as blood trickled out of her mouth. Tara didn't even see the Brainless devouring her; tearing out her entrails, ripping the tissue and meat from the corpse. She only saw the beautiful face that looked tranquil and half-asleep. It was like she knew something that Tara didn't. An end to suffering. An end to pain.

Tara watched the Saints around her, fighting in vain against the onslaught of monsters. The fire of the Troop Transport flickered behind her, only slightly warming her cold body. Tara took one last look at Joshua. He had to be dead. It was hopeless. Everything here was hopeless. Everyone here would be dead by the day's end. Even if they weren't, she truly had nothing now. Tara pulled her pistol from its holster and observed it. Each little crevice of the pistol served a purpose. Every little factory-made line—the nozzle, the hammer, the clip, the trigger—it all served a purpose. But what purpose did any of the chaos around her serve?

Machine guns rattled somewhere, a world away.

Maybe this was the end of the fighting. Maybe it was better to go out the easy way than be eaten alive. Maybe Joshua would understand.

Her hand shook as she put the handgun in her mouth. As soon as she tasted the iron, she immediately yanked it out and sobbed. But she'd made her choice. Tara laid her head on Joshua's body and started to put the gun in her mouth again.

Gasp.

Joshua's torso inhaled deeply, and Tara pulled the gun away. She immediately sat up and saw his eyes open.

"Josh?"

She panicked while watching her lover's burnt body breathe life loudly, as if he had just awoken from drowning. "Josh!" Tara took him into her arms. "Josh! Baby? Can you hear me? *Baby?*" Josh breathed hard and didn't look at her, instead looking blindly at the sky.

Suddenly, light blue veins flashed in his face like neon lights. His eyes began glowing the same color.

"Josh?" Tara panicked. The look on his face became one of pure horror as his body began to pulsate. He began screaming at the top of his lungs. The sun gleamed on his forehead as he gyrated violently on the ground.

Gabriel turned around and looked at the fidgeting and screaming Joshua, and Tara swallowed hard as she watched her lover helplessly. He continued screaming as the light blue veins showed through his skin, flashing.

PESTILENCE

Pestilence walked through the interior of the main building, followed by her fellow deviants. Something was wrong. Why hadn't they left yet? What the hell was Dagon doing? The plan was that the Brainless hordes that she controlled would hold off the Saints while the creature carried the equipment back to The Ninth Circle. The deviants should've been gone before the Saint forces even attacked. There weren't enough actual deviants to hold off that many Saints.

Pestilence saw Dagon and the other deviants strapping the equipment onto the creature. The long, giant thing was locked in fortified restraints, not revealing much of its elongated physical form.

"Dagon, *what the hell?* We should be gone by now!"

Dagon looked in her direction and sniffed. "Oy, you're a real pisser, ain't ya?"

"We have to get going. Now."

Dagon smirked. "And why is that, love? Sounds to me like we're winning out there."

Pestilence almost got into Dagon's face right then and there. "They're gonna bring in the heavy artillery soon. We're gonna need more than Brainless when that happens, and we don't have much other than that up our sleeves. Maybe a few weapons we can steal from here, *tops*, but with the remaining brothers and sisters—"

Dagon indicated the creature with his head. "What about this?"

"The creature? No. I've already told you, no way. I've told you, I can't completely control it! I let that thing loose, it could just as easily eat us! Get our people out of here *now*!"

"You givin' *me* orders, love?"

"So what if I am? You wanna survive? Azrael is here too!"

This seemed to catch Dagon's attention. "Now, how do you know that?"

"A whole division of our Brainless was just taken out in the sewers. They *burned* to death. There's only one person that could've caused a massive explosion like that and survived. He's out there, Dagon, I feel it,"

Dagon looked deep in thought at this, then grabbed his walkie. "Begin wrapping up, gents. Party's over. Azrael is he—"

The ground began to shake.

"What was that?" one of the deviants asked before the ground rumbled again. Pestilence knew but didn't answer. She turned to go to a lookout point instead to see what she already knew was happening.

ESMERALDA

Esmeralda ran out of bullets in her assault rifle. She threw it to the ground.

"Shit!" she screamed before getting out her sword and running it through another Brainless. Exhaustion made her limbs heavy, but she would not give in. Gabriel dug an ax into Brainless flesh next to her as the horde continued its relentless assault. Goddamn it, why wasn't the Tank Suit Unit here yet? Was Morgan really so vindictive?

Of course he is. The small thought entered the back of her mind. Morgan was really about to let her die like this. Esmeralda briefly glanced at Gabriel as he swung an ax into a Brainless. She had made the right choice to be with him. Even if Esmeralda hurt Gabriel in the worst of ways, *he* would never leave her to die like this. She briefly watched her lover as the fight raged on. He'd risked his own life to come down here and fight by her side; Morgan never would've done that. Gabriel loved her like she loved him. Even if they both died today, she'd made the right choice.

Esmeralda stabbed another Brainless in the mouth. They just *kept coming.* There was no end to them. There was a reason Pestilence was feared among the Saints, and *this* was easily that reason. Brainless crawled over the corpses of other Brainless, not seeming sentimental or mindful of the other creatures' well-being. It was hopeless; there was no end to them. No end at all—

A sound whistled overhead. Suddenly, Brainless parts flew through the battlefield in a fiery blaze. Esmeralda's hopes lifted as she saw a lone blue tank suit standing above the chaos. A red flower of fire bloomed among the bodies with an ear-deafening roar. The tank suit continued its way forward and fired its cannon again, setting another part of the battlefield ablaze. The Brainless took notice of the towering tank suit and began to head for it. The minigun arms twirled and cut through the creatures like paper. Why only one tank unit, though? Esmeralda looked inside the cockpit and saw Private Marie Vasquez piloting the machinery. A smile crossed her face as she watched her student take out clumps of Brainless. Marie screamed while blasting away as many Brainless as she could. She was making a dent!

Then a missile whistled through the air, headed for the tank suit. Marie noticed it just barely and tried to get away.

Boom!

Esmeralda looked on in horror as one of the tank suit's legs blew off. The cockpit toppled to one side. She looked up—the deviants had rocket launchers. *Shit, they've reentered the battlefield.* Esmeralda looked to one side and saw a line being cut through the Brainless as Pestilence marched forward with a small group of deviants behind her, all of them firing into the Saints. Pestilence's skin turned a chrome color and her arm turned into a blade. She began cutting through Saints as easily as Eric would cut through DDs.

"Shit," Esmeralda muttered. She felt her limbs grow heavier and the sting of the Brainless scratches on her back as she started toward Pestilence. Sweat stung her eyes and made it hard for her to see ahead of her. There was only one thing causing the Brainless to launch such a concentrated attack on the Saints, and it was Pestilence. Esmeralda moved her hair out of her face and clenched her left hand around her sword tighter with every step.

"Ezzy! What're you doing?" Gabriel called out. Esmeralda looked backward and put her right hand up briefly, a small grin on her face as she began for the leader.

Before she knew it, a Brainless grabbed her raised hand with its jaws. She yelped in pain as she lobotomized the Brainless with a swift swing of her sword. Pain didn't matter. Esmeralda looked briefly at the holes in her hand as she was tackled to the ground by another Brainless. She struggled to push the Brainless off her back and stabbed it in the forehead with a knife using her bad hand. The hard feeling of the metal handle against her mutilated flesh made it scream; she dropped the knife after the motion. Then she grabbed her sword with her good hand, lifted herself off the ground, and continued her way forward, feeling dizzy still from the tackle.

Everything in Esmeralda's body hurt and screamed a thousand promises of pain as she headed toward the metal-skinned menace. Feeling in her bloodied hand began to numb as she lost the ability to move her fingers. Didn't matter, though; she was going to get out of this alive, of that she was certain. She wasn't going to lose. Not now, when life was finally starting to go her way. Today would not be the day she died.

Esmeralda lifted her sword and began running toward the metallic woman, swinging her sword for her neck while Pestilence wasn't looking. A metallic clang rang out as the sword hit. It didn't even so much as dent Pestilence, despite Ezzy's best effort. The deviant turned her head, taking notice of the wounded sergeant. The chrome-covered woman then pushed the sword off her neck and swung her blade arm at Esmeralda. The sergeant blocked, feeling her sword shake slightly in her hand as she held Pestilence at bay with it for a moment. In an instant, she threw her body into another strike against the metallic woman only to hear another metallic clang as the sword hit the woman's torso. Pestilence looked down at the blade and punched Esmeralda off, the bruises already on her face igniting with pain. As the sergeant turned away from the inertia of the hit, the white-haired deviant swiped her arm blade at Esmeralda's back, slicing a nasty cut into it. The sergeant yelped in agony and quickly turned around, swiping her sword at Pestilence's face with all her might.

Dink.

It was a different sort of sound as the blade lodged its way into Pestilence's metallic cheek. A small bit of blood trickled onto the blade as Pestilence knocked Esmeralda off her.

Explosions rang out on the battlefield as more tank suits showed up to wreak havoc on the Brainless and deviants. Pestilence quickly swiped her blade arm diagonally, slightly quicker than before. Ezzy narrowly blocked it, and soon the deviant followed with another strike. Then another and another, both of which the sergeant barely was able to block. Her opponent was good, and it was obvious who the better fighter was. Esmeralda tried desperately to hold her own in the battle of blades, but Pestilence continuously barraged her, each harder to stop than the one before. The sergeant's arm gave in while attempting to block an attack and Pestilence's blade sliced into her shoulder. She slowed and dropped to her knees, exhaustion finally taking hold. Snow fell and blew through the wind as she sank to the icy ground and felt her knees dig into it. She was finished. She knew it. Esmeralda breathed hard, bleeding, as Pestilence stood over her, watching.

"Well, if you're gonna do it, then do it, bitch," she growled. Pestilence stared at her silently for a second, then began winding up to slice off her head.

A single shot rang loud and clear through the air, almost above the other sounds of gunfire. Pestilence dropped to her knees, blood staining her white military coat as she fell to the ground. Her skin turned back to normal as she winced and moaned in pain. She breathed heavy, shaky breaths as she clutched her side and looked at her own blood. She climbed to her feet and began running, but another shot hit her in the back, sending the white-haired woman face-first into the snow.

Esmeralda looked up and saw the girl who had punched out Morgan crouched on one of the rooftops, holding a sniper rifle. Her vision then blurred as she sank into a deep, dark abyss.

BRENDEN

Eric and Brenden moved swiftly through the halls of the Westbrook factory, weapons at the ready. Explosions blasted outside as they moved through the coldly lit area.

Brenden breathed out in frustration. "I'm not seeing anything so far, you?"

Eric remained silent as the two carefully moved through the empty hallways. The two then turned a corner and Brenden's eyes caught onto something unexpected. He and Eric rushed to the DD corpses on the ground. Brenden looked over them carefully. They were surrounded by boxes of equipment and were all fairly well armed, but a mixture of bullets and burn marks filled their bodies. One corpse was completely blackened, with a fairly large stab wound through his abdomen.

Brenden couldn't help but chuckle, relieved that he himself wouldn't have to deal with these dead DDs. "Well, looks like Jared's been through here . . ." He trailed off when he noticed the way Eric's tilted his head and how he licked his lips, analyzing the scenario. An unreadable, almost wild look came to his eyes as he studied the corpses. It unnerved Brenden.

"Eric?"

Eric turned around and began stomping off.

"*Eric?*"

DAGON

Dagon continued to study the battlefield from the high window of the factory. Shit, those tank suits were changing the tide of battle. The DD units with rocket launchers had been disposed of by the tank suits sending missiles their way, which also sent parts of the factory up in flames. Other tank suits sprayed gunfire into the Brainless, putting significant dents in the horde. The blue tank suit on the ground had almost been broken into by Brainless, but a whole new unit of the Saints' ground forces swept in and saved the pilot, now adding their fire power to the fight. The Devil's Deviants were losing, and fast. Even the mighty Pestilence had been brought down in the fighting.

The deviant to Dagon's immediate right looked at him with desperation.

"Sir, what should we do?"

Dagon remained silent, mesmerized by the chaos of the battle below.

"Sir?"

Dagon's eyelids flinched for a brief moment. He felt nauseous. Their forces were getting torn apart in minutes. Pestilence had been right about the heavy artillery. If only she hadn't been taken out, maybe they could've used the creature. Even Dagon could admit letting it loose without her controlling it was a terrible idea, even as a last-ditch effort. No one would be safe at that point. It was possible everyone here could die. A part of him wanted desperately to retreat. So desperately . . . but at what cost? What sort of things would Lucifer do if Dagon called for a retreat now? He may have no choice but to unleash the horrifying monstrosity with how quickly they were being wiped out. Nothing could stop that thing.

What to do . . .

Dagon swallowed after a moment's contemplation. Releasing the creature might be their only option now.

"Undo the restraints on the creature," he said. "Then run like hell."

The deviant beside him widened his eyes. With good reason too, admittedly.

Dagon nodded his head to confirm what he just said. "Do it. It's our only option now. Ready the rocket launchers, gather up as many weapons as you can. We make one final—"

A sound interrupted Dagon, catching his attention and that of every other deviant in the room. There was a familiar deviant standing in the doorway, holding his gut, which looked burnt. A glowing orange knife was stuck in his back. Dagon recognized the deviant as one of his scavengers.

"A-Azrael . . ." The scavenger deviant looked pitiful as he whimpered and sniveled. "It's Az—"

Whoooooosh.

The deviant, screaming, burst into flames. The other Devil's Deviants in the room looked on in panic as the deviant burned alive before them, twisting and turning before falling to the floor. Silenced shots burst from the doorway, hitting the deviant closest to the burning man. Before Dagon could even pull his own pistol out, Azrael's familiar face, covered in blood and soot, appeared and then disappeared. Gunfire rattled as his blurred figure approached a deviant to Dagon's right and sent his head flying. Azrael appeared behind another deviant on Dagon's opposite side and slit his throat. Dagon and the remainder of his men fired in their enemy's direction as Azrael used the now-dead deviant before him as a shield. A pistol with a silencer appeared from behind the corpse.

PchooPchooPchooPchoo.

Pain ignited in Dagon's shoulder and gut. He went down immediately as the shots dispatched the rest of his comrades. Just like that, a sense of quiet returned to the room, save for the flickering flames and Dagon's own moans and cries. The rat-faced man's breath shuddered as he clutched himself, warm blood rushing past his fingers. The corpse Azrael was holding fell face-first with a graceless thud. The orange scythe in his hand transformed into a rod.

"They got *you* behind this operation, Dagon? Shit, no wonder you're losing out there," Azrael said. The click of a lighter sounded off in the air.

Dagon grunted in pain as he tried to turn himself toward Azrael's looming figure. "If—if it isn't the fucking traitor . . ." The sizzle of a cigarette being puffed on filled Dagon's ear.

"Who betrayed who first, I wonder? Either way, we're on opposite sides now."

Dagon did his best to look at the soot-covered boy standing over him, who had now begun to kneel so Dagon could see his face: messy black hair, orange eyes. Azrael tilted his head.

"I never liked you, and you? Well I think it's fair to say you don't like anyone, so let's cut to the chase, yeah? *You're* gonna tell *me* what Lucifer has all of you doing all the way out here. And you're gonna tell me sooner rather than later." Azrael took a puff of his cigarette.

Dagon chuckled through his pain. He had a pistol on his side . . . maybe he could do what so many had failed to do in the past. "Yeah? Why's that?"

Azrael's face, despite its smirk, kept its darkly serious demeanor. "I think we both know why, Dagon."

Dagon's grip was now firmly on his pistol. He began to laugh. "Yeah?"

"Yeah."

"*Fuck you!*"

Dagon pulled out his pistol and pointed it at—

Boom.

Dagon howled and clutched his hand. His hand! *It was almost completely gone!* Bones stuck out of exposed flesh as Dagon screamed in horror and rolled on the ground.

Azrael scoffed. "Gunpowder. You should've known that was a bad idea." Azrael took another puff of his cigarette before continuing. "Tell me, what were you assholes planning by attacking this factory?"

"*Eat shit!*" Dagon cried out.

Azrael's eyelid flinched for a moment before he tossed his cigarette aside. In milliseconds, Azrael grabbed the deviant's good hand and one of his glowing knives, twirling it in his fingers.

"All right."

Stab.

Dagon cried out as the boy in soot jabbed the knife into his hand. Then Azrael stood and kicked him to his back. "Bet you're wishing your only ability wasn't breathing underwater right now, huh, Dagon?"

Dagon looked at his hand. The knife was lodged in the concrete floor under his palm. He cried out in pain.

"You're probably thinking, 'That shot to my gut will kill me in a few minutes. I don't have to tell him dick.'" Azrael stood over Dagon, breathing in through his nose. "What you don't know is, you may die, but I'm sure as hell not making it painless."

Fingers jabbed into Dagon's shoulder wound. He screamed as Azrael dug his thumb into the mangled flesh. "Tell me what the DDs are doing in Westbrook!"

Dagon continued to scream.

"*Tell me!*"

Bam.

JARED

Jared stared in bewilderment at Dagon; the deviant's head had exploded in front of him. Viscera, chunks of brain, and blood dripped off Jared's face as he blinked at the fresh cadaver.

"Off the deviant corpse," a familiar voice commanded.

Jared breathed hard, still gathering his bearings. "He . . . he could've told us what the DDs were doing here . . ."

"I could give a shit. Off. The. Corpse."

Jared swallowed and stood up, searching with his eyes. He slowly raised his hands and turned toward the area the gunshot came from. There was Eric, dressed fully in enhancer armor with his helmet off. A pistol in his hand, directly pointed at Jared.

An exasperated Brenden rushed around the corner, almost out of breath, looking terrified at the situation. "Eric! *What're you doing?*"

Eric and Jared kept eyes on each other. Jared caught his breath and nodded. "You gonna shoot me with that pistol, Eric?" Eric's face remained cold. "You *know* what I can do to firearms . . ."

Eric smirked, then pulled the gun off Jared. "You're right, I do." He threw aside his pistol.

Brenden put his hands up, eyes shifting between the two. "Boys . . ."

Then Eric pulled out a rod and pressed a button, unfolding his sword.

"Eric!"

"I'm merely following orders, Sergeant Schumacher. Our orders are to kill every deviant here. I still see one right in front of me."

Jared folded his lips, still breathing through his nose. "What's this about, Eric?"

Eric's smirk remained. "I'll give you ten guesses."

Jared studied the boy before him and swallowed. A dull ache began in his chest.

"Deersmouth." Jared breathed out and nodded. "It—it's not my fault she died, Eric." His face twitched as he stared at the man in front of him. He frowned and shook his head. Memories of her body in his arms flooded him. His throat felt dry as his breaths shortened. His eyes began to sting. "I know you think it is, and you have *every right* to. . . . But I did *everything* I could. Everything. It's not . . . *Jessica* wouldn't want us to figh—"

"Nobody gives a shit what that *cheating bitch* would want." Eric's smirk faded and his breaths became heavier. "Pull out your scythe . . . so I can kill you like a *man*."

"Eric, th-this is insane!" Brenden added, seemingly a world away. "You—you're gonna be in a lot of trouble as i—"

"Doubt it."

Jared breathed in through his nose, nodding. There was no use. No point in trying to avoid the inevitable. Somehow, he always thought he'd be more prepared for this fight. Always thought he craved this fight. At this moment, though? "That's what you want? A fight?" he asked solemnly.

Eric tilted his head. "As good a time as any. Think anybody on our side gives a *shit* if you walk outta this battle alive?"

Brenden came in closer, still keeping a safe distance. He knew better than to get in the way. Not like there was anything *he* could do about this. "*Hey!* I said knock it off! Deersmouth was *three years* ago—"

Jared pulled out his scythe and pressed the button. Immediately Brenden turned toward him. "*Jared!*"

Eric chuckled. "Emo Bitch has balls after all." The swordsman began to close the space between them. The two young men began to circle each other.

Brenden looked at a complete loss. "*I'm ordering both of you to stand do—*"

"Shut the fuck up, Brenden. Go be a drunk hoe somewhere else." Eric's smirk returned to his face; he never broke eye contact with Jared.

Jared focused on his opponent. "Stay out of this, Brenden. It's been a long time coming."

Immediately, Brenden shut up. There was nothing he could do but watch. As the two circled each other, memories of the one they both lost began to creep into Jared's mind. Jessica would roll in her grave. One of the two men was going to die today. Jared wasn't sure who deserved death more.

EPISODE 18

CONSIDERATION

AYLEN

Aylen watched as the battle ended as quickly as it started. Once the tank suits arrived on scene, the deviants and Brainless were done for. Before she knew it, the gun fire and explosions stopped and there was stillness in the air. The fire from the burning Troop Transport continued to flicker, but now it wasn't alone. Multiple fires were strewn out on the battlefield as dying cries echoed. The surviving Saints looked up at the carnage of dead DDs, Saints, and Brainless. Aylen had never seen so many bodies in her life. Snow and ash blew through the chilly wind as the heat of the battle drew to a close. It was over. The battle was over.

Someone in the distance began laughing hysterically.

"We—we won? *We won!*" another voice in the distance yelled.

Aylen stared at the dead. Did they? Did they really? She saw the Saints with their guts strewn out across the snow. She saw bullet holes, bodies blown apart, dismembered, burnt—just about every type of dead there could've been. Gabriel held an unconscious Sergeant Rodriguez in his arms; a young soldier who had been blown to bits was now unconscious in the center of the courtyard after writhing in pain for a long time; Marie was helped out of her tank suit by her fellow pilots after apparently suffering a broken leg; and Adrien was still alive down below with blood running down his cheek. A few of the Saints cheered while shooting deviants that were on the ground.

"*Yeeeaaah, bitches!*" someone screamed through the air. Celebratory gunshots rattled.

Captain Gatton sat on the ledge of his tank suit's cockpit and drank from his flask.

Did they really win? Jonathan was dead. Aylen was supposed to go on a date with him after training, but now that would never happen. She'd never see that goofy smile of his again. A part of her mourned her friend deeply. A boy she barely knew, but a boy she never would forget. A deep sense of regret overcame her. She couldn't help him. She'd tried in vain, and he ended up dead. 'Cause of her. It was like Beth all over again. Now another friend was dead because of her too.

Aylen continued to look around the battlefield. There were some noticeable absences. Jared wasn't there, neither was Eric, neither was Brenden, and most frighteningly of all . . . the white-haired woman from earlier was nowhere to be found. Aylen panicked as her eyes searched the battlefield, yet she couldn't find the woman she'd shot. What happened to her? Why was she not there? *What the hell happened to the woman with white hair?*

JARED

Jared and Eric stood still with their blades ready, waiting and anticipating the other's attack. Brenden watched silently in the corner, probably sensing that he could not stop the inevitable.

Jared remembered the first time he met Eric. He dared say he was almost jealous of him back then. Eric was good looking, fit, rich, had a good life before the war between Saints and Devil's Deviants. Jared's life was hell every step of the way. Perhaps that was why his ability seemed so befitting him: the fires resembled everything that had happened in his life up until the point Jessica saved him from death. Even before Project Suncloud, Jared had a shit life, a shit family, and a shit childhood. Yet here was this guy who seemed to have it all. His greatest prize? The lovely angel named Jessica hanging off his arm, who Jared wound up loving more than he had ever loved anyone in his life. As fate would have it, he was lucky enough to eventually get the girl of his dreams after she nursed him back to health. Admittedly, that wasn't the only satisfaction he got from ending up with Jessica.

It had felt *so* good to take something away from someone who had it all, just so they could see what his pain was like.

What Jared saw in front of him was not the Eric from back then, though. And the Jared who stood in front of Eric was not the same either.

"What's the matter? You gonna make a move?" Eric smirked, standing in battle position. The title of "Saint" that had been given to both of them was misleading; neither man was in any way a saint. But then, who was?

Snow fell outside as Jared heard the battle die down. The deviant clenched his weapon tightly, but kept his mouth shut. There was a momentary silence as the two held their ground, waiting for the other to make a move.

"Fine. I will." Suddenly, Eric shifted his weight, and Jared knew the battle had begun.

Within a second, their weapons clashed as Eric struck at Jared like a snake toward a mongoose. He spun for another slash and Jared blocked it again. The two struggled for a moment, then one of them slipped and a flurry of strikes blurred their movements. They ceased being two soldiers and became two tigers attempting to land the killing bite on the other's throat.

Jared spun his red-hot scythe toward Eric only to not land a single blow, despite his speed. Eric was the best. *That* was evident. Jared heated his scythe and set it on fire, waving the flames toward his enemy's face. Embers flew and barely missed Eric, who only grinned and kept attacking, knocking the scythe out of the way. Before Jared could even register that his move had been deflected, he felt the wind get knocked out of him as Eric tackled him. The two burst through the wall behind them and fell for what seemed like a mile. Air whistled through Jared's ears before he felt his back slam onto some cold and hard machinery.

Eric stood and wiped his bloodied lip. Jared felt nauseous and attempted to regain his bearings.

Whack.

Jared grunted in pain when Eric's boot slammed into his gut.

"Let's up the stakes a little, shall we?" Eric growled. He kicked a lever to the side of the machine and they began to move. Shit, they were on a conveyor belt. Eric tugged on Jared's hair and pulled him up. A full-blown enhancer armor-assisted punch smacked into Jared's face. "*That's* how you throw a punch, buttercup." Another punch followed. The belt shook underneath them as they moved. Jared heard a machine sound behind him that he couldn't see and then heard a huge stomp as they neared whatever it was.

"Fight back!" Eric wailed on Jared again. "*Fight back! Come on!*"

For a brief moment, Jared saw Cerberus punching him instead of Eric. Eric smacked him across the face again. An image of Cerberus grinning at him briefly passed through his mind. Jared fell onto his back on the conveyor belt. The thumping sounds crept closer. Eric leaned down and grabbed his neck. Jared felt blood trickle from his face as Eric looked down at him, wide-eyed. "Oh no, don't you pass out yet. Don't you pass out yet, Emo Bitch. I'm not done with you!"

Eric breathed hard and looked ahead. "Got a surprise for ya, J-Boy. Remember Ronald Brown's execution?" He looked down and grinned. "It's something like that."

Jared finally tilted his head to look at the machine making those ominous thumps. A factory compressor slammed down and crushed the belt not too far from him. Eric's face went deadpan, and he swallowed.

"This is for killing Jessica."

Jared watched as the machine got closer and closer. His heart pounded with fear as he helplessly watched the compressor come nearer. Every time it descended, the belt beneath him shook slightly from under him. He couldn't get up. . . . He couldn't—

Suddenly, Jared went flying and landed on the ground with a hard thud, his spine tingling.

"Nah, just kidding, I ain't gonna kill ya . . . *yet.*" Eric grinned. "I will say, though, I *was* very upset when Jessica died. Very *fucking* upset," he said while delivering a kick to Jared's face. "She had to go and get captured on *your* watch? Had to die in *your* arms?" Eric picked Jared up and sent him face-first into what looked like some kind of spout. "*She's dead because of you!*"

Eric threw the deviant into another piece of machinery and Jared slid down onto his back. He could hardly feel the blows, now. "*Jessica's dead because of you!*" Eric screamed. Seemingly somewhere distant now—

Cerberus breathed in his cigar smoke and nodded. "You're gonna spend a lot of long nights wondering what we're doing to her. It's gonna drive you bonkers . . . then when you find out—"

Jared shook his head, blinking back into consciousness and breathing hard.

"Y-you have a birthday gift, J . . ."

"That's not important, Jess. Save your strength. We're gonna get you home, you're gonna be okay . . ."

"I-it's under a loose floorboard in our apartment. In our bedroom. I—I was looking forward to sharing your eighteenth with you . . ."

With a shuddering breath, Jared remembered Jessica as she was: her brunette hair, her pale skin, her hazel eyes. His eyes began to burn. Those two weeks they spent on the beach, those long nights they spent in each other's arms, the way she stared into his eyes back then. She had *wanted* to go into the armory. He couldn't stop her . . . she wanted to go in. Then when she was captured, he fought tooth and nail to bring her back . . . and Cerberus snapped her neck while she was in his arms.

Jared didn't kill her.

Cerberus did.

Cerberus killed Jessica. Cerberus killed Jessica in Jared's arms. For a moment, while he stared up at Eric, Jared saw Cerberus standing in front of him instead. Jared spat out blood.

"Still with me, Emo Bitch?"

Eric was out of breath. Jared was sprawled completely on the floor, head spinning. His hands began moving on their own. Jessica had loved Jared. He had done everything he physically could. It wasn't his fault.

Jared lifted his aching, bloody body, spittle filled with drool and blood dripping from his mouth as he rose.

"Get up," Eric muttered. "*I said get up!*" Eric bellowed with a throaty voice, marching toward him and grabbing his hair.

But Jared didn't kill Jessica. He didn't kill—

Jared's fist connected with Eric's face, coupled with an unholy growl. Then another, then another. Eric headbutted Jared, causing him to stumble back, then kicked him in the stomach. Before Jared could recover, Eric flung his body and tackled Jared into the machinery. Jared brought down both his fists onto Eric's back and threw him off him before sending a knee into Eric's face. He spotted a chain hanging nearby and grabbed it, using his speed to wrap it around Eric's throat. He clenched his teeth as Eric's body buckled, making croaking noises as Jared pulled on the chain.

"*Motherfucker!*" Jared growled, tightening the chain around Eric's throat, making it cut into his own hands. The blond's face began turning a purple color, his mouth foamed, his eyes bulged. No . . . this was too easy. Eric deserved to feel this more.

Jared unwrapped the chain and slammed it into Eric's head, forcing him down onto his side, coughing. He slammed the chain into Eric a few more times, then threw it aside and kicked Eric's stomach, watching intensely as he gasped for air. It wasn't enough, not nearly enough. Rage filled every inch of Jared's body . . . and Eric needed to suffer. Then he knelt down over Eric and brought down his fists. One after another after another. Jared screamed, only half aware of what he was doing as he pummeled Eric's face. In flashes, he imagined it was Cerberus.

A stabbing pain appeared in Jared's side, and he screamed. He looked down. Eric had planted his knife into him, then pulled it out. Jared rolled off him and the two men caught their breath, Jared groaning and clutching the bleeding knife wound in his side while Eric coughed and regained his breath.

The two looked at each other. Both of their bruised and swollen faces dripped blood and drool as they stared at one another with hate. This fight was going to kill them. Neither man would walk away from this in one piece. The two backed away from each other and staggered up, using the nearby machines to help them get back on their feet. Jared could tell every bone and muscle in Eric's body was screaming in pain, just like his.

Then Eric looked at his sword and picked it up, kicking Jared's scythe over to him in the process. The young men eyed each other again, breathing hard and shaking. The silent exchange between them continued as Jared picked his scythe back up and lit it on fire. The two weakly began circling each other again.

PESTILENCE

Emily ran as fast as she could through the forest behind the Westbrook factory, leaving a trail of blood in the snow behind her. Her body shook from the pain, and she had already thrown up once. Her head spun and her throat burned as she struggled to breathe. Two gaping, bleeding bullet holes were inside her, one in her stomach and one in her shoulder. The shoulder one would heal. The stomach one, however . . .

Emily shuddered to think about it as she leaned against a nearby tree. Her body was covered in cold sweat. The Devil's Deviants had lost. They had *actually* lost. Emily would not go home. She would not see her daughter's birthday. She tried to shake off the thought as her mind turned to the mission's main objective. It was still completely possible for the Devil's Deviants to get what they wanted from this factory extraction. The computer files, at least to Emily's knowledge, had been sent. But there was still the matter of what they had actually come for. The equipment was still on the creature, as far as she could tell.

Her crimson blood filled the snow. Maybe, with her dying moments, Pestilence could still be useful to the cause, to the future, to her daughter. Emily focused her thoughts on the creature in its restraints down below. Pluto had the means to contain it, she just had to get the thing back to him.

Go back to The Ninth Circle, Emily told the creature with her mind. She could feel it: wild, angry, ferocious, mad that it was locked in a cage, mad that it hadn't been fed in days. Most of all, it was mad at Emily for subduing it to her will.

Deliver the items to Pluto, Emily thought more intently; she was having trouble focusing because of the pain. It didn't help that the creature fought back against her, but she was determined to save her daughter's future. She would get this creature to take the items back. She would. She would do it even if it meant using her last moments on Earth doing so.

JARED

The sound of blades clashing rang through the factory as Jared and Eric struck at each other. They threw all they had at each other only to deflect each other's blows, as if their weapons were magnetically connected. Jared's vision faded in and out as he blindly waved his flaming scythe at Eric. Eric, too, seemed to barely be conscious as he deflected the blow from Jared. But they had to finish this . . . once and for all.

The two backed off, out of breath, Jared's scythe trembling in his hands. Everything went dead silent. Both men glared at each other, clutching their weapons. This was it. Both men knew the fight was coming to an end. Whoever could land the next strike would win. Their whole rivalry had come down to this moment.

Jared's breath shuddered as sweat seared into every cut on his body. He was bleeding out through the knife wound in his side. Unless it was properly attended to, it could wind up killing him. Jared felt his life draining away from his veins slowly as he staggered. Eric's cold, unreadable eyes seemed to notice this. He had the advantage. He had Jared right where he wanted him, if he could manage to muster enough strength to finish him off. Yet as he stared, Jared noticed the certain way Eric blinked his eyes. It was possible he'd given him a concussion when pummeling his face into the ground.

On an instinct more primal than the entire existence of man, they charged at each other again and clashed their weapons. This was it. This was the final, determining moment of who would end this feud once and for all. They had tried with all of their might to overpower each other, but to no avail. The two clenched their teeth as they became locked and dead set on killing each other. This was the end. This was the—

A low rumble started under their feet, upsetting their balance. Something burst through the ground and spiraled in midair, knocking both Saints to the ground. Whatever the thing was, it was long, large, and fast, a creature that spiraled above them high into the air. Its skin was a charcoal-black mixed with a sausage-red, and it twisted so fast Jared couldn't clearly see the shapes on it. Then, when the spiral motion slowed, he realized it almost looked like thousands, if not millions, of Brainless bodies combined together and spliced. Torsos stuck out, hands, fingers, eyes, legs, limbs, innards, bones, veins, and various other human body parts pasted together. At its height, the creature then split in four ways like a banana to reveal thousands, if not millions, of heads inside, more human-looking than Brainless. Each flap had large black talons that looked almost like scorpion stingers on the tip.

Then every head in the flaps of the Brainless monster opened its mouth at the same time and screamed in synchronization so loud that Jared's ears began to ring.

Were they going to have to fight that thing? Now? Just like that, all of the energy went out of Jared, and seemingly Eric too, as they both lay on the floor. Neither had anything left to give as they watched the giant with silent horror, briefly looking at each other with baffled looks before turning back to the gargantuan beast in front of them.

The creature burst through the roof of the factory and disappeared from view as quickly as it came. Jared's vision faded as debris from the ceiling began to fall, and his body gave out as he rested his head on the floor. Everything blurred into nothing.

AYLEN

Aylen watched as a gigantic creature broke through the top of the main factory building, barely keeping her balance as the floor beneath her rumbled. The creature twirled in midair and opened up to reveal thousands of twisted faces. It was definitely a Brainless, but it was frightening how big it was. She couldn't help but watch it with her jaw wide open. The creature howled, sounding like millions of people screaming at the same time, before twisting and crashing down into another building, making the ground shake. In moments, it faded into the distance as quickly as it came, crashing through the rest of the factory buildings in its path before anyone had time to react to its appearance. It seemed to go in a direction that avoided the Saints altogether, as if it was willfully avoiding them.

Aylen shuddered to think what would've happened if the thing had decided to attack instead. How would the Saints even fight that thing? How could they, with the state they were all in? Aylen remembered the photo that Jared had taken in the condemned city. The big blur that seemed like it was the size of a skyscraper among the cityscape. She wasn't sure it was that big now . . . but it was still bigger than it had any right being. The rarest Brainless that Jared had ever seen: the Level 5 Centipede Brainless, as he called it. That thing seemed bigger than the barrier around Salutem. If it was set loose on Salutem, humanity would be screwed. Something that big and alive shouldn't exist. Something that . . . *horrible* . . . shouldn't exist. It was the scariest thing she had ever seen.

Aylen watched, mesmerized, as the creature disappeared on the horizon, and she prayed that she would never see it again.

PESTILENCE

Emily watched the creature as it raced away. Her plan worked. She smiled to herself, feeling her body grow colder as she watched the Brainless disappear into the distance. When it was gone, she pushed herself off the tree she leaned on and began a journey through the snow. Her steps were weak as they crunched the snow. She grasped her bloody stomach as she attempted to keep some semblance of balance. She would be dead soon. It was a fact. A cold, hard fact. There wasn't any denial of it.

Emily continued walking the lonely path out into the wilderness and felt her legs give in suddenly. She rolled down the snowy hill and left a trail of blood along the way. While rolling, she could only think of two people. The only two people that mattered to her, the people she would never see again.

Paul, Stacy . . . I'm sorry, Emily thought before her head hit a rock. Everything faded to black after that.

CERBERUS

The Devil's Deviants lost.

Cerberus breathed heavily after hearing the news. After a long and hard fight with the Saint Organization, the Saints came out on top. That only meant one thing: All the DDs at the battle were dead. *Pestilence* was most likely dead. Morningstar would be very unhappy to hear that. Then there was Death and his daughter. Cerberus couldn't imagine how those two would take the news. It had all failed. Even though Pluto got the computer files he needed, the damage and loss to the deviant community was too heavy.

Cerberus rubbed his head in his hands and lit a cigar. The brothers and sisters at the Westbrook factory had died in vain. Meanwhile, the Saints and the UWF lay in bed together with some sort of new deal. Cerberus blew smoke into the air while thinking things over and finished the cigar before making a decision. Morningstar should hear the news from him. She was close to Pestilence and Death; she should know.

He set out into the rest of the bunker, preparing himself for waterworks from Morningstar. As the giant man approached her quarters, he heard talking from behind her door. She was with someone? Not that it was any of his business, but this surprised him at the very least. Other than himself, Blasphemer, and the Gilmore family, Morningstar kept to herself most of the time. Blasphemer would not be the type to visit, and the Gilmore family were probably grieving by now. The voices inside sounded jovial, and it sounded like the second voice was male. On paternal instinct, Cerberus knocked on the door.

Within seconds, Morningstar came out with a huge grin, holding a cat. "Cerby! Come in, we were just playing with Jelly."

Cerberus lifted his eyebrow. "Jelly?"

Morningstar held up the cat. "Jelly!"

He looked a moment at the cat, who fidgeted in her hands, and shook his head. "I hate cats."

"Aw, come on, Cerby! Don't be a sourpuss, she's really cute!"

Cerberus entered the room and saw a sight he did not expect: Triple Six sat on the ground holding a cat toy.

The boy looked up with a grin. "'Sup, Cerbs."

Cerberus felt nauseous. What the hell was *he* doing here? "Six, go practice your vines on some targets. Need you sharp. Morningstar and I have some things to discuss," he said.

Triple Six shrugged. "Whatever you say, boss man." He stood and walked past Morningstar, smiling at her. "See you around." The young man then left the room, closing the door behind him.

"Cerby, what'd you do that—"

Cerberus slapped Morningstar. She clutched her cheek in horror as the large man moved in closer, frothing at the mouth. "*Why was he here?*"

"Wh-what?"

Cerberus grabbed her by the arms. He felt his hands shake with anger. "Triple Six! *The hell was he doing here?*"

Morningstar was wide-eyed and breathed quickly. "He—he's my friend—"

"Friend?" Cerberus laughed in disbelief. He let go of Morningstar and clutched his head. Shit.

Tears came to Morningstar's eyes. "He—he knows a lot about cats, he's been helping me with Jelly . . ."

Cerberus pointed to the door. "*That boy is not your friend!*" he barked. Cerberus froze, seeing the shock and fear in Morningstar's face and realizing how much he was shaking her up. He calmed down best he could, breathing heavily. "That—that *psycho* has no friends. He enjoys killing, he *enjoys* causing people pain. You *don't* know him."

Morningstar shook her head. She was sobbing now. "H-he's not like that! He's sweet and kind and he's *my friend!*"

"Friend?" He scoffed while shaking his head. "Do you know what your '*friend*' has done?

"I don't care!"

"He's tortured daughters in front of their fathers, he—he's disemboweled people for sport, he's murdered more people than I can—"

"*And how's that any different from you?*" Morningstar yelled at him. Cerberus was taken back by this. "*You're a killer too!*"

Cerberus was at a loss. He breathed hard, glaring at her.

"That's not—"

"Not the same thing? Is that what you tell yourself?"

Cerberus scoffed and shook his head, mouth open. He didn't know what to say.

Morningstar composed herself a moment, feeling her cheek. A hurt look haunted her eyes. "Y-you may have been there for me for a long time. Y-you may have watched over me, taken care of me, but you are *not* my father! *I can make friends with whoever I want!*"

Cerberus felt like someone had delivered a swift kick to his testicles. Not her . . . Cerberus blinked repeatedly.

"Star, I-I'm trying to protect yo—"

"What? By coming in and *slapping me*? We're not related, *you can't—*"

"Sorry, but I do what I have to if you're making *dumb fuckin' decisions.* You're too damn important to me to—"

Morningstar stepped closer, getting into his face. "I'm *not* Austi! Stop pretending like I am!"

Cerberus blinked repeatedly at this. A subtle, dull pain started in his chest. Low blow. His eyes began aching as the girl in front of him shook her head.

"Just get out. Out of my quarters."

He stood in disbelief and watched Morningstar give him a death glare through tear-filled eyes. Then he nodded his head.

"Okay. Know what? You're right. You're *not* Austi. . . . So when that boy hurts you, and he will, don't you come cryin' to me. You're sure as hell no daughter of mi—"

"*I said get out!*" she screamed.

With that, Cerberus immediately headed for the door, slamming it on the way out. She could find out the news about Pestilence on her own.

ABEL

It was nightfall by the time the Saints arrived back on base. Admittedly, it was a surprise to Abel that they made it back at all. Looking at the quickly drawn plan he'd made, he knew it wasn't terribly well thought-out. If they were given more time, they could've . . . Abel grimaced. He'd been sweating it all day. It could've been better. Somehow, it could've been better. It being a bad plan was probably part of the reason Li signed off on it. It was lucky the Saints made it back at all, a fluke. And they somehow won? Somewhat of a miracle.

The Saint leader could not celebrate the miracle, though. Between unsettling reports about a gigantic Brainless and the heavy casualties the Saints had suffered in the battle, it was hard to see it as a victory, though the UWF seemed pleased as punch. Of course, there were other reasons Abel could not celebrate the victory of Westbrook.

Abel stood at his son's hospital bed in the infirmary of the Saint Organization base. Joshua's eyes glowed light blue as they continued to stare sightlessly at the ceiling. A blanket covered what remained of his body. The Saint leader thought of Denise for a moment and how she'd died: blown to pieces by a rocket from the deviants at Widow's Mountain. The irony of the situation was tragic: Both mother and son were blown up.

Hot tears come to Abel's eyes as he thought of his loss. Joshua's eyes continued to glow that unnatural blue. Abel recognized it from his days in the Anthrodi War: Cherubine poisoning. It was a mysterious chemical from the Anthrodi, one they'd used in high-pressure beams that would dissolve entire lines of infantry into nothing. Direct exposure to the chemical on its own without the Anthrodi's weaponry also had lethal effects. The scary thing was it worked more like a disease than a poison. Anyone infected had an unpredictable death sentence, but though unpredictable, it was definite. The catatonic phase may or may not pass.

Apparently, Cherubine had been mixed into whatever bomb had gone off on Josh. Faith told him that the chemical had kept Joshua alive, but his time was limited. If he ever woke, his body would always be in pain. Very slowly, the poison would shut down what remained of his bodily functions until, eventually, he would die. The kindest thing would be if he died soon and never woke up, but the chemical could take months, even years to finally kill someone off. In the meanwhile, the infected's loved ones would have to watch them slowly wither away. Would have to watch them suffer.

Who would put such a thing in a bomb? Abel wondered while tears rolled down his face. He grabbed his son's remaining hand.

"Joshua . . ." Abel sniffed, attempting to maintain his composure. "Joshua . . . I don't know if you can hear me, but we won." Abel smiled weakly. "The Westbrook factory is no longer overrun with DDs, and the UWF is putting more money in our pockets. Your idea worked." Abel did his best to continue to smile. His son's hand felt lifeless in his as Abel rubbed it with his thumb. He nodded and put his free hand to his mouth to try to keep from losing composure. "Your idea to get money from the UWF worked. You're a proud leader."

General Quinn sniffed again, his voice trembling with every word. The Principal Overseer then pulled something out of his pocket. It was small and weightless in his hand as he placed the pin in his son's hand. "For your honor, your vigilance, and your sense of duty, I'm naming you captain." Abel looked into his son's lifeless face. "That's what you always wanted, right? To be captain?"

Abel shook, no longer able to keep his composure. He let his emotion finally come out. He loved his son. He truly loved his son.

AYLEN

As nightfall came after the air transports sent the Saints back to base, there was a good, albeit uneasy, feeling among the Saints. They had survived. They went through hell and survived. Medics treated everyone as soon as they arrived on the air transports, rushing those wounded worst to sick bay. Despite the heavy losses, Aylen heard talks of celebration among the Saints. There were some who remarked on the Centipede's appearance, but most just seemed to be thankful to be alive.

As the survivors of the battle trickled out of their air transports to meet with lovers and friends, she couldn't help but feel a little lost. There were some who were reunited with loved ones, and some who looked among the crowd but seemed to be unable to find who they were looking for. People hooted and hollered. A vibrant energy of glee could be felt at a fever pitch, but Aylen did not share the sentiment. How could she? She watched her friend die. She watched so many others die. A creature of frightening proportions had appeared out of nowhere today, lives were cut short, the Saints had many wounded, yet people were *celebrating*—people seemed to be acting like everything was fine.

Not everyone, though.

From afar, she saw Brenden get off a Troop Transport. He saw Adrien and ran up to him and began talking to him; he held the redhead's face, only to be pushed away by an angry Adrien, who stomped away. Gabriel had Sergeant Rodriguez's arm around his neck as they limped off into the base.

Aylen felt some sort of strange feeling come over her. The world kept turning, despite those that had died that day. Life went on. It would continue going on. Tomorrow would be just like any other day, despite noticeable absences. Faces never to be seen again that would only live on in memory. Crickets sounded in the night air as Aylen continuously searched . . . for what? She did not know.

Aylen's eyes then found a familiar woman in a white lab coat. Dr. Lancaster walked over to her with a furrowed brow. "Hey, Aylen, how're you doing?"

Aylen probably looked worse than she thought. She nodded her head. "Okay."

Faith lightly smiled despite her furrowed brow. "Can I get you anything? Hot cocoa, maybe?"

Aylen shook her head silently. There was a momentary silence as Aylen stared off into space.

Faith nodded. "You know, my offer on being my apprentice still stands—"

"Okay, I'll do it," Aylen interrupted. This response seemed to surprise the doctor. "After my training, I wanna do that."

Faith studied Aylen for a moment before opening her mouth. "What about Legion?"

Aylen breathed out and closed her eyes hard a moment before opening them. "Today . . . I wasn't fighting Legion. Was fighting a bunch of other people . . ." Aylen shuddered, then braced herself, looking down. "The—the people that got killed today weren't Legion. Unless it's Legion, I don't wanna be a part of it." There was silence as Aylen breathed out.

Faith licked her lips in thought and looked down. "Okay," she responded before looking up. "Do you wanna get something to eat?"

"I, um . . . I just wanna be alone right now, i-if that's all right. I . . ." Aylen looked up and saw a sympathetic look in Faith's eyes. She thought about Johnathan. "I'll be at the top of the main building, if anyone needs me."

Faith looked her up and down and nodded. "Okay."

Aylen made her way to the place Jonathan showed her. The sea rushed in and out as it crashed on the rocks below. She looked out onto the horizon. The moon lit up the sky, creating a veil across the world that was a dark blue rather than black. It was quiet out here, except for the sea. As she stared into the distance, thoughts of the boy who asked her out the night before—was it only last night?—crept into her mind. Last night, he was right next to her, smoking weed and cracking dorky jokes. Now . . .

"What're you doing up here?"

The croaking voice came from behind her. She looked over her shoulder to see Eric's muscular form standing in the moonlight. His voice was almost unrecognizable, like he'd lost it from screaming or something. Bandages covered his face and his blond hair swayed in the wind. He was holding a glass bottle filled with clear liquid, and was hunched slightly in a way that indicated he was in pain.

Aylen scoffed. "The hell happened to you?"

Eric smirked politely. "Rough battle. Why you out here by yourself, Monro?"

Aylen rolled her eyes and looked away. "What do you care?"

Eric came up next to her and leaned on the railing, sighing. In the moonlight, his bruised and battered face looked contemplative.

"If I'm not mistaken, we *were* friends once, weren't we?"

Aylen scoffed. "Yeah, before you tried to use me for sex—"

"Jared's words, not mine."

Aylen breathed in through her nose, taking a moment to think about what to say next. "There's rumors you and Jared beat the heck outta each other, that true?"

Eric grinned slightly. "In the interest of protecting my hearing, as they say in old movies, I plead the fifth."

Aylen looked out into the sea. "Secrets . . . why am I not surprised?" There was a momentary silence. "You know, they may have been Jared's words, but I have more reason to trust Jared than to trust you, and he's an asshole who barely gives two craps about me."

Eric took a swig of his bottle of clear liquid and scoffed. "If I was trying to use someone for sex, I would've gone after Beth, not you."

Aylen felt offended. Like that statement trampled on her already wounded pride. "That supposed to make me feel better?"

"Not calling you ugly, Beth seemed easier is all—"

"You take that back about Beth!" Aylen hissed, glaring at Eric. He merely sighed.

"Sorry . . . didn't mean it like that. Point is I'd pick a girl more . . . *open* 'bout her sexuality if I was just trying to fuck her. I was more interested in other things about you—"

"Which is why you tried to *fuck me* on the second date, right?"

"Well, I just did that 'cause I am the way I am." There was a contemplative moment where Aylen stirred in her bad mood before Eric then began speaking again. "Why you up here, Aylen? Everybody is celebrating, why aren't you?"

There was a moment of quiet as Aylen looked out into the dark, remembering Jonathan and the other casualties of the day. Her breath quickened just thinking about the boy she failed to save. "I don't want to celebrate what happened today." She shook her head before digging her nails into her arm, remembering the dead eyes that had stared back at her earlier.

"I heard about your friend. I'm sorry I called him a palooka."

"What's it matter? He's dead, anyway."

Eric laughed lightly and nodded his head. "I suppose."

"So many people . . ." she started. She realized she was shaking. Eric seemed to take notice of this. "So many people died today." Her eyes began tearing up as she thought of every dead body that she saw on the ground. "I—I couldn't save Jonathan . . . y-you know, I—I tried, he was right in my hands. Then Captain Webster cut him off of me, said he was dragging me down to the Brainless horde. I—I know he was right, but—but I tried to save him!" Aylen's lip curled. "Just like Beth . . . it's *my* fault he died . . ."

Salty tears rush from her eyes as she began shaking. Aylen dug her face into her arms as she leaned on the railing. She heard what sounded like liquid moving around in a bottle. Aylen looked up and saw Eric holding the bottle of liquor in front of her.

When she hesitated, Eric looked at her with a furrowed brow "Here. This'll help."

Aylen grabbed the bottle and took a swig, then another. Even as she pulled her mouth away, she still felt terrible. Then Eric's arm wrapped around her shoulder and rubbed it slightly.

"It's okay. Let it all out, Aylen. Let it all out."

He felt so warm. Aylen leaned into his warm body as tears slipped out, feeling his comforting embrace in full.

PESTILENCE

Emily's vision returned as she slowly opened her eyes. She was alive? An orange light flickered at her side, and she soon felt the pain pulsing through her body. Her throat was dry and her head, stomach, and back were sore. Heat radiated from her and cold sweat drenched her body.

"Easy, dat's a nasty fever you got," she heard a woman say in an islander accent.

Emily felt warm blankets on her and her vision began to focus. She was not outside, but rather in what seemed to be a tent. Shivers overcame her body and she felt herself choke like she was going to throw up. A purple hand held out a small bucket, and Emily took it and vomited.

"We almost lost you a few times when we dug the bullets out, you know."

Emily's eyes adjusted as she saw a cloaked woman in front of her with vibrant purple skin. She had four yellow eyes and a calm smile on her face. "If not for my ability, you'd be dead right now." The woman then held a bowl to Emily's lips and tipped water into her mouth.

Emily pulled away from the bowl. "Wh-where am I?"

"With some fellow brothas and sistas, my friend."

Emily's vision felt hazy as she looked around the tent. "A deviant colony?"

The purple woman nodded. "Of sorts. We found you not too far from the factory where they had dat big battle. Is a shame what happen. So many people died," the woman said through her thick accent. "Were you in dat battle?"

Emily glared, breathing hard. "Yeah. . . . If you were so close, why didn't you fight?"

The woman shook her head and a light chuckle crept out of her mouth. "Us? No. We don't fight. We only do what we need to survive."

Emily laid back her head onto the pillow she rested on. "Figures."

At this, the purple woman laughed. "No, sista, your organization an' mine, we don't share the same values. *We* believe in peace. We raise no hand against fellow deviant or human. Deviants are just humans chosen to overcome greater obstacles. Peace is our ultimate test."

The white-haired woman's ears perked. "Wait . . . I've heard this kind of rhetoric before. Don't tell me you're—"

The woman smiled. "We're the Brotherhood of the Emerald Light."

Emily then noticed the green handprint on the cloak the woman wore. Oh. That made sense. She was in a camp of the Brotherhood of the Emerald Light. Great, stuck with a bunch of wackos.

"Wh-what're you guys doing this far north? You're a *long* way from Neolympus."

The purple woman simply smiled. "Oh, sista, I'm afraid dat story's too long right now. You must get rest." The purple woman got up and bowed her head. "May the Emerald Light shine upon you."

Emily watched as the woman left the tent and stepped into the snow outside. Emily breathed hard and felt woozy, throat hurting and her body in pain. She really thought she was a goner. The heater shone a warm light on Emily and she closed her eyes. She was alive. She would be able to see her family again. Emily smiled as she lay in the makeshift bed, drifting away again into a deep sleep.

JARED

After getting the last of his wounds tended to, Jared limped over to the cafeteria, his side still aching. Apparently Eric didn't stab him too deep and Jared's deviant healing factor had already begun to work its magic, but holy hell was he in pain. More or less unnoticed, the boy in black slipped into the dining hall and got some dinner. With a little trouble, he ate in the cafeteria as he watched other Saints hoot and holler and drink themselves silly. Everyone was in a lively mood. Couples were making out, practically having sex with clothes on. For a moment, Jared thought of how similar the cafeteria was to college parties. He understood it. It was a hard battle. Many people died and many people didn't think they would make it. People were alive.

He wondered what Aylen was doing. If it weren't for her, Gail probably would've killed him with that little incident in the sewers. Jared searched the room and watched Gail from afar as she laughed at someone's joke with a drink in her hand. Between almost killing him and Pestilence getting taken out, Faith's twin must've felt all sorts of glee right about now. He watched as she and some Saint he barely recognized met lips like they were trying to breathe air from each other's lungs. In the interest of not breaking Faith's heart, he wasn't gonna do anything about Gail trying to kill him . . . this time. But if she ever tried it again, blood ties wouldn't be enough to save her. Then again, that'd be tough. She *was* tight with Abel. Might be too tricky to pull off without people immediately blaming the resident deviant. It wasn't a secret they hated each other.

As Jared continued to watch the kiss, though, a part of his brain immediately turned back to Aylen. He let out a heavy breath as he thought about her. All in all, there wasn't much that he could say. Aylen survived the battle.

The Sharpshooter Unit was hit hard, yet she survived. Maybe Jared had been stupid for the last couple of weeks. Maybe he didn't have to push her away like he had. His wounds under his bandages hurt as he thought of the fight he and Eric had. Jared didn't kill Jessica. Cerberus was the one responsible. If anything, something about that fight made Jared realize that truth. He wasn't to blame for what happened. It was not something in his control. He didn't need to do what he'd done to poor Aylen. He didn't need to push her away like that. She . . . she didn't deserve how he treated her at all.

Maybe he should try to find her and apologize for how he had been acting. He didn't kill Jessica, he wouldn't kill her. Maybe it was okay to let her in close. The first step was going to be to apologize. Not like he had anything better to do. Tara and Joshua were in the infirmary, the latter on death's door, and no one else was really worth talking to with how stupid drunk everyone was.

He was making his choice when Faith appeared in the room. She watched the celebration with a smile on her face, then noticed Jared and headed toward him.

Jared cleared his hoarse throat. "Hey, Faith."

"Jared, how're your injuries, hun?"

"I'm fine. H-have you seen Aylen around?"

Faith looked Jared up and down and nodded. "I did see her, I think she needs some time alone, though, and you're in no condition to go too many places other than here and your quarters."

Jared sighed. "I *need* to apologize to her, Ma. I've been a real dick."

"You *need* to get rest. You got *stabbed* today, J. Eric could've killed you."

Jared shook his head. "I gotta make things right."

"Jared, I'm serious, maybe talk to her when—"

"*Ma, please . . .*" he said, his hoarse throat burning. Faith stared into his eyes as he stared as hard as he could into hers. "I gotta do right by her. I gotta do right by Aylen. Please tell me where she is."

Faith sighed and softly rubbed his back. "All right. . . . Last I heard, she said she was going to the roof. She did look like she needed some comforting. I don't know what's going on with you kids, but if you can't climb those stairs, don't push yourself. I *don't* want you to fall."

"Got it. I'll be careful," Jared said through some pain as he stood and almost slipped. Faith momentarily assisted him. "I'm fine, Ma. Really."

She backed off and nodded as Jared limped out the cafeteria and made his way to the main building. Everything hurt as he headed to the stairs and began to climb them. He had to stop a few times because of jolts of pain from his side that ebbed and flowed. He checked the time on his phone: 9:40 p.m. He had a plan: He would tell Aylen why he had been acting like a jerk. He would help her understand. He would make things right. Jared climbed the floors despite the pain and saw the roof door ahead of him. As soon as he got to the top of the staircase, he reached for the door handle and grabbed it firmly. He would tell her everything. He would explain every—

Thing.

Jared opened the door and saw two figures moving frantically in the moonlight. A male figure and a female figure, synchronized as the male moved his bare waist back and forth behind the female. Grunts and moans filled the air. Jared stared in horror as he realized who was standing in front of him. What female was leaning against the rail and had her bare bottom revealed in the moonlight, and which male he recognized moving inside her.

AYLEN

Aylen breathed heavily and moaned as she felt Eric behind her. She needed this. Needed this so bad. Everything in her body synced up with every motion he made. Everything in her wanted him at that moment. It felt so good. . . . Felt so—

Suddenly, Eric stopped. "'Sup, Emo Bitch." He laughed while still in position.

Aylen's eyes widened as she looked over and saw a familiar silhouette in the doorway. Jared stood silently without a word, his wounded face unreadable. Without a word, he then began to limp back into the base.

Aylen's heart skipped a beat, realizing what she was doing. This was a mistake. Aylen made a mistake. She moved out of position, pushing Eric away and pulling up her pants in shame. She got carried away and— *Crap. Crap. Crap. Crap.* She was a little tipsy and could feel it as she burst through the door and ran to Jared, who was making his way down the steps with his back to her.

"Jared! Wait!" Aylen's head spun a little from the alcohol. Jared continued his way forward silently. Aylen caught up with him and attempted to grab his sleeve. "Jared!" He shook her off and continued his way forward. Aylen grabbed Jared's arm again. "Jared, please! Stop! Please!"

Jared turned around sharply. The whites of his eyes were red. Bandages and dried cuts peppered his slightly bruised face. "J-Jared, I—"

"Um, I just came up to say that I apologize for how I've acted over the last couple of weeks," he said softly. "I thought I was keeping you safe by keeping you away. Oh, and one more thing—"

Jared pulled Aylen into a kiss. It was rough and passionate, making her heart stutter. There was a soft moment as the two interlocked, kissing with everything they had.

Then Jared pushed her away.

"I love you," he said as if he spewed venom. Aylen froze as she looked at Jared in disbelief. He began to back away, a lone tear drop sneaking out of his eye, his lips trembling.

"That being said, don't you dare come back to my quarters, and stay the *fuck* out of my life." His voice broke and trembled as his face scrunched. He then turned around, clutching his side, and disappeared down the staircase.

Aylen felt breathless as she leaned against the wall and felt a wave of emotion come over her, making her feel like she was choking. She messed up. She messed up bad. The sound of footfall came from the top of the stairs and Aylen saw Eric coming down with his pants buckled, laughing a raspy laugh.

"Part of me was wondering if he'd show up or not. But damn, that worked out like clockwork."

Aylen felt the blood go out of her face as she looked at Eric, tears running down her cheeks. "Y-you planned this?"

"Admittedly, it worked out even better than I planned. But hey, what can I say? Payback is a bitch . . . and you played along *perfectly*, Monro." Eric leaned in closer. "But as for any more sword lessons?" He stopped and then put his mouth to her ear. "I'll consider it."

Eric grinned through his teeth before heading down the stairs and disappearing. Aylen stood in shock of what happened, still breathing hard. She . . . she made a mistake. She made a— Aylen felt herself drop to the stairs, broken and hyperventilating.

That night, Aylen made her way to Faith, who arranged for Aylen to go back to sleeping in the training barracks. Afterward, she returned to Jared's private quarters to find her things neatly packed outside of his door. He was serious. Aylen took her things and went back to the female recruit barracks to be greeted by a sullen Marie, who had a cast on her leg, and crutches. She'd heard about Jonathan but the two didn't talk about it more than a brief mention before sitting in a dreary silence, wallowing in their own miseries.

Aylen lay in her cot that night and thought of how much her life had changed within the last few months. A few months ago, she'd lain in bed in a college dorm, roommates with her best friend. Now, she was in a military base in the middle of nowhere. She had killed. She had fought. She had seen bloodshed. A few months ago, she had never heard of the name Jared Griffin. Now, he was all she could think about.

Sorrow filled her as she thought of everything that they had gone through together, good and bad. Sorrow filled her as she thought about all the ways that their relationship fell apart. Those final words ran through her head like a death sentence: *I love you.* She looked at the key-shaped birthmark on her forearm, the one that was almost identical to Jared's, and felt her face crumple. They were supposed to save the world together. Where did they go wrong?

After sobbing into her pillow, Aylen finally shut her eyes and let herself slip into a comforting and dark unconsciousness, far away from the world. Far away from Salutem, the Saints, and the Devil's Deviants.

Far away from Jared.

EPILOGUE

Wolves in the Garden

LUCIFER

Lucifer watched as Cerberus entered his private quarters.

"You summoned me, sir?" Cerberus grunted. Lucifer stared at him for a second. His eyes burned from the fireplace next to him that crackled and kept him warm.

Lucifer sighed. "So . . . Westbrook was a failure."

Cerberus breathed through his nose. "Yes, sir. We did manage to get the files for Pluto, but they appear to have been corrupted. Some sort of anti-hacking precaution the UWF has on the files." Cerberus breathed through his nose.

Lucifer scowled and massaged his neck. The big attack had failed. The deviant goal was now an even higher mountain to climb.

"A shame. And Pestilence is . . ."

"Dead, sir, as far as we know."

The deviant leader chuckled wryly and shook his head. The Saints really had screwed over the Devil's Deviants with this round. He smiled at Cerberus. The large Viking-like man stood silently as Lucifer lounged comfortably in his chair.

"Cerberus, you seem to be utterly *heartbroken* over this recent loss."

Cerberus blinked at this, as if caught off guard. "Sir?"

Lucifer smiled. "I have something to cheer us both up, though! Something I just received not two minutes ago!" He opened his laptop from a side table and showed the text on the screen to Cerberus.

Lucifer,

I know what happened at Westbrook. I know how bad the Devil's Deviants are hurting after the loss of Pestilence. Sounds like the DDs could use a friend in these trying times. What if I told you I'm in a position to get the Saints off your back for good? With a little of your help, of course. Let me know if you're interested.

Your Friend,

A Disgruntled Member of the Saint Organization.

Cerberus read the email from an unrecognizable email address made up of random numbers and shook his head. "Could be a trap."

"Could be," Lucifer said playfully. Then the leader of the Devil's Deviants smiled. "It could also be true too."

End.

ABOUT THE AUTHOR

Nicholas J. Ripley is the frontman of the punk rock band Futilitarian Librarians as well as the author and primary visual artist of everything related to Project Suncloud. Born in Las Vegas to a pair of dancers, "Uncle Nick" has been professionally involved in the arts since the young age of nine years old, when he got his first professional acting and modeling gig. Besides playing with his band and working on Project Suncloud, Nick also writes as a film critic for FilmSnob Reviews. When he is not doing anything artistic, he enjoys watching horror movies, playing old video games, and spending time with his cat/co-author Arya Stark.

To discuss booking Nicholas J. Ripley for media or speaking events, email: projectsuncloud@gmail.com

If you've enjoyed this book, please consider leaving a review on Goodreads. I appreciate every bit of support, and it would mean a lot. Thank you!

-NJR

Website:
patreon.com/ripleyjnick

Instagram:
@nickjripleyofficial

UPCOMING BOOKS

Project Suncloud:

A Hunt for Wolves

A Mourning for Vultures

A Grave for Sparrows

Other Books in the Suncloudverse:

The Vindictive Queen: A Commander Li Origin Story

www.ingramcontent.com/pod-product-compliance
Lightning Source LLC
Chambersburg PA
CBHW031154010826
48971CB00012B/276